JUSU AND MOTHER EARTH

Sharon Ervin

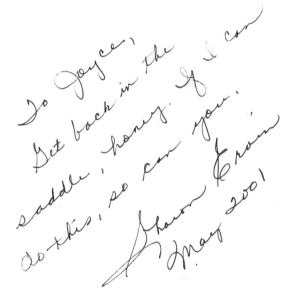

To Joyce,
Get back in the
saddle, honey. If I can
do this, so can you.
Sharon Ervin
May 2001

AmErica House
Baltimore

Cover design by Pat Wershiner

ISBN: 1-893162-87-7
PUBLISHED BY AMERICA HOUSE BOOK PUBLISHERS
www.publishamerica.com
Baltimore

Printed in the United States of America

To my husband, Bill,

For teaching me to choose my races,
to set my eyes on the goal, and
to run...and run...and keep on running.

Acknowledgements:

The Reverend Charles Kapson and his wife, Enid, of Rwashmaire, Uganda, for years of faithful friendship, letters, pictures, and gifts--my brother and sister in Christ whom I will meet someday;

Dr. Paul LeDoux, for graciously sharing his expertise;

Margaret Olinger, for determination after her loss;

Jane Bryant, Ila Pigg, Connie Gordon, Frank McSherry, and Genevieve Kroger for reading and encouraging;

Mary Ann Kerl, who taught me to market on Mondays;

Larry and Frank at the post office for continually tidying my mailings;

Posthumously: Wilbur Martin, the Associated Press exec, and Harold Keith, my mentor, who insisted we achieve only what we attempt;

The Overseas Missions program of the Episcopal Church of the Diocese of Oklahoma, the American Red Cross, and the Peace Corps;

Literary Agent Elaine Markson, who read the manuscript and suggested ways to strengthen it, although she couldn't represent it;

The Johnson County, Texas, contest judge who gave JUSU third-place but said this was the one she would buy, the one she would read;

Florine Hager, other family members, McAlester's McSherry Writers; Lesser North Texas Writers; Sooner Area Romance Authors, and friends who cheered, critiqued, cajoled, sympathized, and even occasionally helped most by ignoring me;

Erica House for writing: "I am happy to inform you..."

Chapter One

"Relax your toes." Ruth Pedigo closed her eyes and tried to lie very still in the quiet of her bedroom. It was nearly three a.m. "Now your feet, your calves. Rest." It didn't matter if she actually slept. There would probably be time for sleep in her new life.

But it was her last night in her own bed, in the safety of her own home, the home she and Mickey bought before their youngest was born. *How old was Donnie now? Next month, June, he would be twenty-two. Old enough. Donnie would look after things.*

Ruth rolled onto her side to gaze east out the upper window beyond the open shutters. Spring in Oklahoma. The damp air was heavy with lilac. A ridiculous time to be leaving. All four children had said that same thing on different occasions.

Outside was only silence. The early birds had not begun to stir. The neighborhood cats who growled late into the night had retired. It was time in limbo, hovering between night and day, neither.

Appropriate.

It was a shame they stopped burying pharaoh's wife with pharaoh, she considered dreamily. She would prefer silence in the bowels of a pyramid with Mickey embalmed to the awful indifference which had consumed her since his death.

He was her focus for thirty-one years. They cooked together, exercised together, made love, even in the predawn hours that fateful morning.

Her eyes stung and Ruth leaned up on an elbow then shifted to sit on the side of the bed, annoyed for giving in to it. She got up, moved through the familiar room, and padded all the way to the kitchen before she turned on a light.

She poured a glass of orange juice, retrieved the sponge and wiped an errant drop from the counter.

Donnie appeared in the doorway. "Can't you sleep?"

She shook her head. He combed his fingers through his rumpled hair which returned to its stubborn disarray. In his pajama bottoms and T-shirt, he looked twelve years old again.

"Mom, you don't have to go."

"I know."

"No one's holding you to this. None of us even remembers your saying it."

She sipped the orange juice. "It's a promise I made to me. I've been grieving for five months. It's time. I can stay here and wait for my own cardiac incident, or I can get off my duff and contribute whatever I've got left to give."

She walked over in front of him, reached up to brush the unruly shock of hair off his forehead with no better result.

"Inside, Donnie, I always knew my life would come to this night. I wasn't certain I would be able to make myself go, leave my family, the comforts and conveniences of home." She reached around Donnie to pat the side-by-side affectionately. "I didn't think I could, not without your dad nudging me." She drew a deep breath. "But here I am, packed and sleepless. I'm going." She leaned her backside against the cabinet, needing the support.

"What about Mr. Belton?"

"Ross is a great guy." She pushed away from the cabinet and shrugged. "He's not your dad. Besides, this is a sacred mission or something."

"Why?"

"I sincerely believe this is God's will. If for some reason, I don't make it back, know that I was doing what I was supposed to be doing...for whatever reason."

Donnie shuffled closer and draped his long arms around her shoulders. She stiffened. She couldn't afford to yield to his tender gesture.

"A few months is not much to give out of a lifetime," she said resolutely, more to herself than to him. "I've had fifty-two years of receiving, a whole life of bests. I guess it's payback time."

"Did you sign up for a year?"

"No. I'm only obligated for three months at a time. I can come home in August. They may kick me out of Uganda before that." She smiled. "Anyway, each hitch is ninety days and I'm taking it one step at a time."

She patted his waist, turned him, snapped off the kitchen light, and guided her son back toward his room. She kissed him good night, again, then returned to her bed and slept soundly from four a.m. until the alarm buzzed at seven-thirty.

Ruth ran through her usual morning routine before rousting a grumbling Donnie. "Come on, we'll have breakfast at that truck stop you like so well before we cross the Red."

The three-hour trip to Dallas was easy, four lane all the way to the farm-to-market shortcut to D/FW Airport.

Flight Seven-twenty-six to London departed at two p.m. Ruth neither wanted nor needed much lead time. She had reduced her luggage to one large duffel to check through, two smaller pieces to carry on and the oversized purse to accommodate the required travel information and incidental reading materials.

There would be a six-hour layover in London before the flight across Africa. Anticipating the hours of travel, she wore comfortable slacks, a sweater over a cotton blouse and her best walking shoes.

Donnie helped her check the duffel and walked her to the waiting area. Half a dozen other people were already there, waiting. It was twelve-forty.

"Honey, I love you." She hugged him. "Please don't drive too fast going home."

He regarded her oddly. "I'll stay 'til the flight leaves."

Recognizing his determined look, she smiled gamely and shook her head. "If you stay and I have a choice, I might chicken out." Her smile faded. "I really want you to go." He started to object again. "Besides," she interrupted the anticipated protest, "the wind's coming up. If you get back early, you can take Charlie to the lake, wind surf before dark."

Relenting, Donnie squeezed her hard. She saw his chin dimple and quiver before he turned and walked away.

She watched her son's retreating back as it melded into the throng of travelers in the concourse. The sight of him was the last vestige of her old life. She could run after him, catch up, beg and win a reprieve. Instead, she wilted onto the edge of a molded plastic chair.

Eventually she sat back, forcing herself to think of something cheerful. Carly's baby. He would be a year old, if Ruth returned on the early deadline. Mickey had done a tour in Vietnam when they were practically newlyweds. She had survived that. Three months away from the baby should be a piece of cake.

Still, Carly's baby was their first grandchild.

Ruth never dreamed she would feel about that baby as she did the first time she held him--his legs muscular at birth, thighs like small hamhocks, miniatures of his grandfather's.

Staring out at the grassy green belt between the runways, Ruth allowed her thoughts to wander.

Carly and Spencer named their baby Michael, Mickey Pedigo's bloodline continuing, his namesake, born three month's before Mickey's death. It was a wonderful name. He was a wonderful baby.

People bustling nearby roused her. A speaker crackled and the clerk called for boarding.

In spite of the ticket agent's urging, Ruth had declined an available window seat. She opted instead for the interior section on Row Twenty-five. Obviously the flight would be less than full.

On board, Ruth nervously stowed the two carry-on pieces under her assigned seat and an empty seat beside her and settled. She watched passengers filing in, observed their frowns, nervous laughter or practiced indifference.

When the flight attendants finally closed the doors, she was disappointed to find the seats on both sides of her unoccupied. A man who appeared to be of middle eastern descent nodded at her from across the aisle on her right.

Across the aisle to her left, a tall, preoccupied young man juggled an armload of books and magazines. He sat on the aisle and seemed oblivious to his surroundings as he spread his reading materials into the two vacant seats toward the window.

Ruth stole another quick glance at the middle eastern man. He stared at her with large, dark eyes. At her glance, he grinned broadly revealing front teeth ravaged by decay. Ruth allowed a little smile and nodded. Hoping to quell any attempts at conversation, she pulled her purse into her lap and focused determinedly on resorting items she had already sorted a dozen times before.

They had been in the air twenty minutes, had heard the pilot's welcome, weather reports for both Dallas and London and the usual spiel and visual aids regarding emergency measures, before Ruth noticed the small dark man again grinning at her. She smiled slightly, tolerantly, then leaned her head back and closed her eyes. She didn't want to speculate about the little man's nationality or his politics, didn't want to consider that he might be a extremist or... No, she wouldn't entertain those thoughts.

With the airplane actually in the air, Ruth felt relieved that at least this step of her commitment was accomplished. She considered this one--entering and staying on the airplane--the most difficult. The first.

She must have dozed because the rustling of someone easing into the seat on her right wakened her. She turned her head and peered.

Flying east, Ruth knew they would lose sunlight rapidly but she was surprised at how quickly daylight was failing. The cabin lights were muted for those who preferred to sleep away the distance. The middle eastern gentleman had moved into the seat next to her.

Ruth looked at him and he smiled again, arching his eyebrows. His teeth made her shiver involuntarily. His fingernails were unusually long and yellowed and he smelled of strong spices. She shifted position turning her shoulder to him and tried to relax again.

A moment later, she felt something warm against her thigh. It was the little man's hand.

"Stop that!"

He grinned.

"No," she said firmly.

"Amer-i-can?" His pronunciation was hesitant.

"Yes."

He nodded, removed his hand, slumped into his seat and folded his arms across his chest, but the sneering smile continued.

Ruth looked around, startled to see the reader on her left watching them. His inquisitive eyes, vividly gray, frowned directly into hers. His face was grim. She scowled back, her anger radiating. With no change of expression, the reader turned his attention back to his magazine.

Unable to settle down again or to get comfortable with the little man right next to her, Ruth straightened her chair back, turned on the overhead light and pulled a paperback and her reading glasses from her purse. Soon the man beside her, his face turned to the front, began to snore quietly. Her stomach felt queasy, a reaction to the man's strong odor.

His snoring, however, lulled her. Gradually her eyes stared unseeing at the pages. The book eased into her lap. Her head drooped, the glasses slid down her nose and her breathing grew even.

Again she awoke with a start, the dark man's hand once more on her thigh. Angry, startled, she jumped up, unsteady on her feet, and grabbed the glasses as they abandoned her nose and fell.

The attendant's cart approached from the front of the cabin in the aisle on the right beyond the dark man. Also on that side, the male attendant helped a woman passenger riffle overhead compartments for something. Ruth could summon assistance which was close at hand. But she wanted to cope. This was her problem.

Her seat mate's grin and leering eyes followed as she grabbed her purse and lunged left into the aisle.

Steadying herself, Ruth placed her purse strap over her shoulder and tried to regain her composure. She held onto the back of the vacant aisle seat with one hand and attempted, with the other, to brush errant strands of her short, dark hair back where they belonged.

Across the aisle, the reader, having lain his magazines aside, stared out at the darkening sky, obviously too immersed in his reverie to notice her. She envied his out-of-body absence.

She supposed she could, even should, complain to one of the attendants. The plane was only sparsely filled. There was plenty of seating elsewhere. She would...could...should ask an attendant to assign her another place.

In the lavatory, Ruth used the hairbrush in her purse, freshened her lipstick, tidied her clothing, and took several deep breaths. She was stalling. She was not accustomed to traveling alone. The dark man frightened her, despite his unimposing size. She glowered at her image in the mirror.

"Toughen up, sweetheart," she said, in her best Bogart. She set her jaw, squared her shoulders, and reached for the doorknob then hesitated, cringing. She'd rather stay there in that private sanctum. Still stalling. Hiding out. It had been her most pervasive instinct since November.

No. No easy outs. She forced herself to turn the handle.

As she wobbled back down the corridor, hampered by the subtle sway of the airplane, the solemn reader stood and stepped forward barring her access to her row.

He was tall, sinewy, his close-cropped, chestnut hair appeared to b prematurely gray. His chambray dress shirt was unbuttoned at the neck, no tie. H wore a navy blue blazer and gray slacks.

He had a long face, a strong jaw and a little cleft in his chin. His mos remarkable features were his eyes, bright gray eyes which bored into her an narrowed as he glowered down his nose at her.

He regarded her so severely that Ruth wondered if she had done somethin to irritate him. Perhaps she had bumped him on her way to the lavatory. She didn think so.

"Sit there." His voice was low, his tone quiet, well modulated. He didn sound angry, but firm. He took a step back to allow her access to the now empt window seat which had been cleared of the periodicals and books which had fille it earlier.

Chapter Two

Ruth looked into the reader's face, trying to understand what he meant.

"Take the window seat." He had a definite Texas drawl. His steely eyes penetrated, looking not just at her, but into her as well.

She glanced at the three seats in his row. He had positioned himself on the aisle and had systematically strewn his reading materials across the other two. The clutter, which he earlier had sorted so methodically, was now heaped into the middle seat.

"I need to get..." she began, meeting the intensity in his eyes.

"Just the two small cases? Under the seats?"

She nodded.

"I'll get them." He turned to enter the center section of Row twenty-five.

The dark middle eastern man, his eyes wide, returned his chair to its upright position as the reader approached, then scrambled over the unoccupied seat and across the aisle to his originally assigned place.

Ignoring him, the reader retrieved Ruth's two small bags, retraced his steps, handed her one case at a time, and waited for her to stow them and sit.

As she sat down and snapped her seat belt, she hoped she was not doing frying pans and fires.

He appeared to be about the age of her older son, Michael. The man was nice looking with eyes and dark lashes most women probably envied. He appeared to have begun the day clean shaven but there was now the shadow of a beard.

Obviously, he was not interested in conversation as he settled and quickly lost himself again in a periodical.

"You're not in your assigned seat." The attractive young woman attendant addressed Ruth in a chastising tone.

"My idea." The reader's voice was gruff as he intercepted her. "Is it a problem?"

The attendant looked at him and her face softened. "No." Her smile was saccharin, as if she had only been kidding. "I just need to change it on our manifest. Doctor, hello! I didn't recognize you. On your usual run, I see."

He allowed a slight smile and a nod. Ruth marveled at the way his smoky eyes melted the young woman whose body suddenly seemed pliable beneath his gaze. He used the half-smile as a weapon to quell the challenge. Ruth wondered what the rest of his arsenal got him.

The attendant beamed. "Will you be staying over in London?"

"Yes."

"Oh, really. Me too."

"I'm sure you'll enjoy your time there. London's great for sightseeing."

"Yeah." She grimaced. "But it's not so hot when you're by yourself, right Will you have any free time while you're there?"

"Not this trip, I'm afraid."

She feigned a pout. "Well, just in case you get loose for a couple of hours I'll give you the number where I'll be staying. Maybe you can squeeze in time fo a quick drink or...or something."

Had he caught the innuendo? Ruth thought so and decided to ignore th patter continuing between them.

Turning toward the window, she realized she should have asked for a window in the first place. The approaching night was glorious. It was nearly twilight ou over the sea, still early back home.

The patter ended. The attendant moved on.

Ignoring the beginning edge of a headache, Ruth found herself studying th reader's reflection in her window. She wanted to catch a catnap but wanted even more to avoid other encroachments. She squared herself in the seat so she coul scrutinize her companion in quick glimpses.

In the stream of the overhead lamp, she noticed his short-cropped hair wa thinning. The corners of his eyes and mouth were cut with wrinkles, probably prematurely etched by the southwest's merciless sun. Obviously, he was a little older than she had first thought.

He was quiet, engrossed in a pamphlet of some kind. The engines droned The lights were dim and the headache annoying. She had aspirin in one of the small cases under the seat but it was too much trouble to look there. She sank into the seat and folded her hands over her purse in her lap.

She felt someone looking at her and her eyes popped open.

"Do you mind?" the familiar twang asked, his face solemn.

"What?"

"This other light. Will it bother you if I turn it on?" He indicated the reading lamp over the seat between them.

The drawl soothed her. He looked at her intently, waiting for her answer.

"No." She felt a little embarrassed to have been suspicious of him in the first place.

He snapped on the spare light. "I like having extra space on the long hauls." He produced a briefcase, tossed it on top of the materials in the seat between them, opened it and began shuffling through its contents. When he looked at her again, she smiled uncertainly.

He said, "You can stretch. You don't have to wear the seat belt now. The light's off." He raised the arm rest. "This way. Give yourself some room."

Wordlessly, Ruth unlatched her seat belt and moved her oversized purse from her lap to the floor. The reader nodded his approval, giving up more of a smirk than a smile, before he returned to his reading.

Ruth declined the earphones offered by the attendant on her next pass. She preferred the drone of the engines.

A half-hour later her headache was worse. She glanced at the literature which absorbed the reader.

The cover of the magazine he held was colorful but the mast unreadable. The letters looked like Russian, not that she had ever had an opportunity for more than a passing glimpse of the language.

An older stewardess arrived with her beverage cart. "Will you have something to drink?" She didn't look at Ruth, but at the reader. He obviously was accustomed to attention from women. Ruth noticed his left hand. *No wedding ring.* She guessed that notable absence probably prompted more and better service in places other than just airplanes.

Instead of ordering, he looked at Ruth and raised his eyebrows asking a wordless question.

"Yes," she said and dug into her purse. Maybe there was a loose aspirin in the bottom. "A cola, please."

A moment later the attendant produced the drink and again turned her full attention on the reader as Ruth continued digging through her bag.

"What do you need?" His eyes were on Ruth.

"Do you have any aspirin?" she asked the attendant.

The woman's smile was one-sided as she turned her attention to Ruth again. "Aspirin or non-aspirin?"

"Excedrin," the reader said firmly. Ruth frowned. She wanted relief, not an argument.

Sorting through items in her pocket, the attendant produced an individual packet which she absently handed to Ruth as she again smiled warmly into the reader's eyes.

Ruth felt embarrassed, as if she were in the middle of the playing field as the second period of this flirtatious event was getting underway. She mumbled her thanks but knew her words fell on unhearing ears as the attendant had again focused her rapt attention on Gray Eyes.

Ruth tossed down the tablets, chasing them with the cola, then reclined her seat, ignoring the reader's concerned expression and gazing out over the clouds which appeared to be confections rather than meteorological formations.

"Would you like a pillow?" The persistently attentive attendant said, obviously trying to get the reader's attention by leaning provocatively over him to address Ruth.

"Yes, please."

"Yes," the reader echoed. The attendant issued one to Ruth, then fluffed an placed one behind the reader's head. He thanked her and handed her a bill from hi pocket. As soon as the girl had moved to the next row, he handed his pillow t Ruth.

"They're small."

Apparently he felt a need to explain his generosity.

The pillow looked peculiarly tiny and white coming from his large well-scrubbed hand. She took it, gaping at his hands. They were manicured. *A siss boy.*

She smiled at the moniker Mickey might have attached to this man. His hai was meticulously cut. The stewardess had called him doctor. Obviously, he wa rich.

"They'll be serving dinner soon," he said without raising his eyes from th printed page. "Maybe you should rest, get rid of the headache before we eat."

She started to argue, piqued by his patronizing tone. This guy certainly di remind her of Michael, taking charge, trying to make her decisions for her.

Conjuring up an image of a boy scout helping an elderly woman cross th street whether she wanted to cross or not, Ruth turned her face, pressed her forehea to the window, and closed her eyes, leaving the reader to his literary clutter or t admire the shapely attendants scurrying back and forth, grinning sillily each tim they caught his eye.

The reader opened his overhead air vent but Ruth kept her eyes closed ignoring him, snatching at the elusive sleep. Her effort was interrupted by the scen of his aftershave which wafted on the air current from his vent. The familia fragrance evoked a deluge of memories.

She drifted dreamily to Mickey leaning against the kitchen cabinet, eating Fritos, downing a beer, talking while she prepared supper. The image was lovely

"I'm so glad you're back."

It was her own voice. Ruth jerked awake. Facing the window, she saw th reflection of the reader looking at her. She faced forward. "I was dreaming." She couldn't look at him. Her peripheral vision detected the nod and movement as h returned to his reading.

She closed her eyes again but was afraid to doze, afraid of speaking out agair in her sleep.

She thought of London. She would have a six-hour wait for the flight to Entebbe. It wasn't long enough for an actual view of the island kingdom. What a shame, actually to be there and to see nothing. Perhaps on the way home, if there were a homecoming. She ignored the recurring fatalism.

Suddenly she opened her eyes to find her seat mate staring at her intently. "Did I say something?"

"No." His face was without expression.

"Do I look like someone you know?"

"No."

"I have a common face. People often think they know me."

"On the contrary," the piercing gray eyes narrowed, "I find your face unusual. You exude an innocence, a naivete." He regarded her soberly. "You are a very attractive woman to be traveling alone. Someone probably should be keeping an eye on you." He half laughed, half snorted, as if his own words surprised him.

Ruth hated feeling the familiar warmth of a blush.

His renegade smile passed as quickly as it had come. "I see that you're married. I'm not coming on with you."

Ruth couldn't contain a low, throaty laugh.

"What?" He looked puzzled.

"The idea of a man 'coming on' with me...it's strange, that's all." She smiled self consciously. His eyebrows arched, but he didn't respond. Had she offended him?

Suddenly, she realized. His hair was styled; his hands manicured, and he was complimenting her. Of course. How stupid of her not to show some admiration, to remark on his fine appearance. She should say something flattering to him, return his kindness. She was embarrassed and her embarrassment showed.

"What's wrong?" He looked and sounded genuinely concerned.

"I'm sorry. I've been awfully self absorbed lately. I certainly should have mentioned, ah, you have a very pleasant face yourself." He looked skeptical and she grew more ill-at-ease. "You're a very handsome, well-groomed young man but, well, with the attendants so solicitous and all, I...I supposed you were getting all the..."

The mercurial smile escaped again, abruptly transforming into a laugh. Ruth smiled uncertainly. He shot another look at her. "You thought I was fishing, did you?" His laugh continued.

Ruth turned back toward the window, swallowing her embarrassment. When his laughter subsided, she peeked at him. He was quiet, but watching her. "'A handsome, well-groomed young man,' you say. Exactly how old do you think I am?" The gray eyes twinkled.

"Twenty-seven?"

He looked at her in disbelief before the low laughter overcame him again.

With a grimace, Ruth turned back toward the window to watch his shadowy reflection.

"I'm glad you thought I was twenty-seven. It must be the lighting." He leaned forward, craning his neck to see her face. "You're not wearing your glasses now either." His eyes had developed a definite shimmer. He was teasing her.

She bristled. "You don't need compliments from me. You're getting plenty of stroking from the attendants."

His eyes glinted mischievously but at least, she consoled herself, he'd stopped laughing.

"They're probably between guys, or looking for a little out-of-town entertainment. They figure I'm alone and might be looking for some of the same."

"Oh?" Ruth again registered surprise and twisted to scour his face. "You really aren't married then?" Her words carried a note of pity.

New laughter burbled in his throat, and he grinned broadly. "Not that I think your question's too personal..."

Was he hedging? Why should he?

She rubbed her palms together. "I'm incorrigibly nosy. Sorry. Maybe I'd better let you get back to your reading."

"No, I need a break. Tell me about your family, your husband."

Ruth touched her wedding band with her right thumb and indexfinger. The ring had not been off that finger in more than twenty-nine years. A familiar lump formed in her throat. "Are you a native Texan?" she asked, forcing the words around the lump.

"Yes. I'm on sabbatical."

"A teacher then? College? A professor? That kind of 'doctor?'"

"Well...yes."

"What's your field?"

"Science, actually."

"And you're going to London?" He smiled suspiciously and she winced. "I read that the World Health Organization is meeting there. Is that of interest to you?"

A smile of genuine pleasure lifted his features and deepened the creases at his eyes. "Yes." He tapped a forefinger on the magazine folded open in his lap, "I'm boning up, as a matter of fact."

"I see. Have you been to W.H.O. meetings before?"

"Several times. Years ago, I argued vehemently against the cessation of small pox vaccinations in the states."

"Oh? You lost that one, didn't you?"

"How would you know that? I didn't think that mattered to anyone here but me--and my wounded pride."

She coughed an apologetic little laugh. "I was relieved. Only my oldest child had to have a smallpox vaccination." Her companion remained silent, studying her. Self-conscious, she said, "What was your pitch?"

"I said if you put four stop signs at a dangerous intersection and there was never an accident at that intersection, it didn't mean you should remove the stop signs."

"Makes sense to me."

"I wish you had been there to vote."

Ruth again regarded the magazines stacked in the middle seat. "Did I break your concentration, talking in my sleep?"

"No, and don't worry, you didn't speak loudly. No one else heard. Who is it who's recently gone away?"

She took a quick breath. "My husband."

"Does he travel?"

"No."

"Are you going to London to meet him?"

She felt the lump forming in her throat. She needed to change the subject. "Actually, I'm going to Uganda by way of London."

"Where in Uganda?"

"Bwana."

He looked genuinely interested.

"Have you heard of it?"

He nodded thoughtfully. "I'm familiar with the area. It's way off the beaten path, probably safer than many places."

"Is it nice?"

He looked at her in disbelief. "The climate's great, of course. But in the rural areas, in villages like Bwana, they're short on luxury accommodations."

"Oh." The Catletts had sent pictures. She had a good idea about the living conditions, the climate, the topography.

"Is your husband in Uganda then?"

"No."

There was a long silence as she scanned her brain for a new conversational direction as he continued studying her.

"Africa is a troubled place right now," he said. "I'm surprised you're going there at all, much less alone."

He waited. He seemed to be allowing her time and opportunity to respond, but she preferred not to explain. Suddenly, he selected a magazine, thumbed to a specific page, and folded it open. "Actually, I'm going to Uganda myself." He didn't look at her as he spoke.

Ruth regarded him sharply. "Into that troubled area?"

Avoiding her gaze, he mumbled into the magazine. "I go every summer."

"To teach?"

"No." He volunteered nothing more.

It was difficult not to pry, to afford him the courtesy of his privacy, but she felt obligated since he had allowed her the same courtesy only moments earlier.

Reluctant to interrupt him again, she still felt the need. "The Excedrin wa a good idea, and thanks for the rescue." She glanced around him, indicating th dark man in the far section.

Without looking up, the reader nodded, rounded his broad shoulders and burrowed into his periodical.

Moody, she told herself.

They each were absorbed in their own musings for several moments before they heard an attendant approaching again, the refreshment cart rattling as it came along the aisle.

Chapter Three

"How's your head?" the reader asked.

Ruth smiled, relieved that he was being friendly again. "Fine, thanks."

"Would you like something stronger to drink, something to relax you, before they bring our meal?"

She started to say yes, then thought better of it. "I don't usually..." Before she could finish, the young male attendant was there with his cart.

The reader pulled loose dollar bills from his trousers pocket. "Two Bloody Marys." He lowered the lap table over the vacant seat between them, took the drinks from the steward, placed one on the neutral surface, and nudged it toward Ruth.

"Are you always so decisive about what other people want?" The question sounded more curt than she intended.

A slow grin commandeered his broad mouth, revealing large, even teeth. "Not always, but I seem to be pretty good at anticipating what you want." He winked and her heart jumped in her chest.

Did he intend the double meaning or was she imagining it? Ruth flashed him the well-practiced displeased look which had curbed unsatisfactory behavior in her children.

"Oh, ho!" He laughed and cocked one brow. "Obviously you are someone's mother. A formidable one, I imagine. How many children do you have?"

Her arched look seemed lost on him. "Four."

"Are they grown?"

"Yes."

"You aren't running away from home, are you?" Mischief sparked in his gray eyes. She turned to look out the window. No one had teased her, flirted with her, in a long time. She felt disloyal to Mickey each time she approved this stranger with her laughter or even the warm, stirrings inside her.

Ignoring her drink, Ruth continued gazing out the window, sorting through emotions, trying to decide on appropriate behavior. In the reflection in the glass, she could see that her seat mate, sipping his drink, was again buried in his magazine.

Maybe she was still too emotionally unstable to be out in the world by herself. She had wrestled with this concern several times already. She always came to the same conclusion.

This trip was necessary. Plan B, the direction she had determined to take when Plan A was over. Marriage and Mickey and their family had been her priority--Plan A. But that life was past. She was the one who had lived beyond it. She tried to shake off the insidious self-pity.

Three of their four offspring were married with families of their own. She could still be useful to them, baby-sitting. Her children and their spouses had hinted at things she might do or not do, say or not say, to make her more tolerable.

Donnie, the only unmarried one, no longer needed supervision or appreciated advice. He'd tried to make that clear to both parents.

All four children offered kind support after their dad's death but, actually, they had inadvertently prodded Ruth into proceeding with Plan B.

Ross Belton also meant well but he, too, pushed her that direction. He said marrying him was the only real option she had. Ross was probably catch--prominent, rich, opinionated, frugal, comfortable plodding in his ruts...No, no, no.

And what good would it do anyone for her to shrivel up at home alone waiting, taking her remaining God-given talents to her grave? She still had a writer's eye, was still able to record her observations succinctly.

After all the soul-searching, Ruth decided to leave it up to Larry Reid, an old college friend with the wire service.

Reid was receptive, once he remembered her.

Her terms made Ruth's an offer Reid couldn't refuse. He would pay only for those articles the service used and he could set the rate of payment per submission.

The Peace Corps people were nice, too. She could maintain an informal liaison relationship with them.

Too, there was the church connection through Father Catlett with whom she had corresponded for fifteen years.

Ruth felt nervous about meeting Father Catlett. The black rector of an Anglican parish in Bwana, a remote area of Uganda, Catlett had repeatedly urged her to visit, though they had nothing in common.

He was a young black man, she an older white woman. His family endured hunger during what he termed "the hungry season," each year before new crops matured. Ruth had never known hunger except the occasional self-imposed restraints of dieting.

Catlett was Anglican, she, Episcopalian. His priest's salary was two hundred eleven dollars a year, when he could collect the full amount. Mickey always grossed six figures.

Ruth and Mickey occasionally sent the Catletts small boxes of groceries and seeds for planting. Two parcels of groceries cost two hundred forty-one dollars to ship and took ten months to arrive. And that was one of the successful attempts during a lull in the perpetual warring among the Ugandans' neighbors. Some shipments never arrived at all.

The priest walked thirteen miles--three to four hours--one way, over roads little more than cattle trails, to serve his congregation. In her Town Car, it took Ruth seven minutes to reach St. Peter's.

Catlett's congregation of twenty-six hundred had been decimated by Slim, his word for AIDS/HIV. Ruth knew five people who had died of AIDS. They'd all lived far from Oklahoma and their illnesses had seemed remote from real life.

As usual, Ruth had prayed to be willing and was surprised to find herself again on an airplane droning its way into a new night, a new darkness; into a world of unfamiliar people and places and circumstances.

She started when her seat mate cleared his throat. From his reflection, she could see he was watching her. *But why?* She was bewildered. *What possible interest could he have in her?*

Chapter Four

"Would you rather have something else?"

The younger female attendant broke into Ruth's musings, indicating the Bloody Mary which sat untouched on the lap table over the vacant seat between Ruth and the reader.

"No, it's fine."

She looked at her companion, but his eyes were riveted on his magazine. His cup was empty. Ruth retrieved the full one and took a sip. It was watery from its wait. She used the accompanying swizzle stick to stir it, then took another sip. Better.

"Don't drink it, if you don't want it," he muttered without looking up. She sipped it again, rolling the tangy tomato flavor over her tongue. It was good.

The attendant addressed them both. "We're about to serve dinner. Would you prefer beef or chicken?"

Without returning Ruth's questioning glance or asking, he said, "We'll have the chicken."

When the attendant had gone, he gave Ruth a boyish grin. "It was no big deal, chicken or beef."

She felt her glower soften. "If you're going to keep reading my mind, maybe we should introduce ourselves. I'm Ruth Pedigo from Bridger, Oklahoma."

"Jack Standish. Dallas." He reached across the vacant seat between them. As her hand slid into his, which was larger and warmer, she shivered involuntarily. He held hers an extra moment.

"The Bloody Mary was good." She smiled crookedly, removing her hand from his.

His smile broadened. "Would you like another one?"

"No, but thank you."

He stowed most of his magazines in the briefcase and shoved it under his seat.

After the meal was on their tables and they'd begun eating, Standish said, "Tell me about your family."

He was just making small talk. She needed to relax. As he'd said, it was no big deal. "We have four children, two of each gender." She took a bite of the chicken.

"And they're all grown?"

"Yes, grown and mostly out of the house except..."

"What?"

She shrugged. "Except when they're not."

Standish nodded.

"And you?" She could certainly be polite too.

"I'm mostly married to my work." He described life in exotic places where he had lived and worked on brief stints, always headquartering out of Dallas, hi hometown. "Now, tell me how you happened to know about the World Health Organization meeting?"

She flushed. "I read. Newspapers, magazines, cereal boxes, shampoo bottles I absorb all kinds of information, more than I need to know about almost everything." She smiled apologetically. "I'm basically nosy."

His gray eyes danced over her face with humor and a trace of something else--admiration maybe. Ruth felt the blush and tried to redirect his attention "How many languages do you speak?"

The grays narrowed before he answered. "Several. They come and go depending on what I have a chance to use. Why?"

She indicated a magazine still in the vacant seat, the one she had noticed earlier and thought to be Russian. "All your traveling...you aren't a spy, are you?"

He chuckled. "No, mostly I do honest work."

"Teaching. Of course."

His face became serious. "You seemed edgy earlier. Have you flown much?"

"Some." She hesitated, then added, "This is my first trip overseas."

"Are you meeting someone?"

She needed another diversion. "Is this Parmesan chicken? It's very good And the snow peas aren't overcooked. My compliments to the man who did the ordering."

He gave her a side-long look.

"Don't you think it's especially good?"

"You have a beguiling way of changing the subject, but I don't get thrown off track that easily. Come on, tell me about this trip. Or are you trying to be mysterious?"

Laughing lightly, she wiped her mouth and took a sip of water. "I'm on an adventure, for a staid Oklahoma housewife. I am apprehensive, less about flying than about when I arrive."

"Are you visiting friends or family in Uganda?"

Ruth thought of Father Catlett and felt a smile tweak the corners of her mouth. "Yes." She gazed past him, "I guess I am."

Jack looked puzzled, but did not press it.

"Dr. Standish?" the coquettish young attendant's voice was terse. She had slipped up beside them unnoticed.

"Yes?" His pleasant smile faded, replaced by a mask of indifference as he turned, obviously annoyed at the interruption.

"Could you come with me, please?" She took his dinner tray and shifted his lap table into its stored position.

Ruth was surprised that, in spite of his apparent irritation, and without asking any questions, he stood, wiped his mouth, tossed his napkin on the tray in the attendant's hand, and followed her forward to first class.

A dozen questions bounded through her head: *what was the Jekyll/Hyde routine with his face? If he were a professor, why did they need him?*

Recalling his manicured nails Ruth wondered, too, why the man wasn't flying first class to begin with?

An older female attendant arrived to clear her tray.

"What happened to Professor Standish?" Ruth asked.

The stewardess smiled, effectively veiling any readable expression. "Doctor Standish should be back right away."

A little miffed at the dismissal, Ruth fluffed both small pillows and leaned back facing the windows, gazing out at the bright nighttime sky.

No matter the weather below, the sky seemed always to be clear above thirty thousand feet. Eventually, she placed the pillows on the few magazines stacked in the middle seat, snapped off all three overhead lights, and slipped off her shoes. She lay on her side, facing the seat, pulled her knees up and curled around them.

The engines droned, the cabin lights dimmed and she let herself drift into a deep, dream-filled sleep.

Someone jostled her to remove the magazines, rearranging her. She stretched but remained cocooned in a dream, basking in the familiar fragrances of her husband's warm body.

*   *   *

The stars were brilliant against a velvet blackness when Ruth awoke. Realizing she lolled over all three seats, she struggled and sat up, stiffly.

Smoothing her hair and wiping her fingers around her mouth, she squinted, trying to get her bearings.

The cabin was quiet, eerie in a kind of half light and the strobe effect of a movie dancing on the screen at the front. Passengers not mesmerized by the movie had assumed various, sometimes peculiar positions in their efforts to get comfortable for sleep.

She needed to use the lavatory.

She might as well take her toothbrush and freshen up. She ran her fingers through her hair--an effort to improve her appearance and to stimulate circulation to her brain at the same time--and located her purse under the middle seat. She didn't recall having put it there. She ruffled through the contents, then decided to take the satchel with her. As she stepped into the aisle, she almost bumped into the male attendant.

"You slept very well." He smiled his approval. Ruth returned the smile. "Your husband wouldn't let us disturb you."

Not fully alert, Ruth nodded. "Good." She was confused. "What time is it?"

"In Dallas, it's nine p.m. Saturday. In London, it's four a.m., Sunday. We'll be landing in less than an hour. Can I get you something?"

Ruth thanked him but declined.

He stepped to one side. "Several people commented on how attentive your husband is. He sat here on the other side of the aisle." He indicated the center row. "He cautioned everyone not to wake you. He had a magazine, but he didn't read. He just watched you. The girls," he indicated the women attendants, "were very envious."

"Oh." She nodded again.

"It's refreshing to see such a devoted couple." The steward's smile was tinged with admiration. He moved on.

Ruth was confused. How could the steward know about Mickey's thoughtfulness. She was drying her face before she sorted out his comments.

She had slept soundly amid recurring dreams of Mickey. But Mickey wasn't there, would never be there again. He seemed awfully real to have been only a dream. *But how had others witnessed her dreams?*

She thought of Jack Standish, the seat mate who smelled so remarkably familiar. *Had he returned to his seat to find her lounging all over the place? Had he removed the magazines? Rearranged her?*

"Oh," she murmured around the toothbrush in her mouth, mortified.

The only consolation seemed that her humiliation would be short-lived. They would be in London. Mr...or professor...or Dr. Standish had been absent when she fell asleep and when she awoke. Perhaps he would not return, in which case, she would not have to worry about apologizing for imposing on him at all. She was annoyed to be disappointed at that thought. He was a kind young man and she merely wanted to thank him, her mature self reasoned.

She laughed at her reflection, then proceeded to dab on fresh lipstick and comb her hair.

Reluctant to venture back into the cabin, she hesitated, then decided this time of day, she could not loiter in the lavatory and deprive others of its availability.

* * *

Her heart skipped as Dr. Standish stood to allow her into their row. Where had all that giddiness come from? She was pleased that her voice sounded calm as she said, "Thank you."

"You're welcome."

"Apparently I hogged all three seats. I'm sorry to have evicted you from the haven you so gallantly provided."

For the first time, she witnessed the spontaneous emergence of his smile, generous lips spanning slowly to reveal large, even teeth. She inhaled sharply.

Why was she behaving like this? Why was he? And why did he keep watching her so closely? Was he flirting with her, or was that just wishful thinking on her part?

Infectious laughter burbled somewhere inside him, and he bowed his head, inadvertently revealing that his close-cropped hair was thinning at the crown. His broad shoulders were slightly stooped, yet he gave the impression of strength. She again upgraded her read on his age. Mid to late thirties. Only a fully mature man exuded this man's kind of confidence.

He said, "I assumed you didn't sleep well last night."

"Right. Did I talk?"

He nodded. "Some."

She clamped her teeth together. "What did I say?"

"I don't believe I've ever felt more appreciated."

She drew a deep breath and began shaking her head, miserable in her embarrassment.

His smile was kind. "It was no big deal. You were awfully glad I was back."

She focused on the back of the seat in front of her. "I wasn't...ah...I wasn't..." Stammering, she paused. He frowned, obviously trying to interpret her question. "Was I..." she tried again.

"Affectionate?" he supplied. The ensuing grin ebbed quickly from teasing to polite. "Not inordinately so."

"You mean 'not inordinately' for married people?"

"That's probably about right."

"Is that why the attendants thought..."

"Probably."

"And you didn't...?"

He shook his head slowly, studying her. "They didn't need an explanation."

Ruth drew another deep breath, this one heralding relief. "Thank you." She exhaled quietly.

"I do need to relay a message, however." His voice deepened to a more serious timbre and he had her full attention. "I didn't let them wake you, but there's a problem with your connecting flight. You may be stuck in London for a day or two."

"Oh." Ruth glanced toward the window.

"Do you know anyone there?"

She shook her head no.

He nodded. "I have friends just out of town. A couple. He's retired military. They have a large country home and have converted part of it to a bed and breakfast. I help them out some, word of mouth, recruiting guests. They're usually booked up, but I may have enough clout to get you a room. They're not far from

29

London. You could do some sightseeing. This delay might turn out to be a blessing in disguise, since you haven't been here before."

Ruth regarded him curiously. How did he know that?

"What is it?" Slowly his puzzled expression gave way to enlightenment "You told me. Remember? You said you'd never flown overseas. You haven' been here before, have you?"

She shook her head but the puzzled expression continued.

"Oh." He ventured another guess. "I didn't think about what your situation might be. Are you on a strict budget?"

"No. I can afford a couple of days. I guess..." He waited for her to complete the thought. "I'm not fully awake yet. I guess I'm still a little confused." She hesitated. "It's not that I doubt what you're saying. I'd just prefer to have, ah..."

"Confirmation?"

She nodded, flustered.

"Don't be embarrassed." He was patronizing her again. "You don't know me You're in a strange country, alone. I could be anyone from Jack the Ripper to Phineas Fogg."

She choked out a little laugh. He regarded her quizzically as she said, "But certainly someone of historical significance?"

He allowed an embarrassed chuckle. "Do I detect a note of disdain?"

She laughed lightly. "Not at all. I admire a strong ego."

He smiled politely, patiently, but his voice sounded more earnest than he looked. "Do you want me to call about your staying at my friends' place, or not?"

Ruth breathed another sigh and hesitated a moment. "No, that won't be necessary. I don't want to put you to any more trouble." He started to object but she did not allow the interruption. "You've been a real knight in shining armor, saving the lady in distress from the dark scalawag," she indicated the middle eastern gentleman dozing at the far side of the airplane, "making all those difficult choices, pain relievers, food, drink; providing ample space for sleep. I've imposed on you too much already. Thank you for being so nice."

She wondered at the sudden, disapproving scowl on his face.

Chapter Five

As they were catapulted through the walkway into the terminal, Ruth welcomed the continued, unsolicited assistance of her new acquaintance. Negotiating a large, unfamiliar airport with someone who knows his way around gave a person an advantage, she decided, as she shadowed Jack Standish through London's Gatwick.

It took her duffel a long time to appear on the carousel. Anxiously, she tried to keep Standish's navy blue blazer in sight as he threaded his way through throngs of travelers, pulling his own bag on wheels, and carrying both of her small ones. She would have thought he had forgotten her altogether except that he glanced back occasionally.

She finally retrieved the duffel and caught up with him at a bank of telephones as he was hanging up.

"My friends can accommodate you, if you care to stay there."

She frowned.

"Or, I made you a reservation at the Browne Hotel in town. It's clean, reputable."

She was uncertain. He grabbed the duffel from her hand and tossed it on top of their other bags situated on a lorry.

"You can make up your mind in the taxi. My friends will collect me, or us, in town."

She stared. "You're developing an English accent."

"I'm very impressionable, when it comes to languages."

"You don't seem the impressionable type."

"It may be a mistake to cast people as types."

She nodded agreement but the motion was wasted as Jack turned and followed the attendant pulling the lorry into the crowd.

Standish's movements seemed quick for such a big man. Maybe he was just decisive. She tried to keep up but kept getting blocked as he wove his way to an exit and out.

England in those predawn hours was damp, terribly foggy, and and smelled of the sea. Ruth didn't know what she had expected. Actually, she hadn't given the British Isles much thought since she hadn't expected to be there for more than a brief layover.

She had to look for Standish at first, visually sorting through people until she saw him, watching her. He had their luggage in a taxi and stood impatiently at the open back door as their eyes met. Ruth's heart plummeted to her stomach and she paused, allowing herself a full view of this man who had been a stranger brief hours before. Marvelously tall and straight, he was ruggedly handsome and exuded blatant charisma.

But where was she going with him? And why?

She recalled a random thought for closer scrutiny.

He had said her connecting flight was canceled. She hadn't verified the information, despite her intention to do so. *This man...this stranger, was whisking her away to an unknown destination in an unfamiliar country on what? Good looks? Charm?*

Sure, he seemed sincere, but what did she know about him?

Then the old doubt flared. *Was she fully competent yet to take care of herself? Was she sufficiently out of grief's suffocating mire to make decisions?*

If she vanished, who would know to come looking for her or where? From this cab stand at the airport, would anyone be able to trace her?

Her children had full lives of their own. Certainly they would be concerned if they didn't hear from her for a while, but they probably would assume, as she had always preached, no news is good news.

Scowling, Standish waved her forward.

What could he want with her? Why did he care if she had a place to stay? She hated thinking he might have evil intentions, but she didn't know of any noble reason for him to insist on taking care of her. Unless, perhaps she reminded him of someone.

The cab driver said something to him and again, impatiently, Standish motioned her forward.

She would have hurried if it had been Mickey urging her but this man was not Mickey, could never be Mickey, despite his familiar scent, the reticent boyish grin and charm. Jack Standish was one of thousands or even millions of men who possessed tiny traces of Mickey Pedigo's persona, his warm helpful way. This Standish was intermittently impersonal, reserved, and currently, again becoming annoyed.

She needed to tell him she'd changed her mind and began culling explanations which might offend him.

She had gotten tougher about that--offending men. She had made Ross Belton angry, finally. Offending him at the last, however, produced clarity. Like Standish, Ross was kind. By responding tactfully to his early overtures, later Ruth had injured him, although not irreparably. She had learned the direct approach was best. Yes, she must be candid with this man and very firm.

She wangled through the other travelers, winding her way to stand in front of Standish. He loomed taller than she realized. He didn't lower his chin to look at her, but glowered down over his Rathbonian nose.

"I can't go with you," she said flatly.

His chin dropped and he fixed the gray eyes, suddenly cold and hard as granite, on her face.

"I don't want to go with you." How much clearer could she be?

He snorted. "White slavers don't pick up American matrons on airplanes."

The statement itself, which voiced her darkest thoughts, made her smile, embarrassed at being so transparent. "No, I don't suppose they do."

His glower softened slightly.

She tried again. "As ridiculous as it sounds, I am not so naive as to go traipsing off with someone I don't know in a strange city, a strange country, without telling someone."

"All right, then. Tell someone."

It was her turn to huff as she looked around. "I doubt anyone will care."

"Exactly."

She stiffened. If she were missing, someone would care, eventually. "I'll take the hotel room in London and try to get my bearings. I'll call the consulate, ask how long they suppose I'll be stranded. You can give me your number at the inn. I can call you."

He studied her a moment, his thoughts shrouded with a look of indifference. "We'll drop you at the hotel."

A quick smile escaped her constraint and she blushed, again glancing around, this time to see if anyone was watching. She and Mickey had never gone anywhere that they hadn't run into someone they knew and she wondered if that someone were observing her now. She looked around self consciously. If the acquaintances were there, she didn't see them. Thank goodness.

People from home, old friends, still teased her about the blush, left over from childhood; persisting, despite the advantages of time and maturity.

For a moment, she thought she detected a twinkle in Standish's somber gray eyes, but as she looked more closely, the veil of indifference returned, and his face again assumed its frown of impersonal detachment.

Was there a warm, natural human being inside there somewhere struggling to get out? She wondered.

In the cab both the driver and Standish shrugged when she asked if she might lower her window.

From what she could see in the predawn, the countryside appeared lush and well organized, not at all like the sprawling plains of home. The air was heavily damp and smelled fishy.

Morning traffic increased only slightly as they neared the business district. The smells took on the musty odor of a large older city.

Dallas, swept by dry wind, usually smelled of dirt and exhaust fumes, o⋯ newspapers and gasoline. London shared some of those, with a dash of damp foliage and the occasional odor of fish, unexpected but not altogether unpleasant.

The incidental uniformed bobby looked as if he belonged on a postcard and she swallowed a giggle.

The buildings, bathed in security lights, were like pictures out of story books. Ruth expected to see a horse-drawn carriage bouncing over cobblestone streets. There were double-deck buses. Despite the early hour, an occasional pedestrian scurried here or there. One had the determined stride of a city dweller in America moving against the clock.

Standish's sudden movement startled her, and she jumped, prompting a reappearance of the teasing gray twinkle before it could be censored. Thumbing through his wallet, he handed her a business card with dog-eared corners.

"The Biscuit Basket" was the name embossed there, along with a series o⋯ numbers which appeared to be address and phone.

"When you're comfortable about your safety, call. I will have them reserve space in your name. It will be affordable."

She stuck the card into her shirt pocket inside her sweater just as the cabby swept swiftly and expertly into a parking place outside a large brown brick building whose marquis high overhead Ruth was not at an angle to read. Both the cabby and Standish stepped out.

Working and muttering together, they recovered her part of the luggage and set it on a carrier which appeared on the sidewalk with a bellman.

Ruth juggled her purse and one of the smaller bags. Jack took the bag and set it beside its mate next to the duffel slouched on the luggage dolly.

"I'll get it," he said, indicating the tip.

"No."

He reached over, closed her purse, and tipped the bellman. "Don't go to sleep now." He stepped back to the taxi.

"What?"

"Jet lag. Don't try to stay on Oklahoma time. Make the switch now. Stay up the rest of the day and sleep when the natives do."

"Then I'll have to readjust to Ugandan time."

"It's only a couple of hours difference, not even a whole continent's worth. The hard part will be staying up all day today. If you can do it, you'll be better off."

"I insist you let me at least pay the cab fare." She fished bills out of her purse and thrust them into the driver's hand. The cabby glanced at Standish who scowled and shook his head in defeat. He slid into the cab which immediately carved a niche for itself in the sparse flow of traffic.

Ruth scarcely had time to mourn over the second thoughts which assailed her as she watched the cab out of sight. The porter was already rolling her belongings through the luggage door and the doorman waited for her at the guests' entrance, greeting her with a drowsy, "Welcome to the Browne."

She got the room without difficulty, a small room with a tiny private bath, already vacant, clean and ready.

The bed looked inviting. Remembering Standish's advice, she laid out fresh clothing--a cotton dress and sweater--bathed, redid her make-up, and even touched up her hair with her curling iron. It was nearly seven o'clock.

Revitalized, Ruth stepped into the hallway and waylaid one of the maids. "Where is the coffee shop?"

The girl looked bewildered.

"Do you speak English?"

"Yes, mim, I do."

"Well, is there a coffee shop downstairs?"

"Beg pardon, mim."

Ruth repeated the question slowly, twice again, before the girl confirmed that the grill was open.

"And is the American Embassy near here?" The girl again looked baffled. "American Embassy?" Ruth tried again.

"I don't know the place, mim."

"Thank you for your help," Ruth said, fishing a dollar from her purse.

"Oh, there's no need of that, mim." The girl's small voice squeaked.

"I insist."

The girl accepted the bill. "If you've need of anything, tea, pastries, the loo, I'm Millie."

Ruth thanked her, wondering what a loo might be. She'd read the word someplace, but couldn't remember in what context.

She needed a lot of advice that morning but had to speak slowly and distinctly and choose her words carefully to be understood. Even then, it took at least two tries. She felt completely disoriented. She didn't know how to use the telephones, had never made an overseas call. She wanted to speak with Carly, maybe even Donnie, try to steady herself with their familiar voices. And she needed to contact Larry Reid at the wire service.

In fact, she could do an article on this little snag in her adventure. It might make a good human interest story, familiar to frequent travelers.

With that idea in mind, Ruth hurried back to her room, jotted her story, edited it and called the desk to get instructions for making long distance calls. Again the questions bore repeating.

She called Donnie with tales of her adventure to date. He seemed mildly interested.

Reid, too, seemed only tolerant when she reached him at his home phone number, thought the travel snag story might be worthwhile, then gave her the number for a typist who would take her dictation.

"But, Ruthy, why don't you wait until morning--that's Eastern Standard Time--to call her." Ruth had forgotten the time difference. A clock on the bedside table said eight-fifteen. Eastern standard was six...or was it seven...no, six hours earlier. Ruth grimaced and clenched her teeth.

"Right."

Despite the oversight, with those minor successes under her belt, Ruth felt ready to tackle something more formidable as she rode the lift to the lobby.

Chapter Six

Ruth read a voluminous *London Times* as she lingered over surprisingly good coffee and a basket of assorted sweet breads in the hotel coffee shop, in no hurry after she learned from the desk clerk the location of the American Embassy and its business hours.

"Are you familiar with The Biscuit Basket?" she had asked the clerk. He looked puzzled and she repeated her question slowly, enunciating carefully.

"Yes, madam, quite. It is a fine period place, of sorts. However, now that the place has such an outstanding reputation, the proprietors no longer have what we term, 'a slow season.' They require reservations at least three months in advance. I have promised my own wife an outing there. We are scheduled in August."

Interrupting her leisure over *The Times*, Ruth opened her purse to search for The Biscuit Basket business card. It was not in her coin purse or in the side zipper pocket where she expected it to be.

When she had searched the pockets of her purse thoroughly, she began laying its contents on the table in front of her. She thumbed through the pages of her passport and checkbook and shook out tissues, even examined the envelopes containing her airplane tickets and boarding passes. The dog-eared little card had vanished. She leaned back, annoyed.

Of course the number would be in a telephone directory. She could look it up.

She glanced at a clock visible in the lobby. It was nearly ten. The embassy would be open.

Armed with directions provided by the doorman, she folded the *Times* under her arm and began walking. Patches of fog lingered, but most had cleared. Vehicle traffic seemed surprisingly sparse for such a large city.

Bells tolled and a carillon rang out. Suddenly she realized. *How stupid. No wonder downtown traffic was light.* "It's Sunday," she said out loud.

Why hadn't the desk clerk said something? But then he probably assumed she knew what day it was. Again she had the strength-sapping thought: *was she competent to be out in the world unsupervised?*

Her steps slowed until she stood still. Certainly she could get around by herself. She was a grown woman, well-educated, seasoned, experienced. Then the deflating thought, most of her experience involved a household, children, adventures in small town America.

Mickey had sheltered and protected her. *Had he shielded her too much?*

She set her jaw. She was not going to be crippled by not having had to cope. Maybe she was handicapped, slightly, but she had character and determination. She

37

could overcome the years of pampering and soft living. Thoughts of Micke
strengthened her.

As she began walking again, Ruth reminded herself he had always said peopl
behave pretty much as you expect them to: considerate, if you expect kindness; fou
if you expect evil. So far, that had been true. She had been suspicious of the dar
little gentleman on the airplane and he had behaved as she might have expected
Standish, on the other hand... Well... He had tried to steer her to the Biscuit Baske
first. And he had seen to it that she had nice accommodations in The Browne.

Also, her faith and natural optimism were assets. Hadn't she always been
generally optimistic about the outcomes of occurrences which first appeared
ominous? Hadn't she not only survived, but embarked on a new adventure, after the
devastation of Mickey's death? She swung her arms and pretended a bravado she
did not actually feel as she put a resolute spring in her step.

"Make believe you're brave and the ruse will take you far..." she hummed a
she strode. Wasn't she in London, a city whose storied history went back, back
back. How much she could recall of England's history? The Battle of Hastings
1066. She winced. Maybe that was too far back.

Straining her brain as she walked, Ruth recalled news stories of the prime
minister addressing parliament one recent afternoon. The quotes made him sound
sarcastic. British humor often eluded her, but she had enjoyed stories about the mar
and his caustic remarks.

Not knowing what day it is should not destroy a person's confidence. It's
Sunday. London is famous for its cathedrals. She had on a dress. She'd go to
church.

Just off Trafalgar Square on the tourist map was St. Martin-in-the-Fields
Ruth got her bearings and set her course.

*   *   *

Back at the hotel later, Ruth selected a dozen brochures from the tourist
information rack in the lobby and retired to her quarters to select her afternoon's
targets. Spreading the pamphlets on the bed, she slipped off her shoes and stretched
out to browse and make a list. She had been reading only a few moments, her head
propped on her hand, when the shrill, insistent blast of the telephone bell jarred her
awake. "Hello," she said uncertainly into the unfamiliar device.

"Not sleeping are you?" Jack Standish didn't bother to identify himself.

"What? And ignore your sage advice?"

"Is that a no?"

"More like a maybe."

"What have you seen so far?"

She didn't know if he was playing detective or genuinely interested. "First let
me say the hotel is terrific and I have a very comfortable room. Thank you. I've

been to Trafalgar Square, to church at St. Martin's and returned. I'm beginning to feel like a local."

"Do you find the language difference a problem?"

She laughed at his apt guess. "I already speak English, you know."

"Your Oklahoma twang is a long way from the King's English."

"Okay, so there's a slight difference."

"Do you have to repeat yourself a lot?"

"I can guess how you know that, seeing as your Texas drawl is probably not any more palatable to delicate British ears than my twang."

He chuckled appreciatively.

Papers beneath her crackled as she moved. "Anyway, I was looking over some tourist information pamphlets when you called. Did your friends have room for you?"

"Of course."

"The desk clerk here gave the Biscuit Basket a glowing endorsement. He said it was impossible to stay there without reservations made months in advance."

"Ah, but you have influence."

"As I told you, the hotel is very nice. I wouldn't want to cause your friends any inconvenience."

"They'll be happy to accommodate you, when you're willing to come. I'll fetch you personally. The only question is when that will be."

Ruth allowed a pained smile. She could not fathom why this man was so set on taking her to raise, especially when the lovely flight attendants obviously were eager to share their time with him. She sat up straight and swung her legs over the side of the bed. "Why are you taking such an interest in me?" The question sounded blunt.

His spurt of laughter was genuine. "Why not?"

"That lovely young stewardess gave you her number."

"Me and probably a dozen other guys. The more pertinent question here is," he lowered his voice suggestively, "how many men have your number?"

It was her turn to chuckle, then she sobered, wondering about the double-entendre. "I'm going to the American Embassy in the morning at ten. I can walk from here, find my way with no help. I want to ask how long they think flights will be delayed. I'll leave my name and number. They can contact me when they have an all clear. I plan to call and do the same with the airline."

"And what phone number do you plan to leave with all these folks?"

She hadn't thought of that. "I guess the number at the Biscuit Basket, if your friends will allow me to stay."

"Do you still have the number?"

"Yes, on the card you gave me."

"And do you know where the card is?"

She smiled to herself. He had to be clairvoyant. She hedged. "Well, I haven thrown anything away so I'm sure I still have it..."

"In the pocket of the blouse you wore on the plane."

"Yes," she murmured, muttering to herself. "Of course. I knew that."

He laughed lightly. "I'll pick you up at the American Embassy at ten-thirt tomorrow morning."

"Jack." Ruth paused, then plunged. "I'm not wealthy."

He coughed. "You've now cast me as a fortune hunter in pursuit of your lif savings, have you?" His hearty laugh rumbled over the line like thunder in th distance.

"Well...I don't understand why you're going to so much trouble. I keep tryin to let you off the hook. You got me comfortably situated here in the hotel. Yo were free."

His rich baritone burbled. "I'm a do-gooder at heart. An incorrigibl do-gooder. I pick up strays and assist the helpless and infirmed."

The taunt stung. "And which am I?"

"I'm researching that."

"I see. Do you always do this stray rescue business on an internationa scale?"

He laughed again and didn't respond.

"I believe I resent your thinking of me as a lost pup." She felt justifiabl miffed.

His laughter subsided. "Maybe that's not what I'm thinking at all."

"So what are you thinking?"

"I guess we'll have to figure that out together. See you in the morning. Don' go back to sleep."

She cradled the phone puzzling. "Don't look a gift horse in the mouth." He voice sounded odd in the stillness of the room. "Oh, yeah? Look what happened to the poor old Trojans.

"Jack Standish seems like a nice man." She played devil's advocate to her more cautious self. "He has a very quick mind.

"But then, some of Jeffry Dahmer's neighbors thought Jeff was nice.

"What could Standish possibly want with me?"

She got up and paced to the tiny bathroom and back, circled and repeated·the path.

"I wish Mickey were here. He read people so well. The children are like me, more trusting.

"I think I'll call Donnie, tell him about the change in plan, give him The Biscuit Basket number." She looked at the clock. "Too early there for him. I'll do it later." She grabbed her sweater and left.

* * *

The receptionist at the embassy on Monday morning was cordial. "We've had a number of queries regarding the freeze on flights to east Africa." She had a clipped West Coast American accent, refreshing to Ruth's ears. "You need to see Mr. Doss, second office on your right."

Mr. Doss was young and from Connecticut. "We're discouraging travel in that area for the time being. Is this trip urgent? Is it an emergency?"

"No." She thought a moment. "Maybe I could fly into another part of Africa and drive."

He paced to the front of his desk, leaned his backside against it and crossed his arms over his chest. "I'd advise strenuously against that. The highways there are not like American highways. You'd need an experienced guide. There are forty-seven tribes in Uganda. Each one has its own language. They cannot understand each other, which is why English is the government's official language. You'd have language difficulties anywhere in Africa. I thought you said this was not an emergency."

Father Catlett would be looking for her, of course. She had no way to contact him to explain the delay. "No." She sighed. "No emergency." She stood and offered to shake hands. "How long do you think this trouble will last?"

He walked her to the door. "Who knows?"

41

Chapter Seven

Jack Standish stepped from a car at the curb in front of the embassy as Ruth exited the building. It was only ten-twenty. She had expected a wait. She felt light-headed when she saw him, and inhaled twice before breathing out.

He stood unsmiling, very straight and startlingly handsome in a light gray sport coat, hounds tooth slacks and a navy blue shirt open at the neck. An impudent shock of dark chest hair curled at the hollow of his throat.

Not wanting him to notice her nervous, unexplained excitement, Ruth focused on the car. She didn't recognize the make. It was large, boxy, a highly polished gray color which oddly enough, matched Standish's jacket. She swallowed and allowed a slight smile. He nodded, gazing at her a long moment as a boyish grin confiscated his features. The look was eager, adoring, and completely unexpected.

Striding toward her, he made no effort to conceal his pleasure which seemed a reflection of her own dizzying rush. In spite of her best effort to think down the rising color, she felt herself blush brightly.

Why did seeing him arouse such a giddy response? She had received eager receptions before--admittedly, most of them in recent years from Carly's cocker spaniel. That thought made her laugh out loud.

Jack held out his hand. Biting her bottom lip to quell her excitement, she walked forward and slipped her hand into his. His touch, his nearness were warm and reassuring, in the damp chill of the spring morning, as he looped her arm through his.

The sky was heavy with darkening clouds. Wordlessly, Standish handed her into the driver's side of the car, but the wheel was on the passenger side. She felt completely disoriented.

Coming around, his eyes caught hers again through the windshield and he paused. They both seemed frozen in a moment of time, staring into each others' faces several heartbeats before she blinked, again blushing furiously. He relinquished a slight smile.

He got into the car and settled behind the wheel before he spoke. "We'll swing by the hotel and pick up your bags." He started the engine and Ruth, still trying to gain control of her giddiness, sought frantically for a benign subject.

"This is a nice car. What is it?"

He pulled out into traffic. "What does it look like?"

"A ghost."

"Aptly put."

She didn't know what he meant. "Isn't it confusing to drive here, with the steering wheel on the wrong side, and different rules, and lefts being rights?"

He shot her a brief, appreciative glance. "No. It's like changing languages. You just have to adjust your thinking a little. Do you want to do some sightseeing before we run out to the Biscuit Basket or would you rather come back another time?"

"I don't know." Ruth felt a surge of the old uncertainty. Jack pulled up to a red traffic light, turned his head to look at her but remained silent.

She avoided his gaze. "There are a lot of things I want to see. One of those is the English countryside, away from all these people.

The traffic light changed. He looked forward and she allowed herself a quick glance at his profile.

Very much like Basil Rathbone, she decided, confirming her earlier impression. He turned at that moment and caught her watching him. She quickly lowered her eyes.

"London is much bigger and more 'today' that I expected." Her words tumbled over themselves and she took a deep breath trying to slow her palpitating heart. She was reacting to him like some goopy teenager. "It teems, like cities all seem to teem. Everyone's in a hurry."

"You expected cobblestone streets, horse-drawn carriages, Sherlock Holmes strolling along?"

He must be aware of the Rathbone resemblance. "Terribly gullible of me, what?"

He chuckled at her imitation of the patois. "I'll bet you're good at languages. You obviously have an ear. Have you ever studied anything but English?"

"I took Latin in high school and French in college."

"Did you enjoy them?"

"Yes. I was surprised when I began thinking in French. No one had told me that would happen."

"Oh, that is a good sign."

They drove in silence for several minutes, allowing Ruth's initial silliness to ebb. "Not to beat a dead horse, old man, but why are you being so solicitous?"

He kept his eyes on the traffic and lowered his voice. "I find you disarming, charming. I imagine people often think so."

She turned toward the window, again trying to overcome the blush. "No one's mentioned it."

"You are stimulating, amusing, a good conversationalist, interested, interesting and..." He hesitated.

"And what?"

He shrugged without looking at her. "Quite striking to look at."

Bewildered, she stared at him. "What?"

"You are a beautiful woman." His voice had an edge of annoyance. "Don't tell me no one's mentioned that."

At a loss, she couldn't think of anything to say.

"Part of your charm is that you seem to have absolutely no idea how attractive you are." Standish's tone was matter-of-fact. "Also, you have that air of innocence I mentioned before, which I find compelling. And, of course, you are married." Before she could reply, he hurried on. "Not just married but what I would call very married. You obviously are not looking for a man." He flashed her a conspiratorial smile. "A lot of women are, and it's obvious. Plus, they usually want to dictate terms."

She remained silent. He shrugged.

"You're going to Uganda. We have a lot in common." He paused but she was suddenly struck dumb. "Of course, too, there is an element of mystery about you."

Ruth began shaking her head. "No, I'm completely transparent. No secrets."

"Not true." He laughed lightly at her surprise. "Example: you choke at any reference to your husband." He looked at her, apparently waiting for an explanation. The heavy, familiar cloud of grief crept over her. He sobered, watching her. "Like now."

Ruth looked straight ahead. Her heart ached at being reminded so keenly of her loss. She didn't want to talk about Mickey. *Not here. Not now.* Besides, it might intimidate Standish to learn she was a widow, therefore, one of those damnable single women.

"I take it you are worried about him or angry with him or..." Jack hesitated. Ruth remained silent, staring forward as if she hadn't heard, trying to keep the expression on her face blank while reining in runaway emotions. He added, under his breath, "We'll discuss it another time."

As he pulled into the circle drive in front of the Browne Hotel, she broke her silence. "My things are down already, in the bellman's area." Perhaps she shouldn't go with him under false pretenses, yet she couldn't think of a graceful way out.

She waved Standish back as he opened his car door. "I'll just be a minute. Why don't you open the trunk."

He stepped from the car and walked around to the back casting a skeptical look at Ruth.

Returning quickly, she directed the trailing bellman to the back of the car and handed him several bills. He tipped his cap and thanked her.

Jack said, "I could have taken care of that for you." She didn't argue. Neither spoke as they got back in the car and waited for an opening in the traffic. As Standish pulled into the flow. Ruth stared straight ahead.

"I'm neither too old nor frail to fend for myself nor too poor to pay my own way." Her words sounded acerbic to her own ears.

Jack glowered at the roadway. "The old, frail crack... You've made severa references to age. Tell me now how old you think I am."

She shot him glance and allowed a tolerant smile. "My oldest child, Carly is twenty-eight. I put you a little older than she is. I've revised that estimate u some. Are you thirty-five?"

"Forty-five."

Ruth made no attempt to hide her genuine surprise as she turned to star unabashedly. "No." She studied his profile. "In all your travels, you've discovere the fountain of youth, right?"

He returned her steady look. "And how old are you?"

The question startled her. "Fifty-two." She cast him a wry smile. "That's no a polite question to ask a mature female."

Approving her, he grinned as he looked back at the traffic. "I doubt you'v ever played the coquette very convincingly. You could have been evasive, ask hov old I thought you were. Some ladies do that and then admit to being about whateve age the gentleman suggests."

"I'll try to remember that. My real reluctance in telling my age is that som people think women over fifty are invisible, even inaudible. I figure if I don't verif my years, I might extend my viable days."

"I see." His grin broadened and he nodded sagely.

When she was quiet for several minutes, again frowning at the highway, shc felt his eyes. "You were more at ease when you thought I was your daughter's age is that right?"

"My son Michael says I give a lot of unsolicited advice to the young. Mayb you've saved yourself that." She flashed him a look. "If you really are forty-five."

Standish extracted his billfold from an inside coat pocket and handed it to her "My driver's license. I am six-foot-three but I'm up from a hundred eighty-five pounds to two-ten. Otherwise, the information there is correct. Check the birth date." Ruth scanned the license. "Now, does it make any difference?"

She returned the billfold to his waiting hand, bowed her head, and appeared to speak to her lap. "Not really. I don't think the invisible-after-fifty theory applies to men. You have plenty of time left." She looked back at him. "And, yes, I am comfortable around young people. I've spent a lot of time with them. I like them."

He returned her look. "And when you found I was no longer one of the young people, you didn't like me any more?"

"Oh, I didn't mean it like that." She stammered, trying to redeem herself. " still like you just as much as I did before."

"Which isn't all that much?"

She turned a chastising look on him. "It's one thing to order a Bloody Mary or chicken for dinner without consulting me." Her tone was brusque. "It's another to keep trying to put words in my mouth. I can formulate and express my own opinions quite well, thank you." Realizing the words sounded harsh, she added, "Even if some people can no longer see or hear me."

Standish's chin thrust upward with a sudden jarring laugh. She smiled. As his mirth subsided, he said, "I rarely laugh anymore. I don't know why not. It certainly feels good. I've experienced a peculiar euphoria from the moment I noticed you trying to extricate yourself from the clutches of the leering middle eastern gentleman. You are very comical, Ruth Pedigo. Most of the time I don't think you really intend to be funny. Something about you makes me want to laugh...and laughing seems to set me free."

"You don't seem like a brooding kind of man."

"No? Well, that's good. Look, speaking of brooding, there's the Tower of London, off over that way."

The conversation from there was laced with historical trivia; Jack's from personal experience, Ruth's from her recent review of the brochures and years of voracious reading.

"Standish," Ruth asked finally, "why did they call you to first class on the airplane?"

"A passenger thought she was having a heart attack."

"And were you able to help?"

"Yes. It was her gall bladder. I told her she needed to have it seen about."

"Oh." She hesitated, giving him a searching look. "Are you qualified to diagnose something like that?"

"Yes."

The lane leading to the Biscuit Basket appeared to be wet. A gloomy overcast had spread across the land, issuing a fine mist which was becoming visible as individual drops.

"Does the Biscuit Basket have a fireplace?" Ruth asked, noticing the deterioration in the weather.

"Several. It might be a cozy afternoon for reading or chess by the hearth. Do you play chess?"

"Not exactly. I played with my younger son when he was in high school. Occasionally I could beat him, but not often enough to hold his attention. Do you play?"

"A little. Do you like games?"

"Very much. I excuse my early performance at chess by explaining Donnie took unfair advantage. He only invited me to play after nine-thirty at night. I'm a morning person. After nine p.m., I'm bleary. Donnie said he didn't do it on purpose--challenging me after my peak--but I suspect he did."

"Here we are." Jack pointed to their left.

Beyond a knoll, Ruth could see a parapet peering from the top of a rampart. She wheezed, gazing at the structure as it rose into full view. "Oh, Jack, you didn' say it was a castle."

"It's not really, but it's quite large and made of stone and feels something like a castle. It's a little tame for a castle. There's neither moat to stop its enemies nor dungeon for torture nor tower for prisoners."

He slipped the car into a parking slot near the front entrance as Ruth continued staring, completely captivated.

Chapter Eight

A sharp-featured man in tweed knickers appeared at the front entrance to the Biscuit Basket. An older man in livery followed, moving directly to the trunk for Ruth's luggage.

Ruth wondered if guests at this obviously posh place often arrived with their belongings in duffel bags. But she was here as a guest, her belongings were so contained and the bellman didn't seem shocked. Perhaps she was not the first.

"Ruth Pedigo, this is my good friend and your gracious host, Reggie Finch." Standish indicated the man in the knickers. "Reggie and his wife Pamela own and operate this cozy little establishment."

Smiling but scarcely able to keep her eyes from the stone wall looming over them, Ruth shook hands with Reggie Finch who looked her over curiously.

Pamela Finch joined them in the entry hall where the guest register occupied an expansive oak library table. A massive, ornate grandfather clock chimed the quarter hour.

Standing at her back, Jack put his hands on Ruth's shoulders. "What room does she have?"

Pamela looked startled. "The Guinevere."

When Jack hesitated, Ruth looked back to find him glowering at their hostess, obviously displeased.

What's his problem, Ruth wondered as Pamela continued speaking, having missed Jack's look of annoyance. Ruth felt sure the woman would be intimidated when she noticed Jack's pique, and he seemed to be getting angrier with every word.

Pamela prattled, unaware. "We had to roust the Bogles. They were nice enough about it. I told them we had a special guest come unexpectedly." She winked at Ruth. "I certainly cannot be called to task for their assuming the special guest was a royal."

Jack allowed a quick smile which broadened at Ruth's muffled giggle as she said, "First time I've been mistaken for royalty."

Intercepting the elderly bellhop who was juggling her luggage, Standish tucked Ruth's two small suitcases under his arm, shifted her duffel into that hand and took her elbow with the free one.

"Come on." He seemed as proud as a parent showing off a newborn. She returned his smile. His glow melted quickly to displeasure, however, as Pamela fell into step beside Ruth. This time Mrs. Finch caught his cross look and stopped.

"I need to see to the meal." A stiffly proper Pamela addressed herself to Ruth. She fluttered her fingers. "Ta for now."

Thinking Jack was over burdened with her bags, Ruth tried to take the duffel. "Here, let me help with that."

He pretended not to hear her as he strode ahead. He hesitated at the parlo doorway to point out the fireplace which stretched six feet from side to side and wa as tall as Jack's shoulders. A dozen logs had been laid and awaited only the flame

"It's magnificent." She whispered, awed. "I've never seen a fireplace tha large. Does the heat drive everyone out of the room?"

"No, but you'll notice the seating is well away from the hearth."

The room was huge, with mahogany furnishings grouped to provide coz corners for two, conversation pits for several and game tables to accommodate a many as six or eight. There was a billiard table to their left, beneath a replic stained glass light fixture.

Bookshelves spanned two interior walls from floor to ceiling some fifteen fee high. A library ladder provided access to the books on the upper shelves.

Tapestries covered much of the broad stone wall between windows. Rut wondered if the hangings helped insulate the room as well as providing artful decor The chamber still seemed drafty. Although there were no occupants, the space wa bathed in light--radiating from sconces on the walls, indirect lighting conceale above long velvet draperies, and lamps everywhere--an effort perhaps to ward of the morning's gloom, she thought.

She trailed Jack up the massive curved stone staircase to a second floo hallway, and past oversized wooden doors with black iron hinges and fittings. She stopped several times to admire the authenticity of the place. She wanted to make notes, to do a story about a traveler's impressions here, a journey back in time.

Jack stood patiently in front of the fifth door on their right. Ruth stepped by him, turned the oversized black key in the huge lock, lifted the latch and pushed the door open.

The room was enormous, with a wall of leaded windows opposite the entry. Rain fell in sheets, but its bleak contribution to the afternoon was lifted by a small, cheery fire crackling in the fireplace which monopolized the room's wall on their right. A love seat at the foot of the bed faced the fireplace.

A stair step was provided for mounting the tall, four-poster bed looming on her left. Ruth smiled at the prospect of sleeping there, snuggled deep in what appeared to be a feather mattress. Jack stood quietly watching her face as she surveyed the room and he smiled an odd half-smile.

She noticed his expression. "What are you thinking?"

"That I like real people." He gave a dismissive snort and continued with her bags to an alcove redesigned as a dressing area.

"Bathrooms were carved out of existing turrets." He nodded toward a door beyond the dressing alcove. "They have all the essentials, including overhead electric heating. I think you'll be comfortable here."

"But they had to evict other guests?"

He regarded her with open admiration. "You already appreciate the Guinevere more than the Bogles did."

Embarrassed again by his frank display of regard, she toured the perimeters of the huge chamber.

His eyes followed her. "Do you need to rest or unpack things before lunch or can we go downstairs?"

Ruth gave him her most appreciative smile. "I think I'll stay here for a while, if you don't mind."

"But I want you to see the grounds. They have a maze--the real thing."

Her glance directed his toward the leaded glass windows. The deluge outside raged with a vengeance.

He looked taken aback. "Probably not the best time to take in the gardens. I could stay here while you unpack, supervise, if you like."

Ruth chuckled. "No thanks. I'll sort through my unmentionables alone, if you don't mind. I may even wash out a couple of things."

"There's a laundry in the basement."

"The dungeon has washers and dryers?"

"Bathrooms and laundry facilities may detract from the authenticity, but they do a lot for the convenience of the place." He showed no sign of leaving.

She moved toward him. He watched carefully as she placed a hand on his firm upper arm and nudged him toward the open door. "Jack, I don't know how I'll ever be able to thank you for getting me in here. I'm definitely impressed. It's marvelous. I want to lock out the world, just putter around in here, absorb the ambiance, pretend."

He gave her an astonished look. "I don't remember ever being invited to leave a lady's bedroom before. Am I being bounced?"

"Sort of." She felt comically apologetic. "You don't belong. You're too today."

"Only yesterday you called me a knight in shining armor. Today you're kicking me out for being too up-to-date?"

"The former was before you produced a castle. Now you're an anachronism, too high-tech for the place."

He looked genuinely injured. "Lunch is at one."

"I'll be down before then, except..."

"What?"

"I don't have a clock."

"What? You started a trip halfway around the world without a time piece?"

"I forgot to bring my wind-up Baby Ben and decided to pick one up someplace. Where better to get a Baby Ben than 'neath the shadow of the real thing."

Jack unbuckled the leather band of his wristwatch and handed it to her. She declined and retreated a step. "I can't take your watch."

He grabbed her hand, turned it palm up and placed the watch in it. "I want you there for lunch." His intensity caught her off guard.

"All right."

He closed her fingers around the watch with one hand while he continued holding her wrist with the other. Her questioning eyes sought his, but he stared at her wrist and hesitated another moment before releasing it. There was something timid, boyish, something very vulnerable about him in that moment and Ruth felt affection swell inside her.

Without looking at her, he set his mouth and pivoted. "I'll see you downstairs before one." He tossed the words over his shoulder with no inflection.

Following, Ruth touched the door as it closed behind him. She latched the deadbolt, then patted the wood before she turned to smile warmly at the room.

"Marvelous!" she whispered. "Absolutely marvelous!"

Chapter Nine

Sitting on a Chesterfield sofa in the parlor just off the entry hall, Standish stood as Ruth descended, her head high, carrying herself stiffly, regally, like a courtesan from another era. Unable to contain it until she reached him, she giggled. He bowed, acknowledging her imagined rank.

Grinning but without saying a word, he gave her his arm and escorted her into the dining room where a liveried footman held her chair at the long table. Reggie Finch was already in place at the head, his wife at the foot. Others occupied several of the twenty chairs lining the table's sides as more guests came in behind them. Casual conversations ignited like grass fires as the diners introduced themselves to each other.

Standish, seated by place card across the table and down three from Ruth, glared his annoyance at Pamela Finch who again seemed oblivious to his displeasure.

Ruth found herself between a large German woman, Mildred Sittle, and a teen-aged boy from New Jersey with acne. Mildred spoke excellent English and proved an able conversationalist.

"Where's youse from?" the boy, David, asked when it was his turn to acknowledge his introduction to Ruth. His words were badly distorted, diverted as they were through his nasal passages.

Ruth smiled. "I beg your pardon?"

"Youse from da states, ain't ya?"

She tilted her head, looking at him, trying frantically to decipher his words. "Where am I from?"

"Yeah, dat's the quession I's astin'."

Ruth grinned broadly trying to contain the snicker which escaped anyway as her brain translated frantically. "I'm from Oklahoma. Bridger, Oklahoma."

"I heard on the noos about doze tornadoes youse had out there in Oklahomer."

Ruth's laughter erupted and she looked helplessly at Jack who smiled, nodding.

"You and Mrs. Sittle seem to be getting around your German/American accents with no difficulty," Jack observed with a droll grin. "You Americans, however, may require an interpreter for your diverse dialects."

Ruth and David laughed merrily into each others' eyes.

He pulled a tissue from his shirt pocket and blew his nose. "I'll slow up on my woids."

"And I will try to enunciate." Still laughing, they shook hands to confirm their agreement.

"Do you play bridge?" Mildred chimed in each time Jack addressed Ruth, allowing no conversation between them. The bridge question was directed at Ruth as they finished lunch.

Ruth was about to answer affirmatively when Jack, who had walked around the table and stood just behind her, touched her shoulder. "Chess, remember?"

"I'm afraid my chess playing is going to be a major disappointment."

"I love chess," Mildred broke in, still seated, twisting around to engage Jack's attention. "And I am really quite good, if I do say so myself. Come on, you handsome man. I'll give you a run."

Standish's eyes narrowed darkly as Mildred hoisted herself to her feet, took his arm and tugged him toward one of the intimate game tables in the parlor. He glanced back at Ruth over his shoulder, his expression pleading. Ruth could only watch helplessly as he was spirited away.

With Mildred otherwise occupied, bridge players invited Ruth to fill out a third table. She partnered with an East Indian man whose opening bid was two spades. Surprised, Ruth recounted her unusually good hand in light of her partner's indicated powerhouse. She hoped he didn't play a weak two-bid. He didn't.

Anup spoke very little English but proved a ruthless player, fairly daring Ruth to keep pace. Despite their language differences, they played well, so well that kibitzers paired to challenge the winners after each rubber.

For Ruth the afternoon flew, despite the weather's decline from foul to worse as the rain gave way to snow. Reggie Finch lit the fire in the massive fireplace which warmed and cheered the guests. Several who had left after lunch returned.

Trying to be gracious, Ruth bit her lips to stifle the pleasure she felt each time she and Anup annihilated another set of opponents. She concentrated, trying to avoid her usual pitfall of knowing what she should have bid immediately after having bid something else. Anup frequently played the hands when the cards ran their way and defended brilliantly, when the opponents won the bid.

Anup had little interest in celebrating individual wins, but remained intent instead on meeting the challenge of their next opponents.

Accepting congratulations each time, Ruth stole glances at Jack, across the room, to find his eyes always on her.

During one break, thinking she might explode with the accumulated successes, Ruth strolled to the chess table.

Jack grinned as he watched her approach, wordlessly acknowledging her exhilaration.

She stepped behind him, put a hand on his shoulder and leaned down, her mouth close to his ear, close enough to catch the scent of him. She felt his muscles tense at her touch. Realizing how aggressive she must appear, she removed her hand.

"It's hard not to gloat." She strained to keep her voice low. "It's harder than I expected not to be 'The Ugly American.'"

He allowed a rolling chuckle.

"How many games have you played?" she asked in a normal speaking voice, straightening to watch as Mildred pondered a move. On the board, the white queen stood in jeopardy.

Mildred glanced up, then back at the board as Jack said, "This is our first."

Mildred spoke to the board. "Chess, of course, requires much more skill and intellectual concentration than party bridge." She lifted an eyebrow at Ruth. "And this civil looking gentleman is a particularly nasty opponent."

"I'm certain of that." Ruth nodded somberly but when her eyes met Jack's grays, she bit her lips, turned around to conceal her smug hilarity, and returned to the bridge table.

*   *   *

Having located pay telephones in the butler's pantry, Ruth slipped in there during the next break to call Larry Reid and dictate the new travel piece written in her room before lunch and neatly folded in her pocket. This one applauded the picturesque inns available in and around London, without specifically naming the Biscuit Basket.

After a quick call to Carly to let her family know her new location, Ruth exited the phone booth, as Pamela emerged from the kitchen, passing through the butler's pantry on her way to the dining room.

"Do you dress for dinner?" Ruth asked as she fell into step with their hostess.

Pamela smiled agreeably. "Usually we do. Yes."

"I didn't bring any evening clothes. I expected to be slogging through jungles, not dining in great halls. Could I sneak down to the kitchen and take a tray to my room?"

"Oh, Dr. Standish would never allow that." The hostess looked as if she were shocked at the suggestion.

Ruth sobered. "What does he have to say about it?"

"I assumed you knew. He is our silent partner, the financial angel who made The Biscuit Basket possible."

Ruth stared at Pamela. "He didn't mention it. I wondered how I was able to draw such a wonderful room."

"The Guinevere is our finest accommodation. He insisted you have it."

Ruth rolled her eyes, marveling. "Of course. I should have known. It is perfect. But I would never have..."

"I doubt you could have refused him long. Women don't, as a rule."

"What?"

"He is accustomed to prevailing with women.. But, then you already know that." Pamela gave her a sidelong look.

Surprised, Ruth shook her head, denying the implication. "No, dear, you misunderstand. I'm a married woman. Surely Jack has more scruples than..." She paused, reflecting.

"Perhaps he feels encouraged by someone he considers his moral equal."

The words stung, as she supposed Pamela intended. The younger woman shrugged. "You are wise, keeping him at arm's length, manipulating him as you do. You realize, of course, he would never succumb to a woman who pursued him. He has a low tolerance for feminine wiles."

This was definitely a British-style sticky wicket. "Does he bring a lot of women in on you this way then?"

Pamela regarded her oddly. "No. Actually, you are the first. And I must say you are something of a surprise. I should not be shocked, I suppose, that he would choose someone who requires no long-term commitment."

Ruth started to object but thought better of it. Her silence seemed to encourage Pamela to continue.

"Of course, the better acquainted we become, the more I understand."

Feeling hamstrung, Ruth held her tongue.

Pamela looked startled. "Oh, don't misunderstand. You are quite a lovely lovely woman."

Considering how ridiculous the situation was and what a corner she'd painted herself into, Ruth laughed. "Thank you, dear. Let me ask and I trust you to be perfectly blunt..."

Pamela nodded somberly.

"Are you afraid of Jack?"

Her hostess remained silent.

"Well?"

"I can never anticipate what will please him, or annoy him, for that matter. He is typical of his class, a gentleman a smidge too smart for his own good. He is an important man. He does important work. I gather he is even famous in some quarters."

Ruth's curiosity was piqued. "A famous college professor?"

"Teaching is only one of his occupations. He has others. I believe that one perhaps, is not the one which earns him the most respect. All I know is that he is sometimes summoned by important people to do important work."

"What kind of work?"

"I can't actually say. Something to do with health."

"I thought you had known him a long time?"

"Well, yes, I suppose." Pamela picked up and buffed a silver serving spoon. "But I do not know him well. He is actually Reggie's friend. They've known one another since Reggie was in the military. Reg was part of a United Nations peacekeeping force sent to break up fighting somewhere. That was before I knew him.

"He contracted some illness which could not be identified at first, never mind treating it. He insists his ailment had no name. Jack had something to do with curing him, although I don't know what, exactly. Neither of them has spoken of it in my hearing."

"Haven't you asked about it?"

"No, really I haven't."

"I see."

"Anyway, it is customary for women to chase after Jack. Sometimes he extinguishes their fervor with insults. He can be quite contemptuous. At one time, I thought he might prefer the company of other men, however, I've not seen any evidence of that.

"Still, I have not known him to behave around a woman as he behaves with you. Certainly I have never seen him so attentive, so intense. Neither has Reg.

"Reggie is getting quite a hoot out of this, actually, seeing the old haughty Jack disadvantaged, laughing spontaneously, acting as if he's smitten like a common school boy. Neither of us understands it."

Pamela ventured a quick assessing look at Ruth who waved the comment off. "I think you've misread our friendship."

Recovering after what she apparently considered her own thoughtless remark, Pamela shook her head. "Certainly I mean no offense when I say we don't understand. If I did understand, I might quite enjoy fate's little joke."

Ruth smiled. "I know how you feel. I feel the same. Left out. Missing the punch line. I don't understand it either. Our only compensation, Pamela, yours and mine, is that the situation is temporary. I'll be out of your hair on the first available flight to Uganda. That's a promise."

Pamela smiled and gave Ruth a pat on the forearm. "Oh, I don't think I really mind all that much now that we've had this little chat. Actually what I probably should dread is your leaving before he does. I have an inkling he may be intolerable if you leave him behind.

"Now, no more worrying about clothes for dinner. I'll just tell everyone we're casual this evening."

Chapter Ten

Ruth came down for dinner in the dress she had worn to St. Martin's on Sunday. She was assigned the chair on Reggie's right, the place of honor. Jack's place card put him next to her. Noting that other guests were assigned generally the same places they had occupied at lunch, Ruth guessed how the one change had come about.

Hosts and guests adjourned to the music room after dinner, a large chamber with a grand piano and deep, comfortable seating. When Anup approached, Jack made a point of standing between him and Ruth.

"Bridge?" Peering around Jack, Anup's round dark eyes conveyed his excitement at the prospect.

Jack shook his head, but smiled. "Mrs. Pedigo must entertain me tonight."

Anup's expression fell as he looked from Jack to Ruth, appealing for sympathy. Ruth smiled but shook her head. "Thank you, Anup. Not tonight."

Jack put his hand on her elbow and guided, deftly side-stepping Mildred, who was hedging their way. "I want you to myself tonight." He directed Ruth to one end of an expansive leather sofa, then settled close beside her. "What do you want to do tomorrow?"

She drew a deep breath. The dinner, cornish hens in orange sauce, had been delicious. She felt wonderful, more content than she had been since...since November. None of that. She wasn't going to allow herself to get maudlin tonight. "I plan to sleep late, take the mid-morning shuttle to town and sign up for a guided tour." When Jack didn't respond, she glanced at him.

His face was very close, the gray eyes partially veiled, his expression impassive, unreadable. Nervously, she hurried on, filling the awkward moment with chatter.

"I know you'll be busy with meetings in town. I want to see as much as I can. If I have two days, all the better."

Without speaking, Jack turned his attention to the musicians who had begun tuning their instruments.

As the sounds of the guest quartet wafted to the lofty ceiling, Ruth relaxed, breathing Jack's familiar fragrance. She closed her eyes and floated. A strong arm eased around her shoulders, cradling her. She imagined the warm body beside her was Mickey's and she nestled close, recalling sunlit days drifting in the boat. Mickey shamed her into holding a pole and at least pretending to fish. She smiled at the memory.

When she got too hot in the Oklahoma sun, she dived over the side to let the water cool her sun-baked body, When she was ready, Mickey lifted her back into the boat, his biceps bunching, always pleased to be reminded that his muscular body still thrilled her.

Dreamily Ruth pressed her nose into the shoulder of the powerful arm draped around her and breathed deeply.

The music ended and the response startled her, calling her back to find Standish removing the protective arm to join his applause with the others. Emotions hammered her--guilt, sorrow--followed by a buoying wave of excitement, lifting her spirits before Standish turned his gray eyes to her face.

Her heart leaped. The girlish joy she felt seemed ridiculous. Jack was nothing to her. An acquaintance. No more. She moved to the edge of the couch preparing to stand, then looked back at him.

His gaze caught and held hers and lingered a long moment before he stood and offered her a hand up.

"Are you a musician?" She tried to stave off the unexpected electricity that sizzled between them as they moved to a table of beverages and tea cakes. She hoped her innocuous question would quiet the bevy of butterflies flittering in her stomach.

"I took the required piano lessons until I was twelve." He poured them each a sherry without asking her preference.

She admired his big, steady hand. "Then what?"

"I became friends with a guy more my size--the bass violin."

Ruth laughed lightly as she took the glass Jack handed her. She tried a sip, raised her eyebrows and smiled her approval. "Not many solos for the bass, are there?"

He returned the approving look and, although his words were innocent enough, the electricity again arced between them. "Yes, as a matter of fact, there are. The bass has a personality and voice of his own. Composers who admire him show their regard by giving him quite a bit to say in certain pieces..." He glanced behind her and his voice dropped. "Oh, no."

Ruth followed his gaze to see Mildred Sittle draw a bead on them from across the room and begin a determined drive their way.

"Come with me." He hurriedly escorted Ruth to a table for two in the game room. "I know, it's after nine-thirty. I promise I'm not pulling Donnie's trick. I just want us to have some time."

Ruth smiled concurrence, surprised that he remembered her younger son's name. The gray eyes met hers and held before his expression opened with a slow, seductive smile. Her breath quickened and she looked away, blushing. She hoped he would think it was the wine heightening her color.

They lingered over the chessboard for a long while, using it as more of an excuse than an entertainment.

"Does your husband enjoy games?" Jack mulled over a move.

"Yes."

He completed his turn. "Is he competitive?"

"Very." Ruth took his queen.

Jack uncrossed his legs, squared himself in his chair and took a hard look at the board. He set his glass on a coaster, glanced at her then back at the board and narrowed his eyes

Half an hour later, Ruth covered a yawn and stretched from one side to the other. "I'm terribly sleepy and the feather mattress in the Guinevere summons. Could we call it a draw?"

Jack glanced at the empty sherry glasses. "How about a night cap?"

She stood. "Please, sir knight, grant me this boon. Let me go until the morrow."

Reluctantly he slid his chair back from the table. "We could sit by the fire."

"I expect a cheery little fire awaits in the Guinevere."

"All right, we can have our night cap by that fire."

Ruth looked directly into his face and faltered, but only for a moment. "Not a chance."

He grimaced. "No harm, no foul."

She smiled wanly, pivoted and, without looking back, walked directly out into the corridor and up the stairs.

*   *   *

Before seven-thirty Tuesday morning, Pamela knocked at Ruth's door. "You have a call on the house telephone downstairs."

The caller, the airline reservations clerk, said flights to Uganda were to resume. Ruth was assigned a seat aboard the second one out departing at six a.m. Wednesday, putting them in Entebbe at eleven-forty. She could call for her ticket and boarding pass any time.

"We depart at six and arrive at eleven-forty? Is it that far?"

"You lose three hours en route because of the time difference. The flight actually lasts something just over two hours."

"Then is there a connecting flight to Kampala?"

"Yes, a short hop."

"I'm a visitor here. Will you give me directions to the place where I am to pick up the ticket?"

"There is an agency, Dunn's, on the corner one block south of the The Browne Hotel. You may collect the ticket there. It is..."

"Good." Ruth interrupted. "The Browne is one of the few landmarks I can find. Oh, and could I possibly have a window seat?" Ruth heard the muted clattering of a keyboard.

"Yes."

"Thank you. I'll stop at Dunn's this afternoon."

Jack had gone to a breakfast meeting in town, but had left a message with Pamela who repeated it to Ruth, word for word. He would entrust her to no other guide. He had devised a day-long tour beginning at ten. She was to be ready by a quarter of, "wearing comfortable walking shoes."

Ruth asked Pamela to repeat the message, then darted upstairs to bathe and dress.

She scarcely noticed as Mildred Sittle rose from her chair at the breakfast table and scurried down the hall.

*   *   *

Jack arrived promptly at nine-forty-five, put Ruth in the open car on loan from Reggie for the day and drove off with a wave and a noisy horn-honking salute to Mildred who obviously had dressed quickly and appropriately to accompany them.

Jack had consolidated the several tours recommended in Ruth's collected brochures into one, daylong excursion.

They drove by No. 10 Downing, and whisked into parking near the palace.

A crowd had gathered to see the changing of the guard at eleven. Jack elbowed his way forward, then put Ruth in front of him. He rested his hands at the backs of her elbows. She felt his warm breath stirring her hair and she again felt the tingling sensation of electricity between them. Big Ben struck the hour but in front of the palace, nothing happened.

A murmur rippled through the crowd. The ceremony was delayed ten minutes. Ten became twenty. Grumbling sight-seers drifted away. Feeling comfortable with Jack so close, Ruth turned her head slightly to say something and caught the scent of him as he leaned closer to hear.

"Do you want to press on?" She worded her question so as not to show her preference either way. It was a strain to cloak the excitement she felt having him so near.

He grinned, obviously also enjoying their proximity. "I'm happy where I am, but we can go if you want."

"How about if we give them ten more minutes to get this gig in gear. No wonder the American Revolution succeeded."

The sound of his laughter sent chills up Ruth's spine. What was the matter with her? She felt adolescent again.

When twenty more minutes elapsed with no signs of the ceremony, Jack suggested they have lunch.

Sitting face to face sharing a wrapper of fish and chips, Ruth tried to keep her eyes off of her companion. He was, she concluded, devastating--so handsome, mannerly, mature, at ease with himself, and with her.

She needed to think about something else. Admittedly, it was difficult with him so close--always directly in front of her, beside her, or even behind her, his ever present scent provocative.

Occasionally her silly thoughts were interrupted by guilt, which she shook off. She didn't intend to berate herself here. She could do that later, when she was alone.

After lunch they followed the sound of excited children's voices cheering the antics of a traveling Punch and Judy performance.

Strolling up behind the seated audience, Jack again positioned Ruth in front of him, resting his hands on her shoulders. Slowly, carefully, his thumbs massaged the base of her neck. She tilted her head to one side, encouraging him, allowing him better access. She felt the warmth of his breath before his lips touched her highly sensitive nape. *What was happening to her? This wasn't what she wanted. Or was it? No, no, she mustn't encourage this...this intimacy.*

But she hesitated a moment too long before her resolve took hold and she stiffened and stepped away from the caress. His muffled laugh followed as she moved out of his grasp.

They spent the afternoon visiting famous landmarks. They tasted culinary delicacies and tramped up and down hills and stairways and ramps, occasionally bumping or touching. Although the sky was overcast, the weather held.

Except for acquiring some souvenirs--including an English-made Baby Ben--Ruth scarcely thought about Bridger, Oklahoma, or her children, or her grief.

Neither did she think of Uganda nor the flight out tomorrow. Her day was full of new sights, of history, of Jack's quick wit and narratives of battles and historical trivia. He was a history buff and seemed to enjoy showing off for her. She basked in the undivided attention of this man, frequently reminded by the occasional comments or stares from passers-by that he was attractive to women; all kinds of women.

This was Camelot, a fairy tale place, and she belonged here, at least for the moment.

"I need to run a little errand." They had just finished tea in a quaint place which, for the sake of tourists, clung desperately to its Nineteenth Century ambiance.

Jack sobered. "Without me?"

She stood and laughed breezily. "Yes, without you. It's just a couple of blocks. You stay here and rest. Guard these packages with your life." She glanced at a woman who was making a rather obvious effort to catch his eye. "Don't be lured away by...by anyone. I'll be right back."

Looking intently into her face, he said, "I couldn't be lured away from you. I'll stay where you say, my only desire to serve you every way you'll allow, awaiting your swift return, your pleasure my foremost concern."

He had made several similar remarks through the day. Coupled with Pamela's comments, Ruth was feeling more than a little perplexed.

A man's ego needs constant care and feeding, she told herself as she left the tea shop. *He thinks I'm married. To him, I am a new frontier, one yet unconquered. It's a game, not important--to either of us.*

She hurried two blocks, past The Browne Hotel to Dunn's Booking agency, picked up the ticket and boarding pass, and raced back toward the tea shop. As she got closer, her feet fairly flew. She panted at the brisk pace. She didn't need to hurry. He would be there. But she couldn't wait to see him...again.

She slipped through the door as another patron left the tea shop, so the bells jingled only once. She froze at the sight of him. His eyes were closed, his head resting against the high wooden back of the booth where she'd left him, his long legs stretched and ankles crossed over the packages he'd sworn to protect.

Suddenly his eyes popped open. Otherwise, he didn't move a muscle, remained still, gazing at her. She recognized the sultry exchange which passed between them. It was an adoring, desirous look which made her heart pound.

Jack broke the spell when he stood and began gathering packages. She walked toward him, frantically searching her mind for away to reestablish their earlier camaraderie.

"Standish, do you have a genuine castle on our tour?" That seemed a good way to regain the amiable mood.

"Next up." Obviously, he saw her concern and was willing to let the heated look pass without remark.

"Jack," she asked as they drove, "do you have manicures regularly?"

He glanced at his hands on the steering wheel and grinned. "The secretaries in my department gave me that for Christmas, part of a inside joke about my hands. They were offended that I hadn't redeemed the gift certificate. I had it done before I left to appease them."

"And is your hair styled?"

"Only at a barber shop near the university. Cleon's been cutting it for twenty-five years, since I was a student."

For some reason, the easy explanations annoyed her. She would like for him not to be quite so perfect.

What Jack termed "a regulation castle," was set upon sweeping, well landscaped grounds. It took very little to imagine swashbuckling sword fights in the corridors, lovers and scoundrels lurking in darkened corners of vast chambers, and the cries of prisoners from both dungeon and tower.

As they were leaving late in the afternoon, sauntering side-by-side across the drawbridge, one of the support chains shifted loudly, making the bridge shiver beneath their feet.

Startled, Ruth caught Jack's coat sleeve and, without realizing it, allowed her fingers to run down the sleeve and slip into his warm, receptive hand which closed over hers.

They walked several yards before she frowned suddenly and peered up into his face. Her joy dissolved to horror as her eyes trailed from his face to his shoulder, down his arm to their clasped hands.

"Oh!" Ruth pulled free, flustered. She looked at his face unbelieving, then angry.

His expression remained stoic, indifferent. He looked at her coolly, then at the path in front of them, not responding in any way to her unspoken accusation.

She hesitated before she began walking again, following him but remaining several paces behind. He glanced back but didn't speak, nor did he wait for her. They drove to the inn, their words stilted, speaking only when necessary.

Later, after dinner, as they sat facing each other over the chess board, Jack said, "Is Mickey Pedigo an affectionate man?"

"I've told you, I don't want to discuss..."

"I know. But this afternoon, when your hand slipped into mine, it was such a natural gesture for you, I couldn't help wondering..."

"Yes."

"What?"

"I said yes. Mickey Pedigo was an affectionate man."

The clock in the hall ticked off the otherwise silent moments.

"You often refer to him in the past tense." Jack's eyes were trained on the board. "He's been absent for some time now, I take it."

Ruth felt her mouth draw. "I'm leaving for Uganda in the morning. My flight goes at six."

He continued studying the board but the muscles in his jaw flexed.

She didn't know why she felt a need to explain. "The airline called this morning. Flights resumed today. They booked me out tomorrow. I picked up my ticket in town."

"The little errand you ran while I sat minding your packages and daydreaming in the tea shop."

"Yes."

"And you didn't think you should mention it?"

"I believe I just did."

65

There was another long pause as both stared at the chess board. His eyes were the color of gunmetal when he raised them to capture hers. "There is a vote tomorrow which I cannot miss."

She met his gaze. "My plans have nothing to do with yours."

"You can surely wait two days. I don't think you should travel in Uganda alone."

"And I don't want to postpone." She glowered at him, then relented a little again feeling an urge to explain. "This might be only a temporary window Fighting might flare up again. Flights might be grounded again. I have to go." She wanted him to understand. "Jack, getting there is what I'm doing here."

His square jaws bunched as he dropped his stare to the chessboard, pursed his lips and regarded the pieces angrily.

She watched him a long moment before she spoke again. "I do thank you, Jack, for everything. You've been a wonderful, wonderful friend."

His eyes shot back to her face. "I'm surprised you can walk away...so easily."

"Do you mean walk away from here or from you?" She didn't want to challenge him. He didn't answer but his eyes were riveted on her. She sighed. "Is this because I inadvertently took your hand this afternoon? That was a mistake, Jack. A momentary lapse."

His steely eyes flashed as they once more caught and held hers. "What's between us is a hell-of-a-lot more than a momentary lapse and you know it. You keep pretending what's happening between us is nothing. But you know you and I are a combustible mix sweetheart, fomenting, simmering. It's obvious even to strangers. Ruth Pedigo, I promise, you and I are not going to end here."

"There is no you and I!" Ruth could feel her color rising. "We were seat mates on an airplane. We passed the time pleasantly there and here." She bit her lips, struggling for control. When she had herself in check, she spoke again.

"Life is like a big highway, Jack." Her words sounded firm, although her body felt like gelatin. "We are travelers who happened to be going the same way for a time. We enjoyed each others' company. Now the road divides. We're just like the flights. We were grounded for a while but now we're ready to resume our regular schedules, our regular lives."

His eyes would not release hers. "I want to be with you."

She met his steady gaze feeling genuine concern. "I like being with you too." She couched the words as she did hoping to mitigate the intensity, the scarcely concealed, sensuous tenor in his statement. She sighed. "The timing is wrong. Maybe someday our paths will merge again."

He glared at her a long time before lowering his eyes to the chess board. When he spoke, his words came quietly. "I can practically guarantee it."

She heard the comment clearly. "Why? Is Uganda that small a country?"

"No, but whites are a minority and tend to gravitate to one other."

"I don't intend to be white in Uganda."

"Oh, yeah?" He glanced up and his voice dripped sarcasm. "And just how will you manage that?"

"I plan to be a colorless, impartial observer writing news stories and features, not some odd duck congregating with a bunch of other odd ducks."

They sat for a long while, each making his moves on the chess board in turn, but silent.

"Tell me about your husband." His voice was low, coaxing.

"I don't want to discuss him with you."

"I want to know about Mickey Pedigo."

"Why are you so persistent about this?"

"I want to know what the competition's got."

Her heart jumped and she eyed him skeptically. He was growing bolder. She needed to put a stop to this, to clarify things. "Jack, this is not a contest."

"I want to know the mark I have to beat."

She grimaced. "Have you never been married or in love?"

He regarded her oddly, his frown matching hers. "Not until..."

Her warning look stopped him.

He inhaled, obviously revising his planned statement. "I tried to talk myself into being in love a couple of times but I wasn't very convincing."

Ruth remained mute, encouraging him to continue.

He leaned back. "The first time was in college. Charlotte was tall, striking, a Sophia Loren look-alike. Very stylish. Quiet. Mysterious. We were twenty-two. My hormones raged. Hers didn't. When we made love, she considered it doing me a favor. Afterward she implied I owed her. She expected me to buy her things as compensation. I did. But it soon became like bartering for goods. Our bargaining destroyed the romance." He squinted at the chessboard and pursed his mouth.

"So?"

"That was it. Her heart-stopping pulchritude was Charlotte's primary asset. She was an important lesson. Looks like hers," he glanced up and narrowed his eyes, "and yours," he stared a long moment before he lowered his eyes again, "compel a man. Physical beauty is tantalizing. But, it isn't enough." He put his elbows on the table and rounded his
shoulders over the chessboard.

"And the second?"

"Hmm," he said, moving a knight. "Mindy was Charlotte's opposite. She was a nurse with an over active libido; short, cherubic, laughed easily, very promiscuous. She enjoyed making love. Made love with just about everyone I knew. She believed in open marriage. Translated, that meant a ceremony did not cancel dating privileges.

"I left her, but I felt the sting of it longer than she did. She was very resilient."

"So after Mindy, you swore off?"

"Off of women?" Glancing at her, he laughed. "No. I just put a moratorium on thoughts of love or marriage. Why?"

"A good marriage is two hearts synchronized, beating as one."

"Yours is a good marriage then?"

"Yes."

"And you are half of a whole heart beating?"

Marveling, she whispered, "That's right."

Jack didn't ask any more questions.

Studying the chessboard, Ruth moved her queen. "Ha!" She whooped quietly, triumphantly. "Check!"

Jack straightened in his chair, alerted from his dark reverie by the threat. Moving a bishop, he grinned. "Check and mate."

Staring at the board, Ruth groaned. "Good grief, I'll never be any good at this. How about Scrabble?"

"I'll beat you at that too."

"What, are you one of those compulsive types who has to win at everything?"

"You keep trying to make me a type. I'm not. But I am truthful and I do play games rather well."

"Maybe, but I doubt you play Scrabble as well as I do." She arched her brows.

He laughed as he stood. "Let me go find us a board."

"What time is it?"

"Have you lost your new watch already?"

"It didn't go with the ensemble."

He turned and walked several paces to view the clock in the hallway. "It's only nine-twenty."

"It's too late and you're too confident. Let's save Scrabble for another time."

He stepped in front of her as she stood and turned toward the stairs. "We still haven't played bridge together. It's your last night. Let me see if the Finches are available, just for a hand or two. How about it?"

Ruth flashed him her disapproving look.

His eyes brightened. "What are you thinking? Right this minute. What?"

"That you intimidate people. You're even trying to shame me, the woman my children dubbed tour guide of the guilt trip. It's not an area for amateurs."

He grinned mischievously. "What do you mean?"

"Giving me that innocent sulk, trying to make me feel sorry about leaving you, subtly implying I should let you win our competitions as consolation. Forget it. I've seen you get away with that with some people but..."

"Who?"

"Reggie and Pamela."

His eyes shimmered. "But not you?"

"No. Not me."

"Then we'll probably clean their clocks." He chuckled.

"Unless we play fair."

"How do you mean?"

"You and I mustn't be partners. It wouldn't be noble."

He grinned. "Are you just generally opposed to winning?"

"Oh, I intend to win. I just intend to win with Pamela as my partner. The girls against the boys."

Every trace of anger or disappointment was gone from his voice and his demeanor. "You'll regret it." He cocked one eyebrow.

She looked straight into his face, openly defying him. "You need humbling."

"You may not be the one for the job."

"Oh I think maybe I am."

Jack's boisterous shout of laughter ricocheted off the ceiling fifteen feet over their heads.

*   *   *

Reggie and Pamela agreed to play as proposed.

Amid glib comments, boasts, threats, needling and wheedling, the men won the first game. Settling to business, the women won the second and third, claiming the rubber and the victory.

"We'll have another run at you tomorrow night," Reggie challenged as Ruth stood. Offering pats of condolence to the losers, she started toward the stairs. "And we won't deal with you so gently then," Reggie called after her.

Ruth's eyes met Jack's. His rounded, a silent query. Did she want him to go up with her? She shook her head almost imperceptibly and turned to climb the stairs. He bounded up the steps between them and caught her arm. "I wish you'd let me hold you," he said quietly, "just once."

She felt the corners of her mouth twitch. "I wish it too."

Incredulous, he brightened. "You wish that I would hold you?"

She shook her head and felt a lump form in her throat. "No, I wish I could let you."

They eyed each other soberly a long moment before they turned, as if on cue, and went opposite ways, she up to her room and he back down.

Jack strode slowly to the music room and sat down at the piano. As Ruth reached the top of the stairway, she cringed to hear the strains of the haunting, "You Are So Beautiful."

Chapter Eleven

Ruth had asked Pamela privately to prepare her bill so she could pay without having to argue with Jack. Pamela slipped it under her door late. It was reasonable--too reasonable, Ruth decided.

Early the next morning, she wrote a personal check for double the amount shown on the bill. She had overheard other guests and knew that even double probably would not cover the usual charge for the Guinevere. She slipped it to Pamela who was setting tables for breakfast. Her hostess pocketed the check without looking at it and hugged Ruth hard. "I do so hate to see you leave."

"And I hate leaving. My time here has been, well, very therapeutic. I'll remember it always." The women hugged each other tightly. "Will you call a taxi for me?"

Pamela nodded but tears made her unable to speak.

Ruth put Jack's wrist watch in an envelope with a note thanking him again for all his kindnesses and slipped it into the incoming mail pouch for whoever was working the desk to find and return to him after she was gone. Then she went back upstairs to gather her luggage.

Jack was standing at the buffet in the dining room pouring two cups of coffee-to-go when Ruth came down again, this time wrestling with her luggage. He hurried to help.

"What are you doing up so early?" She squinted at him. "It's not even five o'clock."

His face was deadpan. "Taking you to the airport."

"Jack, you've done too much already. Maybe with me out of your way, you'll get some rest."

He set the duffel and both cases by the door and gazed at her, the mischievous twinkle back in his eyes.

"Ah, yes. With you out of the way, I will at last be free to make a move on the vampish Mildred Sittle."

Ruth did a double take before she began giggling. "From the stews to Mrs. Sittle? I had no idea you were so versatile."

"I have depths you have not yet plumbed." His face was suddenly serious. "Stay one more day and explore?"

Determinedly maintaining the smile, she shook her head. "I've cramped your style long enough, sir knight."

He looked glum but his words were kind. "It's been pretty tough duty." He allowed a slow smile, "but you may have noticed, I have grit."

Ruth laughed as she watched him add milk and sugar to her coffee. Dear Lord, she was going to miss him. He had become terribly important to her, even in these few days. But she'd been wise not to get more involved than she was. For them, the timing was wrong. She hoped they'd meet again...when it wasn't.

There was very little traffic through the city that early in the day.

They checked the duffel, leaving Ruth the two small cases and her purse to carry. She produced her boarding pass, then reluctantly turned to thank Jack one last time.

"Will you kiss me good-bye?" His expression was unreadable. He stepped close, not waiting for her to object. "I haven't asked much." He flashed the mischievous grin. "Don't you feel obligated, even a little bit?"

She smiled crookedly and presented her cheek for a quick buss. He put both hands on her face and turned it to kiss her forehead and nose. He leaned back to assess her reaction. She knew he could feel her trembling. When she didn't object he tugged her face close and pressed his lips to hers.

Her eyes remained open but averted.

The kiss was tentative. When it was over, he kept his hands on her face, his thumbs beneath her chin, and studied her another moment before releasing her.

"'See you." She said the words uncertainly. Her eyes stung as she scanned his face.

"This is not good-bye, Ruth. You can run, but you can't hide...from me. I'll be right behind you." He watched her darkly, reading her mind, she thought. She certainly hoped so. "That's a promise. I may be momentarily stymied, but I am not stopped. I'll lick my wounds and heal, then I'll resume the hunt. I'm coming after you."

Ruth shivered with what she feared was anticipation. She couldn't tell by his inflection or his expression if his words reflected anger, injured pride or if he were teasing.

*   *   *

The flight to Entebbe seemed brief after the overseas journey. The small plane from there to Kampala was packed. Ruth tried to concentrate on the future but her thoughts drifted again and again back to The Biscuit Basket and her associations there--particularly Jack, who had become so inordinately important.

Deplaning in Kampala, Ruth eagerly breathed the aromatic fragrance of the forests which threatened the integrity of the city, refreshing after the stale odors in the airplane.

The temperature was a mild seventy-three. She knew there was little temperature flux in Uganda, despite its location, perched squarely on the equator. The small nation would be unbearably warm, if it were not nearly four thousand feet above sea level. With mountains looming to fourteen thousand, the air there felt fresh and cool to a woman acclimated to the American plains. She felt cozy knowing the whole country was just a little larger than the state of Oklahoma.

Ruth corralled her luggage in one spot and asked the information clerk about transportation to Bwana. The young man smirked.

"There's a bus." He spoke in halting English and made a disagreeable face. "It goes there sometimes."

"How do I make arrangements?"

"You must ask Riz Diaz. He is the driver. You most assuredly will have to ask once and then again and perhaps many more times. If you hope to go today, you must begin soon and prevail quickly. The round trip takes eight hours. Any driver, even a man like Diaz, prefers to be back in sight of Kampala before dark."

Ruth glanced at the clock on the wall. It was already after noon, twelve-thirty-five. "Where do I find Mr. Diaz?"

The attendant pointed toward a man reading a newspaper with one foot propped against the wall behind him. The man was medium build, average looking. His face was hidden by a grizzled beard and framed by matted looking brown hair.

"The fare is three dollars, American." The attendant's voice carried a warning.

Straightening to her full five-foot-eight, Ruth drew a bead on Mr. Diaz and approached him, smiling.

He, too, spoke English.

"I may have other passengers." He peered at her with eyes so dark the irises looked black. A trench intersected the bridge of his nose making him resemble an angry bird.

"Passengers going to Bwana?" she asked.

"Maybe not." He glanced around. "But perhaps generally in that direction. Others may want to go also. I will see."

"Do you mean now?"

"I will see." He spoke impatiently. "If I can find the others, I will take you."

"Today?"

"Yes, today."

"How many will you need?" But she found herself speaking to his back as he shuffled toward an exit. She was certain he had heard the question and wondered why he pretended he hadn't.

As he drifted away, a pungent odor of human waste claimed the air in his wake. Ruth's eyes watered at the smell. She blinked to dispel the fumes then quickly carried her bags and dragged her duffel outside to wait.

Seeing a bank of telephones, she maneuvered her belongings and made a hurried call to Larry Reid, telling him she had arrived in Kampala.

He was enthusiastically complimentary of her travel pieces from London. "You haven't lost your touch, Ruthy. They were lively, very readable, full of color.

Several of our wire service members have asked when they can expect more from Pedigo."

"I'll send as many as I can. Please try to remember who I am when they come."

He laughed, then lowered his voice. "Ruth, this is my home phone number you know?"

"Yes?"

"What time is it there in Uganda?"

"Almost one in the afternoon. Why?"

"On this end, we are nine hours earlier, remember."

"Oh," Ruth said, doing the math quickly. "Larry, I'm so sorry. I didn't... Well, it won't happen again anyway. This is probably the last time I'll have access to a phone for a while. Lucky you. Sorry."

He laughed, forgiving her as they said their good-byes.

She started to make another call, hesitated, took a deep breath and cradled the receiver.

Diaz wasn't gone long. On his return, he led several men, women and children, all clamoring in unrecognizable dialects and all smiling and nodding at Ruth. Puzzled, she smiled and nodded back.

As Diaz drove an ancient Merry Miler van into the commercial bus dock for loading, Ruth fished three one-dollar bills from her purse.

Of the others, the seven who apparently were passengers must already have paid, as they filed onto the aged transport in front of her without offering a fee.

"That will be fifty dollars." Diaz held his hand out for her fare.

Ruth's eyebrows arched as she studied the man. "The attendant inside said the fare was three dollars."

"I drive. He does not. The fare for you is fifty dollars."

"None of the other passengers paid."

"They have no money."

"So you're charging me for all of them as well?"

"All right," he conceded angrily. "Forty dollars!"

"No."

The driver's shoulders slumped and his voice became a whine. "Truth be told, Madam, it costs thirty dollars, American, to make the trip to Bwana. You are the only one who wants to go. These only come to keep you company. They live here. None in Bwana. They like to ride. When I have space, when there is no fighting, I see no harm."

Mulling it over, Ruth saw a certain benevolence in Diaz' reasoning.

"I will pay you twenty dollars."

He looked around, scowled at Ruth then screwed up his face and nodded grudgingly. She dug into her purse.

The mixed collection of travelers hooted their approval as Ruth placed the currency in Diaz's hand--which he shook in the air as a sign of victory--and lugged her baggage to an empty space immediately behind the driver. Several people offered to help with the duffel and suitcases but she waved them off genially, preferring to hoist the bags alone.

She was glad most of her cash was not in her purse, which seemed to draw longing looks from many eyes, but was secured instead in a money belt about her waist, as per Pamela's instructions.

When Ruth returned her billfold to her purse, the glint of something metallic inside caught her eye. After she opened a window, settled in her seat, and the loaded bus had groaned its way into the traffic, she dug into her purse.

The shining object was Jack's wrist watch which she had so carefully left in the mail pouch for return to him. Holding it, she smiled. It was a fine, practical watch, very dependable; a battery-operated device which displayed the day and date as well as the correct time. Jack had scrupulously synchronized it with the authentic Big Ben under her own watchful supervision only the day before.

Obviously he had smuggled the watch into her purse during their early morning shuttle to the airport. Always watching after her, even absentee, he remained the ever vigilant knight valiantly providing for the inept lady.

Her smile broadened as she fastened the watch onto her arm. If her purse should somehow wind up misplaced, Ruth did not want the watch lost. Like the money belt, she would wear this gift close to her person.

Leaning up over Diaz' shoulder, she again shuddered at the man's overwhelming odor, but tried to ignore it in order to ask her question. "Do you know a white man who visits here? His name is Jack Standish."

The driver shook his head, no. "Many white men come to Kampala City."

"No, this man travels into the rural areas beyond Kampala. He knows Bwana."

"I know of no white man by that name."

"Perhaps he lives here sometimes and you have not had occasion to meet him."

"Oh yes, Madam, if he lived beyond Kampala City anytime, I would know him. There is no Jack Standish." His words were definite.

Ruth settled back in her seat. Obviously Diaz did not know everyone in rural Uganda, but his certainty gave her an odd unease.

She often practiced mental discipline, willing her mind to other subjects when it latched onto a thought which she would rather it did not entertain. Jack's parting words, his tenderness, the kiss, were difficult to circumvent, even with her most practiced method. She would save those moments to savor later.

The bus had no shocks or struts or whatever cushioning features it may have once had, and the seats were hard. The conditions made it even more difficult to flush the persistent thoughts of Jack and his peculiar promise.

* * *

Three hours into their trip, as they bumped along a pock-marked asphalt road, Ruth marveled that the other passengers would be so bored in town that they would volunteer for such a torturous outing, packed together as they were. Most, after their initial excitement ebbed, gazed dully out the windows. They spoke to one another occasionally, marveling in hushed tones, and pointing to landmarks, craters in the landscape, burned grass or fire-gutted structures.

Reverently, they repeated one word over and over. Their attitudes and faces indicated to Ruth that the word was probably death.

The rutted road deteriorated to dirt. Ruth saw bare-footed black children dressed much like little American children in housing projects playing around grass matted huts or occasionally a stucco structure.

Women wrapped in colorful fabrics tended aging stands of corn, pulled weeds, picked fruit, watered. Banana trees bent under the weight of their yield. She saw clusters of men--old men and very young ones but none of middle age--talking together in coveys.

The people on the bus called and waved wildly out at the residents, sometimes pointing to Ruth and calling the attention of the bystanders to her. Gradually it dawned on her. She was the only white person there, not just on the bus, but anywhere. It surprised her not to have noticed sooner.

Runners apparently had raced ahead across country to announce the bus and its cargo.

When her fellow passengers began chattering excitedly, Ruth peered out the front windshield to see a familiar landmark, a mud brick structure with a tile roof. She had seen the building before, in pictures; photos enclosed in missives from Father Catlett and his family. It was the parish guest house in Bwana.

Much grander than the priest's home, the guest house had windows with shutters, the practical kind which swung closed to defend from the wind and rains in season.

An electric line looped into the house through one corner of the roof. Ruth smiled. "Home, sweet home."

Then the tall, gangly form of Father Catlett appeared, loping toward the guest house. He fumbled with his collar as he ran, trying to secure the button at the back of his black shirt and to greet the approaching bus on time.

Like Catlett, others ran toward the guest house. Seeing the bus seemed to have alerted everyone in the community. They swept in from all directions, giggling and waving and chattering noisily as they came.

They were dressed in various kinds of clothing. Some of the women were dressed much as American housewives did in the nineteen fifties, in flowered print dresses and aprons. Some were wrapped in serapes. Some carried babies on their hips. Some balanced bundles on their heads. Some hurried ahead of trailing flocks of children.

The men, some bare chested, wore khaki work trousers or cut-off pants of one kind or another. Two young ones wore what appeared to be breechcloths, scarcely covering themselves.

Like the grown-ups, the children wore a hodgepodge of clothing.

The bus rumbled to a stop, gave a noisy gasp and a shudder and suddenly became silent and still. No one moved. No one spoke. Diaz pivoted in the driver's seat to look at his lone paying customer with an air of expectation.

It was her move.

Ruth stood, gathered her belongings and shuffled to the door. The lanky priest opened it, then retreated several paces to allow her room to step out.

Recalling their correspondence and pictures, Ruth hesitated on the running board and tried to pick which were Catletts as she scanned the expectant glowing black faces gaping up at her.

She felt a surge of emotion. In only a moment of time, she loved those faces; trusting, courageous, innocent faces, from the full round cheeks of toddlers to the ancient ones scored by years of sunshine and laughter and pain and grief.

Chapter Twelve

Father Paul Catlett, a very black, very thin man with large, round eyes, watched with obvious anxiety as Ruth stepped from the bus. Dozens of observers inside and outside the transport stared at her, spellbound.

Catlett withdrew several paces more, respectfully. The others clustered behind him, not frightened, Ruth decided, but not willing to be first to face her. Their unsmiling faces all seemed darker, more sinister than she had imagined.

The passengers on the bus and Riz Diaz remained silent, as if they realized they were watching this strange woman take a monumental step, from her old life, onto the fertile ground of Bwana, Uganda, and into her new one.

Dragging her duffel which bumped down the step in the bus doorway, she placed one foot on the ground and smiled up at the priest tentatively. Father Catlett returned the smile, revealing long, narrow white teeth. He waited for her to speak or to otherwise orchestrate this first meeting.

Ruth put her duffel, suitcases and purse on the ground, smiled broadly at Father Catlett and opened her arms. His smile mirrored hers as he stepped forward to embrace her, stooping to wrap his long arms around her shoulders as she slipped hers about his slender waist and lifted her face to touch her cheek to his.

The throng of onlookers murmured happily behind him before they broke into cheering and a frenzied chatter.

The passengers on the bus hailed friends on the ground and conversations kindled through open windows along both sides of the Merry Miler. None of the passengers risked getting off and none of the villagers attempted to get on.

One arm around Father Catlett, Ruth inhaled the warm aroma of the man. He obviously bathed frequently but worked hard in the out-of-doors. There was also a smell of school, of papers or pencils or ink or something she could not immediately identify.

Of course, she realized, *Father Catlett and his wife could read and write English.* Ruth knew they often wrote letters and conducted business for those who lacked the necessary skills.

The Catletts both were adamant that each of their five children have as much schooling as he or she could absorb. Ruth recalled that from their early correspondence, fifteen years before when she and they first became acquainted, before there were Catlett children, even before their eldest, Mary, was born.

Ruth had reread those early letters in preparation for this trip.

As the celebration continued, a reticent woman came out of the crowd and Father Catlett introduced "my beloved wife, Ossie."

Ossie did not look at Ruth at first and Ruth waited. When Ossie glanced up shyly, curiously, Ruth smiled. "Will you welcome me with a hug?"

79

A slow smile crept over Ossie's face as her bright chocolate brown eyes locked with Ruth's. Both women took one pace forward, wrapped their arms around one another, squeezing and grinning their exuberance.

Ruth could feel tears coming but she gulped them back, afraid of offending her new/old friends. When they separated, however, Ossie swiped at her own eyes with the back of her hand before she beckoned her children forward to meet their visitor.

Most of the Bwanans had never seen a white woman before and stood in a kind of stupor, studying her curiously. Ruth smiled into each set of eyes and tried to memorize names with faces as Father Catlett called each person forward, one at a time, for introductions. She shook each hand but there were too many and their names too varied to retain many of them.

She would have time, she told herself. She would have plenty of time here among these people to learn their names.

*   *   *

Ruth knew that, initially at least, she was to live in the parish guest house and that was where the Catletts eventually escorted her.

The house had a dirt floor on which her shoes left prints in the brush strokes of recent sweeping. There was a narrow hospital bed.

Ossie glowed when Ruth commented on the fine bed.

"A gift to Father from a generous benefactor. A man who worked for an oil company in the low country."

So Ossie did not call her husband by his Christian name but referred to him as Father Catlett or simply Father.

Also in the house were two straight-back wooden chairs and a small lamp which stood resolutely on a bedside table.

"The electrical service comes and goes at its own will," Ossie said. "You must not rely on it too extremely."

Ruth struggled to contain her laughter, a result of the joy bubbling within her. She did not want to offend Ossie.

A two-burner hot plate sat on a long trestle table which was handmade and elaborately carved. The table also held an enamel wash basin, assorted dishes, two pans, and also served as a pantry for canned soups and fresh, oversized fruits and vegetables. The dishes and pans appeared to have been recently washed and there was the distinct smell of people having occupied the house.

"Have you had other guests?"

Ossie shrugged, obviously not wanting to answer. Ruth waited. "Travelers, soldiers, refugees."

Ruth maintained an approving look which seemed to give Ossie confidence.

80

"You must boil your water. Even the water in which you wash your vegetables should be boiled first. It must make bubbles for twenty minutes, English, before it is ready." She pointed to a jar of water on the table. "This is to be sufficient until you boil water for yourself."

Ruth thanked Ossie for the supplies and continued admiring the house which consisted of the main room and an odd closet with windows. She was curious about bathroom facilities. Ossie anticipated her question.

"Women share a latrine, an outhouse, only a short walk from here down the hill. Come. I will show you."

She led the way about twenty yards down a cleared, well-trampled path to a frame structure. There was a lavatory with a single pipe running into it and three stalls.

"We have modernized it for you," Ossie said with some pride.

Ruth smiled. It was primitive but clean, smelled of disinfectant, and obviously was carefully maintained. "This is very nice."

Ossie beamed with pleasure. "Come, I will show you where we bathe."

They climbed another hill. Upstream from the latrine area, Ossie pointed to an outcropping of rocks arranged to screen and dam the bubbling brook.

"We wash our bodies here." Ossie indicated with a sweep of her hand. "Further down the water is the place for washing clothes." She looked eagerly at Ruth's face. Ruth smiled, aware that Ossie was as sensitive to her facial expressions as to her words.

"Water could be carried to the guest house and heated for you, if you want it." Ossie continued her study of Ruth's face.

"What do you do when the weather turns cool?"

Ossie looked puzzled. "The weather does not turn cool."

"Of course not. It's like this all year round." How could she have forgotten? She knew how stable their temperatures were.

"We have the rains."

Ruth chuckled, laughing more at herself than at her guide's bewilderment.

"I forgot that the weather here remains constant. Does the water remain the same temperature as well?"

"Except in the mountains, where ice forms at its hems."

"May I?" Ruth indicated she would like to walk closer and touch the water. "Yes."

At the edge of the stream, Ruth scooped a handful of water. It was cool enough to be invigorating, stimulating to the skin.

Ossie watched. "This part is entirely private for women, except for small boys with their mothers."

Ruth nodded. "I will bathe with you at first, if that's all right."

"I sometimes wear a large kimono which allows me to wash beneath it. The garment also serves for drying."

Ruth would manage just fine. She would bathe in loose clothing at first, while she was self-conscious about the color of her skin among woman who had never seen it before.

That first evening, Ruth planned to write an article for Larry Reid and to record in her journal her first impressions of Bwana, the village and its people. Instead she entertained a steady stream of visitors, all bringing gifts of welcome.

There were brightly colored mats and wall hangings and baskets, all handmade.

Ossie explained. "The mats may stack one upon the other for sleep when one does not have a bed."

Ruth decided she would roll them together for a sleeping bag/bed to carry with her when she traveled.

Many times during the evening, Ruth apologized that she had no gifts to offer her visitors in return for their kindnesses. However, they seemed satisfied to shake her hand, to listen to her voice, to gaze at her white face and study her straight, dark hair. All of her visitors treated her with great respect. Some came alone, others in family groups or with friends. Many, even very old ones, spoke some English and were pleased when she seemed to understand their words of friendship and welcome.

At last, when Jack Standish's wrist watch read eight-thirty, the parade of visitors ceased. A short time later, the light from the small electric lamp faltered and failed. Ruth changed into her oversized cotton nightgown in the dark and stepped outside, a saucepan in her hand.

A small boy sat cross-legged on a mat just outside her door. He leaped to his feet and bowed slightly as she emerged. "Mother, I am Artemis." His English was good. "I am your guide. I will stay here at night to watch while you sleep. I will escort you when you are awake."

"How old are you, Artemis?"

"Nine years."

He looked small for nine. Shirtless, he wore large khaki shorts gathered and tied with a piece of rope at the waist. She could have counted his ribs through the thin layer of skin. His legs were slightly bowed and spindly with knots of muscle. His feet were bare. His face was round, cherubic and he had large, alert brown eyes. She couldn't help smiling at his intense stare.

"I want to go to the women's latrine, Artemis, also to draw water in this pan to boil tomorrow when the electricity returns."

He stepped smartly onto the path.

"I will take you. I will draw the water from the stream and return you safely. If the electricity does not come tomorrow, I will collect wood to make a hot, hot fire for boiling your kettle."

Ruth thanked him. With great dignity he trudged down the well-worn path, escorting her to the outhouse.

Before allowing her to pass, he took the saucepan and proceeded upstream for water, leaving her to conduct her personal business at the latrine unassisted.

When Ruth emerged, she found Artemis crouched on the path leading back to the guest house. He stood, bowing slightly, and turned to usher her on the return.

The boy stopped at her door. Groping in the darkened house, Ruth placed the pan on the trestle table, found her way to the bed, slipped off her shoes and lay back.

How strange, to find such comfort in knowing the small boy guarded her door. The door had no lock but that had seemed of little consequence. Now it seemed of even less.

She knew the scripture. *God's protection is sufficient.* If He were to allow a thief to break into a house, seven guards watching could not prevent it, and if He did not allow it, a gang of burglars could not enter. Still, Ruth felt comforted knowing Artemis was at the door, and she slept.

In the early hours, she dreamed of Mickey but her mind's picture of him was dim. The image of Jack Standish intruded, vivid, arrogant. Against her will, Ruth found herself reaching out to the more potent image. She roused feeling disloyal, angry that Jack should dominate her dreams.

She lay on her side, her head propped on a thin pillow over her arm, and listened to the watch on her wrist ticking.

Of course, she soothed her troubled conscience. It was not the man at all, only the hum of his watch which conjured dreams of Standish.

At home, in Bridger, she might have gotten up, gone to the kitchen for a drink. Here in this strange place, she lay quietly, thinking. After a while, she gave in to her grief and wept for all she had lost; the old loss and, now, the more recent one.

* * *

Ruth awoke early to voices whispering excitedly outside her door. She rolled up to sit on the side of the hospital bed which seemed tall, narrow and spindly. Her legs dangled high above the floor.

Artemis peeked inside. "Mrs. Catlett and her children wish to take you visiting."

"What are you doing, Artemis?"

"I am boiling the water. Already two kettles have been prepared and poured into our jug."

She nodded, stretching. "Thank you. But, Artemis, when will you sleep?"

"In the daylight, Mother." He frowned at her with a surprised look on his face. "Those who do not sleep in the night, must sleep in the daylight. Those are the only times there are, here in Uganda."

Studying his puzzled expression, she smiled. He seemed concerned that she should not know such an obvious answer. Or maybe he wondered at her asking such an obtuse question.

"Of course." She wasn't sure if she was complimenting him for being so astute or reassuring him that she was aware of daylight and dark. "Will you sleep in this bed, then?"

His eyes widened and he shook his head. "No, Mother. I will sleep on the floor."

"Then you must have the mats." She pushed herself off the bed and looked around for the mats which had been gifts from the villagers. She stacked three together and pulled them over underneath the trestle table, working around her billowing nightgown. There, he would be out from under feet which might traipse in and out, including her own.

Artemis hurried to help as she stacked all six mats, one on top of the other. Pleased, he looked at her with unshrouded admiration before he remembered. "Mrs. Catlett waits for you."

"Tell her I will be right out."

Ruth slipped quickly into her clothes and ran a comb through her short, dark hair. Using a little of the water from the jug over the basin, she rinsed her face and brushed her teeth before she stepped out into the dazzling sunlight to greet Ossie, the Catlett's eldest child Mary, and an assortment of others.

Ossie smiled her timid smile and spoke softly. "Come."

Ruth followed as they led her sightseeing. Ossie spoke haltingly at first, describing families who lived in the huts along the main thoroughfare of the village.

"And this is Father Catlett's office." Ossie gestured with her hand as the group stopped in front of a small, adobe-looking structure. Faces looked at Ruth expectantly and she openly admired the building which they seemed so pleased to point out.

Father Catlett appeared in the doorway and, after a greeting, gently dismissed his wife and children. Others remained close, watching. He placed a hand on Ruth's arm, perhaps demonstrating their equality. She felt flattered in this place where women seemed to be considered inferior.

Many of those who had followed, drifted off after a few minutes, their curiosity apparently sated.

The priest led Ruth through the three-room building which housed his office and schoolrooms for young children and for those older ones who could not afford or who had not yet been able to pass the test to be accepted to a boarding school.

"The nearest boarding school is in Ula, nearly thirty miles distant. Our Mary is only thirteen but she will soon be qualified to test. Of course, it is more difficult for women to obtain the scholarships, especially such a young woman."

Ruth could not hide her surprise. "Do you want her to live away from you?"

"Want her to?" He bowed his head. "No. For her future, she needs education. But, no, we do not want her to live away from us. Many things can happen to a young girl away from the protection of her family. That is why she must qualify for the school at Ula. It is a church facility. Children there are carefully looked after."

Mulling over this information, marveling that she took secondary schooling for granted, Ruth walked in silence for several moments before he interrupted her musing. "Do American school children study Uganda?"

"Not in any great detail."

"We are an emerging nation."

She heard the pride in his voice. "Yes. Uganda has great potential. It is a beautiful country, lush and green."

"We are called the pearl of Africa." Gazing at the mountains around them as if taking inventory, Father Catlett frowned. "But Uganda bears the scars of war and the need of education."

Ruth patted his arm. "All countries must endure growing pains, just as people do. I saved your letters and read them again before I came. I was amazed at how your English has improved. You have made much progress through the years."

"Yes." The admission did not seem immodest, only the verification of fact. "I have learned much of the English from you, from your faithful writings to me."

The priest seemed agitated. Something was troubling him and, seeing his distress, Ruth held silent waiting for him to broach the subject vexing him.

"Now, Mrs. Ruth," he said finally in a businesslike tone, "can you tell me how we in Uganda might emerge more quickly and without so much difficulty, so much bloodshed, as our neighbors."

"I do not know of any shortcut." Her somber tone matched his. "If a child has difficulty learning to read or to do arithmetic, what is the solution?"

He flashed a frown. "He must study, try harder."

"What if he wants to give up, to surrender to his ignorance?"

Catlett regarded her with annoyance. "If he is gifted, he must endure, in spite of difficulties."

"I believe it is the same with nations."

"But must there be so much injury? So much death?"

"All of life is difficult, Father Paul."

He smiled, apparently at her familiar use of his name. They continued walking in silence until Ruth spoke again. "Why is English Uganda's official language?"

"Uganda has forty-two tribes."

Mr. Doss at the embassy, had said forty-seven, but she did not mention it.

"Each tribe has a language of its own. Occasionally words in one language are similar in another, but not often.

"English was most agreeable to the parties in government who must do business in the world, but not to the people of villages like Bwana. However, when we learned you were coming, people in Bwana demanded to learn the English so that they could speak with you and understand your words.

"We knew you were a great woman because you shared our love for our Lord Jesus Christ and because you showed love to us. You sent us seeds and gifts and money. You encouraged us when things were difficult in our government.

"You were unlike us, yet you signed your letters, 'Your sister in Christ.' These people cheered when I read those words aloud in the congregation.

"You became one of us, though apart from us. We knew you from your writings and from the pictures of your family, of your children as they grew."

Father Catlett stopped at the crest of a hill overlooking the village and indicated Ruth should regard the view. "When your son Michael married, we prayed for him earnestly. And for Carly and for Anna on the occasions of their marriages. We pray for Donnie who is unmarried because he has no wife and because he is yours.

"When you lost your beloved husband, we wept for you and wished you here for our comfort to you."

They began their descent from the knoll, walking in silence for several moments, each again occupied with his own thoughts. It was the priest who broke the quiet.

"We are highly honored to have you here. When you chose to come to us, you made Bwana enviable among all villages."

"Thank you. You make me feel as if I belong here. You make me feel very comfortable among you."

"You did not bring many books." The statement was more than an idle observation. It rang of criticism. But he was right.

"No, not nearly enough."

"You must tell us stories then, of America."

"Yes."

"You must share with the children and the adults as well." He allowed a slight smile. "And you must share with me."

Ruth chuckled, nodding her agreement.

Over and over again that day and on succeeding days, Ruth was pressed by her hosts to describe her home, her house in Bridger, the community, St. Peter's and to speak about the members of her family. She wished she had pictures, magazines, anything to help answer their questions.

"All children are required to go to school in America?" Artemis repeated in amazement after one afternoon story session during which Ruth described classrooms in America. "It is too great an honor to bestow on all children." The idea seemed to annoy him.

Ruth regarded him closely. "Why does that make you angry?"

He snorted in disgust. "Possibly some boy in America does not enjoy school. It is wrong that he should be required to attend, wishing he were not, and that I should be here, wishing that I were."

Ruth got out a yellow legal pad, a pencil and a ballpoint pen which she placed on the table in front of Artemis. Sitting beside him, she printed the alphabet in capital letters at the top of the first page of the tablet. "Copy those. Let's see what kind of a student you will be."

His dark eyes rounded, he snatched up the pencil and began.

During the day, Bwanan children begged Ruth to read to them from the few books she had with her: two mysteries, an AP style book and a Bible. She wished she'd brought a book of fairy tales, particularly Aesop's Fables; a book of nursery rhymes, a set of encyclopedias, the Narnia Tales and many more. She repeated those stories she could recall over and over again as accurately as she could remember them.

She wished for magazines and catalogs for the adults who asked about American super markets with their "shelves and shelves of marvelous foods;" about department stores filled with an abundance and about the fable that everyone in America was rich enough to purchase things in those stores every day.

Few of the children in the village had ever been to a grocery store. Even those who had, were in families too poor to actually purchase many items there.

One night Ruth found herself wishing desperately for Tootsie Pops. In frustration, she made a wish list and mailed it to Ross Belton, with a letter asking if he would ask people to send things. She described Bwana, many of the people individually and the transportation difficulties.

Over the first ten days, as she studied the Bwanan life style, Ruth was impressed that women did so much of the labor--planting, weeding, coaxing the crops, tending the homes, cooking, rearing the children, carrying the water and generally providing.

It was then, too, that she noticed how few men there were in Bwana. Those tended herds of cattle whose hip bones often protruded nearly through their hides.

Some people in the village had lesions, the kind she had seen in pictures of AIDS victims. The sores frightened her at first and she asked Ossie about those people.

"They have the Slim," Ossie said simply. "They will die. But then we shall all die. The Bible says it is so."

Gradually, after several days and many more sightings, Ruth grew accustomed to the symptoms. Philosophically, Ossie was right, of course. But then Ruth still felt the bitter sting of death and separation which she had experienced only too recently, close up and personal.

Chapter Thirteen

During her first weeks in Uganda, Ruth tried to cast off memories and focus. She wrote articles about life in Bwana; about Artemis, the enterprising orphan making his own way; about a naive people inclined, in their innocence, to be brutally truthful. She wrote of their diet--bananas, beans, ground nuts, sweet potatoes and the ox blood/rice delicacy which was so hard for her to appreciate--about the gentle climate and the phenomenal growth of fruits and vegetables which fairly exploded out of the ground and grew much larger than their American counterparts.

But at night, her family peopled her dreams, along with a vivid, haunting Jack Standish. She often woke in the dark reaching for him only to be devastated that she had no way to find him.

Perhaps someday, if she made it home, she could find him but doubted it would matter to either of them, then.

The Bwanans couldn't seem to find a satisfactory title for Ruth. "Mrs. Ruth" was difficult for them to pronounce. They seemed to feel disrespectful calling her simply "Ruth." Besides, there was a small girl in the village whose name also was the unusual English name Ruth. To distinguish the woman from the child as well as to provide a title of sorts, the villagers followed Artemis' lead and began calling her "Mother Ruth."

Collectively and individually they spoke the new name with quiet reverence. Ruth smiled at what she assumed was their attempt at honoring her, for even the very elderly called her Mother.

Ruth also wrote stories about Ossie and the women who washed and planted and mothered with joy; about Father Catlett and his congregation of twenty-six hundred, many of whom walked miles to worship services on Sunday and back for Bible study on Wednesdays.

She wrote an account of the two hundred fifty-six in Catlett's congregation who had died of Slim, nearly one-tenth of the membership of All Souls Church, most of them young men.

"Do you think perhaps the Holy Father exacts a tithe of lives from among our people?" Catlett's question surprised her as she and Father Paul followed their usual path up into the foothills one afternoon.

"We know He no longer requires blood sacrifice."

Catlett gave her a dark look. "He is no longer 'satisfied with such,'" he corrected.

"It would be wasteful to sacrifice lives for no reason." Catlett started to correct her again when she verbally plunged ahead. "His ways are not our ways, Father. We see as through the dark glass, not with His clarity."

"It is true." Catlett's tone was woeful.

Ruth also wrote about the music in Bwana, haunting strains in which a low chant gave depth to the melody. She found it difficult to describe the profundity o the music when her readers could not experience the mournful sound.

Along with the many articles, she sent the thirty miles for posting at the trading center in Ula, Ruth mailed letters and occasional gifts handmade in Bwana always including wish lists for books, for seeds, canned goods, fabric and treats fo the children. Although her missives went out regularly, nothing came back; no letters, no supplies from home, no paychecks from Larry Reid. Nothing.

At first timid learning her way around, Ruth grew bolder as she became acquainted with the country and the people. She began to understand snatches o conversations spoken in the local dialect which people found simpler than struggling with the English.

And she began to write about local politics.

"Although there have been no elections in recent months, the people staunchly insist they live in a democracy. There are no government programs to aid the poor or the elderly, yet no one here is homeless or starves.

"Americans argue the benefits and hazards of a socialist society. Here there are no such arguments. There is no socialized medicine, no medical service at all. The closest place for medical attention--with the exception of a smattering of self-proclaimed witch doctors--is Kampala, forty-six miles away, an awesome distance when the primary mode of transportation is a person's own two feet.

"There is little disparity between the richest family in town and the poorest. Bwana has its own form of socialism."

Researching information for this article, Ruth asked Ossie if there were a witch doctor nearby. "I would like to meet one."

The priest's wife swelled to her full height and gazed at Ruth in disbelief for a long moment before she turned and strode back into her house without a word.

"Okay, I'll ask someone else," Ruth muttered with a shrug. But she didn't. There was something in Ossie's expression--fear, disdain, disbelief--which purged Ruth's thought of meeting a genuine witch doctor.

* * *

Tuslan's first visit to Bwana after Ruth's arrival caused a stir. It was the sudden unnatural quiet in the middle of the afternoon which drew her out of the guest house where she had been reading to Artemis about his favorite biblical hero, Samson.

From her doorway, she saw the villagers speaking in hushed whispers as they watched the tall, silent black man who simply appeared in the street.

Dressed in trousers and a shirt too small for such a large man, Tuslan glided along the main thoroughfare on foot, looking neither right nor left except for a cursory glance which swept over Ruth, then withdrew.

"Who is that?" Ruth whispered near Artemis' ear.

"Tuslan."

"Do the people dislike him so much that they do not speak or offer him a drink?"

"They are afraid, Mother. If he is thirsty, he will signal."

Artemis' eyes never left the tall, dignified figure as the man moved down the rutted highway and into the cover of the woods beyond.

The boy's eyes widened with concern. "He was here to see you, Mother."

"Why do you say that?"

"Because you are the one he saw."

Ruth shuddered. "Oh."

She noticed that the populace immediately resumed their digging, tending, washing, bathing--activities they had momentarily curtailed at the arrival and before the departure of Tuslan, whoever or whatever he was.

*   *   *

Her ability to read and write English gave Ruth even greater status in the village. She helped Ossie fill out required government forms and write personal letters for those who could neither read nor write the language.

"Education is the possession most honored here," she wrote in one article. "Great value is placed on children with bright minds. The best are singled out to attend the boarding school in Ula. Mothers weep mixed tears of sorrow and pride when their fifth-grader is judged worthy to continue his education. Such children are absent for many months, even though Ula is only thirty miles away."

"Why are you not in school?" Ruth asked, regarding Artemis thoughtfully as she worked on the article.

"I have no family, no money, no future." He spoke with his usual candor. There was no hint of self pity. Ruth found her conversations with the boy refreshing.

"I have no family either, Artemis, here in Uganda. Perhaps I can be your family."

"Do not worry, Mother, I have sworn myself to care for you all your days. Do not be concerned that you are old. I will provide for you."

Ruth laughed. She had intended to offer him comfort. It had not occurred to her that he thought she the one needing care and nurture.

She finished the feature about the type of schooling available to children in Bwana and of their envy of American children's opportunity for education. As

91

usual, she dispatched the story, thinking it was like pouring water onto sand, with little hope of result.

Ruth picked up a hoe and followed when Ossie went to the fields. The first day, her hands burned with the blisters which screamed their objection to such incalculable behavior. Accompanied by Artemis, not many days passed before Ruth was working, singing, mingling among the Bwanans, unnoticed, unwhite. She enjoyed her relative anonymity believing she was as obscure all over Uganda as she was in Bwana.

Someone, she was uncertain of the identity of the composer, made up a song about her. Melodiously it paid tribute to her white hands, so soft to the touch, to her easy smile and her piercing eyes able to see through any skin to pure hearts which had no color. There was another reference in the song, to the halo which framed her angel's face.

Ruth had not looked carefully until she heard the song. She understood most of the words, sung in Runyandole, the Bwanans' native tongue, but was a little puzzled about the halo reference. She asked the ever candid Artemis who took her to the water to see her reflection.

The dark dye on her hair, the color it had been when she was a young woman, was growing out. The emerging roots framing her face were snow white giving the illusion of a halo. Ruth laughed as she studied her reflection in the women's bathing pool that afternoon.

Preparing their evening meal, she said, "Artemis, I want to color my hair, make it dark again. Is there some kind of tree which has bark which will color things?"

"No, Mother." He paused. "But there are thistle balls in the trees which make an ink when they simmer in oil. They are like nuts but they are not recommended for eating."

"Will you show me?"

"Yes, Mother. I am glad to hear of this plan."

"Why is that, Artemis?"

"If we wash your hair with the color from the thistle balls, perhaps you will live. Women with white hair die."

Ruth shot him a look, thinking he intended the pun. When she saw he hadn't, she turned from the hot plate and walked to the chair where the boy was again concentrating on his reading lesson. She wrapped her arms around his shoulders, swayed from side to side and laughed.

He looked puzzled. "Mother, I like speaking words which please you, but I do not always know which words those will be."

92

She laughed softly. "Artemis, you have discovered one of the universal mysteries of life. Throughout history, men in every culture have had difficulty knowing what words will please women."

His eyebrows shot up with sincerity as he said, "In spite of your confusion as women, we like you very much."

Were those the words of a chauvinist? She laughed. *Definitely!*

The song about Ruth was infectious. Bwanan women hummed it as they worked. Children picked up the words and added their own. One night the men contributed their haunting, harmonizing drone.

The lyrics expanded.

She came to us in the sunlight
Stepped from the golden coach
Smiling on us, her face bright
Embracing us from her approach

She came to light our way with song,
Speaks to us of God and truth
She does love and praise us all day long
We love our own dear Mother Ruth.

Her cool, white hands touch us with grace
Her hair very straight, her eyes very blue
A pale halo shines about her face
And her eyes see through skin to souls made new

Rebecca Marmel, a four-year-old with a piping little voice with what sounded to Ruth like perfect pitch, was humming or singing the ditty each time Ruth saw her. But Rebecca had difficulty with the pronunciation. Chanting gustily, she sang, "We love our own dear Mother Earth."

Rebecca's mother, other adults and older children tried in vain to correct the child's words. She insisted on her version. Thinking it made little difference to the song, others eventually acquiesced.

Ruth couldn't help smiling each time she heard Rebecca sing, her tiny body marching or twirling or swaying to her own tune. Without intending to, other children adopted Rebecca's version. Unwittingly, grown-ups followed suit.

It wasn't long before Ossie greeted Ruth one morning with a cheery, "Hello, Mother Earth." Ossie quickly clamped her hand over her mouth before blurting, "Oh, Mother, I am so sorry!"

Ruth hugged her. "I am pleased, Ossie. The name is my own designation, my very own identity."

Since Ruth did not seem to be offended, the title stuck.

"I belong here," Ruth wrote to her family in Bridger. "Here I am myself, not Dad's wife, not your mother, but Mother Earth. My heart has found its old beat and thrums in sync with these people.

"I am flattered when they sing the song they have written about me. I bask in the regard of my neighbors. I sleep soundly in my primitive little home with the dirt floor, sparse furnishings and no locks. It somehow seems appropriate that a woman at the beginning of a new life in the middle of her normal human span, should acquire a new name, a new home and new people."

As she and Father Paul walked together by the narrow river one afternoon, she told him of her insight. "You were right all along. Right to have me come here. Uganda is where I belong."

He stopped and regarded her, his face pinched with what appeared to be anger. "Bwana is your home now. We are your people." She waited for him to continue. "But you must be wise." His dark eyes burned into hers. "All of Uganda is not safe for you. You must not wander out alone."

She smiled a little uncertainly. She had not seen him so severe before. "Because evil waits for me away from Bwana?" She was kidding, attempting to lighten his dark thoughts. He did not answer her smile, however, and his somber look deepened.

"We are Christians here. Others are not. They do not have Christian kindness. They do not honor Christian beliefs."

"Okay." She was still unsure of what they were talking about. "I never go anywhere without Artemis close by me."

"Artemis is a small boy. He could not defend you. He would only place himself in danger. Because he is an orphan, he, too, must stay near."

"Why would anyone hurt the boy?" Ruth's stomach knotted.

"He would bring a price."

"They would sell him? Someone would buy him? Not in this day and time."

"Maybe not this day or this time in America. He would not bring much, even here. It is easy to see that he is of greater value to you than to any other."

Ruth turned to locate her small companion plodding along several yards behind them, watching alertly for animals, small or large, in the tall grass nearby. Yes, she thought, the boy had great value to her.

Turning back, she found the priest studying her seriously as she met his gaze. "Thank you, Father, for your advice. I did not realize there might be danger to either of us beyond the village. I will be very careful where Artemis and I travel."

Not satisfied with her concession, Father Paul started to speak again, then let the subject drop.

"Father, have you heard of a white man named Jack Standish?"

The priest shook his head. "You must ask Riz Diaz. He would know the whereabouts of such a man, if he is in the country among us."

Ruth stared at the ground. She couldn't bring herself to believe Jack lied to her. He didn't seem the type. She smiled ruefully. It was Jack who cautioned her against classifying people as types. She was sometimes deceived by words when she was looking into a face. Hadn't her own children fooled her with little lies?

The memory of Jack, reassuring in those first days and nights in Bwana, seemed suddenly tainted, as if cleansing by some harsh agent revealed tarnish beneath the once shiny finish.

Before she had tingled peculiarly, anticipating their next meeting. Now it appeared her "tingles" were misinformed and that anticipated meeting was not going to take place after all.

Chapter Fourteen

Ruth had been in Bwana nearly four weeks when runners arrived to announce breathlessly, Riz Diaz was coming in his bus.

They wheezed, scarcely able to speak. There were no foreign passengers, only people from town out for a ride. The bus carried many boxes for Mother Earth.

Ruth thought the excitement surrounding the approach of Diaz and his bus rivaled the arrival of the Wells Fargo wagon in River City, Iowa, of Music Man fame. Children, women and men spilled from every hut and household, women washing clothes in the river and those hoeing maize, men tending their cattle, all swarmed into the village. The throng backed off bashfully as the yellow conveyance rumbled to a stop directly in front of the guest house.

Diaz leaped from the bus as it shivered to a stop. "Mother, you have many gifts! And THERE IS NO FEE!" The onlookers cheered and applauded.

Ruth laughed. Obviously the man had been well paid not to demand that she ransom her gifts. She suspected he might have scarfed off one or two pieces of the cargo for himself as a contribution.

Diaz motioned to several men in the gathering, all of whom accepted their appointments modestly, obviously honored to be selected. At his direction, they formed a human brigade to shuttle boxes from the bus to the guest house.

As they worked, the onlookers counted the cartons, out loud, in English. Diaz presented Ruth with an invoice describing the shipment. As far as she could tell, all sixteen boxes shipped had arrived intact. They were from Ross Belton and the congregation at St. Peter's in Bridger.

Puzzled, she looked at Diaz. "Who paid you to deliver them at no additional fee?" When his look of injured indignation won no sympathy, Diaz stepped nearer, close enough for her to catch the putrid smell of the man.

"Jusu guaranteed delivery." He arched his eyebrows with what he seemed to consider the significance of the statement.

Drawing back, Ruth regarded Diaz curiously. "Jusu?" She asked the one word question in a normal speaking voice. Diaz clapped a filthy hand over her mouth and looked around wide-eyed.

"Do not speak his name out loud. His guarantee is honored by Diaz. Tell him so."

Puzzling, Ruth nodded as she withdrew several steps from the hand still poised where her mouth had been.

Since it was still early in the day, Diaz waved to his passengers, allowing them to get off the bus and mingle with the people of Bwana.

Out of the corner of her eye, Ruth saw Diaz himself hurry into the Marmel home, the hut of a family with four young daughters. The youngest daughter was the four-year-old Rebecca who had dubbed Ruth "Mother Earth."

Moments later Marmel and his wife emerged from the hut carrying Rebecca with them but leaving Diaz alone with the other three daughters. Perhaps they were relatives. She hoped she remembered to ask Father Catlett about it.

Ruth invited Artemis to help her open the boxes. Other villagers milled about, stalling. They appeared to be hoping she might require more than the boy's assistance.

Aware of their interest, Ruth nevertheless wished to examine the contents of the shipment carefully before they were exposed to the general population.

A large box which looked as if it contained a mattress, drew her attention first. Opening it, she and Artemis discovered, not the anticipated bed, but a bicycle. It lacked only the mounting of the handle bars and peddles to be road worthy. Ruth laughed and laughed as she read the card attached to the bike. It was Ross Belton's handwriting.

"I plan to be in Kampala with the overseas mission people July tenth. I expect you to greet me with open arms, transport me to this Eden you have found and give me the full tour. I hope there is transportation available other than the enclosed. If you recall, I was the first man in town to acquire my own golf cart. I am opposed to walking when I can ride. If this is the sole means of conveyance, please have yourself in condition to transport me in comfort."

Ruth read the card aloud to Artemis. When she explained that her friend Ross was kidding, Artemis made much of the joke, laughing and, pretending to be able to read the scrawled words, reciting the message over and over again out loud.

Another carton contained a bicycle basket, a passenger carrier to fit over the back fender, an air pump, extra hardware, a spare tire, pliers and two screw drivers. Ruth clapped her hands, applauding the group and imagining their enjoyment and glib comments as they put this shipment together. Until she opened the second carton, she hadn't known how she would affix the handlebars and peddles.

Other boxes were packed with books, clean used clothing of all kinds and sizes. And groceries. It was Christmas in June.

Watching, Artemis was awed by the abundance. "Your friend must be very rich."

"Many friends who attend my church sent these things."

Artemis looked at her with new regard. "Then you must have many rich friends."

Ruth nodded. "Yes."

Among the clothing were items which fit Artemis. Ruth insisted that he take several T-shirts, also two of the button up kind, shorts and a pair of faded denim jeans, softened by many washings. He folded the items carefully and placed them in an empty pasteboard box. He pushed the box under the trestle table, but that evening and for the next several days, Artemis frequently refolded and rearranged his new apparel. He would not, however, wear any of them, insisting the clothes were too valuable to be worn everyday.

That evening as Ruth and Artemis sat side by side marveling at the contents of a "Highlights for Children" Magazine, one of dozens included in the shipment, Ruth remembered something. "Artemis, who is Jusu?"

The boy's eyes rounded and he stared at her before lowering them back to the page before him. "I don't know."

"Artemis, tell me."

"You must ask Father Catlett. I am a child. I am not allowed to speak of him. It was enough that I was standing with you when Tuslan passed, that he saw me with you."

"What is Tuslan to Jusu? Are they friends?"

"You must ask Father."

More mystified than before, Ruth allowed the boy to return to the magazine's enchanted world--America. But his response and Diaz' words had piqued her curiosity. *Why did the mere mention of that name, or Tuslan's passing appearance, cause such fear in these innocent people?*

The next morning, Ruth delivered a carton of school books to Father Paul. She found him in his office, painfully scrutinizing new government forms. When he looked up, he smiled. The grin broadened as she presented the box into his hands. A continuous chuckle escaped as he picked each book from the box with care, handling them more painstakingly than he might have handled rare jewels. Ruth and Father Catlett browsed through the collection together, discussing which books might be best for which child.

When she was leaving, Catlett fell into step beside her and she remembered her questions about Jusu and Tuslan.

"The word Jusu means magician." The frown which had been absent from his face for a time, was back in its usual station. "There is a man, a mortal, who is thought to hold power over souls. He is called by that name."

"Is he a witch doctor then?"

Father Catlett first shook his head, then reconsidered. "Perhaps. He uses magic to frighten these uneducated people. In truth, he has no power. He heals some. He asks many questions of the injured and the sick.

"He conjures foul-smelling sauces and cooks bits of things in small glass tubes over open flame. Sometimes the contents change colors, sometimes the liquid inside the tube bubbles. Sometimes it makes small explosions. Sometimes Jusu is pleased when these things occur. Sometimes he is angry."

Ruth and Father Catlett walked in silence, each frowning, deep in his own thoughts. She had visions of a painted, feather-clad witch doctor conjuring things in the darkness.

"Where does Jusu do this magic?"

Catlett pursed his mouth. "I do not know. Further, I do not care."

"How do people know where to find him?"

"Tuslan, the tall one who came before."

"Are the people afraid of Tuslan as well?"

"Tuslan has no magic, only that which he steals from the other one."

Again there was silence between them for several paces.

"Why did Diaz visit the hut of Marmel?"

He shrugged. "Diaz is not only the driver of the bus. He also drives a truck across the country."

"And what does that mean?"

"It means he is rich. He is paid forty dollars a month, every month. He is an important man. He carries news between people and from place to place."

"But Marmel and his wife left the hut soon after Diaz came."

"Diaz often requires payment for repeating the news."

"Marmel is poor. How can he pay?"

Father Catlett's eyebrows knitted together. "Diaz uses Marmel's daughters as payment."

"Do you mean Diaz has sex with those three young girls?" Ruth gasped. "Father, how old are Marmel's girls?"

"Leah is fifteen, the others thirteen and ten. They are the ones from whom Diaz will accept favors."

Remembering the foul smell of the man, Ruth shivered involuntarily. "Did he have sex with all three girls today then?"

"Probably so."

"And you allow that?" There was fierce accusation in her tone.

"I was not consulted."

"Why didn't the girls resist or cry out or run?"

"The payment is customary."

"Do the truck drivers always get such special favors when they come?"

Father Catlett nodded. "It is the way to pass news from one district to another." He paused, reflecting, then lowered his voice. "Also it is the way of spreading the disease, the Slim."

"What? If you know the truck drivers carry the disease, why are they allowed to have sex with children?"

"All people must die. It is God's will."

"Well, we don't have to go rushing headlong into it, do we?"

Catlett shrugged.

Ruth walked back to the guest house brooding and silent. She had thought the spread of AIDS over the dark continent could be attributed to ignorance, to the people's lack of knowledge. That assumption, she determined, apparently revealed her ignorance, rather than theirs.

Chapter Fifteen

Among the gifts from America was a lady's billfold. An odd inclusion, Ruth thought and tossed it aside. Later, opening it, she found one hundred dollars in American currency. The cash would bring more than twice its face value on the black market in Kampala. *But where nearby would she be able to spend it?*

She asked Ossie.

"Glouster's Store, seven miles distant. You must go in the company of many others." Ossie seemed alarmed by her own words. "You and the boy must not travel from Bwana alone."

Ruth grimaced. "People keep warning me about some kind of mysterious danger beyond Bwana but the real meaning of the words is hidden. Is there a secret I should know?"

"The men driving the trucks tell many stories of you, Mother."

"It's only natural they should be curious about me, don't you think? I would expect a white woman living in Bwana to be part of a news account on the Ugandan pipeline."

"It is more than idle curiosity." Ossie lowered her voice mysteriously. "You must be watchful. It is easy for them to find you. Some say you are rich, that someone might pay, if you were lost."

It was not like Ossie to be overly dramatic and Ruth wondered at these veiled warnings. "Who would even think of such a thing?"

Ossie shivered and cast her eyes at the floor. "I cannot say. You must not be taken. It would cause much trouble in places you do not even know."

"But I will be safe enough in Kampala, don't you think, when I go to meet my friend who is coming."

"I do not know. I am afraid for you. The drivers ask many questions."

"What kind of questions?"

Tears gathered in Ossie's large eyes. She bit her lips, shook her head and refused to discuss the subject further.

*   *   *

They looked like a caravan preparing to cross a continent Saturday morning as many Bwanans loaded their goods on wheel barrows, carts and on their heads for transport to Glouster's Store where Ruth suggested they might barter their crafts for supplies.

The entourage moved slowly, like a caterpillar rippling over the landscape. Ruth rode her bike with a haughty Artemis perched on the passenger seat behind her calling and waving to other boys making the trip afoot.

As the caterpillar moved over the seven miles, the travelers sang and their voices filled Ruth's heart. They seemed an array of innocent children without a responsible adult to tend them.

When they broke into strains of their song about Mother Earth, she laughed quietly under her breath. Perhaps she was the parent sent to see to oversee these childlike folk. Perhaps that is what God had in mind in nudging her to this primitive land. Whatever her role, she felt content among them.

As they caught sight of the store, Ruth noticed several men loitering on the wooden platform outside.

The men regarded the party insolently as the parade wound closer, pointing and talking excitedly.

Ruth had just attained the porch at the entrance to the store when a large, filthy, bearded white man rose from his hunker in front and said, "Hello."

She gave him a cautious smile. "Hello." As she proceeded toward the doorway, he blocked her path.

Others of her party mounted the platform, crowding, seeming eager to get inside. The half dozen other white men hunkering on the platform watched.

The man who had spoken, grabbed the top of Ruth's arm, and dug his fingers into her flesh just below the tunic sleeve. "I think you will be coming with me."

Ruth shrank from him and his smell, shaking her head.

Suddenly Artemis was there, squeezing his small body between the man and Ruth. She wanted to push the child away, tell him to run, but she needed to remain calm.

She was startled when the point of a knife pricked the man's heavy jowl, the weapon wielded by the boy's firm little hand. Blood spurted as the point of the knife where its tip stuck the man's neck. He quickly released Ruth's arm.

She heard a rustling among the loiterers and turned to see several of the white men begin to stand, then shrink back as the Bwanans produced knives and implements wielded as weapons. The faces of the Bwanan villagers, stripped of their childish innocence, bore a fierce resolve.

"What's happening?"

Ossie stepped forward, grabbed her hand and led Ruth quickly into the store.

The proprietor, another white man, leered at the two women. "What can I do for you, ladies?" His English had a distinctly Australian accent. He looked smug as he focused on Ruth.

Ossie placed her hand-woven mats and baskets on the counter. He glanced at the offered items, nodded and motioned her to shop before turning his eyes back to Ruth.

"How much?" Ossie asked.

"I'll let you know when you reach your limit." He continued staring at Ruth without looking at the Bwanans entering the store but nodded and waved each one off as they placed their wares on the counter.

"And what do you have to sell?" he asked Ruth. It was a civil question, but his manner was surly, insolent. She didn't answer.

She noticed a box in the display case, on the side of which were imprinted the words, "American Red Cross." Looking more closely, she saw that the box contained condoms. Someone had written in black pencil across the face of the box, "$8."

She looked from the box to the proprietor. "Where did you get that?"

"From my supplier." He arched his eyebrows and sneered. "Do you have need of one of those?" Seeing the look on her face, he threw back his head with a nasty sounding guffaw.

"You are charging eight dollars for a box of condoms donated to the people of Uganda by the American public?"

"Each."

"Eight dollars a piece?" Ruth trembled with a sudden fury. "AIDS is epidemic in this country, wiping out thousands. No one in Bwana can afford even one of those."

"By the time this scourge is over, there may not be many blacks left on the continent." He winked. "Some say it is God destroying them. Who am I to argue with God?"

Ruth turned her back and walked away as the proprietor laughed, again too loudly.

He hinted at God's wrath. Obviously, the man had no idea what that meant. Glancing back, her irritation ebbed and she felt a consuming pity for him.

Ruth did not want to reward Glouster by purchasing things at his store, however, his goods were the only ones available within two hours of Bwana.

Artemis came inside. Ruth peeked out to see the white loiterers had dispersed. The Bwanans remaining outside had put away their weapons and the fierce looks on their faces but remained alert.

Ruth again regarded Glouster and decided not to purchase much, but the look on Artemis' face as his small hands caressed first one item and then another, weakened her determination.

She regarded the boy tenderly. She loved him more each day, completely, from his kinky black hair to the pale soles of his black, black feet. His forehead was high and broad; his eyebrows expressive, rising and falling with his animated conversation. His large dark eyes danced with his enthusiasm for life. His long black lashes gave him a cherubic look when he slept mornings on the mats beneath the trestle table in her house. He still insisted on keeping watch outside through the night and would yield his post only at first light.

She decided his small size was a result of having been undernourished as a toddler. From stories, she knew he had survived on scraps from tables where families had barely enough to feed their own households.

The boy appreciated everything she shared with him of what seemed, by comparison to other homes, a vast abundance.

Browsing through Glousters, Ruth by-passed candy, the six cans of peaches on a shelf, vegetable and fruit juices and a tin of crackers. She had received many similar items in the shipment from Bridger. She did, however, select a bag of marshmallows and jars of pickles, one sweet, one dill.

"Would you like to have shoes?" she asked quietly as they wound their way into the mercantile part of the store where she gathered thread, needles, pins and buttons.

He smiled brightly, signaling a humorous answer. "No thank you, Mother. These feet do not need shoes. If they did, Father Catlett says, I would have been born with hooves."

Ruth laughed lightly, watching the boy's eyebrows arch at having pleased her.

Ossie and most of the others had finished shopping and had bartered with Glouster to settlements which left him grinning when Ruth and Artemis approached the counter.

The man eyed her playfully. "You may take all of that, in exchange for the boy."

How ironic. If it weren't for Artemis, she wouldn't be buying anything from this man. She pondered so long that Artemis looked into her face curiously. She shook her head. "How much do I owe you?"

Without looking closely at the items, Glouster said, "Thirty-five, American."

"Too much." She placed the items on the counter and turned to leave.

"Thirty."

She pivoted to settle an indifferent look on the merchandise, as if it were inferior. "Five."

A low whine slipped between Glouster's lips. "I would starve if I sold these goods for less than twenty."

"Not interested."

He bucked up. "Fifteen and you are taking advantage of a poor man."

Ruth considered a moment, then pulled the billfold from the pocket of her loose fitting tunic, opened it and counted out the bills.

"I didn't see the needles," Glouster said as he began sacking her purchases. "They will be four dollars more."

A man's voice growled behind her. "Jusu ain't gonna like you cheating this one. Tuslan's outside."

Ruth turned to stare at the speaker, the bearded man who had accosted her in front of the store. One of his eyes was swollen and there was dried blood at his nose and the tiny puncture in his neck.

Glouster studied the man. "Is this her, then?" Glouster gave Ruth a sweeping new appraisal.

"Only one I know about. You?"

"Take your purchases and go," the proprietor snapped, staring at Ruth. His gaze dropped to the floor then back to the display case. "Here, I'll throw in that box of personal items you asked about."

Surprised, Ruth scanned his face then wordlessly nodded.

He drew out the box of condoms, took the lid from underneath, secured it and handed the box to her carefully.

"How much?" she asked.

"My gift to you." He lowered his voice so, she could barely hear him. "And to Jusu." He leered.

She started for the door. The last of the Bwanans in the store had shuffled out when Ruth stepped back to catch Glouster's attention. "Who is Jusu?"

Glouster regarded her suspiciously as if it were a trick. "He is one who cuts out a man's heart and holds it beating in his two hands." Wide-eyed, Glouster obviously was impressed by his own words. "He puts that heart into whom he pleases. The one dies. The other lives. Jusu is God."

More confused than before, Ruth turned and walked slowly, thoughtfully out of the store.

She had read very little about black magic or sorcerers or evil spells. She considered it all tripe.

She expected superstitious mumbo-jumbo from uneducated blacks who frightened each other with their ghastly tales. She didn't know why she had expected better from Glouster just because his skin was white, or she supposed it was, under the layers of dirt.

He had lived among them too long, had gone native, she supposed.

She was glad that she lived in Bwana among Christians and relieved, too, that her Bible was one of the books she had brought along. She reminded herself to read it before sleeping that night.

Chapter Sixteen

Ruth wrote and sent to the wire service the story about finding the Red Cross condoms donated by Americans on the shelf at Glouster's, merchandise the proprietor sold for eight dollars each to a population which needed them desperately and could not afford that price.

She carried the box from hut to hut--beginning at Marmel's--speaking with each of the families about Slim, and asking that they use the condoms to protect themselves from outsiders who might be carrying the disease.

The day after their trip to Glouster's, Marmel's oldest daughter Leah and two older people in other households came down with a sudden, ravaging fever.

When Ruth heard, she fished aspirin from her supplies and distributed them, with instructions for their use.

On the third day, the initial sufferers were worse, hallucinating, writhing in pools of sweat, trembling with chills, and there were new cases.

Ruth took charge. "They must have lots of liquids. They must drink as much as we can get down them."

For small children who refused to drink water, Ruth provided canned fruit juices sent from America.

After three nights of the mysterious, excruciating illness, one of the first victims, an old woman, died. Marmel's daughter and another older woman seemed to recover. Meanwhile, more villagers fell ill.

Alarmed, blaming herself for their exposure to the illness, which she assumed they contracted at Glouster's, Ruth went from house to house trying to identify the problem, to curb the outbreak. More and more people went down with the disease.

The strong regained their senses after three days. The old and the very young succumbed--two other old women, the oldest man in the village (who had not even made the trip to Glouster's) and two toddlers.

Guilt ridden that she had instigated the trip, Ruth cooked meat broth, which her mother had called "beef tea," and fed it to the weaker victims hoping to restore their strength as a dozen more people came down with the disease before week's end.

Ruth watched Artemis closely and begged him to stay away from the homes where people were infected. He agreed, but insisted on accompanying her when she visited those same huts. Minding her as nearly as possible, he remained vigilant outside the doors.

Ruth and Artemis gargled antiseptic mouthwash to keep from ingesting the germs and scrubbed to keep their hands clean as they moved from house to house, patient to patient.

Ruth's heart leapt into her throat early one morning as she stepped out of a hut where she had spent the night tending to the sick to see the tall, silent Tuslan, standing in the road. He watched her emerge from the hut but did not approach. Her nerves were frayed and she thought him wise to keep his distance.

On the morning of the eighth day, villagers murmured together in the street.

"What is it?" she asked Father Catlett as he passed.

"Jusu was here."

"When?"

"In the night."

"Why?"

"To visit the sick ones."

"Did he do some kind of voodoo?"

"No. He took blood from some and jars of water."

"Whose blood did he take?"

"One was Marmel's wife."

Ruth walked quickly to Marmel's and stepped inside, as she had when she had tended Leah, the oldest daughter and first to be stricken. "I understand that Jusu was here."

Marmel sat on the floor propped against an upright beside his wife who lay on a mat on the floor, her eyes bright with fever. He didn't speak, only nodded.

"Why did he come?"

His eyes rolled. "To see her."

"What did he say?"

"He did not speak. He stabbed her. She bled."

"Show me where."

Marmel's wife held up her finger, then pointed to a needle mark in the bend of her elbow. Ruth regarded the wounds curiously.

"Marmel, why did you allow him to come into your home, to examine your wife?"

"Even when I am well and strong, I do not oppose Jusu. No man does and lives."

On the ninth day after the visit to Glouster's store, there was no new case of the fever. Relaxing a little, Ruth realized her vigilance had taken a toll. She felt the fatigue of the long nights beside mats, tending patients to give rest to caretakers who were sometimes sick themselves.

Before dawn the next morning, Ruth walked slowly to the guest house, lay down on her bed fully clothed and fell into a restless sleep.

Artemis brought Ossie to her. Ruth saw them both wavering in a dreamlike state, moving quietly about the house, speaking in whispers. Late in the night strong, unfamiliar hands held her head and forced her to choke down strange, foul-smelling potions.

The large, shadowy illusion moved soundlessly, always in the dark. Occasionally Ruth heard the form chanting over her in the night. The chant heralded the cool cloth with which shadowy hands sponged her burning skin.

Half conscious, half asleep, she soon welcomed the sound of the approaching chant, knowing the hands and the sponge would follow. She roused enough once to ask if he were an angel. She heard only a muffled grunt.

She didn't care if he were or not. Surely he served her as an angel would, she thought dreamily.

The house was bathed in crimson when she next opened her eyes when the walls didn't swim. Artemis sat in a chair beside her bed reading his magazine. He looked up and a smile broke over his small face.

"Artemis." Her voice sounded hoarse to her.

Artemis grinned so broadly, his gums showed. "I am most glad to hear you speak clearly. You have been very sick. You must rest."

"All right."

With that, she slept, quiet slumber replacing the restless churning of the fever-induced sleep.

Artemis was gone and Ossie was there with soup when Ruth woke again. Ossie helped her lean forward and propped pillows behind her.

"You must eat," Ossie ordered and began ladling soup into her mouth. When Ruth had eaten half the bowl without objection, she waved Ossie off. "I need to rest a minute." She slumped back into the pillows. "Thank you for taking care of me."

"Artemis and I watched together every day."

"You were wonderful, especially in the nights." Ruth blinked against the daylight. "You were very strong, very patient."

"No. It was Artemis."

Ruth scowled. "No. Your larger, stronger hands comforted me. You chanted while you bathed me. I cannot believe the water which cooled me was only a dream."

Ossie gave Ruth a hard stare, turned her eyes away, then back. "Jusu came." She whispered the words and looked frightened. "He came in the night when you were fitful." Ossie looked around, as if fearful of being overheard. "He made me leave. He made me go home to sleep. He said he would watch. I was frightened. I did not tell Father. I did not know of the bathing. I only know when I returned each morning, you were not dead. You were clean and resting and quiet.

"Artemis would not leave." Ossie continued, whispering hurriedly, intently. "Jusu told him to go home. I waited. Artemis was stubborn. He said this was his home and you, his own loving mother, his Maawe, that he would not allow Jusu to remove your heart while it continued beating. He said he was pledged to care for you for the rest of your days, whether they were few or many. He would not leave you.

"Jusu said he would care for you. He forced Artemis to sit outside, guarding as he does every night. Artemis was frightened but he told Jusu boldly that he would come to check you when he wanted, if Jusu allowed it or not.

"It was a foolish thing to speak to Jusu's face. Jusu can take the heart from a man..."

"I've heard all that," Ruth interrupted impatiently. "Where is Artemis now?"

"He is with my children at the water. He is only a child, Mother. When I told him you would awake today, I sent him to my Mary for food. I told him to go to the water and wash and put on fresh clothing to please you. He was very tired from his long vigil."

Ruth drew a deep breath and settled against the pillows. She needed to remember something. Something about the dark figure chanting, but she couldn't think what it was.

She might have been afraid if she had roused and found a feather-clad black man conjuring spirits over her. She was glad she had not.

Then, before she could entertain another thought, she slept.

Chapter Seventeen

Ruth's head swam when she attempted to stand that afternoon.

How many had died? She wondered, sitting on the side of the bed, her feet dangling above the dirt floor. She wanted to know. How many was she responsible for having murdered by taking them to Glouster's that day.

How many days had passed since then? Was the disease still sweeping Bwana? Had Glouster and the other white men also fallen to the mysterious illness? And why had Artemis not become ill when he had spent so much time around those who were?

She frowned, fighting the recurring headache which seemed to pound, flashing bright lights, blinding her. She ran her hands over her clothing and found she was awash in a large gown which covered her modestly from neck to knee but there was nothing underneath. She did not remember the garment.

Gradually, Ruth overcame the headache and the swimming images, lowered her feet to the floor and hobbled to the straight-backed chair positioned at the trestle table. Just the little effort of getting from the bed to the chair sapped her strength.

Picking up the pen, she pulled the tablet over in front of her and began to write.

She wrote a news story about the apparition in her fevered nights, of the elusive yet ever present, ghostly Jusu, the chanting witch doctor with strange nocturnal bedside manner.

As she wrote, Ruth realized she had little information about the black magician who held sway over even the marauding white men of the area. *How far did his influence extend? And why?*

Her head throbbed. She wanted to go home. Bwana was her home now, these her family and friends.

She wanted to go to Kampala to meet Ross Belton when he came, but she mustn't mention it for fear of leading the willing Bwanans on yet another treacherous outing.

Maybe Ross could tell her what to do. No. Ross would urge her to go home with him.

She might.

She mustn't.

Her head pounded. Using the back of the chair, Ruth struggled to her feet and shuffled back to bed. Perhaps she should rethink this project, this new life. But she didn't need to do it right now. She would, she determined, as soon as she was stronger.

*   *   *

A week of leisure and rest passed, including the Fourth of July--with no celebration, no picnics or fireworks. With renewed strength on that morning, Ruth whispered a wistful, "Happy Birthday, America."

The temperature was seventy-five or seventy-six in the warmest parts of the days and the mercury fell no lower than sixty-two at night. It was balmy, almost like springtime at home and Ruth was content to allow her body to mend.

Relieved of his nursemaid duties, Artemis played with other children, for the first time in his life, Ossie told her.

"Artemis has always been serious," Ossie said, "not really ever a child at all. Now that he has adopted a mother for himself, he seems more comfortable in the roll of little boy."

Ruth worried. "He's awfully small for his age, don't you think?"

"He will grow, now that he basks in your love. You will see."

There was a clamor as Mary, Benjamin (Ossie's oldest son) and Artemis raced toward the women, shoving one another and giggling.

"Mother." Artemis gasped with his excitement. "They asked me to go with them to the clearing woods to cut trees for the cooking fire." He paused to catch his breath. "They have said I may use the saw."

Ruth patted his face and smiled into his luminous eyes. "You must be very careful. A saw is a tool, not a toy."

"Yes, Mother." She detected a note of disdain, familiar from voices in her earlier life. *Was his inflection more like Michael's or Donnie's?*

Occasionally Ruth received letters from those people who had once called her Mom, one from Carly with pictures of their grandchild. But it seemed as if those were part of an earlier life, a dreamlike existence which was long ago and far away.

Later Ruth mused. "I am surprised that I do not grieve at this separation from my own children." Ossie scraped vegetables over a pan of water, then chopped them into a pot for stew. Baby Christina sat beside her on the ground rattling metal measuring spoons, mixing an imaginary batter in a small, empty metal pan.

Ruth ran her hands over the nearly dry clothes swaying on the clothesline. "Maybe it's because I know they are happy and achieving goals they've set for themselves. If I were there, I would probably argue with them about their priorities. I would try to tell them what is worthwhile and what is not."

Ossie didn't look up from her vegetables. "When one is an adult, she has experienced success and failure and knows which things are worth the risks and which are not. We want to tell our children which is which. They do not want to hear what we found of value. They want to experience for themselves the feeling of success and failure.

"We want to save them from the disappointments. However, if they do not know disappointment, perhaps they cannot appreciate accomplishment."

Ruth smiled at her friend and confidante and took the clothespins off the first item on the line.

"You are very wise, Ossie. I cannot tell how old you are. I know your Mary is thirteen years, but you look only a little older than that yourself."

Ossie turned a brilliant smile on Ruth, an unusual concession. "I am thirty-two years."

Ruth swallowed her astonishment as she folded the shirt and tossed it in the laundry basket at her feet.

"My daughter Carly is twenty-eight." She brushed her hand over the next shirt.

"Oh? And is she the one with the baby son?"

"Yes. Have I bored you with stories of my grandchild?"

"Not at all. In your fever, you spoke lovingly of Mickey. I could not tell if you spoke of your grandson or of your husband."

The baby rattled the keys loudly.

"Where is your nose, Christina?" Ruth asked, gazing at the toddler. Christina stopped stirring her imaginary mixture and put a tentative index finger on the tip of her nose.

"Yes, Christina. That is very good. What a smart girl you are."

The baby grinned, flashing four pearly white teeth, two on top and two at the bottom of her small budlike mouth.

Removing a pair of trousers from the line, Ruth felt rather than heard the children's first screams which shattered the familiar hum of the warm afternoon.

Ossie leaped to her feet, threw an ear of corn and the knife into the pan of water in front of her. She grabbed the baby and bolted down the path to the woods to meet the screaming children.

Simultaneously, Ruth tossed the trousers into the waiting basket, picked up the basket, then dropped it and ran after Ossie.

She finally saw them, Mary, running, carrying Artemis. The boy was silent, his round eyes frightened. His arms locked around Mary's neck, he bounced nearly out of her arms as she galloped toward her mother, sobbing as she ran.

There was blood on both Mary and Artemis. The blood confused Ruth. With all the screams, she couldn't tell which of them was the source of the bleeding, although common sense should have told her, she realized.

Ruth ran by Ossie and reached the pair first, grabbed Mary's arm and shouted directly into the girl's face. "Mary, which one of you is hurt?" She could not be heard over the incessant wails of the other two Catlett children following. From behind Ruth, Ossie shrieked at all of the children.

Mary shoved Artemis into Ruth's arms.

Ruth turned him, looking for the source of the blood. "What happened?"

"I was careful of the saw, Mother." His voice was low as he directed his words into her face. "I forgot to be careful of the tree. When it fell, my foot was where the tree wished to be."

Ruth's eyes traveled down his body to the foot.

Blood pumped from an open wound above his arch. The top of the dark little appendage was streaked with black. His foot appeared to have been crushed.

"Jusu." Ossie screamed the name, clutching Ruth's arm and turning her. "You must take him to Jusu."

Holding the boy's diminutive body, Ruth peered into his face, then examined his shoulders, arms, trunk. Splotches of blood diverted her attention to one place, then another, but his foot seemed the only casualty.

Blood pumped from the open wound rhythmically--with each heartbeat. Realizing that, she became alarmed all over again and felt her heart thrumming blood through her own veins.

Other people arrived and surrounded the two women and the boy. Ruth tried to get a grip on her runaway fear. "Benjamin, get a plastic sack from my house, off the doorknob. Run to the high stream. Fill the sack with frost from the stream bank. Quickly! Quickly!

"Daniel, dump the materials from the sewing box on the table beside my bed. Bring it. The box and lid."

She designated two women to make a litter for the boy, to fit across the handlebars of the bicycle. People ran in separate directions, set upon their tasks.

"Bring the bicycle," she called to Marmel who had already darted toward the guest house in search of the vehicle.

One woman brought clean linens and urged Ruth to wrap them around the boy.

Shock. Of course. She hadn't thought. They needed to keep him warm.

Another woman tore strips for a tourniquet.

Looking at the many hands and many heads working together, Ruth felt a rush of love. She held the boy more tightly and rocked him in her arms as warm tears rose in her heart and spilled from her eyes. She gazed down into his dark little face.

Artemis watched her expression solemnly. She swallowed the tears stinging her throat, swiped at her eyes and forced a reassuring smile. "Everything will be all right." She held her words, forcing them to come slowly. "We will find Jusu. He will fix your foot."

"Yes." The boy's eyes brightened. "Jusu made you well, Mother. He will make me well also, if you will ask him."

She nodded. "Yes, darling, I will ask him." Suddenly with a new thought, she looked around the gathering crowd in horror. "Where is Jusu? Where do I find him?"

"West to Savanron, to his clinic." It was a man's even voice which spoke with authority. Tuslan had materialized as if he were a genie summoned. There was no question. Tuslan was the person most likely to know the whereabouts of Jusu.

"Savanron," several voices repeated.

"West? How will I know which direction when the road divides?"

"West." Tuslan repeated with a wave of his arm. "Always choose the road west."

Twenty-six miles, Ruth thought frantically. *Rutted, terrible roads.* She looked at Artemis. His eyes were focused on her. His wavering smile mirrored hers.

She snatched one length from the mound of cloth strips, bound it around the boy's ankle as a tourniquet and stuffed others in her pocket for the trip.

How long could a tourniquet remain tight without damaging the foot? Was it twenty minutes? It needed to be loosened every twenty minutes, she thought, but her mind sprinted erratically and she couldn't be sure. She would loosen it every twenty minutes and hope for the best. She checked the time on the wrist watch on her arm.

It seemed a long wait before all the components essential to their journey were gathered. Actually, it was only seven minutes on the watch.

With few unnecessary words, hands secured the quickly devised litter to the bicycle's handle bars. Ruth put the bag of frost in the sewing box, used the palm of her hand to form a trough and gently placed the heel of his injured foot in the hollow. She wanted to stabilize his foot as much as possible.

"Get back," she ordered as soon as the boy was secured to the litter.

Ruth wobbled a little as she took off, then found amazing strength somewhere inside as she began to pump, propelling the bike along the rutted dirt road.

Ossie handed Christina to Mary and gave her instructions, then Ossie began running in the bicycle's wake. Many ran behind them for a while, until the rider hit her stride and began to out pace them.

As others abandoned the chase, Ossie settled into a steady gait, falling farther and farther behind, but continuing.

When she reached the ten-mile marker, Ruth stopped to catch her breath and to release the tourniquet. Blood surged from the open wound. Ruth shuddered, grimacing, then, again realizing Artemis's eyes were on her face, she smiled, patted him, righted the bicycle and pushed off again.

She was glad the boy did not require verbal encouragement. Her lungs burned with the exertion of their ride. She had neither strength nor breath for talking.

She stopped a second time at the outer mark of Savanron, seven miles outside the village, again released the tourniquet, watched the blood spurt and caught her breath.

As she rode into the village, residents looked up, surprised at the unlikely conveyance racing toward them. Ruth had no time for explanations.

"Jusu," she called to people at the roadside. "Where is Jusu?"

Fingers pointed, all in the same direction, eventually indicating a large mudded hut in a cluster of smaller thatched ones.

She stopped in front of the mudded structure, braced the bicycle with trembling legs and began to unbind the wrapping securing her passenger to the litter.

An old man and a young girl who had watched her ride into town came quickly. Wordlessly the old man grasped and steadied the bike. The girl's nimble fingers helped loosen ties around Artemis. When he was free, Ruth scooped the boy into her arms. Leaving the bicycle with the old man, she darted through a canvas-like covering over the front door and plunged into the dim light inside the hut.

The antiseptic smell assailed her. A wood and fabric screen defined the waiting area, open at each end. Ruth quickly stepped around the screen and nearly bumped into a gurney on which a man lay sleeping.

A large figure in green surgical clothing with its back to her stood over a basin at the far end of the room, apparently washing his hands.

Ruth had expected a shriveled, bent little man, not this dominating figure looming before her.

No matter.

"Jusu?" She was scarcely able to breathe after the wild ride and with fear for the boy pounding in her chest. "Help me. Please help me."

The figure turned.

Above the surgical mask covering the lower part of his face, she saw striking gray eyes, the same eyes which often pervaded her dreams. This was not the help she sought, not the witch doctor, the magician. This was merely a white man. A teacher, he had said...of science.

Then a new thought intervened. *Could Jusu be a white man?* No one had said he wasn't. No one had said either way.

"Jusu?" she repeated in disbelief. The gray eyes swept from her to the boy, settling on the injured foot as the masked countenance nodded slowly.

"Yes." His voice was familiar.

"Jack Standish?" she wheezed.

Again he nodded. "Yes."

Chapter Eighteen

Keeping his hands up, palms toward one another, the man snagged a second gurney with his foot and pulled it toward them.

"Put him here." He indicated the table. It was covered with a long sheet of clean, white paper. Ruth placed Artemis on the table and straightened his clothing and his limbs. The boy winced when she straightened his bloody foot but he did not cry out. Jusu's eyes and full attention were directed at the open wound as he worked his hands into latex gloves.

He touched the appendage, examining the wound. "The foot is cold." He shot Ruth a curious look.

"It's been in ice."

He nodded. With his nod, Ruth felt overwhelmed with relief. He was going to help. She studied him dully. She had never seen Standish in short sleeves, only in a coat and tie. The shoulders on this man were square; his arms, extending from the short sleeves of his surgical tunic, well formed, capable. If strength were required, it was obvious, this Jusu would make the boy well.

Ruth felt peculiar. The gurney swayed before her. Her joints felt loose. Without realizing what was happening, her knees buckled and she sat abruptly, unceremoniously on the tarpaulin covering the dirt floor. She remained upright, just unexpectedly sitting instead of standing.

"Lie down, right there." Standish gave her a quick glance. "On your back. Head down. Bend your knees. I'm going to need your help."

She did as he said. Her thoughts were confused. *He's going to need my help,* she thought queerly. *I've already done all I can do. I can't do any more.*

She recalled the old adage she had repeated to her children. "Can't never could."

He needs my help. She replayed his words in her mind. Her thinking was muddled. *Do you think you can? Yes,* she thought. *Can do,* she thought. But her body did not respond to the command to sit. She raised her head and tried again.

"Lie still for a few minutes." The command was brusque. "We don't need you yet. Rest until we do."

We needing her was entirely different than he needing her. *We* was the man and the boy, her own precious Artemis.

Yes. She would rest until they were ready. Then she would help.

She closed her eyes--her head down, her knees flexed--and breathed deeply. Nerves quivered through the muscles in her legs. She was accustomed to riding the bicycle, but not at that speed over that distance. Too, she had ridden very little since her illness.

Time passed.

The man spoke quietly to the boy, telling him a story, Jack and the Beanstalk, as he cleaned the wound. She lifted her arm to glance at her watch. She must have flown to have gotten there so quickly. A motorized ambulance might not have done that well over that road.

Looking at the watch, Ruth felt confused all over again about an altogether different subject. *What was she trying to remember?*

Oh, yes, the watch. It was his watch. Not Jusu's watch, of course. Jack Standish's watch.

No one had ever heard of Standish. They told her so. It was terribly disappointing. She consoled herself a little by thinking if she could not find Jack Standish, she would not have to return the watch. *Was that good thought better than the bad thought was bad?*

Jusu had been in Bwana, they told her. When she was ill, Ossie took care of her during the days. But at night Jusu was there chanting in the darkness. It was Jusu, Ossie said, who applied wet cloths, who bathed Ruth through those dark, harrowing nights.

She had not seen him herself, but she had heard his chant, the magician's song over and over again. The magician's hands were gentle, caring hands, lifting her, shifting her from soiled sheets to fresh ones; tender hands; dark hands.

No one told her Jusu was white. They didn't think of him as white. They knew him, feared him, trusted him.

Jack Standish was arrogant, rich, white.

Jusu was not.

How could they be one man? They were not even alike.

Her thoughts wrestled in her mind, tumbling, one prevailing first, then the other.

Jusu's voice interrupted. "We need you to scrub now."

She rolled onto her hands and knees and up. On her feet, she shuffled to the basin, cuffed her elbow-length sleeves once and dipped her hands into the antiseptic solution. She did have to scrub to remove the blood which had dried around her fingernails.

Jack Standish had manicured nails on the airplane.

Don't think about it, she told herself and shook her head in an effort to dispel memories of Standish. She wavered with the effort.

"Can you come now?" He sounded a long way off, somewhere outside.

Like a zombie, she shook off the excess solution and walked to the table. He pointed at a box of latex gloves. It took her a minute to pull them on.

"Tell him a story." His words were crisp, deliberate.

She began with no hesitation. "Once upon a time a man named Manoah and his wife wanted a son." Samson was the boy's favorite hero. He asked her to read or tell the story again and again. She always began with the man and the woman who wanted a son. Artemis loved that part.

Ruth watched his face closely when she told him the story. She loved the boy's dear, mahogany face, his generous mouth and round, dark eyes. Thinking how she loved him, she smiled at him tenderly. He smiled back. The man glanced up, noting the exchange. He rolled the boy onto his side, bared a small hip and gave him a quick shot before either Artemis or Ruth could object.

"And did they get the son they wanted?" the man asked.

Ruth nodded. "And finally, when they had prayed many times and had waited a long, long while..."

Without interrupting her narrative, Ruth responded to each of the man's requests as he manipulated the injured foot, lining up toes, pressing with his fingers, squeezing, pushing, twisting. The boy lay quietly, his eyes closed, his face relaxed as if he were asleep. Ruth continued the story.

"Hold this tightly." The man interrupted when it was necessary. "See those splints? Hand me a large one." "Mop my forehead, please."

When she finished the story, Artemis didn't open his eyes.

The man did not ask how she felt or in any way call Ruth's attention to herself. She wondered how she had ever thought him sensitive.

Yet he was the same man who had rescued her from the pawing seat mate on the airplane, provided her a place to stay in London...

No, that was not this man. That was the other...

She didn't want to think about him. But here he was beside her and occasionally, as he worked, she caught a whiff of the familiar scent, the one which reminded her of Mickey. At the thought of Mickey, she hesitated, stalled for a moment.

"Hand me the four-oh suture."

Where was Mickey Pedigo?

"The number is in bold white lettering on the blue box. The four-oh suture, please."

Oh, yes. Mickey Pedigo was gone. And he left her again, over and over again, nightly, in her dreams. Some nights Mickey's memory paled, replaced by the tall, gentle darkness, sometimes chanting.

She looked around. There was the dark blue box. She picked it up and handed it to the masked figure.

Their aroma was the same, Mickey Pedigo and Jack Standish. Fragrances usually smell different on different bodies. Ruth knew that.

Wild-eyed, breathless, Ossie lunged through the doorway, skirted the screen, burst into the surgery and surveyed the odd scene.

121

"Mrs. Catlett, stay outside until I call you." Jusu's voice was quiet but full of authority. Ossie retreated. Ruth was overwhelmed with relief to see Ossie had arrived.

Ruth watched the man stitch the boy's foot where the skin had been laid open.

Again she was reminded that their scents, Mickey's and Standish's, were the same. It was the scent that drew her. And when she had the fever, she had caught a trace of that same fragrance wafting from the witch doctor. That was the thing she had been trying to remember.

Her arms itched. Her head ached. Blood had spattered over the table, soaked into the clean white paper which had covered its surface. The serum was smeared into her clothing, on her skin and in her hair. She looked at the boy.

As he finished stitching the foot, the man turned his head. "Rosamond!"

Ruth started at the unexpected shout.

A stately young black woman pushed aside the curtain covering a doorway and floated into the surgery. The man said something to her and she disappeared the same way. Moments later she returned and handed him something which seemed to be alive, wriggling.

He took the handful of moving things and placed them on the boy's swollen foot.

Ruth took a step closer. "What is that?"

"Leeches."

She glowered into his face. "What? Why?"

"To reduce the swelling. I don't have anything for it. Our supplies are limited. Mother nature helps us get around some of the deficiencies."

Ruth made an awful face but didn't take her eyes off the foot, now alive with the leeches.

The man concentrated on the injured area.

"Be glad we have live tissue. It's more repugnant to clean out an area of dead tissue. Maggots do a very thorough job without damaging live skin, but the idea of them is nauseating to some people. Nature is quite remarkable when we call upon her."

Ruth's back emitted silent screams before the doctor finished dressing Artemis's leg. Then the enigmatic man peeled off his surgical gloves and uncovered his face and head to reveal a somber Jack Standish.

"What happens next?" She peered at him in quick, unbelieving glimpses, squinting against the persistent headache.

"When he comes out of the anesthetic, the pain will be excruciating."

"Has he been asleep all this time?"

"Since we gave him the shot."

"Then why was I telling the story?"

"That was for my benefit. I enjoy the sound of your voice. And to help distract you."

She gave him a shaky smile. "Do you have medicine to help him cope with the pain?"

"I have some. It will help. But you will be the best medicine for that." He glanced down at the boy and stroked his shoulder. "The pain's going to be terrible and he's awfully young. He'll try to be brave for you. You must distract him with stories, games, whatever you think will keep his mind off his foot."

"What else?"

"He needs to stay here for a few days. I want to keep an eye on the stitches, that open area. You saw the splint. It's a primitive substitute for a cast. We must keep the foot immobile for six weeks. He must not put any weight on it."

"Will it heal? Will he be able to walk normally?"

"I think so. The human body is a marvelous piece of machinery. If you touch two bones together, they will knit themselves. All we have to do is line them up correctly and keep them touching and immobile. I don't have an x-ray. I had to place the broken bones together by feel but I'm pretty sure we've got it right."

She felt confused. "I thought you were a teacher."

"I am."

"I thought you taught science?"

"Surgical technique."

"On feet?"

He exhaled. "You may have noticed, we are not fully staffed here. I am the only surgeon available. We will have to make do with my meager skills." He raised his eyebrows.

Recognizing the arrogance in the mischievous twinkle, she allowed a wry smile.

Rosamond reappeared, again moving silently through the covered door.

"Move him to the back," Jack ordered brusquely. The woman's eyes narrowed as she regarded Ruth. "Keep him comfortable. Mrs. Pedigo will return in a little while. If he awakens, come for her."

Still glowering at Ruth, the woman nodded, ducked her head and began gathering the strips of soiled fabric strewn about the gurney.

"Wash your hands." His voice reflected his ire. "Move the boy first." Again she nodded sullenly.

Ruth was too tired to think or to speak.

Chapter Nineteen

Jack Standish placed his hand in the small of Ruth's aching back and nudged her through a doorway covered by heavy fabric, down a hall toward another covered doorway. As they walked, he wrapped an arm around her waist. "You're thinner."

She leaned into his strength and attempted an appreciative smile. "There was a time when I would have given a lot to hear those words."

"The fever often leaves people without an appetite. Are you eating?"

She nodded but a gnawing memory evaded capture. At least for the moment she couldn't think of the questions she wanted to ask.

He ushered her into what appeared to be a small bedroom. *It had a full size bed, the first she had seen since...how long? Since the Guinevere.*

Ruth frowned up into his face.

He looked around the room oddly, as if considering it for the first time, then hurried to straightened the bed coverings which had been pulled up carelessly.

Struggling with, then overcoming the obstinate bottom drawer on an aged bureau, he coaxed out clean pillow cases and quickly changed and fluffed both pillows which he left atop the bedspread.

"This is where I sleep." He took her elbow. "Lie down here for a while and rest. I'll find you something to eat."

She started to object.

"You're spent." He waved off her words. "You came a long way. You stood in the surgery for nearly two hours. You need to rest. Lie down. It doesn't matter if you go to sleep. Lie still. Close your eyes. Rest."

He was doing it again, making her decisions for her. *She was a grown woman. She should assert herself.*

Still, the bed looked inviting. The room was cool and darkened by heavy fabric coverings over the two casement windows high on one wall.

She could use a rest. She didn't trust the woman, Rosamond, but Ossie was here. *How had Ossie gotten there so quickly?* Someone with a vehicle must have come along and given her a ride.

"Will you ask Ossie to watch Artemis?"

"Yes."

Ruth walked over and pushed the mattress experimentally with one hand. She turned, sat on the edge of the bed and took a deep breath. Without a word, Jack knelt in front of her, untied and pulled off her boots then lifted her legs, pivoting her onto the bed. She inhaled deeply and stretched. He left the room and returned with a quilt which he put over her.

She would rest, she agreed in herself, but only for a few minutes. She glanced at her wrist watch, then at Jack who paused in the doorway to meet her gaze.

"I need to give you back your watch." Her voice wavered and she looked at him with a puzzled frown.

He smiled, stepped to the bureau, picked up a watch identical to the one on her arm, and buckled the strap around his wrist. "I have one, thank you."

He stood another long moment looking at her face, then turned and walked out of the room. She stretched again, trying to get the kinks out of her muscles. It was wonderful to see Jack again. He always seemed to make things better.

* * *

Unwillingly, unwittingly, Ruth dozed, vaguely aware of every sound, every shadow whispering through the darkened room until gradually her body yielded and she relaxed into a deep slumber.

She opened her eyes suddenly, alarmed by her strange surroundings or a sound or a smell. She leaned up on one arm and rubbed her eyes with her free hand.

The room was completely dark except for a votive candle valiantly fending off the pitch blackness of the night.

Ruth felt a stare burning into her. She scanned twice before her bleary eyes brought into focus the scant outline of a figure in the doorway. "Who is it?" Ruth rubbed her eyes again, trying to translate the vision into a familiar form. No one spoke as the apparition drew back and became part of the night.

Ruth sat up and steadied herself for a moment. She slid her feet into her boots, then stood without tying them. Her feet hurt. Her calves were tight. Her thighs objected to supporting her full weight. She still wore the shorts and camp shirt, her usual uniform of the day. Sluggishly she walked to the shrouded doorway. The curtain was drawn back halfway.

She retraced her steps from the afternoon and wound her way back down the hallway to the surgery. It was empty and also dark, except for the faint glow of another votive.

Targeting the outside door, she walked into the chill silence of early, early morning. The warmth of a new day was coming, but now the temperature hovered near sixty. She shivered. *Why hadn't someone wakened her? Had Artemis called for her? Was he awake? In pain?*

She turned back toward the house to find the ghostly figure again framed in a doorway. "Rosamond, why did you not speak?" Ruth's vexation was scantily concealed in her tone. There was no response. "Are you mute? Or perhaps you do not speak English."

The woman smirked. "I speak when I choose. Yes, as you see, I do speak your precious English."

"Yes, you do. And very well. Thank you. I understand some of the dialects, but I still cannot string enough words together to speak any of them adequately."

126

The two women stood still, each silently evaluating the other. Rosamond was first to break the silence. "What did you do?"

"When? What do you mean?"

"To enchant him? What spell was it?"

Ruth was taken aback. "Do you mean Artemis?"

The dark woman in the doorway winced.

"No, of course not. You mean Jusu. Oh, no, Rosamond, Jusu is not enchanted. You misunderstand. I am clumsy in Uganda. The customs and the language are new to me. He sees my ignorance, thinks me helpless. He is a caring person, a man of compassion. It is his nature to help those who need help."

"No." The black woman objected sharply. "He has no regard for ignorance. There is no need. Jusu has power."

Ruth started to interrupt, then hesitated, allowing Rosamond to continue.

"He nods and there is life. He frowns and death follows. He has not this compassion. He despises the weak ones. Often he will not help when they come. He sends them home to die. He shares his power only with the strong."

Ruth studied the beautiful black face. It was firm, with fine, proportionate features atop a long, slender neck sweeping to prominent collar bones visible above the wrap of her serape.

Perhaps six feet tall, Rosamond carried her unusual height proudly, haughty and straight.

Her serape followed the lines of her slim figure, narrowing and swelling at appropriate places.

"Are you Jusu's woman?" Ruth dreaded the answer.

"Perhaps."

"My dear, you needn't feel threatened. I am well beyond my days of being attractive to men. Sweet daughter, I have children older than you."

For the first time, Rosamond's face revealed something other than contempt. Hurt, maybe. Her black head bowed. "I am not his woman. Jusu does not want me."

"Certainly he does." Ruth took a step forward before Rosamond snapped her head up again, a warning. Ruth stopped but continued speaking. "Isn't it you he calls when he needs assistance? Doesn't he want you beside him when he has a difficult case? Whose hands did he trust with the care of the small boy who required so much of his skill, his power, for repair?"

Rosamond again assumed her regal posture, head and chin high with pride.

Ruth nodded. "The answer to those questions, Rosamond, is you."

"Jusu has no sons." The girl spoke the words earnestly. "He will allow no one to give him sons. I want to make a child with him. I tell him so. Many women have spoken to him thus. Even white women in Kampala City invite his pleasure.

But he will not allow it. In my country, all men want sons. Is that not true of men in America also?"

Ruth nodded. "Yes, most men in America do want sons."

"Jusu comes from America. He is there many months each year. He has no sons there either. He is able to plant the seed. I know. I have..."

"Well," Ruth interrupted nodding, then cleared her throat. She was a little embarrassed at the intimate direction their conversation was taking. She already knew more about Jack Standish than she thought altogether seemly, a word Mickey's mother used. "Rosamond, you are a strikingly beautiful woman. Don't you have a husband?"

"I have had two husbands. Both went away. Both died."

"I am so sorry. You must have been very young."

"I married first when I was fourteen years. He went away and was lost. I married again when I was seventeen years. He was afraid of death. He escaped, made his way into Zaire. Some say he died there."

"And you are afraid to marry again?"

"No. I have been alone now three years. I could marry others but I desire only Jusu."

"Rosamond, isn't Jusu a little old for you?"

The girl stared at her with disbelief. "He is beautiful to behold. I peek sometimes when he bathes. He is strong and straight and marvelously made. His manhood..."

"Wait." Ruth held up a hand to stop the words.

Rosamond cast her eyes at the ground. "My body weeps to receive him."

Neither woman spoke for a moment. Ruth maintained her silence. She had nothing to say.

"One night I went into his bed, after he slept." The younger woman's voice was soft, almost apologetic. "I was very still, afraid to anger him. When my courage came, I moved closer until I could feel his warm breath on my skin. My body filled with the scent of him. I trembled I touched him and he grew strong. I longed to welcome him.

"He awoke with a start, much as you did tonight in that same bed. He leaped up as if I were a serpent. He ordered me out. He said I could not return to his house, ever."

"I ran away. I cried for many days. I sent messenger after messenger begging him to forgive me, to allow me to return, to assist him in the surgery. I swore I would never again seek his favor in any other way."

Brightening, Ruth began nodding. "And he forgave you, didn't he?"

"Only because Timmons would not let Jusu cut off his leg. I told Timmons Jusu had promised his good leg to another. In truth, Jusu wanted Timmons to live."

"You told that lie intentionally?"

"Some lies help."

"Is Timmons alive today?"

"I told Jusu I would make Timmons come to have his leg removed only if Jusu would take me back as his assistant. For Timmons' sake, Jusu allowed me to return. He removed the leg. Timmons lived, until he stumbled with his crutches and his elephant stepped on him."

Ruth stifled the involuntary smile. It wasn't a funny story, of course, but she thought of news reports in America every day involving all manner of fatalities. At home, she had never heard or read an account of anyone dying in an elephant mishap.

But whatever was she thinking? She was not concerned about elephants. "Rosamond, where is Artemis?"

"What?"

"The boy. Where is he?"

"In the infirmary for recovery."

"May I see him?"

"I will show you, but I cannot enter there tonight and possibly you should not."

Ruth was suddenly alarmed. "Why, Rosamond? Is he not recovering well?"

"The boy is all right. Jusu is sleeping there also. I think you understand..."

Ruth nodded, then waited for Rosamond to lead her back through the surgery, another curtained doorway, down a hall into another votive-lighted room which smelled of rubbing alcohol.

Following the sound of heavy breathing Ruth could see mounds of white bedclothes in two of the three narrow hospital beds set side by side with only walking space to separate them.

Waving Rosamond back, Ruth tiptoed to the smaller figure and gazed down, allowing her eyes to adjust to the darkness as she interpreted the shape of the familiar head belonging to Artemis. She shivered. The larger figure in the next bed stirred and sat up quickly.

"Lie down here." Standish spoke in a stage whisper as he abandoned his berth beside the child and moved to the next bed over. Shoeless, he wore a T-shirt and khaki trousers.

Ruth first pulled the sheet up over the boy's exposed shoulder then, seemly or not, she sat on the edge of the bed next to his, the middle of the three.

"Lie down," Standish ordered again. She didn't want him to rouse the boy, so she slipped her feet out of her boots and stretched on her side facing Artemis. Without realizing it at first, she nestled into the warmth the man's body had left there, and pulled the cover over her.

"He's doing fine." Standish's voice was quieter. "I wanted to be nearby. The pain will be intense when he wakes up. I'm glad you're here.

"He called for you, roused enough one time to reach for you. I thought we might have to wake you. I went to look. You were sleeping so soundly, I didn't want to disturb you until we had to."

Ruth didn't want to talk. This was a peculiar situation. *What would her children think if they had a sudden glimpse of her here in this room at this moment.*

And wouldn't it shock the old duffers Sunday school class?

And what about Ross Belton? He considered her stodgy. He would be surprised. She chuckled a little to herself.

Standish stirred. "What is it?"

"Nothing," she whispered. "I'm sorry. Go to sleep."

*   *   *

Artemis wanted to be brave for her, that was obvious, but tears filled his eyes over and over again that first day as he lay immobile in the bed in the infirmary.

He would not allow Ruth to leave his bedside, insisting that she maintain some kind of physical contact with him every moment for the first several hours. From a straight-backed chair placed between the beds, she kept one hand on the child and he slept. When she shifted, removed her hand for only a moment, he cried out.

She was terribly relieved to see the tall, black nurse when the young woman came to check on them. "Rosamond, come put your hand on his back, please, like this, while I go to the bathroom."

The clinic had a crude type of indoor toilet, devised by someone who understood both the structural and anatomical designs of the two subjects and something, too, about gravitational flow. Although they bathed elsewhere, the residents had the luxury of an indoor stool. Ruth appreciated the facility, a substantial change from her accommodations in Bwana.

Absent for those few moments, Ruth heard Artemis scream.

She washed her hands and hurried back to his room to find both Jack and Rosamond trying to comfort the boy. His shrieking stopped only after Jack stood aside to allow the child to see Ruth scurrying through the doorway.

Chapter Twenty

Ossie returned to Bwana on the bicycle the morning after their wild flight to Savanron, carrying the news of Artemis' condition.

Ruth remained vigilant at the boy's bedside. When his pain was too great during those first two long, grueling days, Ruth cradled him in her arms, humming or singing softly. Twice she glanced up to find Jack standing in the doorway watching. Self-conscious, she ignored him.

Jack did not go to bed at night in the infirmary with Artemis and Ruth but as the nights wore on and Ruth was up repeatedly comforting the child, she welcomed the respite in the predawn hours, when Jack appeared and ordered her into the next bed to sleep, allowing him the middle bed, next to the boy, to take over the patient's care.

"The work you do here," she whispered one predawn morning as she edged toward sleep in the far bed, "is it legitimate medical practice? Are you a medical doctor?"

He stood studying the sleeping child. Without looking at her, he said tersely, "Yes, I am. Why?"

"People are afraid of you. They talk about you in whispers. They describe you like Mary Shelly described Dr. Frankenstein. They say you hold beating hearts in your two hands, that you choose who lives and who dies."

"I see."

"Are you doing experimental work on these people? Are you Dr. Mengele returned?"

"I am not." His answer was terse.

"Do you come here then for the adulation?"

He was quiet a long time, still poised over the boy, as Ruth lay in the darkness awaiting his response. He nodded at the sleeping Artemis, then sat, kicked off his shoes and lay down on the middle bed between the woman and the boy. He stretched on his back and locked his hands behind his head.

"No. People in the states admire me enough--give my ego all the stroking I need. I don't come here for that. I come to remember, to see first hand my work making a difference.

"In Dallas a surgeon doesn't have much time for individual patients. People wheel a sedated body into the room, I do the procedure dictated by a chart, they whisk that one off to recovery and wheel in the next. I tend to forget I'm dealing with human beings, that families and friends pace the waiting rooms and pray in the chapel. Sometimes they pray for me...for me to do especially well what I routinely do pretty well without their prayers.

"I'm not here doing experimental work or medical research. I damn sure wouldn't come all this way and live in these conditions for any evil purpose. I come to recharge my battery. People--frightened, injured, sick people--come to me. Also..."

"What?"

"You need to sleep. You can hear me lecture another time."

"Why do they call you the magician?"

"I don't know how that started. I have the training to perform certain feats. From the knowledge of my own limitations and the supplies available, I know which injuries or illnesses are likely to be fatal and which can be overcome. If I lack either the skill or the equipment, people are permanently maimed or die. There's no magic. People here are naive. Like a lot of Americans, they think doctors know more than we do. Actually, I can only give an educated guess no matter where I am, then I make all the effort my ability and resources allow."

In the half light, gazing at the ceiling, Ruth smiled. Having turned his face toward her, he saw the smile. "What are you thinking?"

"You were coming to recharge your batteries when we met. You were primed, in your do-good mode, and I popped right into your line of sight."

He rolled onto his side facing her and rested his head on his arm.

"No." He crooned, lowering his voice to a quieter tone. "There is actually no do-good mode. And you don't fit anyone's idea of a helpless female. I noticed you first in the airport, telling your son good-bye. Something had you in knots. It didn't seem to be a conflict with the boy but more some turmoil inside you.

"Although I thought you were attractive, I planned right then to steer clear of you. When people, particularly neurotic females, learn I am a medical doctor, they often solicit advice. Discussing their medical experiences, their symptoms helps them pass the time on a long trip. In an effort to protect myself, I avoided you at first. You seemed content to keep to yourself. Then I became curious."

She smiled. "When did you notice the little masher?"

"He eye-balled you in the airport, bumped you once, but you weren't paying attention. That's when I figured you must have several kids. Moms get conditioned to people in their space and learn to ignore it. I noticed the ring, knew you were married.

"When he began moving in, I decided I might need to protect you from him, rather than me from you. By then I had more or less adopted you, taken you into my area of responsibility. I didn't like the little creep bugging you. When you went to the lavatory on the airplane, you provided the opportunity I needed.

"Because you trusted me so quickly, I assumed maybe you were...well, mentally challenged." She started to object but he grinned broadly. "Once we got settled, you didn't insist on talking, which was all right with me.

132

"Gradually, when we did start talking, you proved to be conversant, well-read, refreshingly candid, guileless. You were self-effacing and it was no act."

"Hence the crack later about liking 'real people.' I see." Ruth turned her face toward him in the dim shadows cast by the light of the votive candle. "So from your experience and training, you knew Artemis would be all right from the moment we arrived yesterday, right?"

She hoped she had changed the subject subtly enough not to alert him. His recounting of his personal impressions of her had become a little embarrassing.

He smiled and cleared his throat. "No." He yielded the subject but hesitated long enough for her to realize he was wise to her. "He's a brave kid but you are the positive variable in his situation."

She laughed, a self conscious little warning.

Jack cleared his throat again and shifted to a less personal tone. "Bacteria thrive in this climate. An open wound, especially one in the tender, hospitable body of a child, invites germs to set up housekeeping. Artemis is an orphan. It is likely, if you had not been there, he would not have been brought to me at all, certainly not as quickly as you got him here.

"At best, I might have seen him in time to stop the infection by amputating the foot or the leg. Worst case, infection would have already killed him before I saw him, even though he might still have been breathing.

"I am not a particularly religious man but I have strong regard for the power of human love among those who enjoy that attribute."

Ignoring the extraneous comment, Ruth turned her face again toward the ceiling. "I do love Artemis." She stared thoughtfully. "I came to Uganda expecting...well, a lot of things. Other things. I did not expect to love anyone here, much less..."

She didn't finish the thought.

"You seem to develop strong ties quickly."

She frowned but didn't respond.

He peered at her in the dim light. "Have I made you blush?"

She didn't answer.

"You've shown a genuine concern for Father and Mrs. Catlett and their children, certainly."

She nodded. "Hmmm."

"And it was you who went from house to house dispensing aspirin and forcing liquids when the fever broke out."

She sighed. "Guilt. Pure guilt. If they hadn't gone to Glouster's with me..."

"You don't know that. The sickness might have been in the water right there in Bwana. In fact, I suspect it was."

She propped up on her elbow and turned wide eyes on him. "What makes you think that? Did you test the water?"

"Yes. I don't have the results yet. I'm growing cultures. Weren't you curious about why some who didn't make the trip to Glouster's got the fever and some who did go didn't get it?"

She sat up straight and looked at him intently. "Yes, but I thought it was spread by contact. I couldn't figure out why Artemis didn't get it."

Jack smiled. "I asked him if he had been drinking plenty of water. He likes canned fruit juices and, since you have an abundance of those, he'd pretty well given up water, as long as the juice lasted. Anyway, I imagine the water in your home was perfectly safe."

"Oh." She nodded recalling the outbreak and her pleasure that Artemis seemed immune. "We boil ours, the full twenty minutes."

"Not everyone is that conscientious."

"I insisted everyone, sick and well alike, drink lots of water."

"And you drank from their jars when you visited the sick, right?"

She lay back again. "Yes." Relief was thick in her voice. "Well, I'll be. And I thought the outbreak was my fault. Thank heavens. But how did it stop?" She turned her face to regard him again.

"Household bleach."

"In the water supply?"

"Yes. Tuslan guessed the source of the outbreak and administered the cure."

She was quiet a long moment. "You knew about our pilgrimage to Glousters?"

"Yes."

"Who told you?"

He chuckled quietly. "Everyone. They also speculated wildly about your accepting an entire box of condoms."

She popped up on an elbow again. "They weren't for me."

He grinned. "I was pretty sure of that."

"I can't have children anymore, anyway."

Jack laughed. "Contraception is not the only reason to use them, you know."

"Exactly. I was concerned about my promiscuous young friends and that awful disease. The fact is, there are none left. They have been widely distributed, just as the original donors intended.

She sighed and became silent. "Bleach in the water..." She relaxed, stretched beneath the sheet and turned onto her side, facing Standish. Gradually her breathing became slow and steady.

"Oh," she mumbled, "thank you, again." Another pause. "Sorry about the Mengele crack." She became silent, yielding finally to the elusive sleep.

She was breathing heavily before he said very softly into the darkness, "That's okay about Mengele. You can call me anything you want, as long as you call me."

*   *   *

"I have a problem," Ruth confided as she and Jack walked out into the sun Saturday afternoon, the eighth of July. The clinic was empty for the moment. Artemis sat on a gurney in the reception room teaching Rosamond to play checkers and rollicking with win after win, freeing his usual caretakers for a breather.

"What is it?"

"I am supposed to meet a friend from home at the Kampala airport on Monday. I don't want to leave Artemis. Also, I'm a little nervous about traveling to Kampala alone. Ossie told me that there had been rumors..."

"It's best that you stay with the boy."

"What I was wondering is, well, I know that you have a car. Do you ever let Rosamond drive it?"

"I'll pick up your friend at the airport."

"What about your patients? The clinic?"

"You'll have to treat any patients who show up. You were there when we did Artemis' stitches. It's monkey see, monkey do. That's what I tell my students. Just do what I did."

Wide-eyed, Ruth started to object, saw the playful smile on his face and grimaced instead, provoking a low, rumbling laugh.

Chapter Twenty-One

His brows furrowed, Jack studied Ross Belton from a distance.

Belton was easy to spot, a white man from small town America, wide-eyed, paranoid in the Kampala airport. Jack stood stock still sizing up the visitor.

Average height, Belton was sixty-ish, with a prominent belly, pudgy and soft, like most American men his age. His watery blue eyes peered nervously from behind wire-rimmed glasses, scanning the flood of travelers as they washed by him. He was looking for her, for Ruth Pedigo. Had he not commanded her to meet him there, with no thought to what difficulty it might impose on her.

Jack's eyes narrowed as he glared at his quarry. He didn't like the man even before he met him which was, he admonished himself, not fair. But, then, he hadn't liked Belton even before that; before he had seen him.

Regarding the visitor now, he felt annoyance, anger, maybe even jealousy. Envy about almost anything had abandoned Standish long ago. Yet he envied this soft, presumptuous intruder.

Belton knew Ruth Pedigo, had known her for years. It was likely Belton knew all about the mysterious absence of Mickey Pedigo and might even cast some light on Ruth's reluctance to talk about her spouse. Yet Jack didn't want to hear it from this pudgy interloper. He wanted Ruth to be willing to confide in him herself.

It seemed ludicrous, unconscionable to him that Mickey Pedigo, or any man for that matter, could have walked away from this woman, even a soft, weak man enticed by the sirens themselves.

His disgust with both Belton and Mickey Pedigo fostered new anger.

Jack shoved through the throng and, in only a moment, stood staring down his nose at the man. He forced a smile, introduced himself and explained his presence.

The building was noisy, the loud speakers calling flights, shouts, bells, buzzers and machinery. Belton frowned back at him, without offering to shake hands, nodded mutely and pointed to three bags at his feet. "Bring those."

The visitor seemed content to allow Jack to hoist the heavy luggage to a cart, unassisted, wheel it to the parking and load the same into the back of the Land Rover.

"Get in." Jack felt and sounded less than gracious.

"I have back trouble." Belton provided the unrequested explanation as Jack settled in the driver's seat. "I wouldn't want it to flare up here. Lifting those heavy bags could sure do the trick. I'm in insurance, you know. Makes a man cautious."

Standish grunted assent, indicating he had heard, but offering no comment as he started the engine.

Belton tightened his seat belt. "I assume you have befriended Ruth Pedigo."

Standish stared at the highway, broad concrete for four miles before it diminished to broken asphalt two-lane. He jammed his foot to the accelerator. "Yes."

Belton's neck popped with the abrupt acceleration. "She can be delightful and difficult, headstrong. Have you had differences with her?"

"No."

There was a long silence before the visitor spoke again.

"Actually, Ruth's husband Mickey was my closest friend. We started out as vestry men together in church, belonged to most of the same civic clubs for probably twenty years. My wife and I didn't have children. Mickey and Ruth let us help out a little with theirs. Great kids. Just real fine kids."

Jack nodded, wordlessly.

"Mick was devoted to his family." Belton looked out at the passing landscape. "Ruth, of course, was his greatest joy in life, even after twenty-five or thirty years of marriage and a houseful of rug-rat/ankle-biters."

Jack did not speak, seemed not to breathe, waiting.

"He spoiled her, of course, as any man might. She kidded him about it. They were often thrown up to the rest of us as an example of ideal marital love, companionable, a sample of what the religious institution of marriage is about." Belton turned his watery eyes back on Jack and fell silent.

Standish continued to stare at the passing road. "So?" It was the first word he had uttered in several minutes.

"After he died, Ruth was understandably..."

Jack turned an astonished face toward Belton, the piercing gray eyes silencing the visitor. "Died?" Standish fairly shouted to be heard above the road noise as he repeated, "Died?"

Belton regarded his host over the tops of his glasses, frowned and nodded uncertainly. "Massive coronary. The day after Thanksgiving."

"Mickey Pedigo, husband to Ruth, is deceased?"

Belton stared at Standish who suddenly jammed on the brakes in the middle of what had deteriorated to a rutted gravel road. The Rover lurched. Standish wheeled the vehicle onto the grassy shoulder and turned his full attention on Belton, who looked startled.

"I assumed if you and Ruth were acquainted... I thought you knew, of course."

"She has refused to speak about her husband. I knew he was absent. It never occurred to me..."

"Weren't you curious that a woman like Ruth...well, that she was here in Uganda alone?"

"Hell yes, I was curious. I've asked her, again and again." Standish sputtered, anger and relief mixed in the emotion in his voice. "She refused to talk about him. I assumed he'd left her."

Belton's laugh began as a rolling chuckle burbling from his throat. The sound grew to a loud guffaw. "Don't be ridiculous. What man in his right mind would... Obviously you don't know her very well."

Jack sucked in a breath, squared his shoulders, leaned forward and grasped the steering wheel so tightly that the veins in his hands protruded. "It would have made things so much... Why didn't she tell me?" He wondered aloud, speaking to the open road in front of him.

Belton shrugged his narrow shoulders. "I guess she didn't want you to know."

Jack turned his face to regard his passenger with real concern. "What difference would it have made?"

"She's an attractive woman. Maybe she wasn't ready to get hit on."

"And giving the appearance of being married... I even commented on it, more than once, her being safely married."

"Look," Belton interrupted, "they were very close. She was devastated by his death."

Standish turned his full attention on Belton. "How do you mean?"

"Oh, she was a brick at first. She comforted everyone: their children, his siblings, his mother, friends, everyone. She made funeral arrangements, got his estate in order, helped Michael get familiar with his dad's cases at the law office, handled insurance claims, paperwork. I watched, kept trying to get her to let go, to grieve. She wouldn't do it. She held strong for three weeks before she caved."

Belton hesitated. Standish kept eager gray eyes on him. "Then what?"

"The onset of the symptoms I'd been waiting for. Ruth was full figured, what you might call a 'buxom' woman. She lost weight. She stayed home, let the answering machine field her calls. She dutifully wrote thank you notes for all the remembrances, but she hid out.

"Gradually, she began walking. People reported seeing her out about in her neighborhood. I thought that was a good sign. I tried to call, but couldn't get by the machine.

"Then she was spotted striding to the city park, two miles from her house. After that she ranged as much as eight miles from home at a time.

"She came back to church, cordial, but remote. She wouldn't let anyone in, if you know what I mean."

Standish nodded. He did.

Belton drew a deep breath and continued. "I kept trying, God knows. I'd been a widower for three years. It's lonely when you are accustomed to sharing everything with someone. I knew what she was going through. I knew I could help, console her, if she'd just let me. She wouldn't. Wouldn't let anyone.

"She kept losing weight. I worried at first, afraid she had diabetes or something. I kept a close eye on her. But her color was good, her nails and hair seemed fine. All that walking was redistributing the fleshy part. The only change I could see was that she just kept getting prettier.

"I wasn't the only one noticing. There's a whole herd of eligible men in and around Bridger, old men, young men, all men. They came out of the woodwork, asked about her, asked if I thought she might be ready to go out with this one or that one, casually, you know."

Belton gazed out at the scenery and the pedestrians striding along the highway. "Now I'll tell you something. Dating has changed a lot in the years since Ruth or I dated. I was shocked when I started taking ladies out after my wife died. The word dating had taken on a whole new meaning. I knew Ruth wasn't ready for that. I tried to tell them.

"Some of these fellows asked her to dinner, to the ballet, the symphony out of town, to church picnics. She was gracious but very up front. She was not interested. Broke some hearts, mine included."

Belton looked at Jack earnestly, his expression a question. Staring, Jack snorted a laugh and nodded. He restarted the engine, shifted into drive and guided the Land Rover back out into the traffic lane.

"The next thing I knew," Belton glared at the landscape, "our priest told me she'd come up with this crazy notion about Uganda. I really think she'd been bouncing it around in her head for quite a while before she told anyone.

"Years ago I encouraged her when she started this idiotic correspondence with this black man. I mean, I had no idea it would lead to this, this irrational trip. I was a damn fool to have encouraged her but back then how could I have known?

"From the little I've seen so far, I can tell you she doesn't belong here. Not at all." Belton suddenly stiffened in his seat, interrupting himself. "Great heavens, look!" He pointed toward giraffes off in the distance.

Lost in his own thoughts, Jack squinted at the road ahead. "Where should she be?"

"What?"

"I said where do you think she should be, if not here?"

Belton sighed. "Ruth has a lot of life left in her. She has a fine mind. She has a lot to contribute, wherever she is. I'm going to try to talk her into going home with me. I want her in Bridger where she belongs, with me and her family. Her kids miss her. We all do."

Jack looked at the man again, this time with a certain regard. "I see. Will you be able to convince her to go?"

It was Belton's turn to cast a respectful eye.

"Maybe, but I could sure use some help. Depending on how close you are, I thought you might be able to help encourage her to leave. She wheedles her way into people and she burrows deep. I imagine she's probably carved a place for herself here, even with you, if I'm reading you right.

"I've read her articles. The local paper runs everything she writes that comes over the wire service. One of our own, you know. Her accounts of her adventures here are hot topics of conversation in every beauty, barber and coffee shop in town."

Jack nodded, swerving to avoid a large pothole in the road. Negotiating this stretch was taking all his skill. He slowed down. The road got worse. He needed time to think, to revamp his approach. He no longer felt any need to hurry.

Belton continued. "We want her back. That's what I'm doing here where whites are probably at risk just for breathing in and out. Can you help me talk to her?"

Jack shook his head and his eyes narrowed. "I don't think anything I say has much influence. She pretty well calls her own shots. We met on the plane to London. She was pleasant but very reserved, didn't mention her husband's death.

"In London her connecting flight was canceled. She flatly refused my help. She was fine with that, but I wasn't. I couldn't get her out of my mind, kept after her until she let me help.

"We had one day together, sight seeing. I never spent time with anyone I enjoyed so much. She was relaxed, funny, quick, you know." He looked to Belton for agreement.

Taking his eyes off the road for just that brief moment, one wheel of the Rover dropped into a crater of a pothole, jarring their teeth, and rolled on through, continuing.

"Sorry."

Belton waved off the apology. "I know exactly what you mean. It's obvious you're a little smitten. I understand. I asked her to marry me."

Standish offered a feeble smile. "What'd she say?"

"She was coming to Uganda. Like I said, I'm familiar with some of the mental gyrations of grieving. I figured she was floundering, grabbing for something to put meaning back in her life.

"I told her coming over here didn't make sense. She could contribute, send money through the church. She didn't have to make a personal appearance.

"I was too late. She'd already thrashed it out, already made her decision. She was determined.

"I asked her to think about marrying me. She thanked me for being such a good friend and said she would.

141

"She's had more than six weeks now. Surely that's long enough for anyone to think, especially anyone enduring the kind of deprivation the people have here."

Jack allowed a wry smile. He thought of the expression on Ruth's face as she looked at the boy Artemis before the surgery and later, holding him in her arms, comforting him. It seemed ironic that the pint-sized orphan had accomplished what two mature, prosperous men had not been able to achieve. It was Artemis who had won her heart. She loved the boy. *Where was the deprivation in that?*

Belton was again studying the landscape. "I've worried myself sick over her. Every time I heard about diseases, the rampant spread of HIV, the killing over here, I've felt a foot in the seat of my pants, kicking me to get over here and save her from herself. I can feel the rumblings, the political unrest, like thunder in the distance warning about a coming storm. I want to get her out of here in one piece.

"I actually signed up for this deal and came all the way over here to try to talk some sense into her. She needs to come home, back to civilization.

"America isn't perfect yet." Belton spoke as if practicing on Jack the argument he was preparing for her. "We have needy people there too. Besides, the conditions, certainly the roads, are better, more familiar, if nothing else. And she'd be safer, back with people who love her."

Jack turned a questioning look on Belton. "What is her mission here exactly? Her goal?"

"Hell if I know." Belton hesitated, staring at Standish. "She wrote back and forth to this Anglican priest for years and for years he begged her to come for a visit. This fellow, Catlett, was willing to have Mickey as well, but he kept the pressure on Ruth to come. Do you know him?"

"Not well, I'm afraid." Jack made a mental note. He needed to get better acquainted with both Catletts.

"She didn't want to come. Mickey offered to bring her. Turns out, she was scared to death of it. But somewhere along the way, she made a silly promise to herself or to God or something. If Mickey died before she did, she would come to sacrifice herself to his memory or to repay God for their wonderful lives together or some damn thing.

"I really think she came kind of like old elephants go off to the elephant graveyard, caught a whiff of her own mortality and resigned herself to this being the end of the road."

Both men were silent for several minutes.

"I had a talk with Donnie, her younger boy, a week ago," Belton said, rousing again. "He gave me the gist of their conversations the day he put her on the airplane. If he put the right spin on it, she was resigned to her fate. She implied she might not be coming home."

Standish swung the Rover into the turn, the last leg to Savanron. Both men were silent as they drove the last few miles, each entertaining his own thoughts of his reunion with Ruth Pedigo.

Chapter Twenty-Two

Ruth came out of the clinic door as soon as she saw the vehicle. She searched Jack's face. He gave her a wavering grin and nodded, provoking her curiosity.

Turning to Ross coming around from the passenger side, Ruth smiled warmly and opened her arms for a hug. "How was your trip?"

"Miserable...until now," he said, squeezing her tightly. "Holding you makes up for every dime and all the sweaty palms. You know how I hate flying."

She hadn't remembered any phobia, but laughed lightly and guided him into the clinic as Jack trailed them, again juggling all three of the man's suitcases.

Belton wrapped an arm around her then backed off and eyed her critically. "You've lost more weight. I've never seen you this tanned before." She was in her usual khaki cargo shorts, camp shirt and jungle boots. "You look good."

"Thanks. Did Jack tell you why we're here in Savanron? About Artemis?"

They sat in the reception area of the surgery, in chairs arranged around the walls. Rosamond had treated or postponed patients so remarkably, no one was waiting.

Ross failed to respond to Ruth's question at first as Rosamond appeared with tea on a teak serving tray. He did a double take and his expression softened as he scanned her exceptional length and comeliness from her head to her feet, then back. When he finally tore his eyes from the younger woman, he shook his head in response to the question.

"Artemis is Ruth's ward," Jack supplied as he reappeared. He had put Ross' bags in his own small bedroom.

"What?" Ross peered at Ruth.

Ruth shot Jack a warning look. "Not officially. Actually, Artemis is my guardian rather than I being his. He is nine years old and insists on guarding the door of my house every night. I adore him."

"Oh, you're talking about the shrimpy black kid you write about all the time?"

Ruth frowned at the description and the revelation. Obviously Ross had read about Artemis and, apparently, more than once. "Yes. He was injured last week. His foot was crushed by a falling tree. I brought him here. It's the nearest medical facility. Jack put him back together and calmed me." She smiled at Standish who returned a private glance. "Now he can't get rid of us."

Jack regarded her strangely. "I think Artemis will be ready to travel by next week. But you'll have to be very careful to keep the wound clean and dressed and to keep that foot absolutely immobile."

Ruth flashed him a puzzled smile before turning her attention back to their guest. "Ross, will you be able to stay, go back to Bwana with us?"

"Afraid not. I have to rejoin my group in Kampala on Wednesday. I hadn't realized how far out in the sticks you were. Is there any reliable transportation here at all?"

Looking mildly chagrined, Jack snorted. "Thanks."

"Oh, no offense. I meant public transportation. Standish, I didn't appreciate you properly before. I'm not very observant as a rule but even I noticed we saw only a dozen cars on the road after we got into the rural area. Don't let my big mouth talk you out of taking me back to the airport. How far are we?"

"Forty-six miles," both Jack and Ruth said in unison.

"It's more than a nice stretch of the legs," Ruth added.

"How do these people usually get there from here?" Ross grimaced, obviously anticipating the answer.

Ruth raised her eyebrows and grinned. "It's the most common means of transportation in Uganda, Ross. They walk. Why do you think everyone around here is so trim?"

"I really hadn't thought about it." He stole another long look as Rosamond reappeared. "But I did notice, believe me."

* * *

Ross talked most of the afternoon, catching Ruth up on news from home, praising her articles which appeared often in the Bridger paper. One of his suitcases contained letters and gifts for her from friends in Bridger. Seeing the contents, Jack seemed to feel more kindly toward their visitor.

Ruth checked on Artemis several times through the afternoon, hoping Ross would inquire about the boy, but he didn't. Finally, she suggested Ross accompany her to the infirmary to meet the child. He was less than eager but did not voice an objection. To Ruth's annoyance, Standish seemed particularly pleased by Belton's lack of interest in Artemis.

Ruth introduced Belton to Artemis who offered to shake hands. Reluctantly, Ross finally allowed a quick shake then, without realizing it, he rubbed his open hand on his trousers. Jack turned his face to hide his smile and Ruth shot him a threatening glare.

"Would you like to play checkers, sir?" Artemis asked.

"No, I'd be no match for you. I haven't played checkers in years."

"Gin rummy? Old maid?"

"No, son." Belton's expression grew stern. "I'm really here to see Mrs. Pedigo. I don't have long. I want to visit with her as much as possible. Maybe another time."

"Are you staying?"

"Only until Wednesday."

"Then you will be back again?"

"No, afraid not."

"When is the 'another time' we can play then?"

Turning away from the boy without answering, Ross caught Ruth's arm and escorted her from the infirmary as Jack settled on the side of the bed. "Deal the cards. It's my turn to win."

Ruth smiled as she heard the boy's rolling giggle and his very Americanized response. "Sure, like that's going to happen."

*   *   *

Belton didn't question sleeping arrangements as he closed himself in Jack's room that night.

Nearly asleep in the bed next to Artemis, Ruth did not stir when Jack entered the infirmary and, as usual, took off his boots and socks, peeled down to boxer shorts and a T-shirt and settled on the far bed. Ruth made a concerted effort not to look at Jack's legs, which she found spectacularly attractive. She slept in the oversized cotton sleep shirt mysteriously acquired during her illness. The three of them had often slept aligned that way together in that room since the accident.

"Why didn't you tell me your husband was dead?" Jack's voice rasped into the darkened room.

She hesitated, lying still and quiet for a moment. "When?"

"On the airplane, for starters."

"I was having my own pity party. I felt sorry enough for myself. I didn't need sympathy from perfect strangers."

"Ah, then you did see me as perfect?"

She smiled at the ceiling. "Not."

"Later then, at the Biscuit Basket. You were aware of my interest in you."

"I didn't think my private life was any concern of yours. Besides, you indicated you were comfortable with me because I was not only married, but because I was, as you put it, 'very married.'"

The far bed groaned as he shifted his weight, turning onto his side to face her. "I was interested in everything about you and you damn well knew it."

"You were a kind man who took me under his wing. I was very unstable, emotional, uncertain about whether I could meet the upcoming challenges I had set for myself."

"I'm remembering particularly when you snuggled up to me the night we listened to the string quartet?"

"You were wearing Mickey's cologne. You smelled like him. I was relaxed, for the first time in days. In weeks. I was snuggling with him, not you."

Jack rolled onto his back and stared at the ceiling. "I suppose it was the same thing when you took my hand on the drawbridge. Why didn't you tell me after that?"

"London for me was like Camelot, Jack, an imaginary perfect place. For the first time, I felt some relief from the awful, consuming grief. Those days at the Biscuit Basket were the first I had enjoyed since Mickey's death. That was where I began wanting to survive."

"You were with me. Did I make a difference?"

"Yes, but I was ashamed of the feelings I had for you."

"When we kissed good-bye at the airport?"

"Yes, then, too."

"Ashamed that you liked me?"

"That I liked any living man. I felt as if I were being unfaithful."

"And after you came here?"

"I began adjusting. I liked Uganda. The Bwanans were innocent, like children. I could see why God sent me. I didn't dwell as much on Mickey, didn't miss my old life so badly. I began living again in the here and now." She turned her head toward him.

"I wondered about you. I asked Diaz and truck drivers passing through, everyone. No one had heard of Jack Standish. I couldn't imagine why they hadn't but I resigned myself to the idea I probably would not see you again."

"After you were in Bwana, you heard the natives talk about Jusu, didn't you?"

She returned his gaze. "No one said Jusu was white. Even if they had, I never would have suspected he was you. I thought Jusu was a witch doctor. The stories were frightening. I certainly didn't care about meeting him. I did want to see you."

"Spoken like you really cared."

"What, cared about seeing you again? Certainly I cared. But what was I supposed to do? You're the one who knew your way around. Why didn't you contact me?"

Jack was silent for a long moment. When he spoke, his voice was apologetic. "I thought you were married. Obviously something was wrong. You seemed vulnerable. I didn't want to take advantage of that vulnerability or of the uncertainty you were sure to be feeling in a strange country among new people." He flashed her a tight smile. "A single man can cavort with some married ladies. Dating a married woman obviously has certain advantages. Other men's wives are low maintenance for a bachelor, low risk for commitment. You, however, were like a magnet, drawing me almost against my will.

"When we were together, I laughed. I got angry. I felt odd stirrings of passion, jealousy. I didn't even know I was capable of those emotions. I experienced a whole spectrum of sensations.

"But you kept me at arm's length. You kept yourself physically inaccessible. Intellectually, I accepted that. Emotionally, well that was a different proposition."

He hesitated a moment, then continued. "Did Mrs. Catlett and Artemis tell you I came when you were ill?"

Ruth smiled at the ceiling. "Yes. Well, they said Jusu came. I remembered a man's voice chanting, his hands bathing me. It was always dark. I kept my eyes closed, afraid the sight of a witch doctor, even one with such a caring touch, conjuring up black magic or voodoo over me might be scary."

Jack laughed. "I thought you should have been more alert than you were."

"What in the world were you chanting?"

"Nothing important."

"Come on, is it a secret?"

"Let's stick to your secrets for now. You've been here in Savanron. We've been together several days and nights and you still hadn't told me your husband was dead."

"Jack, why are we having this conversation?" She felt peculiarly vexed. "Why now? My husband is dead. There, I've told you. What difference could it possibly make? Does it change anything at all?"

He didn't answer. She hadn't expected him to. She suddenly felt a burgeoning, unreasonable anger and she wasn't sure why.

Chapter Twenty-Three

"You must have slept well." Ruth smiled when Ross appeared for breakfast at nine-thirty. He regarded her oddly. Everyone else had eaten, as usual, at seven. "I slept all right, thank you." He didn't smile and his tone sounded curt. He slid into the lone place set at the table, correctly assuming it was for him.

She tried again. "The melons here are enormous." Rosamond served him a huge half, along with coffee and toast with a citrus marmalade.

He dug into the melon. "Where did you sleep last night?"

"In the infirmary, as usual, in the hospital bed next to Artemis. He was in a great deal of pain at first, with his foot, and I needed to be near to quiet him."

Another bite. "And where did Standish sleep?"

She was getting the picture. "Why do you ask?"

"I'm not pronouncing any judgments here. I'm just curious. I had a little talk earlier with your colored girl." He gouged another spoonful of melon.

"Well, you were in his bed, so he slept in the infirmary also."

"Not in your bed?" His face was becoming flushed.

"No, not in my bed. You saw those hospital beds. They're barely wide enough to accommodate one person."

"But you slept side by side?" His question sounded more like an accusation. He let his spoon clatter onto the plate.

Ruth glowered. "That sounds suggestive and intimate. It's not like that at all. I keep the watch until three-thirty or four while Standish sleeps, then he takes the duty while I sleep."

"I understood that the boy was all but well."

She flushed, struggling to hold onto her temper. "Of course, now that Artemis is recovering, there's less to do."

Belton began to hiss. "I thought if you were going to give it away, you'd at least entertain the legitimate offers first."

Ruth had sat watching Ross excavate the melon and listening to the tone of his voice as it become more and more insulting. Suddenly she was on her feet glaring down at him. "You arrogant, moralizing ass."

"What?" His eyes rounded at her verbal assault but he remained seated. "I'd say that I, not you, was the offended party here, madam." His voice rose as he sputtered. "I treated you with the respect due the wife of Mickey Pedigo. Under the pretense of grieving, you ran off to the wild kingdom to get your jollies, figuring none of your good Christian friends would hear about your romps in the hay all the way over here.

151

"Well granted, I can keep a secret better than most but don't get all high and mighty with me or everyone in Bridger will know what kind of game you've got going here."

Ruth took a step back staring at him in disbelief, then pointed at the door. "There's a supply truck outside. The driver stayed over. Pack your bags. I'll ask him to drive you back to Kampala. I can't vouch for his morality, you understand. I hope his conduct is in keeping with your strict code of behavior."

Belton stood, sneering. "I've got a better idea. Tonight you sleep with me. My bed's a double. Don't deny you've slept in it already. As you can see, the colored girl told me the whole sordid story. Tonight you can provide me the services you give him. I'll give you pointers on dating practices these days back in the states. I might even still consider marrying you, if you meet certain criteria between the sheets."

Ruth stared at the man. *Who was this impostor who had taken over the body of the real Ross Belton? Where was the friend who came by on Saturday mornings early, helped himself to coffee and entertained her while he waited. Where was that Ross?* She trembled, livid at his accusations.

"I want you out of here. Now. Go pack up your stuff and get the hell gone."

She wheeled and almost ran Jack down as he jogged through the door. He caught her arms. "Hey. What's all the racket?" His shirt flapped open over khaki shorts, allowing a full view of his hairy, well-toned stomach and chest. A towel draped around his neck indicated he was just back from
the men's communal shower.

Both Ruth and Ross turned to brace him as he looked from one angry face to the other. "What's happened?" His expression grew serious as his eyes settled on Ruth.

"Ross here thinks I've taken advantage of your hospitality." She sizzled, the words almost steaming as they spewed from her mouth. She clenched her teeth and tried to squeeze by Jack and out, but he held her arm.

"What do you mean?" Jack turned his searching gaze on Belton.

"I'm angry that she came to Uganda and that she's sleeping with you. I'm mad that I stood back being a gentleman, that I didn't take advantage of her before. I should have jumped her bones while she was off balance, but in the interest of fair play, I backed off, waited for her to get her bearings. I didn't realize someone else would take my place."

Ruth rolled her eyes. "Your place?"

Jack frowned at Ruth. "Hey, quiet down, now." His gaze shifted to Ross. "Belton, Ruth and I sometimes sleep in the same room." Standish spoke slowly, his words measured. "She has not had sex with anyone in Uganda. The locals would know if she had and they would tell it. Ruth doesn't wash her hands without it being reported cross country."

"Your girl in there said..." Ross began.

"If she did, she lied. You don't know her. You do know Ruth. Have you ever known Ruth to lie?"

Ross thought a moment, glanced at Ruth, exhaled slowly and lowered his angry, accusing eyes.

"Belton," Jack's tone was conciliatory, "behind her back these people call Ruth 'Maawe.' The word translates, not just 'Mother,' but 'my own highly regarded Mother.' It may be blasphemous for them to love her the way they do.

"You see for yourself how she adores them. She teaches them Bible. They listen because she lives the faith she teaches."

Like Ross, Ruth stared at the floor, her anger suddenly dissolved to embarrassment, as Standish continued. "Here in Uganda, she has been sexually inviolate. It's common knowledge. People discuss it."

Ross risked an embarrassed look at Jack, then settled his gaze on Ruth, his expression grave. "The colored girl made it sound like..." He shook his head, shame written across his face. "Honey, I apologize. Your being gone, well, it's been damned hard on me. I'd told everyone in Bridger I'd asked you to marry me. It was the most public thing I guess I ever did. I offered you everything I had.

"As my wife, Ruth, you'd have a certain enviable position in Bridger. You could have anything you wanted, hold your head up anyplace.

"I was never unfaithful to Dolores. You know that. I can be a damned good husband, a damned generous provider. Most women would jump at the chance for my kind of devotion. Why isn't it enough for you?"

Ruth's face softened as she raised her eyes to his. "I didn't realize... I didn't know where all that venom came from. I'd never seen you so... People here are innocent, Ross. I've gotten used to their, their naivete. They don't question motives. Your ugly invective or whatever that was... Well, it was so ugly, so unexpected. I thought you could see how things are here, the magnificent country, the marvelous climate, the people... I thought you'd love it. I didn't expect you to resent Artemis or Jack or..." She shrugged.

Jack released her arm.

After a lull, her face became sincere. "There is a trucker here who'll take you back to Kampala. You can go to a hotel, order room service, enjoy the frills you've earned, the kinds of things you deserve."

Belton looked properly contrite. "I will, if you'll go with me." He suddenly looked startled. "Separate rooms, of course!"

Ruth smiled and shook her head. "No thanks. I have a nice room here. In some hotels in Kampala, you probably can get a breath-taking view of Lake Victoria. I prefer the view here of one giggling little boy."

Ross's voice fell to a pleading tone. "If I promise to behave, will you please, please let me stay, just until tomorrow? Please."

She shook her head sadly. "Ross, we have only a certain number of beds. Do the math. Can you devise sleeping arrangements more acceptable to your sensitivity?"

"No, no, no." He held both hands up, his palms toward her, as if fending off an assault. "Any way you people work it is okay with me. No more kibitzing. Ruth, to prove my heart's in the right place, I'll even take a turn letting the kid beat me at checkers."

Jack's laugh spewed into the room. "Oh, ho! Maybe you'd better take a couple of practice runs at Ruth or me first. Artemis is a tiger when he crouches over the checkerboard. He gloats. He can be damned insufferable. He's also tough to beat."

Ross narrowed his eyes and glanced at Ruth, then back at Jack. "Have you played board games with that one?" He indicated Ruth.

Jack cocked an eyebrow. "Yes. It's a difficult premise, but it appears the boy's unsportsmanlike conduct is a genetic thing acquired from his Maawe."

Ruth pretended to be annoyed as the two men laughed.

*   *   *

That night Ruth excused herself earlier than usual and was pretending to be asleep when Jack slipped into the third bed in the infirmary. Artemis breathed in and out heavily in his place on Ruth's right as Jack settled in the one on her left. "Are you still angry?" He spoke in a hushed tone.

She flounced in the bed as she turned toward him. "Not about Ross."

"What then?"

"Jack, Artemis is awfully bright and..."

"No, you can not take him home with you."

"How did you know..."

"I have eyes and ears. You telegraph your thoughts."

"Why can't I?"

"He's not a stray puppy you can feed once a day, pet now and then, and forget. His life with a black family in Bridger would be complicated enough. With you, he'd be a freak."

"But what will happen to him when I leave?"

"Like you said, he's very bright. For two hundred dollars a year, you can put him in the boarding school at Ula, give him an education, a profession."

"He wants to be a doctor, like you. He wants to put people's bones back in place with his fingers. He wants to cure fevers. He's convinced Rosamond to work for him when he comes back here to run this clinic someday. He made a point of saying he would stay year round."

Jack laughed softly in the darkness.

Ruth continued, her words coming rapidly. "Father Catlett asked if I would underwrite Artemis' schooling in the states. I want to do it, Jack."

"No. That's exactly what's wrong here now."

"What's wrong about it?"

"When the brightest students are identified, people sponsor them for schooling in other countries. Think what it is for you to come here, knowing you're going home eventually. You endure the hardship, the inconvenience as kind of a game.

"Artemis has never known the kind of wealth you and I take for granted. In Dallas, we get in a lather when there's a glitch in the cable reception, particularly when the Cowboys are playing. You probably don't cook dinner if the water's off for some reason. You feel put upon if an electrical transformer blows and you don't have lights for thirty or forty-five minutes. In Bridger those classify as major inconveniences, right?"

She gave him an affirmative, "Uh-huh."

"If Artemis went to America, he wouldn't come back. Few do. They think they will. They sign contracts, agreements, anything. But after they get away from here, get the training in whatever field, adopt the lifestyle, get used to the conveniences, they don't want to come back. And their teachers and co-workers help them figure out ways they can stay gone. The hosts want to hang onto these valuable human resources. The result is, we drain this country of its best and brightest."

"Then what's the solution?"

"To bring education here, to them. They've already got some pretty good basic education, but the Ugandan kids with potential to learn more--the ones who come from poor families or, like Artemis, from no family at all--have got to have university opportunities in Kampala or Rwabatura or Bwana. Ugandans have to become teachers and priests and doctors and politicians right here at home."

"But that's impossible. It's just not happening."

"You're here. I'm here. Will you be back?"

She hesitated. She had not seriously considered the idea of ever leaving. "Uganda--the people, the music, the smells, everything--it's in my marrow now, a part of me."

"Exactly. If we come, if we encourage others to come, we can make quality higher education available.

"Kids like Artemis are paying attention. He sees what I do. He thinks he might like to do what I do. He's bright. He sees being a physician is just a matter of learning what symptoms require what treatment. There's no juju, no magic. It's plain old rote memory work, the ability to look things up in books, coupled with a dash of common sense.

"It's obvious to him that he can do what medical doctors do. That's a major step. But if you sweep him away to the luxury of life in the states, he won't come back."

Ruth was quiet for a long time. Jack lay back supposing she might have fallen asleep until he heard her sniffling quietly. He rolled onto his side. Her back was to him but he could see her shoulders shaking.

"Jack." Her voice was muffled, "I don't think I can stand being separated from him."

He snorted. "I've always agreed with the poet who said 'love is all we know of heaven and all we need of hell.'"

"But, he's just a little orphan boy."

"Oh no he's not. He's got you behind him now. Besides that, he's a smart little rascal and tough as cowhide. His difficulties have spawned strength and compassion in him without bitterness. You can leave him, once you see him in a good boarding school."

"I don't want to lose him."

Sooner or later, you'll lose him anyway. You've raised kids. You know the drill. He's already half grown." He paused. "Besides, there may be other options."

She mopped her nose and peered at him. "Like what?"

"Let's wait and talk about it tomorrow, in the daylight. We need to get some sleep. Artemis has been re-energizing for several hours already. You've got to get some sleep, be ready to keep up with him."

Jack became silent. He listened until he heard her breathing become slow and deep.

He knew people at Ula. He'd sponsored scholarships there before. He had no family on which to squander his income. He studied the form of the woman in the bed next to him. He might as well squander a little on Artemis. Besides, if all went well, Artemis actually might be the man to take over Jack's Ugandan practice one day. His eyes on Ruth's back, he smiled.

She confided in him more and more, spoke openly about things that troubled her. The chemistry between them was growing. The simmer had become a boil. She didn't realize it. Not yet. That was probably best. In time he would point it out to her. For now he was content being her confidant, a friend she was comfortable to have sleeping one bed over.

But the best thing of all: *There was no husband.*

Chapter Twenty-Four

Ross loaded his own suitcases into the Rover Wednesday afternoon. Ruth followed him outside. Jack would drive him back to Kampala, Ruth again relegated to staying with Artemis.

"It was wonderful to see you." She felt genuinely sorry that he was leaving.

Ross closed the vehicle's back door and turned to regard her soberly. "Come go home with me."

She shook her head. "I'm committed here until the end of next month. If Artemis gets into school at Ula, I may come home then. But I expect I'll sign on for another ninety days, if the wire service will have me. We don't get a lot of feedback here. We seldom see a newspaper of any kind. Your talking about reading my stuff in the Bridger News was
encouraging. I wasn't even sure they could use the stories I sent. It appears so."

Ross shuffled his feet. "And they are good reading."

"Thanks. Anyway, I'll be home eventually. Meanwhile, you know what it's like here. Write to me. Tell me what's going on, especially if and when you see my children."

"I will."

She couldn't read the look on his face. She heard Jack coming from the clinic and started to turn when Ross spoke again. "Kiss me good-bye?"

"Sure." She stepped forward, expecting a tender brush on the cheek. Instead, Ross collected her tightly. He pressed his mouth roughly against hers and tried to pry her lips apart. Startled, she pushed against his shoulders, separating herself from him.

He whispered, "I want you, Ruth. I want you to be my wife, sharing my bed, my life, everything."

She took a deep breath and wheezed. "Thank you. That's a beautiful compliment. It means a lot to me."

"Honey, you used to enjoy playing golf, doing things with people you know and love, people who know and love you. You were happy in Bridger. You could be happy there again. Do you remember at all how nice life is in Oklahoma?"

"Certainly."

"I'll do anything it takes to make you happy. You know that, don't you?"

"Yes, Ross, I'm sure you would. Life in Bridger is wonderful. It would be wonderful with you. And, yes, I remember every detail. I think about home often." She paused. "But here I serve a purpose. I contribute. If nothing else, I'm important to one little boy."

She retreated as he attempted to embrace her again. She heard Jack snort as he walked to the other side and climbed into the vehicle.

Stepping back, she blew Ross a kiss. "We'll talk about us when I get home."

He smiled, recovering. "You'd better hope I don't get an offer I can't refuse before then."

She laughed lightly. "If you get one that good, take it."

"And break your heart? I don't think so."

They both laughed as Jack started the engine. Ruth was acutely aware of Jack's presence during her conversation with Ross and also aware that he neither looked at nor spoke to her before he turned the Rover down the rutted road toward Kampala.

*   *   *

It was nearly dark and Ruth had just finished showering when Jack returned. She noticed the Rover when she came up the path in her nightshirt, carrying her towel and soap dish. She found him sitting in the front room of the clinic, slouched in a straight-back chair, his legs splayed in front of him, his hands, fingers interlaced, over his belt buckle. The only light was that from the lantern on a small table beside him. He glowered up at her.

She smiled. "I'm glad you're back." He grunted a wordless response. "Did you have any problems?"

"No."

"Are you tired?"

"No."

"Angry?"

"I saw you kiss Belton."

"Actually, you saw him kiss me."

"You seemed willing."

"I thought..." She stopped and her smile faded. "What business is that of yours?"

"I want you to kiss me."

"Jack, this is not a competition."

"I'm the one who takes care of you. I'm the one you should kiss, the one you should love."

"No." She spat the word angrily. "I am a faithful wife."

"Faithful to a dead man?" Jack suddenly stood and took a step to loom over her. She tried to go around him to the hallway leading to the infirmary, but he caught her arm.

"I only want you to kiss me." He said the words quietly, guiltily.

Clutching the soap dish and towel in front of her, she clamped her teeth and thrust her face toward his defiantly.

158

Without releasing her arm, he placed his free hand on her neck and slowly brushed his thumb over her lips. She saw pain and sadness mix as he scanned her face.

Her defiance ebbed.

His thumb traced her lips, down her chin to her throat. Gently he tilted her face. He touched his warm, full lips to hers, the soft kiss she had expected from Ross.

Jack raised his mouth to look at her face. She struggled to maintain what she hoped looked like indifference. Slowly he lowered his mouth again. His lips parted slightly but the kiss was again tentative, experimental. As he held her mouth with his, he released her arm and moved his hand to her back, then pressed, bringing their bodies closer.

Warmth and pleasure mingled as Ruth relaxed into the kiss, turning her head until the side of her face was against his shoulder. She luxuriated in his arms, breathing in the aroma of him, a scent no longer associated only with a memory. She wanted to linger, to stay cocooned in his embrace. His arms tightened.

Slowly, deliberately he kissed her face again and again until his lips were at her ear. "Let's go to my room."

She shook her head almost imperceptibly and pushed herself away. "I can't. Maybe someday, but not yet. I'm still half of a couple. Mickey's heart still beats with mine."

"His doesn't, Ruth," Jack said gently. "His doesn't beat anymore at all. That's my heart you feel."

"I'm all that's left of him, Jack."

"No. You gave him children to carry his baton into the next laps of the race. Mine is the life solely dependent on you."

"I never thought of you as poetic." She gave him a puzzled smile.

"And I've never felt like a romantic before." He regarded her oddly. "I've never experienced this...this tenderness, this passion. I've waited a lifetime for you to come, to set me free from my reserve, my inhibitions. With you I am whole, laughing and jealous and complete for the first time."

His biceps flexed under her hands, his lower body taut against hers and she struggled not to give in. She needed to get away from him, to escape this haven of his making.

She didn't speak immediately, trying to get her breath, to get her emotions in check, before she muttered, "I'm glad you've got your own room back."

She stepped around him and shuffled all the way to her bed to cower next to Artemis in the infirmary.

She didn't sleep. She said her prayers; prayed for a long while, thanking God for Mickey, the life they had had together, their children, their successes; for

159

sustaining them in their disappointments--the deaths of her parents and of his dad, crises they had endured together, always gleaning strength from one another. She tried very hard not to think of Jack.

Intellectually Ruth knew Mickey had not left her willingly yet, as she struggled for control in the dark, she felt utterly abandoned.

* * *

Rosamond entered the infirmary soon after first light while Ruth helped Artemis dress. After Ross' accounts of Rosamond's gossip and half truths, Ruth could barely stand the sight of the younger woman, much less indulge in casual conversation with her. Rosamond was treacherous. A viper should not be allowed to slither too close.

"Jusu has patients other places." Rosamond spoke sharply, unaware of Ruth's new hostility. "He has neglected them for you."

"For Artemis, you mean."

Rosamond shot her an accusing look. "He has sent home ones who were sick and wounded. You were in their beds. This morning a driver said Mrs. Catlett and the father beg to know when you will return."

"That cinches it," Ruth mumbled to Artemis when Rosamond was gone from the room. "We are out of here."

* * *

"We need to go home." They were Ruth's first words when she found Jack at the cook stove.

He looked down over his straight nose into her face. "I'll miss you."

She smiled and nodded but didn't say anything else.

"When do you want to go?"

"This morning, if you have time to take us."

"Rosamond!" The willowy form appeared immediately in the doorway. "Finish this." He handed her the spatula, then took Ruth's elbow and guided her outside into the golden morning. He turned her toward the hills north of Savanron, a place they often walked together at twilight, when he was able to get free. "Have you written about me in your articles?"

Looking at him, Ruth again felt a stirring long dormant. "Yes. And about Jusu."

His gray eyes rounded, his interest piqued.

"Nothing about the lurking witch doctor, of course." She smiled. "I wrote about your volunteering your services, about your use of natural medicines, tree root for headaches, leeches for swelling, maggots for cleaning out dead tissue."

"Those things are common knowledge."

"In the medical community, maybe, but I imagine the general public was as surprised to learn about nature's helping hands as I was."

He grinned broadly. "Back in Bridger, Oklahoma, they probably think you're hanging out with a barbarian."

She sighed, "Yeah," before allowing her eyes to rest again on his face. His lips were full, his forehead broad, his cheeks slightly sunken, his nose...

"Jack, in a word, how would you describe your nose? Grecian? Roman? Aristocratic? What?"

"I don't know." He chuckled self consciously. "Adequate."

"Not a very apt description. I'd say Rathbone-ish."

He laughed again.

She adored his rich, well-modulated voice, given to exceptional volume when he was annoyed. She would miss his nose, his face, even his occasional volume. Now, since last night, she probably would miss his lips most of all.

She concentrated on not looking at his mouth, but it drew her. He arched his brows, laughed a little and appeared to read the dilemma on her face.

"You are going to miss me, you know."

"Probably." She made the concession grudgingly.

She could feel his pleasure at the one word concession, and he took her hand. She pretended not to notice as they walked hand-in-hand in silence, each gazing out at the expanse of green falling away below as they climbed.

She broke the hush. "Will we see you?"

"Of course. Now, tell me something of Mickey Pedigo."

She breathed deeply. "I met him my junior year in college, his second year of law school. He was perfect. I didn't fall in love easily, even when my best friend dropped in and out of love twice a week.

"Mickey was unusual, the best looking man I'd ever met. He was only slightly taller than I was, very muscular, what you might call stocky. He had a beautiful body."

Jack grimaced but she plunged ahead.

"He noticed me, too. After the first couple of sightings, he began hanging out with people I hung with.

"It had been my experience that most really great looking guys were insufferably egotistical or stupid. Some were both. Not Mickey. He was funny, clever, smart. You used a term recently that described him best. He was guileless, a man of great integrity, completely honorable."

She gazed across the plains below. "He read people well--their strengths, their weaknesses. Yet, as clearly as he saw people, he was kind and compassionate."

Jack looked skeptical. "I think those traits as being unusual in a lawyer."

"Yes, well, some people think of doctors as money-grubbing womanizers, yet you certainly seem the exception to that." She relinquished a smile in way of an apology. "Yes, he was an unusual lawyer.

"One night he asked me to go to the show, told me not to invite all my friends. It was a date."

Nodding, Jack chuckled, apparently appreciating Mickey's situation.

"We dated nearly two years and both graduated. He got drafted. We got married."

"You didn't sleep with him before you married him, did you?"

The observation caught her by surprise. "Why do you say that?"

"I know you and I'm beginning to get a pretty clear picture of him, too."

"Okay, so we didn't sleep together before we were married. Big deal."

"How was the wedding night?"

She felt a blush but was determined to answer his candor with candor.

"Lovely. Mickey's first priority was that I like sex. He was very gentle, very methodical, very thorough. By the time we'd been married three weeks, I was panting at the door when he got home for lunch. And I wanted him home for lunch, every single day."

Jack's smile became a frown as he stared into the distance. "And you never argued or disagreed?"

"Sure we did. We bickered practically our whole first year. A lot of married people have rocky first years, thrashing out all the little ground rules."

"Like what?"

"'I don't eat vegetables.' 'You have to eat them with every meal.' 'Why?' 'Because my mother said so.'"

Jack winced. "That basic, huh?"

"Oh yes."

They strolled in silence, hands clasped to provide each other balance over the rough terrain. It seemed natural when Jack pulled up, wrapped her in his arms and kissed her. Again the kiss was tentative, unthreatening. When it deepened, Ruth pushed away from him, not quite steady on her feet. He allowed the separation, smiling, before they continued their walk.

"Jack, what did Jusu chant at night when I had the fever?"

He grinned sheepishly. "I'll tell you someday."

"But not today?"

"No. Not yet."

*   *   *

Rosamond was sulking when they returned.

After breakfast, Jack carried Artemis to the Rover and carefully placed him inside, admonishing him again. "The foot is mending well. Your body is building bridges of new bones to link the broken ones. I know you understand."

Artemis nodded, his eyes wide.

162

"You must not allow your body to put any weight on these fragile new bridges. One step could break several at once. Is it Maawe's job to protect the new bones? Is this her responsibility?"

Artemis shook his head, answering in the negative.

"That's right. It is up to you to protect them. You must give them the opportunity they need to grow strong."

Artemis answered gravely. "Yes, Jusu. I will protect them as I protect Maawe. When will we see you again?"

Jack gazed at the boy fondly, then allowed his eyes to travel to Ruth just emerging from the clinic. "Soon. You are probably going to see more of me than you want."

"Jusu?" The boy lowered his voice. "Do you love Maawe?"

Jack smiled warmly and kept his voice low. "Yes, but my love is a secret, between men." As the boy looked puzzled, he continued. "Do you speak of your love for her?"

The boy's eyes rounded. "No. It is a secret for me as well. But someday I will tell her. Someday will you?"

"Yes I will too, someday."

*   *   *

A week later, Ossie fumed as Ruth prepared to ride her bicycle to Vestal, a small settlement ten miles away. "You are growing bolder than you should."

"They have plants they do not recognize." Ruth pumped air into the tires with the hand pump. She paused to read the gauge, then continued pumping. "They have sent word by five runners now. The vegetables are from seeds sent from Oklahoma. I may be able to identify them and give the women recipes for preparing them."

Ossie's face twisted with concern. "Do planters have this problem in America?"

Satisfied with the next pressure reading, Ruth set the pump aside. "Not that I know about, but I'm not much of a farmer. Plus, produce here grows much larger than the same varieties do at home. Uganda is a marvelous garden."

"And your journey has nothing to do with your desire to see Jusu?"

Ruth flashed Ossie a sharp stare and the younger woman relented.

"Mother, you know it is not wise for you to travel alone."

"Ten miles in broad daylight should be safe. I'll be back before night. Just promise to keep Artemis off that foot. He's feeling better and becoming adventurous."

Ossie huffed. "It is a problem with you both."

"We're just a little restless, I guess."

"You were not restless before you went to Savanron."

163

"Hmmm," Ruth hummed, ignoring the suggestion. She had not seen Jack in six days. Ossie faithfully reported tidbits of information she gleaned from travelers who saw Jusu in this village or that one. Stories of Jusu were always worth a meal to a hungry driver.

"Jusu had to make up for time lost when he remained in Savanron so long with the small orphan, Artemis," Ossie reported, repeating the stories the drivers told. "They speak of the great value Jusu places on Artemis to have given the boy so much of his magic."

Ruth laughed at that report, remembering Jack's chagrin when Artemis stripped his last king from the checkerboard. The folk hero did not take well to losing.

Pedaling along the rutted road, Ruth heard a motor humming some distance behind her and moved to what might be considered the shoulder of the roadway--if there had been one--and kept pedaling. The vehicle roared up beside her and stopped. She put a foot down to brace the bike and looked back into a foolish grin on the face of the driver, Riz Diaz.

"Good day, Mother." Diaz tipped the brim of his hat. "I was hoping to meet you on this road. You are traveling to Vestal, is that correct?"

Ruth nodded.

"Put your bicycle inside and I will drive you the rest of the way."

Ruth started to refuse but Diaz interrupted. "It is still nearly, ah, six miles."

She suspected the stammer allowed him time to compute the distance from kilometers to miles for her benefit. She shrugged and wheeled the bike to the side of the small bus, broke open the doors, hoisted the bicycle inside and secured the doors. She was not surprised that Diaz made no effort to help her load her conveyance.

She climbed into the passenger seat. "Are you making a delivery?"

"No, I was hired by three businessmen to do an errand. It is important. It has to do with a large sum of money. I am pleased they trusted me to do it."

"I see." Ruth preferred not to delve too deeply into Diaz' business affairs. She didn't want to be called upon to testify someday to what she knew of his dealings. Plus, she was enjoying the day and didn't care to have him fill the air with bragging.

Hugging the door, she rolled down her window and gazed at the mountains purple in the distance. She could not yet smell the putrid odor which usually accompanied Diaz. She hoped air circulating in the front of the small bus might perpetuate that condition.

There was no other traffic. Soon after they began, Ruth objected as Diaz turned off the road to Vestal. "What are you doing? The sign pointed that way."

He flashed a smug smile. "The bridge is too narrow, too weak for motorized vehicles. We must take the longer way."

"Stop then and let me out. I can go the shorter, quicker way on my bike."

"No, no, Mother." His voice sounded urgent. "I could not allow it. I am now responsible for your safe arrival in Vestal. My driving, does it offend you?"

She thought a moment. His driving was fine. It was the man himself she found offensive. But, of course, she wouldn't say that. "No, you're driving is fine, Diaz. How far must we go out of our way?"

He frowned at the road.

"You can tell me in kilometers, if it's easier."

"No, it's that I do not know exactly. It will be maybe an hour from here but it is the same hour you would have spent pedaling the six miles. The road is very bad."

Muttering that it would not take her an hour to ride six miles, she tried to forget the detour and the company and simply enjoy the sounds and sights outside.

Eventually, nearly an hour and a half later, she saw a settlement. "Is that Vestal?" She had not been there before.

Diaz smiled straight ahead and grunted, a sound she took as a yes.

Several men roamed back and forth, crossing from establishments on one side of the main street to those on the other. The men did not appear to be farmers.

The women were oddly dressed, their clothes more provocative than clothes worn by the women in Bwana. Their hair, set; their fingernails, painted.

When they saw Diaz' vehicle, most of the pedestrians approached, chattering among themselves, pointing, peering. Others spilled from doorways.

Ruth smiled. "People here are like they are everywhere else, Diaz, all eager to see your cargo."

"Yes." His thin lips extended across his face. It was a nasty little grin and Ruth shivered with a vague feeling of foreboding.

"Diaz, where are we?" She intentionally kept the apprehension out of her voice. The main thoroughfare was only a block long and was bordered by what appeared to be a series of saloons. "This is not Vestal, is it? What place is this?"

He didn't answer. Instead, he pulled up in front of the largest frame building and honked his horn.

Immediately a dozen men and women scurried out, then paused to wait. Three round men--one black, one white, one mixed--sauntered out, squinting, obviously not accustomed to the midday sun. They all wore three-piece suits and all gaped at Ruth. She tried to ignore the chills shivering up her spine.

The round white one gave a shrill whistle and a man wearing a green eyeshade and garters on his shirt sleeves emerged from a doorway, walked to Diaz'

165

side of the vehicle and handed him a wad of currency which Diaz quickly stuffed into his shirt.

A husky black woman in a skimpy red dress with a flounce shoved through the onlookers and flung open the passenger door. She grabbed Ruth's upper arm. Ruth tried to jerk away but the woman dug fingernails into flesh in a biting grip, and yanked her from the van to stand subject to the stares of onlookers gathered on the dusty street.

The woman barked a command in a strange dialect. Spinning, Ruth frowned at Diaz who avoided her eyes.

"No!" Ruth succeeded in yanking her arm from the woman's grasp, but the matron swung her fist to back-hand Ruth across the face. The startling blow sent Ruth to her knees.

"Here," the round white man objected, speaking to Diaz who translated for the others. "Don't damage the goods."

Ruth was relieved to hear English but her relief was short lived.

"Shop worn merchandise goes cheap. This is prime. Let's keep her that way. At least make sure no damage shows."

The hefty woman bent over without bending her knees, provoking catcalls and hoots, to snatch Ruth's arm, hoist her to her feet, and turn her.

Stunned, confused, Ruth marched ahead of the woman who shoved her up a cattle track, their destination a small hut in a clearing surrounded by tall grass. The woman thrust her inside.

Ruth stumbled trying to keep her feet, but toppled against an upright on the far side of the barren little chamber.

The large black captor remained at the door, her anger obvious as she raked Ruth with a furious stare.

Chapter Twenty-Five

Ruth sat in the dirt floor leaning against one of the hut's support poles. At first frightened, her fear gradually developed spine and became anger.

She stroked the side of her face. Her cheek still stung from the fat woman's open hand but the blow didn't seem to have done any permanent damage. Her shoulder was sore but moved all right.

She was angry with Diaz. There was no reason to be angry with him, of course. He was consistent. He never pretended to be anything but the scoundrel he was.

Still, Diaz at his worst would never have slapped her. His malice was more the mental, spiritual kind. His physical torment of others seemed limited to the awful smell emanating from him. The man, of course, expressed concern for Jusu's opinion of things. Residents here in this settlement apparently lacked regard for the white witch doctor. Or maybe they didn't know her connection.

Ruth's anger escalated. *Was this a whole community of villains? Where were the good guys, the heroes? There was bound to be one, a sheriff, a ranger, a marshal, like those who tamed tough towns in America's old west. Where was a hero when a woman needed one?* Ruth allowed a wry smile.

Her peril seemed real. She lost the smile.

Finally she was angry with herself for leaving Bwana alone, against the advice of people she respected: Ossie, Father Catlett, Artemis and, yes, Standish. *Where was she? And what did these people want with her? Ransom? Maybe.* But certainly they, and Diaz too, knew the people of Bwana had no money. Besides, these seemed to have plenty of that, considering the wad they handed Diaz. *Why had they paid him? For delivering her? Again, why?*

Maybe they planned to contact the American government with demands. Or maybe they knew she worked for the wire service and thought someone there might pay for her freedom. People in Bwana had spoken openly of her rich American friends who sent supplies and gifts. Maybe word had spread.

Of course. Money must be what motivated her capture. *What had Diaz said? He was hired to do something for a group of businessmen? It involved a lot of money?* She supposed Uganda had laws against kidnapping.

Who would know where she was? She didn't even know. How could Ossie know? Or Artemis? Or Jusu himself? She was supposed to be in Vestal. She was supposed to be home by nightfall. Ossie and Artemis would be concerned when she didn't return on time, but they could not search for her in the dark. Even if she had hope of rescue, it would not come until tomorrow and this was still early afternoon.

The prospect of spending a night here in this hut, alone, was chilling.

The prospect of someone joining her, was worse.

There seemed to be plenty of women down the cattle track, in the village. Willing women. Surely they would not have gone to the trouble, paid Diaz money, to bring a white woman to this place to assault her. She grimaced to think anyone would find her sexually provocative. There was something ridiculous in thinking of herself as a sex object.

What then?

She got to her feet, paced to the doorway and peered out. The beefy woman in red, stationed just outside the door, sat cross-legged in a funk. She gave Ruth a threatening glower. Ruth smiled halfheartedly and nodded.

She could probably outrun this sentry, dart into the undergrowth, follow the road back to Bwana. But she would be too visible on the road and doubted she could find her way cross country. Still, if the situation became desperate, she would have to try.

What if they had some valid reason for waylaying her?

She couldn't think of one.

Where was that rich imagination, that natural optimism when she needed it?

As she paced and considered her situation, she heard a commotion outside and again stepped to the doorway. A delegation of men appeared to be coming her way. Maybe they would explain.

"Hello." She eased back to allow the three round men and three young black bucks with them to enter. The young visitors were muscular. One had cauliflower ears. The round trio fawned and pandered to the young ones, speaking in an unfamiliar dialect. Inside, the six became silent, staring at her. None returned her uncertain smile.

"What's going on?" She looked at the fat white man who had spoken English.

He didn't answer. Instead he and the others looked her up and down as she had seen judges at the fat stock show eye yearlings. She shivered involuntarily under their scrutiny.

One of the young ones said something in the dialect Ruth had not heard before. The round black man stepped forward, grabbed her arm and hurled her into the young man's face.

Scrambling, she pushed herself away from him but he caught her shoulders. Unexpectedly, he grabbed her breasts with both hands.

She shoved him. The shove earned her a swift fist in the stomach from the pudgy white gentleman. She doubled over coughing as the young examiner dropped to one knee to feel her ankles, her calves, her knees and thighs.

"Get away from me you little pervert." Her words prompted a quick smile. He stood and his dark eyes glittered with excitement. He nodded to the three round men, as his eyes devoured her.

168

Forget heroes and rescues. The country was alive with snakes and vermin but nothing was more threatening that this pack. She would escape as soon as they were gone. There was plenty of daylight. She could follow the road without being on it, reach Bwana before dark, if she put a foot into it.

Animated conversation in the odd dialect occupied the men before another of the young stalwarts moved toward her. When he ventured too close, she slapped his face.

She flinched as he shouted and grabbed the corpulent white fist, again aimed at her mid section.

The young men seemed to approve of her objections to their advances. Their sanctions boosted her confidence.

The first two said something to the third young man who had obviously enjoyed the discomfort of his companions. At their goading, he sidled forward, his hand poised to protect his face from another slap. Ruth allowed him to get just close enough before she delivered a knee to his groin.

He doubled over, then dropped to the floor writhing as his two young companions laughed loudly, taunting him. The round black man made a fist and lurched forward only to be intercepted by the other two young men who caught and turned him, both grinning and jabbering at once. They helped their comrade to his feet and all three grinned at Ruth as they nudged the older men forward and followed them from the hut.

After much conversation outside, the round white man dismissed the matron, over her objections. Two of the young men stayed at the door as the others trailed the matron down the path to the village.

Ruth had to reconsider her escape plan. Plan A was based on her certainty she could outrun the matron. But these two strapping young men were another matter. They were like two playful lion cubs who might enjoy a romp in the jungle chasing such inept prey, *but what would happen when they caught her?*

Better devise a new plan. She glanced at Jack's watch on her wrist. Two o'clock. She studied the watch a minute, then unbuckled it and slipped it into her bra. She could use the watch, perhaps as a bribe, later. She looked at her wedding ring.

Her life with Mickey Pedigo, that soft, secure, serene life of luxury and comfort seemed a long time ago. The ring reminded her of that life. She liked having it where she could see it. It represented Mickey, courageous, solid, predictable. *Was she a fool to have come to this remote place where life was such a contrast to the one she had known?*

She had drunk deeply of Mickey's courage, his strength of character. He would be proud of her for having taken his example to heart, for having come. The ring reminded her he would be proud and that he would expect her to use her head to get out of this particular little crunch.

She smiled at the ring. She would leave it where it was--had been all these years--and trust God to keep it safe.

Noise in the village increased as the afternoon passed. The two young men standing watch eventually were replaced by two others and the replacements replaced again before sundown. Each time there was a change, the newcomers leered in at her. She stood boldly and scowled back at them.

Below in the population, new arrivals tuned musical instruments adding their efforts to the noise of shouts and singing and drunkenness.

Ruth's fear heightened as night approached. Over and over she examined the perimeters of the hut, thinking to dig her way out beneath or through the flimsy thatched walls, but each time she peeked out, feet stood where she looked. Maybe they were watching her or perhaps just anticipating ways she might attempt to escape.

The two guards who came just after dark reeked of booze and their words seemed slurred as they spoke loudly to one another. One peered in at her, started to enter the hut but was prevented by his companion who shouted angrily.

If she spoke the dialect, if she understood any of their words, she might try to talk her way out, to pit them one against the other, but she was afraid to attempt to negotiate without having any knowledge of their language. She could pick out only a word here and there as they spoke, derivatives of familiar words.

They appeared to have had a lot to drink. Perhaps, away from the commotion, they would doze. She stayed alert, waiting for her chance.

Just as she was devising ways to elude them once she was out, another entourage climbed the cattle trail and appeared at the door of the hut.

The white round man came with two more strong looking young blacks, one of which had a long scar through his eyebrow and a droopy eyelid. Two of the young, muscular fellows earlier looked as if their noses had been broken sometime and she remembered the cauliflower ears. All three of these carried drinks, smoked cigars and pounded one another on the back after boisterous comments which, having been spoken, triggered suggestive looks at Ruth, raucous laughter and more back slapping.

Drunks were boors in any language.

When one of the young men stepped close to her, the round white one shouted something which might have been a warning. Everyone laughed loudly and the young man eased back but flashed Ruth a toothless grin.

That group left only to be followed at ten by another, then another at eleven. The new guards built a fire which radiated some warmth and light into the hut's interior, slightly lifting the mantle of Ruth's gloom. Guards were spelled every hour.

No pair became drowsy enough to allow her a shot at escape, although Ruth continued to pace the hut waiting for the opportunity she felt sure would come.

They were bound to wear down eventually. In the early morning, she might have a chance. If it came, she was determined to take it.

Close to midnight, she quit pacing and sat slumped against an upright. She needed to conserve her strength to be ready later.

As she worried, she heard yet another group coming up the path. Wearily she stood, preparing for the usual encounter. Instead, two rotund women entered.

The shorter of the two shouted at her in the odd dialect. When Ruth failed to respond, the short one placed both hands on Ruth's shoulders and pressed down, hard. Yielding, Ruth squatted, then sat. The taller woman grabbed one of Ruth's feet and began unlacing her boot. The stout one did the same with the other foot.

"No! No, no!" Ruth kicked and struggled, trying to regain her feet. The two women rolled her onto her stomach before the shorter one rudely planted her broad derriere in the middle of Ruth's behind. Scarcely able to breath, still kicking and squirming, trying to escape, Ruth could not prevent their finally removing her boots.

Allowing her to sit up, the women eyed Ruth's clothing and talked solemnly, obviously discussing her shirt then her cargo shorts. They both were disheveled, spent after their effort to obtain the boots. Ruth knew it would be hard to keep them from taking her clothing, but was determined that the next battle was going to leave tell-tale marks on everyone. She clenched her fists, set her jaws, and waited.

As the two spoke, the shorter woman shook her head, stubbornly objecting to the other's suggestions. Apparently she prevailed. Satisfied with the boots, they left.

If she had run early, in the daylight, when she had her boots and the fat matron was the only guard, she might have had a chance. She berated herself for the delay. She'd better go now, shoeless, before she lost anything else.

She listened, hoping to hear the partying below had diminished. There were odd, occasional lulls but the music and loud voices picked up again after each one. She risked a peek outside.

Two young men stood sentry, one at either side of the door, poised, ready to give chase. She decided to wait a little longer.

Chapter Twenty-Six

The guards changed again. Ruth heard the drone of their voices as the newcomers received instructions from the men they replaced. The new ones refueled the campfire.

Ruth took the wrist watch from her bra and moved it around until its face caught enough firelight from outside to be readable. One-thirty. Later maybe the raucous party would dwindle to only the hard drinkers and the guards would be lulled by her silence.

Huddled against the far upright, Ruth shivered when she heard a new commotion below. The temperature was probably sixty-five or so, the usual comfortable Ugandan night, but she shuddered and rubbed her arms and shoulders briskly.

Loud voices below, excited at first, were calmed by what sounded like a single speaker. Ruth scrambled to her feet, straining to hear but it was no use. She could catch only snatches of their words traveling on the night air, still in the strange dialect.

The two guards outside growled and grumbled to each other, reacting to the speaker's words which sparked noisy discussions in the gathering below.

Ruth started with the crowd's shout of approval. She also heard some dissent. Then, again, voices coming up the trail. Moments later, two men were silhouetted in the doorway.

She retreated to the farthest point in the hut, unable at first to identify the lone figure which slipped inside.

In the light of the rekindled campfire, she recognized a familiar form and exhaled relief as Jack Standish stood before her.

His guide vanished and Ruth and Jusu were alone in the semi darkness. He spoke quietly. "Hello."

"Hello."

"I see you've gotten yourself into another lively situation."

"I should have listened to Ossie and Artemis...and you."

He didn't seem angry. "Yes. Well, don't I keep telling you that."

"Are you here to rescue me?"

"More as a negotiator bargaining for your, ah, shall we say your honor. We've been haggling for some time now."

"I haven't seen any white smoke. Do we have a pope? Or a contract?"

"Sort of. We took a recess. We're down to two options. The head man just informed the general population. The jury is deliberating."

Her eyes scoured his face. "I don't even know what's going on."

"No one's talked to you?"

"No one's been willing to speak English, until you." She was trying to be patient. "Except for the round white guy, they seem to speak a dialect I don't recognize. Where are we? What's happening?"

He smiled, an obvious effort to soothe her. "This is Momburg. You are quite a premium here, it seems. Some local tycoons put up a bounty, paid Diaz a substantial sum to procure you."

"Why?"

"He assured them he could. He's the one who sent word the people in Vestal were not able to identify their crops. It was true but they did not think of asking you to solve their dilemma."

"This was Diaz' idea?"

He waved her silent and shook his head. "No. The original idea seems to have come from someone else. I don't know who. It's someone close to you. Diaz was just enterprising enough to think of a way to snag you once he heard they were interested." He shifted his weight from one
foot to the other.

"Do you want to sit down?" she asked. "You look tired."

He waved off the offer and continued speaking, staring at her, apparently trying to read her expressions. "A white woman is something of a phenomenon here, as you may have noticed. The local males have become quite curious about your various parts. They've heard stories, very lewd, very specific stories, that yours function differently than the black variety."

"That's ridiculous."

He held up his hand indicating she should be silent. "Over several weeks, the stories have whetted the appetites of a number of curious fellows. Some bright boy thought of a way to cash in on that interest.

"Tonight is the eve of three days of competition and games here in Momburg. Forty contenders have come from many miles for the event. They have trained as if they were preparing for the Olympics for what we might term, a Tough Man Contest. I believe you've met some of the favorites."

The young men she'd seen bore battle scars. She started to speak, to ask the questions tumbling through her mind, but Jack's intensity prevented it.

"The competition's been widely advertised. It's drawn many spectators as well as combatants. The wagering is impressive."

"So, what does all that have to do with me?"

He grimaced. "You are first prize."

Her eyes popped wide and her jaw dropped as she stared at him. "They give people?"

"Women or disabled men or young boys often are awarded as prizes to be the winner's concubines and/or slaves."

She paused, astounded by such an unorthodox idea, unorthodox even in this strange new world. Then she remembered. "You said there's an option." Hope rose.

He nodded solemnly. "Negotiations have gone a little differently than I anticipated but, yes, you have an option. It came to me after I realized it was the only possibility they might consider."

"I'll take it."

"Wait." Again he held up a hand to silence her. "You'd better hear it first. Remember, I was at my wits' end."

"Okay, so what is it?"

"I told them you were Jusu's woman." He paused to watch her reaction.

"You mean your woman?"

He nodded. "I told them I had put up a monetary reward for your return, that the money would be paid through Mr. Glouster. I suggested the reward money be paid to the winner of the contest in lieu of you."

"You bought them off? I'm ransomed?" Ruth brightened. "Good. Let's get out of here."

Standish laughed ruefully. "I wish it were that simple. There was a lot of grumbling at first. They demanded to know how much. I had to make a judgment call. The amount had to be high enough to quell their hormonal interest but not so much as to make them think they should demand more."

"How much had you put up?"

"Nothing, since I had no idea what was going on until I got here. As soon as I knew, I sent a runner to tell Glouster I would stand good for the premium, however much it was, just in case they checked with him before I got back.

"So, we were in the heat of the negotiations when one smart aleck asked if you and I were married before God. He said you preached to women about confining sex to the marriage bed." Jack arched his eyebrows.

She nodded to confirm the truth of that statement.

"Then he declared to one and all that you were not my woman since we had not been joined by what you preached was required: holy matrimony."

Jack regarded her steadily. She remained silent, waiting for him to continue.

"I admitted that we were not married...yet." He hesitated again, apparently to allow her to digest the information. "These people are accustomed to lies and accept liars for what they are. Among them, Jusu has a reputation for speaking the truth."

Ruth shifted her gaze to her bare feet.

In the face of her silence, Standish continued. "Many thought the cash premium was preferable to you. Word has spread that you might be difficult to manage. That premise has inspired glib comments and laughter. Your attitude during the short time you've been in Momburg has confirmed that speculation."

Ruth gave him a harsh look.

He grinned and shrugged comically. "I didn't contradict them."

"Go on."

"There was more grumbling before the smart aleck spoke again. He suggested that if they opted for the cash prize, you should be punished. His idea was that they conduct the marriage ceremony and detain you until you and I share a connubial night which they will somehow monitor. That idea met with enthusiastic approval. I suspect they thought it would be fair punishment for your preaching and my interference and they would have the prize money for consolation.

"Then they again demanded to know the amount. Having had some time to think, I told them I had put up one thousand dollars, American. You may have heard the oohs and aahs."

She nodded. "In a country where truck drivers are revered for making forty bucks a month, a thousand must seem like a marvelous sum." She paused. "Actually, it's probably a good price for a high mileage, vintage model white woman." Ruth peered at his face, curious but reluctant to ask the next question.

He gave her a reassuring smile. "You already know I'm willing." His voice was low, his face solemn. "More than willing."

They stood motionless.

"There are your choices," he said at last. "I told them I needed to talk to you. You may have an improvised, local wedding and one night of wedded bliss with me or you may keep your freedom and take your chances that whatever tough man wins the marathon--which will probably last at least the scheduled three days--will have enough strength left to subdue you."

Ruth turned her back to Standish and ducked her head. "They took my boots."

He seemed impervious to the self-pity in her tone.

"One more thing you might consider." His voice was steady. "You are very important to me. I have never felt for any woman--for any person--this gut-wrenching tenderness, the vulnerability that I feel with you."

She turned suddenly and fixed him with an angry glare, eyes stinging with pent up tears. "I was married for twenty-nine years to the finest man I've ever known." Her voice broke. "This...this blackmail is an insult to his memory. Don't try to make it sound in any way noble or honorable."

Obviously taken aback, Standish swelled to his full height and lurched forward staring into her face.

"Woman, this part of your life has nothing to do with Mickey Pedigo." He seemed suddenly to be giving vent to some frustrations of his own. "I am sick of hearing you and that pansy Ross Belton and the flawless Father Catlett extol the remembered perfection of a dead man.

"Saint Pedigo may have been a prince among men, but he is gone, dead and buried. If he were alive, he probably would come charging in here and deliver you from this place unscathed, but I lack his godlike wisdom. I am only a human being, limited by human imperfection."

Ruth drew a breath to retort but Standish did not allow the interruption.

"AND I am also weakened by another malady which I have not experienced before. Hell, woman, won't you understand? I am inextricably, irrationally in love."

Ruth's mouth dropped open and she took a step back, recoiling.

His eyes locked on her face. "I haven't been able to think straight since I got on that damned airplane in Dallas. You are forever lollygagging around in my mind.

"I was in a frenzy to get to you today. Word of their plan came early this morning. I tried to get to Bwana in time to catch you but I was too late. Even Tuslan did not know at first where they'd taken you.

"Negotiating has been a nightmare. I am a desperate man attempting to bluff with a crowd of professional card sharks. I would have given them anything--money, car, everything I own. All I could think of was getting you back. I never imagined they would take me up on such a tremendous alternative--great for me, that is."

He looked so woeful that she felt a pang of remorse, but didn't know what to say.

"Despite my own feelings in the thing, I tried to do better, for your sake. I suggested every kind of bribe I could think of. This was the only idea that drew any takers.

"I was reluctant to present it to you. Your choices boil down to me or one of them; bad and worse."

She didn't speak, didn't move. He waited, watching her, for a long moment. Finally he drew a deep breath and shuddered. His shoulders slumped and she could see his fatigue. "I'll leave you for a while." His voice was again quiet, controlled. "Let you make up your mind."

Abruptly, he turned and disappeared through the doorway as suddenly as he had arrived.

Ruth crumpled into a heap on the dirt floor and covered her head with both hands. She stayed that way a long time torn by thoughts of betrayal--her disloyalty to Mickey, to Jack, to herself. How could she choose a honeymoon with Jack? She had had her honeymoon.

On the other hand, how could she do otherwise?

She see-sawed back and forth until she was exhausted and it became obvious there was only one acceptable decision. More time passed before she asked the guards to summon Jusu.

Just before two a.m., Jack entered the hut. His eyes searched her face, trying to read her expression in the dim light. "So, we've come to a bottom line, have we?" He spoke quietly and his gaze drew hers.

She looked at him and gasped.

His bottom lip was cut and swollen. There was a dark shadow along one cheekbone. He smiled gamely.

"After we spoke, I went back and presented more arguments. The fat man has little patience." He paused, allowing space for her to speak but she suddenly had nothing to say, so he continued. "The brackets are posted. First rounds begin tonight. The contestants have gotten used to the idea of cash. They seem equally excited about either prize for first place. The promoters will accept your decision. Which will it be?"

She locked her fingers and twisted. "Who will perform this marriage ceremony?" The words sounded ugly as she spat them at him.

Standish straightened and he cut a harsh look at her face. "A holy man from Denan. He's already here."

"Will it be valid? Legal other places or just here?"

"He holds a certificate. It will be valid everywhere."

She peered up at him. "And you're willing to do this?"

"Yes. It is the only way I can think of to keep you from being passed from one drunken contender to the other when the winner has finished with you. If you've an alternative, I'll present it to them."

She was surprised by his candor. She hadn't thought beyond the one proposed atrocity. "What about the law? Is there no chance we'll be rescued by the civil authorities?"

"I sent a runner to Rwabatura from Savanron. I wasn't able to tell him exactly where to find us, if he can interest the police in coming. I told him to contact the Americans as well as any Peace Corps or government people he can find, but only after he had notified the police."

Ruth nodded, tacitly approving his efforts. "What's to say they will not pass me off to the others after you have finished with me?"

He allowed a grim smile. "I mentioned before, I have a reputation among them. Also, Tuslan is a friend, a powerful one. They know they're in jeopardy. Their plan to kidnap you didn't anticipate rousing me. Diaz failed to mention our friendship when they were hatching this little scheme. As long as they detain us both, they are relatively safe.

178

"Tuslan, however, is another consideration. Even in their greed, they will not be so foolish as to take on two strong enemies at once. He will show up sooner or later. That's why they're willing to let you make the choice."

"Is it Standish or Jusu the magician who has standing?"

His gray eyes narrowed. "I'm one and the same."

She sneered. "No. Jusu is a god to these people. You're only a mortal."

Jack's hands balled into fists at his sides. "I assume by your sarcasm that you choose to take your chances with the winner of the competition or gamble that help will arrive in time?"

She reeled, turning her back to him. "No." Anger and frustration muffled her voice. Her head remained bowed as she muttered. "You know you're my only real choice."

Standish exhaled his bated breath. "I'll tell them." He turned and left.

A roar of approval met his announcement, but Ruth heard grumbling beneath the cheers.

Chapter Twenty-Seven

Only a few women mingled in the crowd as the matron in red escorted Ruth down the cattle trail in her stocking feet. The women that were present were not like the Bwanan women Ruth knew or worked beside. These were not women who planted and tended crops and raised children. These were women with jewelry and make-up who smoked cheroots and draped themselves over men. Everyone seemed to be staggering drunk.

Watching them, men and women alike, Ruth wondered how many of them had Slim; how many would be dead in a year; if any of them would live five.

Ruth did not want to be raped but beneath that was her even greater fear of contracting HIV. AIDS had decimated thousands in Uganda, all over Africa, yet the truck drivers who spawned much of it and the women and men who were their sexual partners knowingly continued their promiscuous sexual behavior. Ruth was amazed at their cavalier attitude toward spread of the disease.

She was led to the middle of the main street.

Bonfires burned all around, filling the area with dancing shadows. Many of the onlookers jeered and some cheered as she walked into the center of the throng.

Ruth stepped to the vacant place beside Jack in front of a dried little prune of a man in a comical double-breasted suit which was much too large for him. He apparently was the officiant.

Jack didn't look at her, but stood staring solemnly straight over the head of the diminutive clergyman. Until that moment, Ruth had not actually considered Jack's position in this. She felt a twinge of guilt.

The rite was such a contrast to her other wedding that comparing the two seemed ludicrous. Here, as the odd little man recited words in the tribal dialect she could not understand, men wobbled around the perimeter of the gathering shouting, drinking, making rude gestures and noisy wagers. Occasionally one shrieked with raucous laughter.

Anxious, Ruth touched Jack's hand. He responded without looking at her, his warm hand steady, welcoming as it wrapped around hers.

Quietly, beneath the tumult around them, Jack began speaking, translating the little prune's words. Almost word for word, he recited the Episcopal marriage ceremony, the same one which had joined her to Mickey Pedigo nearly thirty years before. The little man's voice stopped.

Jack said, "I, John Philip Standish, take thee, Ruth Pedigo..."

When he had finished, the wizened one looked at her. Ruth repeated Jack's words, inserting the proper names. The gnome nodded his approval.

Apparently the part in the ceremony about rings was omitted. Jack tugged on her hand as he knelt, indicating she should kneel beside him. The diminutive clergyman pronounced a blessing, touching each of them on the forehead and the shoulders, then he raised their joined hands for the benefit of the spectators.

Ruth and Jack stood amid hoots and catcalls and heightened merriment. Somber, Jack led her quickly back to the hut which apparently was to double as both prison cell and honeymoon suite.

Two women and a man followed, stationing themselves as sentries as the couple went inside.

*   *   *

The hut's doorway was newly covered by a blanket of heavy fabric. *Ah, privacy,* Ruth thought.

Inside, a lone candle revealed that someone had made improvements. There were two metal chairs and a small table on which stood two wash basins of warm water. Ruth's boots, their laces missing, stood resolutely side-by-side beneath one of the chairs.

A stack of thin sleeping mats, layered, occupied most of the floor in the center of the area, presumably their marriage bed. Two frayed cotton sheets were folded neatly at the bottom of the stacked mats.

The hut's distance and even its thin walls provided some muffling of the noise as the revelers in the village below revived.

Ruth faced Jack. "I feel like I'm suffocating; like I have a fever and I'm fighting to get out of a bad dream. I can't seem to wake up."

He smiled into her eyes, his expression calm. "Everything's all right. We'll get a good night's rest and be out of here by morning. We can have the thing annulled in Kampala."

Frowning, Ruth drew a deep breath and glanced around. "I have to ask them to take me to the women's latrine. I'll be back."

He nodded as she removed her socks, retrieved the boots and slid her bare feet into them. She pulled back the new covering over the doorway and summoned one of the women from outside.

Ruth returned a short time later to find Jack sitting stiffly on one of the chairs.

"Lie down," he said quietly, indicating the mats. "Rest. I'll watch for a while."

"Then you don't intend to..."

"We'll see."

Ruth spread one of the sheets over the mats, shook the other out to cover herself, stepped out of her boots and lay down.

Spent, assured that Jack would warn her of any new threat, Ruth curled onto her side. When he moved, she looked up to find he had removed the ammo vest which he wore over his khaki shirt. He rolled it into a pillow and placed it beneath her head. She smiled, whispered "Thanks," and closed her eyes.

The shouting and cheering in the village seemed far away. The scent of Jack's body enveloped her and she felt safe.

While the noise of the revelry below did not disturb her, the roar of the eventual silence was deafening.

She rolled in a half sleep, securing the edges of the sheet around her as she turned. Mickey's fragrance soothed her and she reached out. Her hand touched flesh, not Mickey's furry paunch, but a firm, hairy chest, muscles flexed. She jerked the hand back quickly and tried to sit. Tangled in the sheet, she was unable to push herself to an upright position. A large hand covered her mouth as she struggled to free herself and Jack whispered, "Be still. Everything's okay. They're watching." He pointed up with his thumb, then pushed her shoulder to force her onto the mat. Her head pillowed on his arm, she looked up.

Eerily, it appeared that several eyes peered down at them through the vent hole in the center of the roof.

"What's happening?"

"They're checking on us. They do periodically. I undressed and lay down here beside you to see if that would get us a little privacy."

"And?"

"Not so far."

"What's next?"

"I'm going to kiss you."

Ruth saw his face in the flickering candlelight. She clutched two corners of the sheet at her throat and lifted her chin, offering her mouth.

He tasted of cloves and grass. As his mouth covered hers, his forearm flexed beneath her head.

When he kissed her forehead, she released the sheet at her throat, and allowed her fingers to lace into the hair on his chest. The timid move surprisingly kindled fire in her.

His hand was warm as his palm traced the outline of her neck, over her shirt to her shoulder, back across her collar bone, then down. He hesitated only a moment before he deftly unbuttoned and opened her shirt.

"I'm embarrassed for you to see me." She leaned up and he helped her off with her shirt.

"I've already seen you. I took care of you. Remember?"

"I used to have a nice body. It's gone soft."

"You're a beautiful woman."

Despite his swollen lip, he kissed the swells above her bra. Her breath quickened and became hot in her chest. She hadn't felt this kind of desire in a long, long time.

She encouraged his lips to skim lower. One hand lifted her as the other unfastened and removed her bra expertly.

Hot hands caressed her breasts. Tentatively his mouth covered a nipple and suckled. His breathing became ragged as he peeled away her shorts and panties.

Clothing aside, Jack's eyes and hands browsed lazily.

Her breath quickened as he fondled and trailed his warm mouth over hollows and openings, kissing, caressing.

Before she could no longer think, Ruth forced herself to look, to see if eyes still peered through the vent. She couldn't tell and was beginning not to care.

She attempted to cover herself with the sheet before she realized she was well hidden from prying eyes. Jack was poised over her, covering her. Then she looked at his face.

His eyes were half closed as his mouth explored. His expression was set, his mind focused, lost in passion, no longer aware of anything but the coming pleasure.

He stroked her gently, tenderly and well. She had almost forgotten how it was to soar beyond herself, urged on and up, teasing the insistent ache of want with the breathless whisper of perhaps.

His mouth grew voracious until, finally, he swept the sheet aside and she lay completely naked, ripe in his arms.

Bracing his upper body, he placed a knee between her thighs, coaxing them apart, and she was aware of the warmth of his legs settling between hers.

Slowly, breathlessly, he lowered himself until he found the place of entry. His shoulders and arms flexed and swelled.

He inhaled sharply as Ruth touched his straining pectoral muscles, his ribs, his waist and down to his hips as he probed. The smell of him, the sound of his hurried breathing, his urgency, aroused an urgency of her own.

He paused to gather himself, plunged once, then again, prowling deeper with each thrust. As he filled her, she gasped and trembled and forgot for a moment to breathe.

He drove deep, his efforts full and deliberate. She grew more eager, more welcoming with each lunge. She flexed muscles long dormant to hold onto him, but his fire raged too hot and would not be directed or contained. She settled for moving and moaning at her own pleasure, rocking, undulating, cradling him.

The passion mounted, spiraling up and up until, in an explosion of nerves and colors and lights, she came.

The orgasm didn't end immediately, but continued. She writhed and arched herself to hold on, to prolong the pleasure, to make it last and last...and last.

Finally, mercifully, the ecstasy waned.

Jack lay close upon her, breathless. Sweat beaded on his body and felt sticky against her, but she could not make her arms release him. Her mouth, her arms and her cunt held on until he gave up trying to withdraw.

Ruth turned her head away, unable to look at him. Tears stung her eyes, collected into droplets and spilled.

Jack shifted his weight off of her. She turned, following, desperate to keep him inside her. Leaning on one elbow, he brushed the hair from her forehead. In the darkness, his eyes narrowed when he saw the tears, felt her thin sobs.

"What is it? Did I hurt you?" He hesitated, exhaling. "No. Of course. It's not physical, is it? It's worse than that, isn't it." His voice fell. "It's guilt."

She nodded but dared not speak or look at him. He held his position. She, too, remained motionless.

While neither spoke, each realized that the probe between them was resuscitating, filling again, quickening with new life, still inside her.

Slowly, very slowly, Jack lifted himself up over her, again bracing his body above hers. Keeping her eyes averted, Ruth began to move with him, rhythmically, again meeting his thrusts with her own eager welcome. Sobbing, she allowed her hands to caress his pulsating body.

As they again approached the pinnacle, she reached high over her head. The tips of her fingers touched the upright, well rooted to support its part of the hut. Stretching, she gained a handhold on the pole, pulled, arched her back and heaved herself upward to prolong the moment, to milk every drop of his manhood, as they again climaxed nearly simultaneously.

Moments later, gasping, finally winning his release, Jack rolled off and stretched beside her. Neither of them spoke. Eventually their breathing slowed and she forced herself to look at him.

His eyes were hooded, glazed, but full of her.

He reached for the top sheet and spread it over them, covering their nakedness. They lay mute, side by side on the mat, touching, maintaining physical contact, sometimes only with their fingertips.

Gradually, when they were quiet, she met his veiled gaze and gave him a tremulous smile.

He grinned broadly. "You never cease to amaze me."

"Do you mean the sex?"

He laughed lightly. "Yes, this time I mean the sex."

"Wasn't it normal, the way it usually is?"

"Normal? No. I've never seen a woman quite as...as uninhibited. It's a good thing you were a faithful wife. Released on an unsuspecting public, you might've killed a lot of men."

"Sex didn't kill Mickey. That's not why he died."

185

Jack's face grew serious. "I can think of a thousand worse ways to go. Why did you cry?"

"I don't deserve this...this kind of pleasure." She hiccupped. "It's wrong for me to have so much...so much, all over again...to feel this kind of joy, this kind of love."

He exhaled before she realized he had been holding his breath, obviously afraid of what she might say.

She gave him an apologetic smile. "I love you, Magician." She said it quietly, sadly, a grudging admission, then laughed ruefully at a new thought. "It seems, Jusu, that mine is one of those beating hearts you hold in your hands. But this time it's not just a physical thing. This time it's also a soul to do with as you please."

Jack gave a quiet, triumphant laugh, as he thrust a fist into the air. "That's all I ever wanted--those two things--your heart and your soul. Nothing more."

"Did you mean it when you said we could have it annulled."

He was suddenly apprehensive again, sobered by her words. "You do or you don't want it undone?"

Silent for a moment, she murmured, "I don't."

He sighed with a light, relieved laugh. "Good. I think annulments are easier for people who don't consummate. We're beyond that now."

She offered a weak smile. "What will we do?"

He laughed out loud. "Spend the rest of our lives together. Make the best of it."

"But where can we live?"

"I have a home in Dallas."

"I have a home in Bridger and family, too. Oh, no." She groaned with a new thought. "How will I explain you to my children?"

He laughed at the prospect of each new dilemma. "Maybe we should sleep on it."

"I need to clean up."

"Why don't you wait. We might want to make another run at it."

She smiled. "Practice? It seemed to me like we pretty well had it right the first time."

He turned and slowly lifted himself over her, smiling into her face. "And the second and..."

"Again? How old did you say you were?"

He looked apologetic. "Well, I've waited a long time."

She giggled, laced her fingers into the hair on his chest, and pulled him to her.

* * *

Tuslan, tall and silent, pushed aside the covering and was silhouetted in the sunlit doorway of the hut when Ruth awoke. She lay spooned beneath a sheet, her back nestled comfortably against Jack's chest and stomach, his arm over her. They were both naked.

She patted his hand and he roused. "We have company."

Jack glanced at the door. His eyes only slits, he grinned.

For the first time, she saw Tuslan smile, revealing a mouth full of large ivory teeth.

Sealing the sheet snugly around Ruth, Jack sat up. "Are we out of here?" Tuslan nodded once, still grinning. "Come, wife." Jack rose triumphantly naked from their marriage bed. "We have things to do."

Stretching, she watched with a proprietary sense of pride as he dressed. Could this marvelous specimen actually be hers? And she, his? Somehow, in the daylight, rested and satisfied, that thought seemed unbelievably pleasant.

When he was ready, he grinned down at her. "Tuslan and I will guard the doorway while you slip into your clothes. Then we'll escort you to the latrine where we will guarantee you the opportunity for a long, leisurely period of dusting off."

Wordlessly, Ruth smiled her approval.

Chapter Twenty-Eight

"It's the first week in August," Jack reminded as he and Ruth made their way back to Savanron two weeks later, about dusk. "We need to make plans."

Ruth and Artemis were staying at Jack's clinic which enabled Ruth to travel with Jusu as he made his rounds. They were talking as they walked back from a small village which was inaccessible by vehicle.

Ruth shifted the back pack hanging off one shoulder. Jack, his pack properly affixed, reached over to take hers. She yielded it grudgingly. "I haven't paid any attention to days passing. I've lost all track of time. Why do we care about the date?"

"Because it's time I thought of getting home for the fall semester."

She looked at him stricken and slowed. "I hadn't thought about your leaving." She shook her head. "Jack, I can't leave yet. There's too much work to do here, too many stories that the rest of the world needs to know." She watched him intently. "When Ossie talks about planting this fall, I imagine myself at her side, Artemis within calling distance." Her face darkened. "When does he leave for Ula?"

"The fall term beings in ten days."

"What? Oh, Jack, everything's changing. I thought I was safe from that here where life seemed so changeless."

They walked a little further, Ruth staring at the path, Jack watching her. "I don't know how you can say that."

She ignored the comment. "You don't need to worry." Her voice wavered. "I'll be here, easy to find next spring, when you return."

His pace, which had slowed with hers, stopped. "I'm not going without you."

Ruth's brows knitted over the bridge of her nose as she regarded him solemnly. "But you have to go back. I don't."

"If I don't show, someone else will take my cases, my classes."

"Jack, just because you are not privy to the private lives of the people you repair doesn't diminish the importance of repairing them. You save lives there. Important lives. Your work here is more of a hobby, isn't it?" Ruth gazed up into his face, frustrated.

"Woman, you are my life now. Where I have to be is with you. Everything else is secondary." He looked at her earnestly. "I managed without you before because I didn't know any better. Come here."

She hesitated.

He took her hand. "Let's sit a minute." He indicated a fallen tree beside the path, ran a stick beneath and behind it to assure no unwanted creatures lurked, then dropped both packs. He threw one leg over to straddle the tree trunk while Ruth sat in front of him, both feet forward, hands folded in her lap.

He did not touch her as he spoke. "When people I knew fell in love and I didn't, I figured being unable to love was my big deficiency. We all have strengths and weaknesses. Reggie Finch can't carry a tune. His voice can't find the notes. That's Reggie's primary deficiency.

"I couldn't love. Until you came along, I simply couldn't find the notes. Something inside me began reforming the moment we met, like a damaged vein cuts a new course to repair itself. I could almost feel the physical change taking place inside me each time I was with you.

"It startled me at first, but gradually I've gotten used to loving...to loving you. You made it so easy." He leaned forward and gave her a peck on the cheek. She turned her face to him for a long, provocative kiss.

He glowered playfully. "Don't get me lathered up. I want you to understand this. My problem is I want to shield this love thing. I can't remember ever being so selfish, of feeling so protective of anything as I am of what we have. I like these feelings you have begun in me." He looked into the distance for a moment, then back at her. "Now that I've sung the notes, I don't want to go back to being tone deaf."

"But your work, Jack, the surgery, the teaching..."

"By the time I was ten years old, I knew I wanted to be a surgeon. My dad was a doctor. I had a knack for it. From then on, repairing bodies--birds, animals, then humans--was my first priority.

"Along the way, occasionally teachers and others said I had a gift. It wasn't enough for me simply to learn their techniques. They said I had a responsibility to expand their teachings and to pass that on to others. They urged me to work and do research and teach. I knew they were right. I devised novel ways to conquer barricades which bodies sometimes throw in our faces. It was easy. Natural.

"Sex, music, sports, other interests alternated in and out of second place in my life, but nothing ever challenged for first. Surgery and medicine were my primary allegiance. I've devoted my life and energy to that calling."

Ruth gazed at the lush foliage around her. When Jack paused, she glanced at him and was surprised to see tears in his eyes. She remained silent.

"You elbowed your way into my life so profoundly, I cannot even remember my earlier dedication to my profession." His voice was husky. He cleared his throat. "If you're staying, I am too, regardless of the consequences. I won't be without you, not ever again."

"I don't want that kind of responsibility. You can't let me dictate your obligations."

"You're not deciding much, only my location. I am going to sleep beside you at night. If you're in the states, I'll be there. If you are in Kampala City, Bwana, Savanron, wherever you are, I'll be in that place when I sleep."

"But my work is here."

"That's it, then. We'll stay."

"But your work is there, training new surgeons."

He shook his head. "You have family and obligations there. If you can abandon yours, I can mine."

"It's not the same."

"Sure it is. Your influence on the lives of your grandchildren is every bit as important as my influence on fledgling surgeons, maybe more so. Those tender young twigs need you there bending them to a proper shape."

She smiled at the analogy. "Here I have Artemis, a twig well worth staving. You said I may have saved his leg or even his life. My effort in his behalf may wind up helping hundreds, even thousands of Ugandans, if he has the drive and the ability to become a doctor." She grinned. "And I will secretly take credit for a tiny bit of every contribution he makes."

Jack nodded. "The same will be true of your influence in the lives of your family and friends in Oklahoma or Texas or..."

"That's another thing," she interrupted. "I'm Oklahoma born and bred. We Sooners have a natural aversion to our braggadocios neighbors south of the Red River. I feel strongly about your work, but I don't want to live in Texas. I can't ask you to live in Bridger."

Jack took her hand and kissed the tips of her fingers. "Pay attention. I will lodge where you lodge. Your people will be my people and your god, my god. Uganda, Oklahoma, Texas notwithstanding, you and I are a lock."

"Jack, this whole situation is ridiculous. You are a young man. You need a young woman who can reproduce your brilliant genetic make-up, give you a house full of little clone surgeons with your abilities."

"And which of your children is the replica of you?"

"Well..." She started then stopped, puzzling.

He smiled. "Exactly. Do you recall my telling you about my goals in life?"

She nodded.

"Did you hear anything in my plan about reproducing. I never cared about having kids. I know a brilliant genetic engineer who probably could clone me, but what if that poor little sprig lived his whole life without someone like you to enlighten him, to make him laugh, to guide him to human love, to teach him to sing the notes?"

She gave him an exaggerated grimace. "He would probably concentrate on surgery and teaching, uninterrupted, to the benefit of all mankind." She stood and strolled over to lean against a banana tree, away from his hands stroking her skin.

Jack watched her movements, studying her various parts with obvious appreciation. "You have brought a new dimension into the tunnel that was my perspective of life." He smiled again. "I'm like a race horse who always ran in blinders. You removed them. Suddenly I can see the stands and the people and the other horses for the first time."

"And are so distracted, you're forgetting to run your race," she finished, pitifully shaking her head at the simile.

He arched his eyebrows. "But there is so much more to living. It's like the old song, 'There were bells on the hill, but I never heard them ringing... 'til there was you...'"

Ruth walked over in front of him. He remained seated on the fallen tree but swung his leg around so he faced her squarely. She put her hands on his shoulders. He propped his on her waist, separated his knees, pulled her close and buried his face in her stomach.

She laced her fingers into his hair. "This should never have happened. I..."

"What did you do?" He tilted his face so he could see hers and splayed his hands on her buttocks, pulling her tightly against him. "You felt a religious nudge, like nudges you've responded to all your life. That nudge put you on an airplane. We met. Did you lead me on, lure me with your feminine wiles?" They both laughed lightly at the suggestion. "You did not.

"Did you elect to stay in London, let me to talk you into my bed? No." He regarded her soberly. "When we reached Uganda, did you track me down and seduce me, as any red-blooded female would have been justified in doing? Did you cajole me, tease me into marrying you?

"Who do you think is responsible for all the peculiar machinations that placed you in front of the gnarled up prune of a preacher that fateful night? It was all too well ordered to be happenstance, don't you think, oh close friend of the Almighty?"

She grimaced. "Even with all that, I should not have given in..."

Gazing up at her, he shook his head, allowing a salacious grin. He stood and picked up both back packs. Slowly he began walking and she fell into step behind.

"I don't remember your giving in, at all," he said. "What I remember is you shivering in a sheet, struggling against a physical need which had been seducing both of us. I doubt I could have restrained myself. Before I took off my clothes, maybe. Unbuttoning my shirt, getting out of my pants that night, I was driven by a desire which I can guarantee was not holy. I'd been fighting it since D/FW. When we were alone in that hut after the ceremony, I was going to have you or bust."

Her eyes darted to his face. "But you wouldn't have forced me, not if I'd resisted."

"I think it's better if we don't speculate about that. What I didn't realize was that you were damn near as ready for me as I was for you."

"Well, I was your wife, after all." She smiled timidly. "It was my responsibility. A wife is expected...required... to perform certain duties, even as unpleasant as they may be." She laughed lightly, looking at the ground.

He grinned. "Your responses, all that heavy breathing were born out of your sense of duty? You certainly fooled me." His eyes twinkled mischievously. "And here I thought all that time you enjoyed it."

She grimaced. "Well, no one had wanted me that badly in a long time. And I hadn't been that...needy. And the circumstances were conducive...."

"Nothing in all that about being in love? Would you say love played any role in your responses? Or was it just lust?"

"Yes." She muttered and he looked at her questioningly. "Okay, I loved you ferociously that night. I was like an animal caged for a long time who suddenly got sprung."

His tone dropped and his face grew sober. "And do you love me now?"

"Yes."

He arched one mischievous brow. "Ferociously?"

She sputtered an embarrassed half snort, half giggle. "Yes."

They walked in silence as Jack's face became solemn with a new thought. "The only thing that bothers me...well, I can't seem to get it off my mind. I keep wondering...."

"What?" She regarded him, feeling genuine concern. He shook his head, apparently trying to shake off the thought but she prodded him. "Come on, tell me."

"It's sophomoric. It's too childish to say it out loud."

She brightened with an insight. "Jack, I told you, I was a virgin when Mickey and I married. He held back at first. He wanted me to like sex. He took things slowly, cultivated my natural inclinations, my curiosity. He soothed my inhibitions. He loved me patiently in those early days until he turned me into what he called, 'a player.'"

They stopped walking again. Looking at each other, Jack's face was solemn. "Did I move too fast for you?"

She regarded him smugly. "Your timing, your entire performance on our wedding night was perfect and you darn well know it. Quit fishing for compliments."

Jack grinned. "Your first husband was a wise man to take such good care of you. I appreciate that. I like Mickey Pedigo."

"You would have." She smiled warmly. "A college roommate of mine came to visit when Mickey and I had been married a couple of years. We were gaggling like girls do and she asked me what kind of lover Mickey was. I said he was terrific. She said, 'As compared to what?'

"I got tickled when I realized the answer. As I told her, 'No wonder he was so good. He was the only game in town.'" Ruth looked at Jack seriously. "Until you, I'd never had sex with anyone but Mickey. I'd never wanted to."

"But you wanted to with me?"

"I didn't care about anything else, not people watching, not drunks fifty yards away, not the threatening circumstances--not anything."

Ruth turned and looked up the path but Jack gave no indication of wanting to move, so they remained as they stood and she began to reminisce. "When the kids were grown and out of the house, our lovemaking slowed down. It was passionate but not as frequent. Mickey and I had always been close, physically, spiritually. But there was no more wild, frenzied groping. Our lovemaking was tender, familiar, comfortable. Not like...."

She frowned into his face. "Mickey and I made love early that last morning." She said the words quickly, like a confession which needed to be rushed. "Two hours before the coronary." She bit her lips, clamped her hand over her mouth and shrugged, watching Jack's face, waiting for condemnation or sympathy. Her chin quivered. He stood still and quiet, never taking his eyes from her face. Tears welled in her eyes, then dried without spilling.

"When Mickey died," she scrambled over the words, "I was reconciled to being celibate. I didn't mind. He was all I'd ever known. At fifty-two, I figured I was too far over the hill to learn new techniques, adjust to anyone else."

Jack continued regarding her somberly and his voice was reverent. "Maybe it was your thinking that way that drew me to you in the first place. Tell me, what did you think of me at first?"

Her melancholia passed in the face of his question and she swiped at her eyes. "I thought you were like my son Michael, looking out for someone you thought needed a keeper."

"But did I appeal to you physically? Did you think I was attractive?"

She shrugged a little indifferently. She didn't want to make this too easy for him.

"When I was young, I didn't care for tall men. They made me uncomfortable. I was attracted strictly to stocky, muscular types, my height or only slightly taller.

"Our sons are both tall, closer to your height than to mine or Mickey's. As the boys grew up, of course, I began feeling very comfortable around rangy guys.

"You would have intimidated me when I was young. You simply would not have appealed to me then. On the airplane, however, I thought you were a very nice piece of work. I didn't feel threatened, even when you blocked my path. You loomed over me like my sons do. I just wondered what you wanted."

"You did like looking at me?"

194

She shook her head with a haughty grin of her own. "You know you're great looking. The stews kept verifying that the whole flight."

He raised his eyebrows and pressed. "I knew what they thought. I want to know what you thought."

She reached up to place one hand on his chin, tapped her index finger on the pucker of skin at each side of his mouth and looked into his eyes.

"You have amazing eyes. They trespass, penetrate into a person's mind and soul. They captured me, despite my effort to look away. I didn't want anyone to see into me like that.

"But the way your mouth puckered when you kidded me, aroused something, a tingling long dormant. That pucker was so damned sexy.... This little bell somewhere deep inside me started jingling. I wallowed in the scent of you, pretended it was not you but Mickey. But I did not allow myself to look closely at the puckers until after the marriage ceremony. When I did let myself look, all was lost."

Jack snorted. "You controlled yourself admirably on the airplane and at the Biscuit Basket. I was aching to get my hands on you. I thought you weren't interested, that you were immune to my charm."

She bowed her head. "You kept helping me. That was very sensitive." She looked up into his face. "That's when you reminded me of my older son. It didn't hurt, of course, that you wore Mickey's aftershave. The scent was familiar, soothing. It also made me aware of your whereabouts every minute.

"Later I tried to attribute all kinds of evil motives to your persistent offers of help. I couldn't understand why a man of your youth and obvious appeal would be so determined to help me. I decided you thought I was rich and were after my money, that you were going to grab me and hold me for ransom, that you felt guilty about someone else and were trying vicariously to make something up to them through me."

He laughed lightly and lowered his head, encouraging her to continue.

"Yes, I found you attractive. But it was a lot more than your physique."

"What else?"

"I liked your kidding me. I liked that you kept gulping back your laughter and that you finally gave into it." She smiled. "I've always admired stick-to-it-tiveness. You pursued me with dogged determination.

"At the Biscuit Basket, Pamela told me you attracted women in droves but you never brought them there. I was flattered, baffled and very nervous, but I still couldn't figure out why me.

"To cap it all, when you kissed me good-bye at the airport, I twittered like a school girl.

"By the time I got to Uganda, I was completely disgusted with myself for being so infatuated. I was a mature woman. It was ridiculous for me to entertain a bunch of romantic illusions about you, but I kept doing it anyway."

Jack swung the backpacks over his shoulders and stepped out in front to lead her as the walking path narrowed to single file. He looked back at her over his shoulder. "You did think of me then, in Bwana?"

"Yes. And dreamed about you. I felt like a teenager, all hormones and giddy, goofy thoughts."

He snickered. "Good."

"I thought I would get straightened out when I got settled and began to turn out some serious writing, but I kept thinking of you, night and day. I asked. No one had heard of Jack Standish. I could not imagine why you might have lied to me, if you had. I couldn't come up with a plausible explanation. But I consoled myself that I had survived losing

Mickey, I certainly could survive losing someone I had known less than a week.

"I got so attached to Artemis so quickly that I decided I was trying to lavish love on anyone who wandered into my life and better him than you."

Jack turned around again and regarded her seriously. "Ruth, Artemis did well on his entry tests at Ula. I wanted to wait to tell you and him together. The dorms are open now to accommodate families who must bring their offspring before the rains."

Ruth was again plunged back into harsh reality.

Jack continued quickly. "I received a note from the dean. Artemis was especially good in English language skills, which will be a big advantage to him. Even though he's only nine, they placed him in classes for children in the sixth and seventh grades. He shows a lot of potential. I have the letter of acceptance. I'll show you when we get home."

She was going to miss the little scamp, her shadow. Suddenly preoccupied with thoughts of Artemis, Ruth squeezed by Jack on the path and trudged along in thoughtful silence.

"I thought you'd be pleased to know he'd done so well." Jack stayed close behind her.

"Yes, I am."

Neither spoke for several minutes.

Jack was the first to break the quiet. "I think we ought to go back to your telling me how I won you."

She snorted a half laugh and looked back at him. "You are so egotistical."

When he didn't argue, she grimaced, then smiled remembering. "I was curious about how you would look without clothes." She felt self-conscious about admitting that. He leaned around, trying to see her face. She knew he could tell she

196

was blushing. "I hadn't seen you in less than a coat and tie until the afternoon Artemis was injured and we came to the clinic. I have a clear mental picture of you in your scrubs. Your arms and torso were beautifully developed. The hair on your chest peeped over the collar of your shirt taunting me."

"Some women prefer hairless men."

"Not me. I wondered, hoped you had hair on your stomach too. Very sexy.

"To make matters worse, Rosamond told me she sneaked around and watched you bathe. She described your, ah, attributes. The mental image she sketched was so provocative, I interrupted her. I was already interested. I didn't want get overstimulated.

"Anyway, standing in front of that little prune priest or whatever he was, I knew you were taking a desperate way trying to prevent my being the village playmate. I appreciated your sacrifice and promised myself not to make you go through with stage two.

"In the hut, I was nervous, frightened, excited, exhausted. I wanted you to hold me but I didn't think I could allow myself that luxury, afraid of how I might respond. You suggested I lie down. I had been keyed up for hours. With you, I knew I was relatively safe. I would rest. You would sit. We would both be okay.

"When I woke up, you were lying beside me, naked, touching me, whispering. I smelled your delicious body. I wanted to tell you you didn't have to, that you'd done enough--too much--already. I didn't say it because I didn't want you to stop. I simply didn't have the fortitude. You were so warm and you smelled so good and...

"Making love with you was like beginning all over again, brand new, back to the early days with Mickey. You needed me. You took my breath, along with my reason, self consciousness, everything." She paused and their eyes met. "Surely you know all this without my...." She hesitated again.

"Go on."

"Your body was so strong, so demanding, so fulfilling, so... I can't reduce it to words. You were there. You know how it was. We soared together into that secret, celestial place, the out-of-mind experience."

He nodded. "I wanted you to tell me it was that way for you. I needed you to."

She turned her head enough to see the satisfied smile on his face.

* * *

Ruth wrote to Larry Reid. She would be back in the states at the end of the month. She wrote to her children as well, but she didn't mention Jack. She wanted to tell them about him in person.

Monday, August fourteenth, was to be Jack's last scheduled clinic day. On Wednesday Ruth and Jack would take Artemis to Kampala to buy him a proper wardrobe.

Wildly excited at the prospect of school, Artemis was equally saddened by the anticipated separation from the only mother he had known.

Jack had to be away all afternoon giving inoculations in a remote village. He had not returned by the time Ruth went to bed.

Rosamond woke Ruth at midnight. Artemis was calling for her in his sleep. Ruth hurried into the infirmary to check but he was resting quietly by the time she got there.

Two young male patients in their early twenties occupied the other beds. Ruth sat in a straight back chair beside Artemis' bed for a while. When he rolled onto his side and whimpered, she eased onto the bed and stretched out beside him, spoke quietly and stroked his head. He relaxed and they both slept.

Jack went directly to their bedroom when he got home tired and hungry at two a.m.

"Where is my wife?" he asked the long apparition in the doorway.

"With Artemis. Shall I wake her?"

"Is he ill?"

"No."

"Get me a glass of milk. I'll get Ruth."

Rosamond nodded and turned, concealing the evil smile which crept over her face.

Jack slipped into the infirmary and to Artemis' bedside. Looking down on them, he was suddenly angry.

Ruth lay on her side facing the boy and he was facing her. The boy's mouth, near her breast, sucked his thumb in his sleep. His other hand rested on her waist.

Jack removed the boy's hand from Ruth's waist, awakened her and lifted her from the bed. Her eyes, squinting in the flickering light of the votive candle, peered up at him. "What's wrong?"

He shushed her, carrying her back through the surgery and down the hallway to their room. He put her carefully on the bed. A glass of milk sat on the bedside table.

"Tell me what's wrong?" She sat up, stifling a yawn, and tried to appear alert and interested. Seeing her valiant effort and her genuine puzzlement, Jack's anger dissolved as he sat on the edge of the bed. "It's good that I know you so well." He smiled quietly, untied the ribbon closure on her gown and methodically unbuttoned the tiny pearl buttons securing the front. Watching his hands, Ruth felt a rush.

He bent and touched his mouth to one exposed nipple. Placing her hands behind his head, Ruth pressed him closer and drew a quick breath. The gown fell away.

Without taking his eyes from her, he stood and stripped.

Moments later, smiling, Ruth stretched luxuriously as her husband rolled up over her.

The apparition in the doorway withdrew into the darkness, her mouth set in anger, and walked purposefully to the infirmary.

Chapter Twenty-Nine

Rosamond went directly to Artemis' bed. He lay as Ruth had left him, on his side, his thumb in his mouth.

She gazed at the boy for a long time before she soundlessly stepped out of her shoes, untied her serape and allowed it to melt to the floor.

Naked, she slithered onto the bed and stretched beside him. He shifted fretfully.

Slowly, gently, Rosamond snaked her long lithe body close to him. She removed his thumb from his mouth. Holding one bare breast in her hand, she touched the tip of her nipple to his lips. His eyes still closed, he opened his mouth, and welcomed the breast, immediately attempting to milk it with his tongue. She picked up his small hand and placed it at her waist. As he suckled, he made a soft mewling sound. Rosamond guided his hand down, down, over the smoothness of her hip to her thigh, then slowly brought it back, placing it on her other breast.

The boxer shorts Artemis wore as pajamas were big for him. He seemed roused but not yet awake. His mouth sucked rhythmically at one breast while his hand fondled the other. He allowed Rosamond to remove the shorts, which she tossed onto the floor with her abandoned serape.

She was content to lie there for a long while, anticipating, planning.

After tonight, Artemis would be hers. Ten years her junior, one day he, not Jusu, would be the one spoken of around the fires at night. When Artemis spoke then, they would listen as they listened now to Jusu. And she, Rosamond, not a pale-skinned foreigner, would be admired, envied as the new magician's woman.

Not only was she pleased with these thoughts of her future, Rosamond breathed deeply with her fantasies of this night, despite the fact this was not the man she wanted. She had dreamed of this many times, always with Jusu.

Remembering those fantasies in detail, she pressed closely against the boy. Deftly using her hands, she kindled his wakefulness and aroused his small penis.

She had seen results of the boy's blood tests. He was clean, free of the Slim, the awful disease consuming her people. She would be sure he remained clean, as she herself was clean.

Her hand caressed his neck, his small shoulder, brushed over his ribs, down his narrow hip. Opening her hand on his buttocks, she drew him to her. He sucked harder at her breast. She found it pleasing to know that she would be his first.

His breath quickened and a fever of desire stirred within her. She felt his small probe hard against her leg, searching. She guided it with her hand, to the opening it sought. He sucked the harder and his hands became alive, hot little hands, flying over her. They were not the man's hands she wanted, the ones at this moment caressing white breasts, but Rosamond encouraged the small hands to explore where they liked, pretending they belonged to Jusu.

As his boy's penis enlarged, she caught Artemis up in her arms and turned onto her back situating him on top of her. His mouth refused to release the breast, even as his small phallus wriggled into the deep, moist darkness.

Rosamond closed her eyes and ceased to be concerned about the silence she had imposed so diligently before. She spread her legs and caught her heels on the sides of the bed, allowing the boy's hips to settle between her thighs.

Instinctively he brought his knees up under him and used them to thrust himself into her. He lost the nipple and, for a moment, rooted like a pup separated from its teat until hers was recaptured.

Writhing, she swallowed the moan which threatened to escape her lips as she moved beneath him, using her hands to make his child's appendage more pleasurable for her.

It would grow. *Wasn't she anointing it now, at this moment?* This man's organ would be devoted to satisfying her. She would visit him in Ula. She would sneak into his quarters, into his bed, as often as he wanted. He would worship her, just as Jusu worshiped the white one.

Wait. Wait, her mind cautioned. This was not the way Mother Earth captivated Jusu. *What method had she used?*

The boy's thrusts became a striving. His mouth released her breast. Tiny cries of pleasure escaped each time he lunged. He pumped faster and faster until he convulsed and cried out. She muffled his cry, clamping her hand over his mouth. The tremor of pleasure sent spasms, shockwaves of joy radiating from his pelvis through every part of his body. His small form was soaked with perspiration as he collapsed on top of her, his ear against the breast which had beguiled his mouth before.

His rapid breathing subsided.

"Thank you," he whispered, nestling, his mouth again searching for the abandoned nipple. "Thank you, Maawe."

Rosamond grabbed his shoulders and rudely shoved him over and off of her. "What?" She gasped. "What did you say?"

Leaning back, Artemis stared at Rosamond in disbelief and fright. He snatched at the sheet wadded at the foot of the bed and pulled it up over his nakedness. "I thought..." He stammered, stopped, started to speak again, thought better of it and lowered his eyes in shame. Something moved in the next bed. Rosamond turned to look.

Both of the other patients assigned to the room, young men older than Artemis, knelt on their beds watching breathlessly, holding themselves. The one in the nearer bed, his eyes wide with anticipation, stared at Rosamond, allowing his gaze to travel the entire length of her nakedness. Boldly rearing up on his knees, he pushed his shorts down.

His penis, much larger than Artemis' was primed and ready. He fondled himself, allowing Rosamond a full view of all that his body promised, then lay back motioning eagerly for her to come to him.

Ignoring the young man, Rosamond slid her feet to the floor and stooped, fumbling for her serape. Hastily wrapping it around her, she hurried out the door, down the hall, through the surgery and into the night.

*   *   *

"Mother, I thought it was you holding me last night in the dark in my bed," Artemis said when Ruth carried his breakfast tray to him at seven.

"I was here, Artemis. When you had trouble sleeping, I slept beside you until Jusu got home."

"I had a dream, Mother. It was like no dream I have known before."

The youth in the next bed spoke. "It was no dream. We saw this dream. Four do not dream together."

As the boys began relating the events of the night, Ruth's eyes grew wide with horror and disbelief, but their detailed accounts were convincing.

Knowing of Rosamond's marginal standing with Jack, Ruth wanted to avoid alienating him further from his assistant. She set out in search of the girl to get some kind of an explanation.

Rosamond had left before daylight, had told one she was going home to visit her family and another that she was going in search of her lost husband.

The young woman knew Artemis would be at the boarding school in Ula. Ruth could only guess why she had instigated such an atrocity. Rosamond was always there watching, her eyes afire with jealousy. Ruth, and Jack too, tried not to display affection toward one another when Rosamond was present but there were times when they did not realize she was watching.

Perhaps Rosamond, seeing the boy's potential, was staking her claim on Artemis for the future. Ruth thought the idea had merit but she didn't want to say anything without more than her supposition.

When Rosamond did not show up by mid morning, Jack recruited an older woman, Teresa. He used other assistants occasionally, when Rosamond was away or when their work required additional help. Teresa had shown great skill as a physician's assistant. Besides, he only needed her to finish out this summer, one more day.

Jack seemed pleased. "I wanted to ask Teresa to work for me before but I didn't want to offend Rosamond as long as things were running smoothly. Teresa agreed to come back next May, if and when I return."

The transition was made with few problems.

That afternoon Ruth had a long private talk with Artemis, the sex talk she had perfected by repetition with her four natural children. She invited questions and the boy, with his usual candor, asked many. She answered frankly.

She did not discuss with Jack the events of the eve of Rosamond's disappearance. She assumed the boys spoke to him about it, but he did not mention it to her until Wednesday morning as they loaded the Rover for the shopping trip to Kampala and on to Ula to take Artemis.

Ruth introduced the subject. "I thought Rosamond might be back to see us off."

Jack's face tightened and his eyes narrowed to slits. "It may be best if we have seen the last of Rosamond."

"Jack, hell hath no fury..."

"In the last couple of days, I've asked questions I should have asked a long time ago. Rosamond conspired with Riz Diaz. There is talk that she helped arrange your kidnapping. She was terribly angry with the way things worked out. She did not foresee the price I would pay for your freedom. Tuslan plans to speak with her about that."

Ruth thought of the desperation which drove the girl to such an extreme. "Have you heard anything of Diaz?"

"I doubt anyone will for a while. Tuslan has people searching for him, as well. He wants to talk with his old friend but Diaz seems to have gone to ground. I doubt he or Rosamond will be seen around here for quite a while.

*   *   *

Tuslan drove Ruth, Jack and Artemis from Savanron to Bwana to exchange tearful good-byes, particularly with the Catletts and Marmel and his wife and daughters, then on to Kampala for shopping and to Ula.

Talkative on the early legs of their journey, Artemis grew silent as they neared Ula.

They arrived on the campus late in the afternoon. Artemis got out of the car, awed at the sight of the brick buildings which, he remarked, appeared to have no roofs.

Ruth's hands nervously brushed his neck and shoulders, like a mother goose preening her gosling. Watching them, Jack turned away. Ruth glanced at Jack. "What are you laughing about?" Knowing full well, she pretended to be vexed.

"Just watching the consummate mother at her work."

"I see. Well, maybe someday we'll critique your performance at something."

He leaned close to her ear. "I believe you've already done that, with exquisite moanings, if I recall correctly." He stepped back to watch. Raising his eyebrows, he grinned at the reliable blush which crept from her collar to her hairline.

She tried to squelch a smile. "The people in Bridger speculate correctly. You are a barbarian."

He laughed lightly.

Ruth soon found what she had suspected, that the bright buildings, the glistening campus were false fronts for the cheerless, impersonal dorm rooms with their tile floors and cinder block walls.

Having seen the school's picture brochure, Ruth had purchased colorful plaid bedspreads for twin beds and a matching valance to place above the blinds covering the lone window, hoping to brighten the place. Also, she had insisted they purchase a large, colorful bulletin board to enhance at least one of the drab walls. Despite those additions, the room seemed determined to remain dismal, depressing.

Watching her efforts, Jack finally intervened. "Beauty is in the eyes of the beholder, my love."

She turned, puzzled, and followed his gaze to Artemis.

The boy was meticulously placing his new clothes in the drawers in the bureau assigned to him. Lovingly he ran his fingers over his name tag before he carefully positioned it and his school supplies in, on and about one of the two desks provided. Ruth considered the room desolate. Obviously Artemis saw it differently.

"My name is Sam," a timid voice croaked. Ruth, Jack and Artemis turned as if on signal.

The boy in the doorway was taller and darker than Artemis, and painfully thin. His eyes were wide and his mouth trembled with the strain of first meeting.

"Hello, Sam, I am Artemis." Artemis held out his hand.

The new arrival took the offered hand and breathed in and out once, quickly. "This is my first term. My math is good. My English is not good."

Artemis smiled and nodded his approval. "Perhaps we will help one another."

Sam's shoulders appeared to relax and his face, too. "Have you seen the toilet?" Artemis shook his head. "Come, I will show you."

Jack could scarcely contain his laughter. Ruth finally relinquished a grudging smile of her own.

"He's holding in for my sake, trying to hide his excitement." Ruth smiled ruefully. "He's trying not to hurt my feelings but I can tell he feels like turning cartwheels up and down the hall."

Jack bit his lips. "I hope he doesn't. Cartwheels might damage the foot."

Her eyes grew bright as she gazed at him. "He scarcely even limps now, Jack, thanks to you."

He returned the smile. "Anything for you, Love."

As the boys returned, Artemis chattered, wondering aloud that there were bathing facilities "right here on our floor, inside the building."

205

Standing behind Ruth, Jack wrapped his arms around her and chuckled out loud before he whispered near her ear. "We need to get going." When she clouded up, he quickly added, "We don't want to cramp his style, Maawe."

She wilted. "It's not like I haven't been this path before. I cried every darn time. First days of kindergarten, with each of them; first church camps when we unloaded them all giddy and excited into hot, mosquito infested cabins, and finally into college dormitory rooms that all looked remarkably like this."

Forewarned, Jack remained placid as Ruth and Artemis hugged and wept, then hugged again.

Finally, Ruth swallowed and pushed the boy to arm's length. "I will write to you at least once a week and send you lots of packages."

"Maawe, do not worry. I will succeed. I have never known such wonderful accommodations. Did you see the bathing room?" She nodded. "Is it not marvelous?"

Marvelous? Yes, marvelous. Ruth pondered. Except for his time in the infirmary in Savanron, Artemis had never had a bed of his own much less a chest of four drawers or a desk. Now he had them all at one time in one location, with a bathing room under the same roof.

"What are you going to do next?" She had found it best on these occasions to focus attention, hers and the child's, on the future.

"I will arrange my book shelves." He waved his hand indicating the small wooden stack shelf on the back of the desk. "I need to locate the books we purchased, to arrange them properly. I must write my name in each one to show that they belong to me. These books are full of wisdom and I am their owner." He hugged himself. "Oh marvelous day."

Jack's shoulders shook again with mirth, as he turned his back to Ruth's pitiful glances.

His eyes darting from the desk to Ruth, Artemis continued. "Maawe, when you return in the spring, I will be a scholar. I will know many things, even, I think, some things which you do not yet know."

Ruth nodded agreement and squeezed the boy, kissing his head and face playfully. "Yes." She risked a look at Jack who was helplessly trying to quell his laughter. "I'm sure you will think you know more than I do by next spring, my son, but I may fool you. I may study harder during your school year than you do. Then we'll see who is the quicker learner."

Artemis' face wrinkled sentimentally at her use of the word "son." His face reflected concern for another moment before his eyes narrowed to field the challenge she issued. "We shall see, Maawe, when you return; when the heat of the Oklahoma summer drives you home to Uganda."

Ruth turned toward Jack. "Will we be back?"

206

"I want to come but you know my new policy."

She directed her eyes from Jack back to the boy's eager face. "Well, I guess for everyone's sake, I'll see you in the spring, Artemis, whether I want to come or not."

Jack and Artemis exchanged knowing looks, then grinned, raised and lowered their eyebrows and gave each other a high five.

Chapter Thirty

"When will you begin using your new name?" Jack asked as they flew from Entebbe to London. He held Ruth's hand in both of his as he gazed at her profile.

Looking straight ahead, she smiled. "My passport, all my photo I.D. has me as Ruth Pedigo. I thought I should keep using that name until we got home and had time to change it officially."

"You're not stalling, are you?"

"What?" She regarded him skeptically. "Why would I?"

"Hedging your bets in case your barbarian behaves inappropriately in civilization."

She turned her head quickly, stared at him a moment, then allowed a slow, knowing smile. "I haven't seen you unsure of yourself before. This is a whole new concept."

"You're dodging the question."

"No, my love, I'm not stalling or hedging any bets." She leaned toward him and lowered her voice. "I've never required my husbands to audition."

He grinned crookedly. "That's popular now, you know. Living together. Tryouts."

She laughed lightly. "I've heard."

"So, if you'd held auditions, would I have gotten the job?"

Again she chuckled, a taunting sound. "Your lovemaking sets the standard for all men." She leaned closer. "Besides that, nude, you have no peers."

He put his hand at her waist and slowly moved it down her abdomen. She stiffened and shot him a startled look.

"Just releasing your seat belt." His eyebrows arched. "The light's off."

She glanced at the seat belt light, and smiled warily before another thought made her serious. "Jack, will you tell me now what it was that Jusu chanted when I was sick."

He rumbled with a deep, throaty laugh.

She prodded. "Come on."

"It was a loose Runyandolean translation of some words I vaguely remember from a long time ago."

"What words?"

He began to chant softly. "With purity, with holiness I will practice my art. I will go to the sick...work for their benefit. I will abstain from every voluntary act of mischief and corruption, particularly from the seduction of females... specifically this female...especially this female...at least for the present moment this female."

"What kind of lyrics are those?"

"It was sort of an emergency rendition of part of the Oath of Hippocrates. A time or two there, bathing you at night, alone, I was hanging onto my personal and professional integrity by my fingernails. That little ditty, in Runyandole, was like slapping cold water on my face."

She sighed, admiring him openly. "I'm looking forward to a couple of days in London."

"My thoughts exactly. But we may have different motives. I'm eager for time alone with you in posh surroundings. You, on the other hand, are just trying to delay the inevitable confrontation with your children."

"Oh, I don't think it will be a confrontation, exactly. They have their own lives. My lifestyle, no matter how bohemian, won't matter to them, once they have a little time to digest the news.

"That's a funny thing about parenting, Jack. You bring babies into the world and they disrupt your whole life. They are dependent on you for everything. If you're wise, you don't fight it. You give yourself over to them completely.

"Then, little by little the world captures them. Their minds, their bodies, their imaginations push you away, stiff-arming you, kicking, squirming, struggling to escape, to be on their own. It's very hard to turn loose since you've sacrificed so much, devoted yourself to their needs.

"Mickey used to say the better parent you are, the less they need you as they grow and discover their own wings.

"Finally one day you accept their rejection. You share a history but they are no longer your children. They are people; special friends, ones you know and like awfully well.

"Anyway, my life now actually has very little to do with theirs." She leaned her head back against her seat and turned, studying his face. "My life now centers on you. You have set the tone. 'Wither thou goest...' and all that scriptural stuff you disavow but which you can quote when you want to."

"That's funny." He leaned his head against the back of his seat to gaze at her, and lifted her fingers to his lips. "That's exactly what I was thinking. My life now revolves entirely around you."

It suddenly dawned on her: he was traveling light. "Hey, where are all your reading materials?"

"I brought along a different kind of distraction this trip." He kissed her fingers again, grinning.

Chapter Thirty-One

"I need a wedding band."

Jack stood braced, wrapped in a towel, in front of the sink in the dressing area of the Guinevere Suite at the Biscuit Basket Inn outside London.

In a light robe, Ruth lounged on the love seat watching him shave, admiring him. He seemed very tall and sinewy and firm. She admired his familiar chest and stomach, his marvelous legs, so deliciously masculine. She marveled all over again that he had wanted her.

"A ring?" she asked. "I didn't think you'd want to wear the insignia of the conquered."

As he rinsed the safety razor, his piercing eyes captured her reflection in the mirror. "Yes, I want the traditional brand, show the world I am lawfully hogtied." His face became serious. "Actually, I want an outward reminder of the bond between us."

Ruth frowned at her wedding band, the one Mickey had placed on her hand the night they were married. Through four pregnancies and several cases of hives which caused her hands to swell, she had never removed that plain gold circlet. Now she simply considered it to be pulling double duty, representing a second husband in marriage, as well as a first. Apparently Jack didn't agree.

"I have an idea." He dried his face, studying her in the mirror. He took something from his dop kit and walked to the love seat, then sat tentatively on the edge beside her.

She watched two droplets of water which had avoided the towel run an erratic path through the hair on his chest. "We can have an official ceremony, if you want, or we can do it right here, privately, simply."

She wasn't sure what he meant. "What?"

"You can put the ring fingers of your hands together, end to end. I will slide Mickey's ring from your left finger to your right, without actually removing it from your body. His ring will remain intact on your right hand, a reminder of your life with him."

He opened his hand to reveal two plain gold circlets. "Then I will put this ring on your left hand as a symbol of your marriage to me. And you can put this other one on my hand, making an honest man of me."

She didn't speak, just sat silently frowning at the two simple symbols resting in his large palm. Her gaze shifted to Mickey's ring which represented nearly three decades of married love.

She thought he spoke to relieve the awkward silence between them. "You can think it over. Whatever you decide about your ring is okay, but I want a wedding band. I feel a little foolish putting it on my own hand. Will you do it for me?"

Wordlessly she nodded, reached out and selected the larger ring from his open palm. She took his left hand in her left. "With this ring," she whispered hoarsely, "I thee wed." She swallowed the knot in her throat as she slid the ring easily over his knuckle and into its proper place.

Jack smiled wistfully, gazing at his new ring, and waited, obviously for some signal, some additional word from her.

She placed her right ring finger end to end with her left and looked at him, her eyes moist.

"Thank you." He smiled only slightly as he coaxed and tugged trying to remove the old ring from its trench. Finally he put her finger in his mouth and wet it round and round. Grudgingly the old ring moved.

She again placed her fingers end to end. He slid Mickey's ring onto her right hand where it settled finally, reverently in its new location.

Sliding his ring onto her left hand, Jack repeated, "With this ring, I thee wed."

Ruth witnessed the transfer without a word. "Not a very auspicious occasion." She held up both hands and her eyes shone as she admired her rings.

"Maybe not to anyone else." He slid from the edge of the sofa to kneel on the floor beside her. He wrapped both his arms around her legs and lay his head on her lap.

With her index finger, Ruth followed the line of his ear and trailed down his square jaw to his chin, back to the fullness of his bottom lip. He caught the roving finger carefully between his teeth and closed his eyes a moment before he rolled back on his heels and stood. "How about a shower? I'm fixing."

She smiled indulgently. "This is ridiculous. Just looking at you makes me giddy. Am I ever going to mature enough not to be such a pushover?"

Jack laughed, pulled her to her feet, and pressed her against him. "I hope not."

"You're going to think I'm one of those fast women always on the make."

Coaxing her out of her robe, he stroked the smooth length of her, arched his eyebrows and crooned, "Yeah."

* * *

They planned to stay three nights at the Biscuit Basket. Except for meals, the first two days they kept to themselves rather than mixing with the other guests.

Reggie and Pamela, pleased at the news of Standish's marriage, honored their preference and saw that their privacy was not disturbed.

"They're having formal dinner and music tonight," Ruth said the morning of their last day in England.

Jack rubbed his hands together. "Okay. Let's go buy ourselves some proper duds and party." It seemed he was back to reading her mind.

They shopped separately and met for lunch at the tea shop they had enjoyed before. Ruth had her hair fixed and nails done. Jack got a haircut but declined a manicure saying, "Manicures are for sissy boys." Laughter spewed and tears prickled at the same time. In spite of his questions, she didn't try to explain.

He dressed early to clear the bath and dressing room for her. When he slipped into the white dinner jacket which set off his Ugandan tan, she wheezed. "You do clean up nice."

"Just trying to keep up. You set a fast pace."

"Don't kiss me, Jack. Go on downstairs. If you touch me like that, you're going to get mugged."

Laughing, he released her. "Will you be long?"

It was Ruth's turn to laugh. "Not long enough for you to get waylaid by any wandering stewardesses, so don't even think about it."

*　　*　　*

Jack was standing at the foot of the stairs when Ruth appeared at the head. His look was enough, although he and several others complimented her verbally through the evening.

Dinner was served at small tables in the music room. Jack and Ruth were seated with Reggie and Pamela, both of whom commented on his new ring

A rhythm and blues combo--piano, drum, saxophone and vocalist--began playing as dessert was being served.

Pamela pointedly addressed Jack after a couple of numbers. "They're pretty good, aren't they?"

He smiled agreement.

She winked at Ruth. "But they're missing something."

Jack didn't see the wink. "No. They sound fine."

"Reggie asked them to bring along a friend of yours."

"Oh yeah? Who's that?"

Reggie stood as the selection finished and strode to the microphone. "Tonight we have a special treat. My friend Jack Standish is an accomplished musician and needs only our encouragement to sit in for a set."

Jack laughed at the drum roll as a sturdy little waiter wagged in a bass violin which towered over him. Laughter rippled through the audience at the picture. Jack ventured a querying look at Ruth who raised her eyebrows. "You don't want to embarrass Reggie."

With a sheepish grin, Jack stood and strode out to join the group. They conferred, agreed, and Jack pulled the big mahogany instrument into his arms.

Pamela was right. Ruth realized at once how the oversized violin gave the group's sound depth. Jack's eyes moved between the music on the stand in front of him and the strings beneath his hands. He appeared to caress the huge instrument which swayed, melding to his body.

Pamela leaned toward her. "I might be a trifle jealous, were I you."

Ruth didn't answer, enchanted to see the way her husband embraced the bass.

The vocalist sang huskily "Someone Like You." The words spoke of the singer's worldwide, lifelong search for a mate, "someone exactly like you."

As he strummed the last measure, Jack's gray eyes met Ruth's and crinkled with a tight smile. Her blush all but singed her hairline. Reggie and Pamela grinned broadly at each other, then at Ruth.

* * *

The flight to Dallas was uneventful except that Ruth got noticeably quieter the closer they got. Donnie would be at the airport to meet her.

"Remember, when I introduce you to him, play it straight," she reminded Jack again.

Seeing how solemn she had become, he agreed.

"I just need time to lay some ground work before I tell them. They'll probably all be in Bridger tomorrow and I can explain you to everyone at once. I think that's probably the best way to do it."

"Am I going to be that hard to sell?"

She didn't answer, instead asked another question. "When are you coming?"

"No later than Wednesday. You have until then to get your secret told. I, on the other hand, am going to shout it to the world, buttonhole people on the street, tell everyone I see."

She laughed. "I love you."

"Despite the shotgun wedding?"

"It was memorable, certainly not your traditional do. I don't believe I ever heard of the bride being the one coerced."

Jack kissed her cheek. "We goes with what works."

* * *

Ruth spotted Donnie as soon as she exited the tunnel. As he hurried forward, she threw her arms around him and hugged him tightly, surprising them both. Wearing a half smile, Jack stood back, watching.

Donnie picked up the small suitcase she had set on the floor and started to turn her toward the concourse when she balked. "Donnie, this is Dr. Standish." She turned boldly to face Jack's gray eyes. "Jack, this is my younger son, Donnie Pedigo."

As the two men shook hands, Donnie eyed Jack curiously.

Ruth stammered. "Dr. Standish has been working in Uganda. Ah, he lives here, in Dallas."

"Oh." Donnie nodded, his face blank, his curiosity assuaged. Ruth glanced from one to the other, then her eyes stayed on Donnie. Something in the bones around his eyes reminded her acutely of Mickey.

"It seems like I've been gone a long, long time."

"We've missed you, too, old girl." Donnie's flippant attitude and words and his laugh cut the mist gathering in her eyes. "Have you got a claim check? I'll go get the rest of your luggage. Just the duffel? Is that all?"

She nodded but didn't take her eyes from Donnie's face. Jack produced claim checks from his coat pocket, prompting another curious look from Donnie.

"She checked the other small suitcase too," Jack corrected, "the mate to this one."

As the boy again turned toward the concourse, Ruth bit her bottom lip, then wheeled to face Jack, unable to hide the pain she knew was visible on her face.

He offered a gentle smile. "It's all right. It'll be an adjustment. We expected that. Shall we shake hands or dare we risk something more personal?"

A step forward and she threw her arms around his neck. Catching her up, he lifted her feet from the floor.

She giggled. "Hanging out with a barbarian is just one harrowing adventure after another."

He lowered her feet back to the floor.

She patted his face, fingering the mounds at either side of his mouth. "I hope I can endure until Wednesday." Biting her lips, she hurried down the concourse to catch up with Donnie.

After he claimed the once stiffly new duffel, now blackened by many hands over many miles, Donnie escorted his mother out into the blistering August heat, across a parking lot to his Cougar with the shallow trunk which would not accommodate the burgeoning duffel. He tossed it instead into the back seat.

Ruth breathed deeply. "I've forgotten how wonderful America smells. The air is marvelous. But isn't it awfully hot?"

"It's only ninety-seven degrees. Yesterday was a hundred and seven. A cool front came through last night."

"Gosh. It takes my breath. Are you hungry?"

"I can always eat, Mom, if you are."

"No. Actually all I really want is a session in front of the jets in my whirlpool. You cannot imagine how many times I've thought about stepping into that tub."

He glanced at her as they waited at a traffic light. "You look different, tanned, all rosy, actually kind of buff, for you." He laughed self consciously, prompting a smile as she looked at him.

"Would you like me to drive?"

"Not unless you want to. Did you drive any in Uganda?"

"Only my bicycle."

"Maybe I'd better, until you get your land legs back. You didn't like it there much, did you?"

215

Ruth was startled. "Oh yes, I did. Honey, I loved it. Didn't you get my letters? Didn't you read the articles?"

"Sure, but I figured you were just blowing smoke, writing stuff to get by government censors. Judging by your letters and all, I figured you'd re-up for at least another three months."

She mouthed a noncommittal, "Uh-huh."

"Well?"

"Well, things were more complicated than that." She wanted to tell her story once, to all of them at the same time. "Will everyone be home this weekend?"

"Yeah, but not until tomorrow. Anna and Darrell both had to work today and Karen did too. Karen and Mike might run over late tonight or just meet us at church in the morning. Carly and Spencer and the baby will try to make it for the ten-thirty service. Carly said little Mick's up by six every morning which will give them plenty of time. We all figured you'd like us being in church together, your first day back and all."

"Is the house ready? Did you put clean sheets on the beds? Clean the bathrooms?"

"No." He grinned. Ruth flashed him her warning look. "Dutch's folks have a cleaning lady once a week. I called and laid my sad story on her: Mom gone three months, accumulated grit and grime, etc. She came yesterday and worked some wizardry on the place. I did the yard. Things look better than when you left."

Ruth smiled. Donnie had always been able to improvise, when he had to.

She was not prepared, however, for the flood of memories which washed through her as they turned onto Windsor Way and she saw her home.

She had always thought of their house as a cottage nestled among the trees. Suddenly it looked huge. Eight rooms and two and a half baths full of comfortable, luxurious furnishings and state-of-the-art appliances.

Donnie hit the button and the garage door opened. The garage was empty. *Where was the car? Mickey must not be home from golf.*

Stupid, stupid, Ruth fretted. The car was right there, behind the second garage door. What mean tricks her mind played from time to time, taunting her. She remembered distinctly. Mickey was gone. Oddly that thought had lost its gut-wrenching pain. There was something mitigating. *What was it?*

Jack. Of course, Jack.

Jack could not replace Mickey, did not expect to, but something strange was happening to her. Suddenly the memory of Mickey did not supersede Jack.

At this moment, both men were only memories, each with a charm and allure of his own. But they were not comparable, in her mind or in her heart.

A woman, any woman, would be proud to claim either of those two men as husband. Preposterous to have somehow, miraculously, attracted both.

216

"It looks good, don't you think?" Donnie's question interrupting her thoughts, startled her.

She sighed deeply. "Yes it does. Oh, honey, the yard is beautiful. Everything looks wonderful. And I'm so glad to be here."

Outside the air-conditioned Cougar, the hot air blasted her rudely. She had never realized how oppressive Oklahoma Augusts were.

Despite her excitement at being home, Ruth felt peculiarly fatigued. Jet lag again. In London it was seven hours later. Six o'clock in Bridger, it was one a.m. at the Biscuit Basket. Four in the morning in Bwana. No wonder she felt sapped.

The cool air in the house gave her boost. She was home, safely back in her own cozy nest. But everything had changed. Circumstances were altogether different now than when she left. Hope had returned in lavish abundance to replace the quiet desolation.

Was Jack alone responsible for the difference, or was it something inside of her?

Ruth speculated. In this mix, she seemed to be the ingredient most changed by the intervening time and miles.

Chapter Thirty-Two

Stripped for her long anticipated bath, Ruth was surprised at her reflection in the wall mirror behind the tub. She turned to check various angles.

She was much more solid, thinner than before Uganda. Eying herself, she took a deep breath and straightened. Her once full, firm breasts were soft and drooped woefully. Birthing four nine-pound babies had left her with only a hint of the hourglass narrowing of her waist. Of course recent walking and bicycling had tightened her tummy, hips and thighs. There was no remedy, however, for the road map stretch marks. It was a mystery to her that this body still aroused so much pleasure.

"I wish Jack could have seen this body before..."

But Mickey had appreciated and gotten full benefit from her agile young woman's body. She shrugged. Jack seemed content with the leavings. He often commented on how beautiful she was, words which prefaced their love making. She smiled thinking of him.

Obviously he was drawn by something other than her waning physical attributes.

Ruth eased into the bath and soaked a long time, calling the ten-minute whirlpool jets cycle repeatedly and running the water so hot her skin turned bright red.

Later she put on a cotton T-shirt and a pair of old shorts, which swallowed her. She would need some new clothes and should, perhaps, reclaim a few pounds. That probably wouldn't be hard.

Donnie ordered a pizza delivered. Food prepared and brought to your door, another luxury Ruth supposed she would never again take for granted.

The filtered air in the house seemed sterile after living outdoors for three months, but recalling the awful heat, Ruth did not suggest opening windows.

She snuggled into her wing-backed chair beside the fireplace with a piece of pizza and a cola. She thought of Artemis. He would love pizza and cola. Of course, the ambiance was better in winter with a fire in the fireplace, but August temperatures definitely discouraged that.

She wanted desperately to bring the boy here, to this room. Someday, she would. But deep inside, she knew Jack was right. She recalled a story about how Eskimos ruined good sled dogs by taking them into their igloos at night. There seemed an elusive parallel.

Donnie seemed restless, prowling to the kitchen and back to slouch on the sofa. It was only eight-thirty but Ruth was again brutally aware of the lag. "Do you have a date?"

"Nothing important."

Wiping her fingers on a napkin, Ruth walked over to tousle his hair. "I'm going to bed early and, anyway, I enjoy having the house to myself." She pushed his shoulder. "Go. Do. Just remember we have church in the morning."

"I'll be in before one." He grinned broadly as he grabbed his car keys.

He had been gone only a few minutes when the telephone rang.

"Mrs. Standish?" a woman's voice asked. Surprised by that name, Ruth hesitated. Wrong number. That was her first reaction. Then she was thankful that Donnie had gone out. If he had been there, he would have answered the phone. But, of course, he would have told the caller she had the wrong number. He probably wouldn't even have remembered Jack's name or made the connection or... "Yes."

"This is Meryl Jacobs. I'm volunteer coordinator with the Metropolitan Symphony Association here in Dallas."

"Yes?"

"Dr. Standish is a longtime patron of ours."

"I see."

"In all the years he's supported us, however, he's seldom darkened the doors. His mother, of course, always makes full use of her tickets. A charming woman. We all adore Mrs. Standish. But I digress.

"When our volunteer called Dr. Standish this evening to solicit his continued support, he agreed cordially, as he always does." The caller lowered her voice to a confidential timbre. "Sometimes, just between you and me, he has been brusque. Of course we understand. We all know the kind of pressure he must be under. Such a dedicated man."

"Yes." Ruth smiled thinking so far her end of the conversation had been easy.

"Usually Dr. Standish tells us where to send his tickets. He gives them to different people every year. So, I was more than a little surprised when the volunteer called me back and said he had told her to check with his wife about where to send the tickets.

"Well, there hasn't been even one line in *The Dallas Morning News* about Dr. Standish marrying. Of course, you probably know, he has been 'Mr. Eligibility' around here for many, many years." The woman seemed embarrassed. "Well, maybe not many, many years.

"Anyway, naturally, I thought the girl must have misunderstood. We called around, did a little discreet checking. No one knew a thing about his marriage. We couldn't reach his mother.

"Finally we were forced to give up on subtly altogether and I called him myself.

"He confirmed that you and he had married quietly, out of the country, quite recently. He said I needed to contact you for a decision on the tickets. He gave me this number."

Ruth chuckled. *Married quietly, out of the country, indeed.*

"I see. Well, Mrs. Jacobs, I think you probably should send the tickets to Dr. Standish this year."

"To his home or his office?"

"His office."

"Would you mind giving me that address, as long as I have you on the phone and all."

Ruth laughed self consciously. "I don't know the address."

"Don't give it another thought. I'll look it up. I am so delighted to know that you all will be attending. You will be such a drawing card."

"Good. I'm glad we can help."

"Oh, Mrs. Standish, the doctor is always so good to help out with every kind of community fund raising project. I serve on several boards. He's famous for his generosity. I have not known him to be terribly interested in music. Could that be your influence?"

"No, he enjoys music very much. He even plays--the piano and the bass violin."

"Why, I had no idea. I don't believe anyone has ever mentioned that to me before. I guess that pretty well guarantees Dr. Standish will be attending the performances with you?"

"I hope so."

"Oh, Mrs. Standish, this is going to be such a coup. Those of our members who are acquainted with your husband speak terribly well of him. I personally have very much wanted to meet him. I will have the tickets sent over to his offices first thing Monday morning. And, please, if I miss your arrival on opening night, come introduce yourself. I can't tell you how pleased we all are at the prospect of your being with us this season.

"Oh, and of course," she added as an afterthought, "you have our very best wishes on your marriage."

After appropriate good-byes, Ruth hung up the telephone and allowed her pent-up laughter to bubble into the room.

"Obviously they haven't heard the tales about Jusu the magician holding beating hearts in his two hands.

"As to his musical talents, I probably should have mentioned that Dr. Standish chants a really melancholy dirge in witchy Runyandole." She began laughing all over again.

*   *   *

221

As tired as she was, Ruth expected to sleep well at home in her own bed but the bedroom seemed stuffy, cluttered, haunted. And she didn't want to sleep alone.

She wondered what Jack would think of the house, of this room. It was hard to visualize him here. *Would memories of Mickey be too pervasive?*

She didn't know what difference it made. Jack wouldn't be living here anyway. The commute, one hundred forty miles one way, was too far.

Restless, she got up and went back into the den.

The woman with the symphony had been solicitous. Obviously she was pandering, worming her way into someone's good graces.

Ruth suddenly felt as if she knew very little about this man she had married. *Did he have an elaborate home in Dallas? Something showy, in keeping with his circumstances?* She turned on a reading lamp beside the sofa and walked over in front of the darkened fireplace. *Probably.*

She muttered to herself. "Did you expect he lived in an adobe hut with a tin roof in Dallas too?" She glanced around at the den's furnishings scarred by events which prompted a deluge of memories. *Would he find this house and its furniture quaint? Too modest?*

And what about his mother, the other Mrs. Standish?

Ruth sat tentatively on the front edge of the wing back. She had not thought of breaking in a new mother-in-law.

She adored Mickey's mom. Maybe Jack's mother would be like Doris, accept the new additions to her family with quiet grace--a daughter-in-law, four grown grandchildren, three grandchildren's spouses and a great grandchild.

"I doubt any woman is that gracious." Ruth slumped back in the chair and looked around. She probably wouldn't like living in Dallas. She had never wanted to live in a large city. This was where she belonged.

But, then, she'd adjusted to dirt floors in Bwana and to accommodations at the posh Biscuit Basket in London.

The idea of a season of symphony music pleased her. She wondered if he had thought of that when he referred Mrs. Jacobs to her. *Was he trying to make the city seem attractive, to lure her there? Maybe.*

He said he wouldn't call until Sunday night. He didn't want to interfere with her preparing her family for his arrival.

She could call him, but she really didn't want to. Tonight seemed reserved for wallowing in memories, for expunging any residual bits of grief.

When she had last been sleepless in this house, pacing to the kitchen for juice, she had not even imagined such an unexpected, remarkable development in her life. And Jack Standish certainly could be termed "an unexpected, remarkable development."

Thinking of him, of his face, his laughter, his scent, she smiled and shivered with pleasure. Then she went to bed.

*   *   *

Ross Belton was the first person Ruth saw as she and Donnie walked down the hallway leading to the church school rooms at St. Peter's Sunday morning.

"Pedigo. When'd you get back?" Ross shouted from the parish hall door some forty feet away, prompting other early arrivals to turn and immediately begin talking at her, all at the same time.

Ruth smiled, shook hands and hugged people in turn without attempting to answer the barrage of questions shot gunned her direction. New people regarded her peculiarly. The hallway filled with a surge of congregants emerging from the early service, adding their questions to the onslaught. She just kept smiling.

"Did you meet Father Catlett? Is he really eleven feet tall?"

"Was the weather wonderful?"

"You lost weight. Were you there for 'hungry season.' That's the worst time to go."

"Did you get diarrhea from the water? I hear everyone who goes spends the first week in the john."

She stopped listening as the questions peppered away one after another.

"People, people!" Father Thomas shouted above the din, and elbowed his way through to lock a protective arm around Ruth's shoulders. "The Inquisition was less unrelenting. Give a girl a break."

He turned her around and pushed her ahead of him to his office, drawing a throng of followers like the pied piper. Gently he shoved her inside, then swung the door closed in the face of the continuing barrage of questions and comments.

"Whew." He pretended to be fatigued by the frenzy. Ruth laughed and thanked him.

He laughed with her. "I know they want to know all about it, but the hallway is hardly the right forum. You can speak to the vestry Monday night, if you will, then perhaps the women's guild at their luncheon. Let me see when that is." He shuffled through pages on his desk calendar. Someone rapped quietly on the office door, then opened it.

"She'll want to see me." Ross gripped the door to prevent its being closed in his face as Father Thomas responded quickly. "I have information for her."

"All right." Thomas stepped back allowing Ross to enter. Others in the hallway seemed to have dispersed to their various destinations.

"As soon as I got home from Uganda," Ross spoke earnestly, "I called around until I found someone who had connections with Medical Community Hospital in Dallas. They're an arm of the university medical school. I tracked down a surgical nurse who knew your friend Standish."

223

Ruth held up a hand to halt Ross' recitation but he would not allow the interruption.

"You need to hear this." He shook his head, making his jowls quiver.

"Ross, I really want to go to Sunday School."

He glanced at his watch. "Give me ten minutes. The coffee line's out the door. We have that long."

"Okay." She shifted her weight from one foot to the other. "What."

"This woman said Standish was a great surgeon, probably the best she's ever seen and she's been around there a dozen years."

Ruth nodded.

"But," he emphasized the word, "she said he is impossible to deal with, insists on having everything his way, is terribly hard to please; won't take suggestions, even when there's a chance he might be wrong."

"If that's the case, I imagine he's got his hands full of lawsuits, malpractice being what it is these days." She regarded him skeptically. "And he probably doesn't have many patients. Right?"

"Wrong." Ross continued excitedly. "Everyone wants him, if they can get him but he takes off all summer, every year. If you can imagine the ego..." He shook his jowls again. "The gall of the man.

"His travels are common knowledge among the staff. No one else takes as much leave as he does. Hospital administrators look the other way. They don't criticize him or allow anyone else on staff to."

Smiling a plastic smile, Ruth looked at Father Thomas, then eased down to the edge of one of the chairs in the comfortable, time-worn office. Taking their lead from her, both Ross and Father Thomas sat also as Ross continued talking.

"Anyway, this nurse said most surgeons are terribly egotistical but that Standish wrote the book. She said in the prep rooms there is a definite chain of command. The orderlies answer to the scheduling nurses in the cage who answer to the floor nurses who answer to the surgical nurses and so on. The surgeons, of course, have final say and receive bucket loads of respect, depending on who they are.

"This woman said when Standish enters the area, a hush falls over the place. People practically genuflect. His arrival is just short of being a religious experience." Ross dropped his voice and slowed his delivery with the next statement.

"Ruth, the man loves being idolized.

"If he speaks to anyone at all, which is rare, according to her, everyone listens, like the old E.F. Hutton ad. But he doesn't usually waste his breath on the peons. The paying customers are pretty groggy by then. She said he occasionally changes the order of the schedule or something but he doesn't talk to them much, just to his students who troop around after him like ducklings following a mother duck, clucking and bowing and scraping."

Ross suddenly seemed to run out of story.

Ruth nodded. "Is that all?"

"Isn't it enough?"

She laughed. "It certainly sounds like I got away from that brute just in the nick of time."

Ross looked annoyed. "I thought that information might be important to you."

"It sounds like he does his job well and co-workers and patients appreciate it. I don't consider that account exactly derogatory, do you?"

"Well, no, not really, I guess, except that he's got a reputation for being something of an arrogant ass." Ruth's mouth dropped open and she looked at Ross significantly. He grimaced under her scrutiny.

"Okay, I know. That's what you called me that morning in Savanron. I admitted I said some things I shouldn't have."

She nodded.

"You said you forgave me."

"Right. But that term probably should be reserved for worse behavior than you've described in Jack."

"I thought what I found out might make you feel better now about being home, away from him."

"Jack and I flew back on the same airplane."

Belton looked at her sheepishly. "Well, since he lives in Dallas and it's the closest international airport for you, that's probably not too great a coincidence. Unless, he came home with you." Ross shot a glance at the door.

Ruth stood as he did. "He's coming for a visit."

"Oh, well." Ross suddenly brightened. "Does he play golf? Maybe I can help entertain him."

Ruth smiled tolerantly. "Thanks. Now, may I please go to Sunday School?"

"Sure. I'll even go with you."

"Fine. Thank you, Father, for your private little sanctuary."

The priest again put his arm around her shoulders. "It was the excitement of seeing you again that provoked the mob response. You have become quite a celebrity, with your stories in the newspapers and all. Word will have spread by now. I'm sure everyone will have his Sunday manners back by the time you get to the hallway this time."

* * *

Carly and Spencer arrived with Baby Mickey just before the late service.

"Oh, honey." Ruth's eyes teared when she saw the baby, who was quickly approaching his first birthday. She had missed so much, three months of his first year, the learning year. He grinned, flashing four tiny pearly white teeth and Ruth was reminded of Christina Catlett's bashful little smile.

When Ruth held out her arms to take him, he turned away and buried his face in his mother's shoulder. As quickly as he hid his face, he popped up again with an impish grin.

Instead of trying to coax him, Ruth focused on Carly, drinking in a full view of her own firstborn. "Baby girl." She opened her arms to hug both mother and baby. Again she struggled with and overcame the tears of joy at seeing the prosperous looking young family. Spencer grinned and accepted his hug with kind words welcoming his mother-in-law home.

Donnie hurried ahead into the sanctuary to stake out seating.

As the entourage strolled from the coffee room talking together excitedly, Anna and Darrell came through the double doors from the back parking lot.

Again there was a commotion as members of the Pedigo family fell into each other's arms, embracing and laughing and weeping quietly. Anna had not mentioned that she was expecting a baby. The news was obvious.

Ruth patted her younger daughter's protruding stomach and congratulated Darrell with a brisk hug. "How far along are you and why didn't you tell me?"

Anna smiled demurely. "Nearly seven months."

"You knew then, before I left?"

"I didn't want to guilt trip you. After all, you had four of us. How tough could it be?"

Darrell winced and smiled.

"Oh, ho," Ruth teased, seeing Darrell's reaction, "I guess we know who's catching the brunt of the mood swings." Darrell nodded over Anna's objections and Ruth embraced each of them in turn, laughing.

"Come on," Ruth whispered, squeezing her younger daughter and son-in-law, propelling them toward the doorway. "We need to beat the crowd." She pointed toward the acolytes scurrying, preparing to lead the choir in the processional.

"We'll need two whole pews," Spencer whispered as they moved into the sanctuary. "Carly insists on taking the baby and all his gear." He indicated the bulging diaper bag and the infant seat. "You can only get six in a row and we need to save room for Michael and Karen."

"They might not make it," Ruth suggested quietly.

Carly turned and leaned around from her point position. "Mom, Michael's missed you more than any of us have and we've all missed you a lot."

Ruth and Mickey both had been crazy about Karen. They had suspected when the kids were in high school that Karen would be Michael's wife someday, but it was still a surprise when they set the date. Two years younger than Carly, Michael was the first of the Pedigo children to marry. It was an adjustment, more for Ruth than for Mickey who looked forward to grandchildren.

But Michael and Karen elected to wait until he graduated from law school to start a family. He had begun practicing with Mickey two years ago but, as far as Ruth knew, they were still waiting about a baby.

She was eager to see his face. Michael's was a man's face but, occasionally, in unguarded moments, in certain light, from certain angles, Ruth was able to discern the little boy's face she had cherished. The others' features had changed too much to allow that kind of a glimpse, but Michael's retained a hint of his baby self.

Carly led them to pews near the back, so she could take Baby Mickey out in case he created too much commotion.

Father Thomas slipped back and urged them to sit closer to the front so he could call on Ruth to give a brief report on Uganda and their sister parish.

"I'd forgotten, the parish luncheon is next week," he said. "Maybe you can share your experiences with all of us at one time then."

"I'll be glad to." Ruth helped gather belongings for the shift as her family scattered to vacancies in pews nearer the front.

*   *   *

Michael and Karen arrived in time to trail the choir as the processional opened the service. Ruth had sat strategically on the outside aisle to be available if and when the tardy pair arrived.

She smiled broadly into Michael's face which happened to be at the correct angle in the refracted light from the stained glass windows to give her the view of him she loved best.

She hugged them both, then moved closer to Donnie to try to clear seating for two, but the pew was too crowded. Instead, Michael ushered Karen into seating just behind Ruth where church members shifted over to provide ample space for them both.

They were well into the service--opening prayers, the lessons, the Psalms read in unison--all familiar to Ruth whether in Bridger or Bwana, when they settled back for the sermon.

She must pay attention, not allow her mind to drift. There was a stir as the back doors creaked open and closed. A late arrival. Hardly noteworthy. Those creaking doors had been giving late comers away for years.

"Hello there." She heard Ross Belton's stage whisper. "Up there, near the front."

Her family was all present and in place. This tag-along belonged to another clan. She didn't bother to look back.

She didn't even glance as a tall figure entered her peripheral vision in the aisle. Startled, she caught the scent of him as he eased into the pew beside her.

She straightened and looked at him as he stretched his arm along the back of the bench seat, and suddenly found herself gazing directly into the large, even teeth of Jack Standish's smile.

Chapter Thirty-Three

Ruth leaned toward Jack. "What are you doing here? You weren't supposed to come until Wednesday."

He put his mouth very close to her ear. "I'm not going to toss and turn even one more night without you."

She smiled, flattered, embarrassed.

Donnie leaned around her and looked at Jack. "Hello, Dr. Standish." He reached a long arm across Ruth to shake Jack's hand. Ruth smiled sheepishly. Jack again leaned close to her ear. "Haven't told them yet, I see."

"Haven't had time."

"When?"

"After church. I'll fix breakfast at the house. After we eat, everyone will be relaxed, mellow."

"Except you and me."

"Well..."

"It's okay. Maybe I can lend a little moral support."

She sighed. "It can't hurt. I thought you weren't a religious man."

"Shhh," he admonished and looked toward the pulpit. "It's important to you. I'll learn."

Without really meaning to, Ruth found herself nestling into him. She wanted desperately to kiss his freshly shaved face, to link her arm through his. But Michael and Karen were directly behind them. Instead she fidgeted.

A few tense moments later Jack caught her hand and slid it into the space between them where no one else could see.

Ruth drew a deep breath and, keeping her face straight ahead, allowed a satisfied smile.

Jack tapped on her wedding ring with his index finger without venturing a look at her. Ruth's smile broadened as she shook her head almost imperceptibly. Playing patty-fingers in church like a couple of kids. Feeling giddy and a little naughty, she blushed. Jack grinned mischievously, keeping his eyes turned to the front.

When the priest called on Ruth for a brief report of her Ugandan adventure, she didn't stand immediately, unable to extricate her hand from Jack's. He continued gazing straight ahead, slow to give up the hand.

She spoke only a moment about Father Catlett and his family, of the guest house with the dirt floor, the enviable climate and promised the congregation she would give them details of the trip, complete with pictures and memorabilia, at the parish luncheon the next Sunday.

After the service, people clustered around Ruth in the aisles, welcoming her home, then looked expectantly at her guest. She introduced Jack as a fellow American she met in Uganda. He drew curious looks as he kept his left arm tightly around her waist while shaking hands with his right. Flushed, she introduced him to her children and their spouses, all of whom regarded him peculiarly.

Patrick Montgomery, a local physician/surgeon, hesitated when he heard Jack's name. "Not Standish with Medical Community in Dallas?" Montgomery spoke a little too loudly.

"Yes." Jack turned to meet Father Thomas who had worked his way through the crowd to try to clear the bottle-neck of greeters in the aisle.

Again a little too loudly, Montgomery called out, "Father, be careful of those hands. They're legendary. He's probably the most distinguished surgeon in this part of the country. Of course, I am the only one here qualified to know that. My question is what is the man doing here in our little burg?"

Montgomery turned his birdlike stare on Ruth as if expecting her to produce some acceptable explanation. Ruth had never liked Patrick Montgomery much anyway. At that moment she liked him less. "What are you doing here, old man?" Montgomery pressed closer to Jack who eyed the slight physician indifferently.

"Visiting friends."

Patrick looked at Ruth with new regard. "I had no idea you knew people here. Were you a friend of Mickey's?"

"No."

Jack took Ruth's elbow with one hand and used the other to nudge people aside, excusing themselves as he guided her out of the sanctuary and into the corridor which had begun to clear.

"Say, Standish," Montgomery called down the hall from the sanctuary door, "give me a jingle later. We'll get together, talk a little shop. Ruth knows the number. Hell, everyone in the place knows how to reach me. Wait up, I'll give you my beeper number." Jack didn't look back at Montgomery, acted as if he hadn't heard. Instead, he joined Carly and Spencer at the exit.

Unexpectedly Baby Mickey, riding on his mother's hip, stuck out his fat little arms, signaling he wanted Jack to carry him. Carly looked at Standish peevishly.

He shrugged. "Babies like tall people. Better view."

Opening and closing his hands eagerly, Mickey leaned toward Jack. Hesitating, Standish looked to Carly for permission. When her glare softened, he smiled and took the baby up easily, a man obviously comfortable handling small children.

"Well, that's a shocker." Carly huffed and looked to her husband for some explanation.

Approaching from behind them, Ruth caught her comment and smiled. "Jack's a pushover for kids and dogs. They seem to sense it." She trailed Jack and Baby Mickey out the door. "Donnie, I'll ride with Jack."

"Why?"

"Because he doesn't know the way and I do."

"I didn't know he was going with us."

Ruth smiled. "Yes, he is." She shot Jack a warning look. He ducked his head as he murmured under his breath, "What's more, Donnie boy, I'll still be here when you're long gone."

Carly called loudly. "Mother, the baby can go with you, but he has to ride in a seat belt in the back seat."

"All right." Ruth lowered her voice. "Jack, the Land Rover isn't here. Which car is yours?"

"The black Lincoln with the Medusa."

She laughed lightly.

"What's funny?"

"A Town Car? A little ostentatious, isn't it?"

"It's comfortable, especially if you spend a lot of time on the road."

"I know." She giggled. "I drive one."

He looked at her in disbelief and they both laughed. "Ostentatious yourself. That doesn't really seem like you either."

"Mickey insisted. But you and Mickey are both right. Flashy or not, they're great on the road."

He handed her the keys. "You drive." He then situated baby Mickey in a seat belt on the armrest in the back which enabled the toddler to sit high enough to see out. Jack settled in the passenger seat as Ruth started the engine.

"What're you doing here?" She turned onto the boulevard.

"Away from you, there's no sunshine, no laughing, no joy. Did Mrs. Jacobs call?" He turned his head to check on Little Mickey who was humming and looking out the windows.

Ruth glanced at Jack. "You rascal."

He chuckled. "Did she ask for Mrs. Standish?"

"Yes, she did."

"And did you know who that was? I thought you might tell her she had the wrong number."

Ruth smiled at the road. "It took me a minute but I was charming. I told her we'd be using the tickets and to send them to your office."

"Oh." He eyed her askance. "You're planning to be in Dallas during the symphony season, I take it." It was more of a question than a statement.

"It seemed a shame to waste those wonderful tickets when we both enjoy live music. I only hope they don't ask you to jam with them."

When he didn't respond, she glanced at him uncertainly. His gray eyes twinkled and he was smiling at her, prompting the reliable blush.

"Jack," Her face was suddenly serious, "do you have a large home?"

"Yes. Much too big for one person. It'll probably be about right when your brood comes to call. I don't care about the house. We'll do whatever you want--live there, find something else or we can build. Whatever you want."

She scowled. "I feel like you're getting cheated. I'm getting everything out of this deal."

When he didn't respond, she risked another look. Jack was gazing at the baby who was holding onto his index finger. Jack's voice was barely audible. "Maybe not."

*   *   *

Ruth scurried around the kitchen. Her movements were jittery, nervous, as she layered strips of bacon in her largest skillet.

"Mom, what do you want me to do?" Anna watched her suspiciously. "Why are you so up tight?"

"I haven't fed this many people...I haven't cooked this kind of food...I haven't cooked in this kitchen for a really long time. I'm just a little edgy."

Keeping a wary eye on her mother, Anna began peeling potatoes. "I'll do hash browns and set the table. You want to do a sit down in the dining room, rather than buffet, right?"

Distractedly, Ruth grunted a yes.

Carly appeared in the kitchen doorway. "How many are there? Are you doing biscuits or muffins?"

Anna frowned at her older sister and shook her head slightly. Seeing the signal, Carly didn't insist on a response. "Okay, we'd probably better do both." She retrieved the muffin tins from the lower cabinet next to the stove. Her eyes darted between their mother and Anna curiously. A moment later, she whispered to Anna. "What's wrong with Mom?"

"I'm not sure. She's preoccupied, worried about something. Maybe she's grieving again, being home and all. Who knows?"

"Where did that guy come from?"

Anna shrugged. "I don't have a clue. Did you hear Dr. Montgomery?"

"Yes, and I'm with him. What's this big fish doing in our little pond? How well does Mom know him?"

"Clueless again. Shhh." The girls were quiet as Ruth reached between them to rinse her hands.

232

In less than forty minutes the joined forces produced steaming platters and bowls with sausage and bacon, eggs, hash browns, biscuits and muffins, and gravy.

Donnie jumped up when he saw the heaping dishes bound for the table. "I'll do drinks."

Karen and the men remained in the den watching an exhibition game on the big screen TV.

"Water, milk, juice or coffee, or any combination," Carly instructed, answering Donnie's offer. "Mom and the rest of us in our usual places."

Karen stood and meandered into the kitchen. "I'll help you, Donnie."

"Where do we put Standish?" Donnie asked Carly quietly.

"Mom, do you still have a high chair in the garage?" Carly called, avoiding the question.

"Hmm," Ruth hummed affirmatively.

Carly peeked into the den. "Spencer, please go get the high chair out of the garage and dust it off a little, if you can." She lowered her voice. "Donnie, put Michael in Dad's place." Her voice rose to normal. "Our guest can go on Mom's right. That's okay, isn't it, Mom?"

"Hmm," Ruth assented again without looking at them.

Moving to the den door to summon eaters, Carly frowned to see Mickey, teetering uncertainly, clutch at the visitor's knee. Just as he was about to topple, Standish provided a steadying hand. The child fell, but not abruptly.

"You could have caught him." Carly's grim countenance and tone were accusing.

Jack smiled at Mickey whose face erupted into a broad grin revealing the tiny white teeth as he clamored again to his feet. "And deny him the pleasure? Not me."

Still frowning, Carly was distracted by Spencer's arrival with the high chair. "Where do you want it?"

She was contemplating the chair's placement when Standish entered the dining room. Frowning again, she glanced into the den. There was no sign of the baby. "Where's Mickey?"

Jack nodded his head, indicating she should look down. Mickey was hidden by Jack's body as he toddled clinging to Jack's extended index finger.

Carly hurried to scoop the child up in her arms. "Don't you like babies?"

Jack regarded Mickey soberly. "Yes, I do. I particularly like this one. He's very independent. A quick study for a little guy. How old was he when he started walking?"

"Nine months. Why?"

"Early physical development can be a sign of intelligence in a kid."

Instead of being pleased at Jack's comment, she scowled. "We don't call him 'a kid.'"

233

Jack's eyes narrowed, his smile cooled, and his tone became remarkably impersonal. "Thank you."

Carly bit the inside of her lower lip.

Witnessing the exchange, the others immediately began chattering in an effort to cover the awkward moment as Ruth entered the dining room.

After they were seated, the blessing asked and plates filled, Anna looked at Ruth curiously. "Mother, how did you and Dr. Standish meet?"

"On the airplane."

"Going over or coming back?"

"On the way to London. Going over."

"Were you seat mates?"

"Well, not at first." Ruth hedged tossing an embarrassed smile and a quick glance at Jack. She took a large bite of eggs.

"So, what happened?" Donnie asked, uncharacteristically pursuing the questioning.

Ruth chewed a moment then washed the bite down with a sip of ice water but no one else said anything, waiting patiently for her answer. "A man, an Arabic looking fellow, made unwelcome overtures toward me..."

"Toward you?" Donnie coughed, as if he had swallowed the wrong way.

Ruth glanced over to see Jack fighting a grin and she wiped her mouth. "Donnie, to you I seem ancient but to some very desperate fellows, apparently, I still have some appeal." She shot Jack another dark glance, daring him to speak. She was embarrassed that Anna saw the look.

Donnie continued. "I didn't mean anything, Mom, that just kind of caught me by surprise." He looked around the table at his siblings and their spouses for concurrence.

Anna shrugged at Ruth apologetically and nodded her agreement with Donnie. Diverted, they ate for a while exchanging small talk.

"So, how did you meet?" Michael asked Ruth quietly during the next lull in the conversation. Again, no one else spoke, waiting.

"Jack was sitting across the aisle. He noticed the man pestering me and suggested I sit in an empty spot a couple of seats over from him.

"The lighting wasn't real good. I thought Jack was about your age. I figured he was like you, Michael, doing a good deed for a woman in need of assistance. I was grateful and relieved." She paused.

One by one, as she scanned their faces, they nodded. They understood so far, but obviously were waiting for more. Silent, Jack seemed to be enjoying the replay.

Ruth took a deep breath and plunged ahead. "Jack was busy with armloads of reading materials but, eventually, we introduced ourselves. He was on his way to Uganda too. He goes every year and seemed willing to share some of his knowledge of the place.

"Then they announced that the flights into Uganda had been canceled because of fighting there. I was going to be stranded in London until the flights resumed. I knew no one and very little about London." She paused. "But I didn't panic. I was confident I could fend for myself."

Feeding Mickey, Carly winced. "Mom, that was so dangerous, you being on your own like that, as naive as you are." Ruth frowned at Carly who was concentrating on Mickey's next bite and missed her mother's chagrin. Again Ruth glanced at Jack who smiled, encouraging her to continue.

"Jack invited me to accompany him to an inn outside London where he was staying."

Anna stared at her mother. "Mother, surely you didn't..."

"No, of course not. Jack seemed nice, but I didn't want to disappear from the airport and never be heard from again." She shot him a hasty look and raised her eyebrows. "He seemed to read my thoughts.

"At the airport, he made two calls, then said I could go with him to the Biscuit Basket..."

"The Biscuit Basket!" Michael's wife Karen interrupted, her eyes bright. "Ruth, the Biscuit Basket is famous. It's been written up in all the travel magazines. There's no way you could have turned down a chance to get in there."

"I know that now," Ruth said emphatically, "but I had never heard of the place and I certainly wasn't going off with some stranger."

Jack looked at her sharply and said, "I resemble that remark."

All four of Ruth's children turned dark, astonished stares on him. He returned the looks, puzzled.

"Mickey used to say that." Ruth scanned her children quickly. "He didn't know."

They relaxed but their eyes frequently darted from their mother to the newcomer.

Ruth took another deep breath. "Anyway, Jack had also made a reservation for me at the Browne Hotel in town."

Anna's husband Darrell looked up. "My dad stays at The Browne,"

Ruth nodded toward him. "So did I, the first day.

"Jack advised me not to sleep, to try to get on London time immediately to avoid repercussions of jet lag. I appreciated his advice, although it made for a long first day. Anyway, I didn't realize it was Sunday..."

Donnie whistled. "Ah, Mom. You didn't even know what day of the week it was? I'm losing all the confidence I ever had in you."

"I got directions and set off for the American embassy. The church bells caught my attention and I realized why traffic was so light downtown. So, I altered my plan and went to church at St. Martin's."

Anna leaned forward. "Was it great?"

"Yes, honey, it was magnificent. I have pictures, actually post cards. Anyway, I went back to the hotel to plan my itinerary when Jack telephoned. I figured that's who it was when the phone rang since I didn't know anyone else there and I hadn't reached you all yet. It was too early here to call you.

"By then, of course, I had asked the hotel clerk about the Biscuit Basket. He gave it a glowing recommendation. At Jack's insistence, I let him talk me into staying there Monday night, after my visit to the embassy and contacting you, Donnie, and you, Carly.

"I went to Uganda a couple of days later, on the second flight out. Jack was supposed to be along that weekend. He told me we would probably run into each other again in Uganda, but we didn't. Whites are unusual in that rural area so residents pretty well know which of us is where all the time. I asked people there if they knew him. Oddly, no one had ever heard of Jack Standish."

Jack laughed lightly. "Oh, I'm sure someone had."

"No." Ruth's eyes widened with the emphasis. "Even Tuslan did not say a word.

"You know the Paul Bunyan stories?" She looked at the other diners for nods as they passed platters for seconds and Anna brought the coffee pot to the table for refills. "Well, they have some very scary tall tales in Uganda, full of witch doctors and evil incantations. The Catletts and my other friends hinted at things and kept cautioning me not to go out of the village unless I traveled with a group. Safety in numbers, you know?"

The listeners indicated they understood.

"I kept hearing these very scary tales about a witch doctor they call Jusu. They whispered his name and looked all around when they dared to speak of him. Their favorite tale was that he held beating hearts in his two hands, that it was up to him who received the hearts and lived and who died."

Darrell grinned. "Pretty graphic."

Ruth's eyes rounded. "You're not kidding.

"Then I came down with a terrible illness, along with half the village. I ran a high fever and slept most of several days. In my delirium, I was aware of a person who came in the night and chanted over me and made me eat herbs and gritty stuff and wash it down with foul tasting liquids. The only good thing was, the concoctions eased the aching and lowered my fever.

"Later, Ossie, told me Jusu had come to me those nights, that he would not allow her to stay when he was there."

"Did that spook you?"

"When I found out, yes.

"Anyway, I had befriended this nine-year-old boy, Artemis. Or he had befriended me."

Anna laughed. "In the articles and in your letters, you sounded like you were crazy about him."

"You certainly wrote enough about him," Carly added.

Ruth cleared her throat. "I don't think I can talk about him yet, without crying. He is absolutely precious.

"A tree fell and crushed his foot. Tuslan, the local wise man, appeared out of nowhere." Suddenly she stopped and scowled at Jack. "Was he ...?"

"Keeping an eye on you? Yes."

"For Jusu?"

"Yes."

Ruth had wondered...

She noticed her children's rapt faces and felt prodded to continue her story. "Well, anyway, Tuslan--and everyone else--told me to take Artemis to Jusu. I was frightened about facing the witch doctor but even more frightened about that foot.

"In all the accounts I'd heard of Jusu and his magic, no one, I mean not one person, had ever mentioned that Jusu was white."

A muffled chuckle rumbled in Donnie's throat. The others looked at him, then at Jack and smiled before their eyes settled on their mother, anticipating.

"When I got Artemis to the clinic, I barged in and came face to face with Jusu who, it turned out, was my old pal Standish." She shot a look at Jack, who grinned.

"You're kidding!" Carly looked at Jack for confirmation. "You're Jusu, the witch doctor Mom wrote about?"

He raised his eyebrows, all innocence, and nodded.

Ruth continued. "Well, Jusu/Jack repaired Artemis and kept him at the clinic a week or so until he was on the mend and understood the kind of inactivity it was going to take for him to get well.

"After Artemis and I got home to Bwana, I foolishly allowed myself to be lured out on the road alone. I was kidnapped. Jack came immediately to negotiate me out of a really bad situation."

She paused, biting her lips, then exhaled.

"He arranged for Artemis to attend boarding school. Jack was coming home for the fall semester. He teaches, you know. I was a little goosey about staying without the two guys I had grown to depend on, so I decided not to reenlist for another three-month stint and came home."

Carly went to the kitchen for a wet towel to wipe Mickey. "I thought you were homesick for us, for the baby." She sounded a little offended.

Ruth watched her clean up after the baby. "That's right, too, of course."

Jack stirred. "Isn't there anything else you'd like to tell them?"

Ruth bit her bottom lip and frowned down at her plate which had barely been touched. When she raised her eyes, Carly was looking at her oddly.

Anna glanced at Jack then eyed her mother curiously and said, "Why don't we move into the den where we can be more comfortable?"

Anna and Karen immediately began clearing plates and refilling coffee cups for transport to the den.

Chapter Thirty-Four

After the commotion of changing rooms had subsided, Carly continued watching her mother. "So, what's the deal with your wedding ring?"

Ruth had settled on the sofa to marvel at baby Mickey toddling from one receptive adult to another.

"I don't remember you having two gold rings."

Ruth glanced at her hands wrapped around her coffee mug.

Sifting through snapshots and postcards from Uganda which Ruth had laid on the game table, Donnie turned, glanced at her hands and frowned. When Ruth didn't answer immediately, Anna's attention, too, settled on her mother.

"Michael," Ruth called, summoning her older son who had just gotten off the telephone in the kitchen, "could you and Karen come in here."

He appeared in the doorway, his wife behind him. Ruth motioned them to sit. They complied, obviously puzzled.

In the wing back across the room from her, Jack looked mildly interested, his eyes on Ruth's face.

"I think you have some idea of how much I loved your dad." Ruth looked to them for the anticipated nods. "I didn't want to live without him." More nods. "But we don't get to choose those things. I went to Uganda as an act of contrition, self sacrifice. I had this idea I was going to serve God, sort of payback, appreciation for the many years of joy I had lived, blessed with a perfect husband and the four of you, perfect children."

There were modest, indulgent smiles all around, but her listeners remained silent. Ruth frowned at the floor. "In order to rescue me from the kidnappers, Jack had to negotiate difficult terms." Her audience remained mute.

"He had to pay a thousand dollars...and he had to marry me." Her cup thudded as she put it on a side table.

Jack emitted a satisfied little laugh at the startled looks on the faces of the adults in the room.

Michael stared. "You mean as a ruse?"

Ruth rubbed her hands together. "No, the kidnappers brought in a dyed-in-the-wool clergyman. The audience was drunk and the service was in a dialect I couldn't understand. Jack interpreted.

"They were getting ready for three days of a tough man contest and they were all whooping it up. They had kidnapped me to be first prize." She blushed and smiled sheepishly as they all stared at her, obviously stunned.

Michael's dour gaze remained riveted on her face. "But this marriage wasn't valid, was it?"

Jack leaned forward in his chair and answered firmly. "It was and is."

"You're m-married?" Carly repeated, choking on the words.

"Exactly when did this happen?" Michael aimed his obvious hostility at Jack. Jack met his stare. "July twenty-first. We've been married almost a month."

Carly sank onto the edge of the sofa. "What about Dad's estate, Mom? Did you do anything to preserve it for us or does everything you and Dad had go to him, I mean, if something happens to you?"

Dumbfounded, Ruth looked at each of her children's faces, then at Jack.

"No." Jack returned Ruth's gaze, assuring her before focusing on Carly. He reached inside his coat pocket and produced an envelope. "I had my lawyer draw this yesterday." He handed the envelope to Michael.

"A lawyer did this for you on a Saturday?" Michael sounded skeptical.

"He's a friend of mine."

"And Dr. Standish is the real reason you came back, is that right, Mom?" Anna seemed to ignore Jack, Michael, and the envelope as she pursued the other.

Ruth nodded.

"What is that?" Donnie asked, speaking to Michael who was scanning the contents of the envelope.

"A revocable trust. Mom and Dr. Standish are co-trustees. He's named me successor trustee." He glanced at Jack curiously. "You don't even know me."

"You're Ruth's son. I knew you'd watch out for her. You're also a lawyer, I figured you'd know the drill. We didn't have the time or the expertise for a prenuptial agreement. I understand this is the next best thing."

"I assume this means you have a substantial estate of your own?"

Jack nodded. "Yes. Over the years I've devised some gadgets for use in certain surgical procedures. They've been kind of a nuisance really. The first time, I rigged up a little shop, hired people to make the gizmos. We got them right into use. They were handy and helpful. The little shop grew. After they were patented, the devices produced so much income, they complicated my tax picture.

"All I wanted to do was practice medicine and teach. To do that, I was forced to sell the little manufacturing outfit and put the money in a trust. The trust was set up to receive all my income and pay me an allowance.

"Since then I've come up with two or three more little mechanical gadgets, figured out how to manufacture them with pretty much the same result.

"Anyway, I had the trust reworked yesterday, put your mother on as co-trustee. I brought it for her signature. I thought you'd want to look it over first."

Michael continued turning pages and reading.

Studying her brother's face, Carly said, "What does this trust thing mean?"

"It means that, not only is Dad's estate safe, but that Mom is sole heir to Dr. Standish's assets as well." Michael looked at his older sister and smiled wryly. "It means, Carly girl, that if we play our cards right, instead of worrying about protecting Dad's estate, we may scarf off Standish's pile too."

Obviously troubled by the words, Anna turned to Jack. "You don't have any other family?"

"A mother. She's a widow. My dad was also a physician. He left her well heeled. She has a life estate in my house, if she wants it, then it reverts to your mother through the pour over will that goes with the trust.

"I have a brother and a sister who both have families. I've set up funds to guarantee their kids' educations but they don't need any financial help from me."

Everyone was quiet for a long moment, absorbed in private thoughts. The only sounds in the room were Michael shuffling pages of the trust as he read, and baby Mickey's heavy breathing as he concentrated on unlacing Jack's shoes.

"Dr. Standish, are you going to live here?" Donnie voiced the question but several sets of eyes shot to Jack.

"I intend to live where your mother lives. I've never been married, never been committed to anyone before. This is a brand new experience. A bunch of newly awakened emotions are making me behave a little foolishly. I wasn't supposed to be here in Bridger until Wednesday. I didn't want to wait. I don't seem to give a damn anymore about anything but being with her." He looked at Ruth apologetically.

"I'm a practicing surgeon, well established. I teach in a medical school. I'm willing to walk away from both of those pursuits, if she needs or wants to live here." Again looking at Ruth, Jack smiled and shook his head, puzzling. "Take my word for it, this is a very big deal to me. I realize how ridiculous it sounds. Pimply faced kids smitten for the first time have nothing on me."

Michael began to chuckle, a rolling sound emanating from deep inside as his attention drifted from the trust papers to his mother's face.

"Mom, I have seriously underestimated you." He beamed. "I knew Dad was still head over heels, but I never dreamed you were such a femme fatale. What kind of spell have you cast on this poor unsuspecting man?"

Ruth felt her face flame. "I didn't plan...didn't mean to. I had no intention of..." She couldn't explain what she didn't exactly understand herself. She glanced at Jack. "Would you fix me a Bloody Mary?"

"Yes." He smiled into her eyes and stood as she did. "Anyone else?" There were polite refusals all around.

"Great kitchen," Jack said as they walked through the swinging door alone. "Great house. Very homey. Very you."

"Thank you." Ruth smiled. "Thanks for being here and for backing me up and for being patient and polite and not taking any guff off of Carly and...just for everything."

241

He swallowed a laugh as he hugged her and began to sing softly."I'd-do-anything-for-you, anything-for-you-mean-everything-to-me..."

He'd mixed two Bloody Marys by the time Carly and Anna invaded the kitchen, joining them. Jack excused himself to returned to the den, leaving the kitchen and the conversation to the ladies.

Eying their mother, the girls asked questions rapid fire, not waiting for replies. Ruth began rinsing dishes, allowing the barrage of questions without even attempting answers. Soon, Karen drifted in to join them.

Carly babbled as her questions dwindled "Mother, how could you have married anyone else? And so soon? And not Mr. Belton or someone safe, but a guy you hardly knew? Daddy hasn't been dead a year. You should have told us. We should have had some say in a decision this important. Why, you're not even stable, emotionally, you know."

Carly finally quit to take a breath.

Sounds carrying from the den indicated Donnie had started a game of toss with the baby's Nerf ball, urging Baby Mickey to "Get the ball, Mick."

Ruth looked at Carly, her eldest, who glowered back, obviously close to tears.

"Carly, I loved your dad. You know that. He pampered me to pieces.

"Baby, when we got married he said he was going to spoil me so badly no one else would have me, so badly I would never want anyone else. Then he proceeded to do exactly that. I loved being married to him. I anticipated the births of each of you with breathless excitement because you embodied me and the person I loved best in the world." She paused, blinking, swallowing tears. "It was a great run. I thought my life was over when he died."

Ruth drew a deep breath.

"I didn't intend to love anyone in Uganda, not little black children or tall, narrow adults who struggled to speak English out of consideration for me. But before long, I loved dozens of people. Artemis captured my heart within an hour after I met him.

"But Jack... Well, Jack was a huge surprise."

"How old is he, Mom?" Anna asked quietly.

Ruth turned back to the dishes in the sink. "Forty-five."

"Mom!" Carly wheezed. "You're fifty-two, for crying out loud."

"He knows that. I told him when I could see he was getting interested. I didn't tell him Dad was dead. I let him think I was married. He struggled with his feelings, kept a respectful distance, until Ross showed up and spilled the beans.

"I didn't want to take advantage of Jack. I could see he was a little infatuated. I was sinking fast myself. I held back, tried to help him get a handle on his emotions, but pretty soon he was beyond being reasonable. He was kind and charming and handsome and...well, finally, too good to resist."

242

The voices in the den grew louder as others joined the Nerf ball game and it became rowdy. Ruth again turned from the sink to face the girls. She leaned against the cabinet and wiped her hands on a T-towel, then got a shot of lotion from the dispenser.

"The kidnappers stuck me in this dark little hut. A woman slapped me and a man hit me in the stomach with his fist. I'd never been intentionally mistreated before. I was frightened. Then Jack showed up willing to do whatever it took to get me out of there.

"The men who organized the contest knew I had been teaching the women, speaking against sex outside of marriage, warning them about AIDS. I think they thought forcing us to marry would be a way of punishing both of us, poetic justice.

"They're the ones who set the requirement for my release. It wasn't Jack's idea, but he pressed me to go along.

"When you know him better, you'll see what a wonderfully compassionate man he is. I had grown terribly fond of him..."

"I can see why." Anna interrupted, regarding her mother with a shy grin. "He's definitely a hunk."

Karen laughed lightly, drawing the attention of the others. "I'm sure he's had lots of opportunities with ladies, being a doctor and all."

Ruth nodded. "I think probably so."

"Why did he get so hung up on you?" Carly was staring at her mother again, the tactless question obviously a result of her genuine bewilderment.

Ruth pretended to be as mystified as anyone as she looked from Carly to Anna and shrugged. "I am clueless."

The three younger women giggled at her terminology. Ruth smiled sheepishly. Carly folded her arms across her chest and frowned at the floor.

Anna said, "Mom, none of us ever liked lap dog guys. You're following tradition. This one definitely has spirit."

Carly seemed oblivious to her sister's jibe.

Karen opened and began loading the dishwasher.

Suddenly amid the boisterous noise in the den there came a shriek, mournful "ohs" and "ahs" from the men and the baby's sharp wail.

Carly darted through the swinging door, bolted through the dining room and across the hallway to the den.

Blood oozed from Baby Mickey's lip, but he stood perfectly still, silent, wide-eyed as Jack, kneeling in front of him, spoke calmly, dabbing the injury with a handkerchief.

Carly snatched the child into her arms and clutched him tightly for a moment before leaning him back to allow her a look at the wound.

Little Mickey's eyes widened. Alarmed, he began to cloud up and sputter.

Jack stood slowly.

Carly shouted, "Spencer, what kind of a father are you, letting him get hurt right in front of your face?" She didn't wait for an explanation. "We need to get to the emergency room."

She clamped Mickey's head against her shoulder and shrieked, "Mom, call Dr. Morrison. Have him meet us at the hospital."

Obviously confused and frightened, Mickey let out a woeful yowl.

"Carly," Jack's controlled voice quieted the baby mid breath. "Your baby's watching you. You are frightening him. You're telling him with your body language and your voice how he is supposed react to an injury, to the sight of blood. He's storing that data in that little computer brain of his for future reference. Do you want Mickey to be one of those children (he emphasized the word she preferred) who gets hysterical at the sight of blood?"

Carly drew a deep, quaking breath and bit her bottom lip. Her chin trembled. "He needs stitches." She squeezed the words as tears began a run down her face. "Doesn't he?" The question waffled with her uncertainty.

"No." Jack peered at the baby's lip and smiled at Mickey, soothing the child. "He's busted his lip, Carly, for the first time. I predict the same thing's going to happen again, many times, particularly if he plays sports...or develops a smart mouth."

The men in the room chuckled, muttering agreement.

Calmly, Spencer stepped over and took his son from Carly's arms. She winced as she gave him up.

It was then that the spectators noticed the baby had the Nerf ball clutched firmly in his fat little fists. Spencer laughed and held up Mickey's hands like a victorious prize fighter. "He made the catch! That's my boy!"

The baby grinned, then grimaced at the discomfort. His lip had begun to swell.

Jack spoke quietly to Carly. "You might want to put a little ice on that."

Struggling to hold her tears in check, Carly hurried to the kitchen.

Donnie and Michael crowded closer to take a look at Mickey's lip, laughing and talking about what a tough little guy he was.

Anna took a quick look, then shrank back. "Why is it men seem to take so much pride in wounds?" Carly reentered the room with a sandwich bag of ice and Anna directed the follow-up question toward her. "Are they just perverse or ghoulish or what?"

Carly shook her head. "An injury is some kind of a badge of courage, I guess."

"Like a rite of passage?" Karen, too, seemed perplexed.

"It must be a guy thing."

Spencer smiled at his wife warmly. As she put the ice bag against Mickey's lip, Spencer slipped his arm around her waist and tugged her close.

Ruth looked from one young person to the other before her gaze settled on Jack who was watching her, and smiled.

She was acutely aware of his movement as he crossed the room and eased around behind her. The others were still focused on the baby, who reached out a pudgy hand to pat his mother's face, comforting her. Carly giggled as a tear trickled down her face.

Casually Jack draped one arm over Ruth's shoulder and down across her body, at the same time wrapping the other arm around her waist, securing her snugly. She felt his breath as he placed his face against her hair. She caught the familiar scent of him. She put both hands on his arm across her body and felt the tremor as he drew a deep, deep breath, then exhaled.

Watching, babbling to Mickey, none of the others appeared to notice.

"It's good to be home." She sighed, nestling into Jack, basking in the warmth of him. "Obviously you are a valuable asset around here. And, who knows, we may even turn out to be of some benefit to you."

"Hmmm," he hummed. "And how about you?"

"Me? I'm glad to be in love and anticipating things again. I'm looking forward to the future, adjusting, contributing and, of course," she gazed sideways at him, "to spending summers in Uganda with my other son, Artemis, and that witchy Jusu."

Jack's burbling chuckle rumbled in his throat before he spoke quietly. "Your first trip over didn't turn out to be all that sacrificial after all, did it?" He hugged her tightly. "Looking back, you were actually only required to meet two little conditions."

She craned her neck to peer curiously at the Rathbonian profile.

He grinned down into her face. "All that was necessary was that you recognize God's nudge and be willing. From there on, you had it made."

She turned in his arms, looked squarely into his face and smiled, feeling nudged, warm, and very, very willing.

THE END

245